Book Two in the acclaimed *Hacker Chronicles* series

Redemption

By Philip Yorke

mashiach publishing

philipyorke.org

First published in Great Britain in 2021.
Reprinted in 2023.

0002023

Copyright © Philip Yorke 2021

Mashiach Publishing

ISBN 9 79 837 917 455 2

Set in 12 point Baskerville and Baskerville SemiBold

philipyorke.org

In memory of Billie Jo Elms.

17 July 1973 to 11 March 2021

A friend and victim of the
Covid-19 pandemic.

'Fear the Lord your God and he shall deliver you out of the hands of all your enemies'

2 Kings 17:39

An extract from *The Souldiers Pocket Bible*, printed on the third day of August, in the year of our Lord, 1643, and given to all men fighting for Parliament

MARSTON MOOR
SATURDAY 2 JULY 1644

IN THE YEAR OF OUR Lord, 1644, the second day of July will be remembered long after my flesh is no more and my bones have been reduced to dust.

It is close to seven o'clock in the evening. It is a Saturday, when husbands and sons should be at home with their families; on farms; in forges; anywhere but on the cursed moorlands of Marston, some eight miles outside the great city of York.

As torrential rain lashes the land and lightning illuminates the grey and foreboding sky, more than forty thousand men silently await their doom.

At this late hour, the armies of the King and Parliament are preparing to unleash themselves upon each other. They have been waiting for most of the day. Patiently; silently; nervously; eager not to show their hand too early, lest it gives the other side an unassailable advantage.

And the stench of their fear is overpowering.

Every man fears death before he marches into battle. Sometimes it is visible; sometimes, it is not. But it is there, seeping from every pore, just as surely as pus oozes from a corrupted, fetid wound.

At these times, nerves are tested, and, as men, we discover who we are and what we stand for. As we prepare to meet our Maker, most of us realise glory is not what we seek; it has never been so. The simple preservation of life itself is what we wish for – and to be reunited with the ones we love.

Bravado cannot disguise the sense of powerlessness that grips a man's soul. On the battlefield, he has nowhere to run, no place to hide. The only available pathway will, in all likelihood, lead to his painful extinction – when axes, swords and muskets bite into flesh and reap a rich harvest at a place where all destinies are fulfilled.

In a bid to find inner peace, men like me kneel and pray; we sing psalms, hoping the Lord will accept our repentance and forgive us for a lifetime of sin. For others, it is a moment of torment and angst, of bleakness; it is a time of pleading to whoever will listen, begging to be spared.

Alas, nobody escapes the torture the final minutes bring when the silence is deafening, and we have time to dwell on the many ills we have perpetrated in this vile civil war and our increasingly meaningless life. Long before the cries of "In God's name" or "For the King" strike up, shattering the peace and sending cold pulses racing down the spines of every man who still possesses a conscience.

Many are affected, their rank and social class meaningless at a time that makes all men equal.

Fear consumes almost every one of us. It doesn't discriminate. Regardless of our breeding, we cannot control our bowels and bladders, so we soil our breeches where we stand. For men of war are meant to be humiliated when the rivers of blood flow over our rich and fertile lands.

I have no doubt brave, godly men fill the Royalist ranks and are looking down from the ridge on the massed ranks of the Parliamentarian army. Like my comrades and I, they are sodden; such has been the intensity of the deluge.

As I watch my foe through the narrow slits protecting my eyes from the lashing storm, I cannot understand how committed followers of Christ Jesus continue to pledge their fealty to a Sovereign who does not deserve their loyalty. A deceiver who believes his rule is by divine appointment. Prince Rupert of the Palatinate and the Earl of Newcastle, commanders of the Cavalier army, are also undeserving of the support they receive, for they too are reckless and selfish men.

Our King has been in the ascendency since this damnable and bloody conflict started in August 1642. Parliament has lost many battles thus far. And men like me are deemed to be rebels because we choose to stand up to the tyrant and try to force him to rescind his Catholic ways, rule justly and accept the will of his people.

Edgehill, in the county of Warwickshire, is the one exception. We fought Charles here, bringing our massed ranks to this quiet, unassuming place. But, unfortunately, we achieved nought, only a stalemate. On that bleak day, thousands died. There were no winners, only losers. Men went to their grave for no compelling reason.

And it has been the same ever thus.

Now allied forces, comprising soldiers loyal to Parliament and led by the Earl of Manchester and

Lieutenant-General Oliver Cromwell, and Scots soldiers from the Covenant army, sent south of the border under the command of the Earl of Leven, have an opportunity to deliver a telling blow against the King's northern regiments. These are the devils that just twelve months ago decimated Fairfax's northern armies at Adwalton Moor. I remember our capitulation well; forty-nine of my best, most committed men died that fateful day.

Soon we will know whether Parliament has learned lessons from so many painful defeats: swords are being drawn from their scabbards, our many cannons are being loaded with grapeshot; men are continuing to pray, and all around me, the blood lust is rising.

And all the while, this incessant rain that turns the firm ground into merciless, unyielding mud continues to hammer down.

I look at myself; I am in a sore state. The realisation makes me laugh aloud and recall a memory from long ago about my old Latin tutor. Whenever he needed spiritual guidance or sought to draw strength from his Faith, Erasmus Woodbridge would quietly whisper to himself: "In deo speramus."

It is an apt expression. Even though I know very little Latin, this is something I have remembered for more than twenty years. And it is so true. For who can we trust if it is not God himself?

Hell will be unleashed once the Parliamentarian army has filled its belly and the men of the York garrison, who have swelled our number, are given their battle orders. Their arrival takes the strength of the army to just under twenty-five thousand men.

We are more numerous than the enemy, and our fifty drakes and many mortars will wreak death and carnage when they are brought to bear on the King's foolhardy and arrogant men. Nevertheless, I am confident, for as the day grows longer, the omens and conditions become more favourable.

For some reason, Rupert chose not to attack us when we were at our weakest: that was in the morn when we first arrived, and our command lines had yet to be established, our men were hungry, and our armies were of equal strength. As the day has worn on, we have grown in number and more daring by the hour, not least because reinforcements have continued to arrive, and Cromwell has had us singing psalms most of the afternoon.

He knows only too well how these precious, holy words give us the lift we need before the fighting starts.

It is now seven-thirty in the evening, and the Royalists are in the midst of retiring when the slaughter begins. Their surprise and lack of preparation seals their fate.

Leading the fight for Parliament is Cromwell. His Ironsides slice through the King's men like water bursting through a dam. Such is the ferocity of the Lieutenant-General's perfectly timed charge and the courage displayed by the infantry on the left that Prince Rupert's finest men are powerless to resist our violent advance. They buckle. And that is all the encouragement we need.

The sound of death is everywhere. Thousands of sabres flash in the gloom; gunpowder turns the air grey as muskets are fired indiscriminately, and men from both sides fall from their horses, their warm blood eagerly consumed by the ravenous Yorkshire meadows.

Death is stalking many a soul this evening, all because Charles, the tyrant King, refuses to listen to his people.

As Cromwell's force clashes with Lord Byron's men in the thick of battle, the Lieutenant General lurches to his side. Crimson flows from his neck; the result of a well-aimed musket ball has left its painful mark on this day.

"Drive them back," he yells, barely noticing the stinging sensation pulsing down the left side of his body and the blood that is now flowing onto his leather jerkin. "Send these curs to Hades. Show them whose side God is on."

As Cromwell leaves the field to have his wound dressed, a huge cry goes up. His men are driving the enemy backwards, angered by the injury to their commander, their very own Caesar. As the pressure intensifies, our foe struggles to keep their bodies upright and their footholds anchored in the mud, the spilt blood, intestines and guts of their comrades adding to their acute difficulties.

And all the time, Parliament's forces press forward, a relentless, disciplined and unstoppable phalanx.

For many, it is too much. Facing overwhelming odds, hundreds of enemy troops surrender in the face of the onslaught.

I survey the wondrous scenes. Almost everywhere, it is a similar story: Parliament is winning the day.

As the battle reaches its conclusion, it is becoming evident the King's army has been caught off-guard. Afterwards, we will learn that many troops left their positions in a bid to find food to fill their ravenous bellies, believing hostilities would not commence until the Sabbath day. Their underestimation of Parliament's resolve is their undoing.

It is surprising just how little the likes of Rupert and the Earl of Essex know us. They have been fighting our forces for the last two years – besting us on so many occasions. Surely they should know our armies are filled with thousands of God-fearing, zealous men who have no desire to draw blood on the Sabbath? Give them the chance to fight in the rain on a Saturday, albeit every inch of them will be soaked through to the skin, and they will take it gladly, for Sundays should always be kept as a day of rest and prayer.

While Cromwell is being attended to by the field surgeon, Prince Rupert's famed squadrons of horse continue to be pressed in the centre of the Royalist formation.

In just over an hour, the fourteen thousand-strong Scottish Covenanters succeed in bludgeoning their way through to the most famed troops in the King's army. No quarter is given. Many of the Prince's men die where they sit. They are hacked. They are mutilated. The Scots have a point to prove and a bounty to earn.

On the right flank of the allied line, Fairfax's men are engaged in a far more even struggle. It is only when he breaks free and rides to Cromwell, alerting the newly stitched-up Lieutenant General to his plight, that the tide turns.

Cromwell quickly gains control of his men and, as a disciplined wedge, they plough into the foe, shattering the tenuous advantage the Royalists hold over Fairfax's brave and steadfast men. Hundreds die as they come under sustained assault from Parliament's most formidable fighting force. The sickening sound of swords and axes being hammered into flesh and bone can be heard all along the line, as can the screams of the dying. It doesn't take long before more of the Cavaliers seek to take flight, the need for survival so much stronger than any other instinct.

And so the slaughter becomes a rout.

By thirty minutes past nine in the evening, with the skies continuing to emit tears of unbridled joy, the fighting is at an end, and more than four thousand Royalists have perished. A further two thousand enemy soldiers are held captive, and all of the King's artillery is now possessed by Parliament.

The battle is over.

The tide of the war is turning.

ONE

IT IS PAST MIDNIGHT AND the songbirds retired to their treetop roosts long before I set about seeking comfort and solace in this quiet, grief-stricken place.

I am sitting in a large, sterile room. My thoughts are my own, as I have little to occupy my mind other than study lines of terracotta, web-encrusted bricks that make up the interior wall of a building hastily commandeered to house Parliament's most senior officers, the men who masterminded the full-scale destruction of the King's army some two days since.

From where I am sitting, I have spent a couple of hours scrutinising the crumbling, blistered masonry, measuring every line of mortar, and identifying line after line of imperfection and weakness. While doing so, I have wished and prayed for the torment that afflicts my companion to cease, so he and I can celebrate the magnificent victory he led us to, one that may have swung the tide of this brutal war firmly in our favour.

Alas, it will not be so. Merriment and revelry is the

last thing my friend has on his mind.

Hundreds of rotting, naked Royalist corpses, stripped bare of anything valuable and with their dignity on show for all to see, still litter the bloody killing fields less than three miles away, on the grasslands of Marston. They are waiting to join the thousands who have already been buried in mass pits, with no marker or recognition offered for their courage and sacrifice. In these cruel times, a final resting place, hidden amongst the bracken and many miles from their loved ones, is all that is afforded the vanquished.

The moorland, a nondescript place just south of York, is the site of the first significant victory for those opposing the King's autocratic regime. And, at a time when we should be toasting the heroism and courage of our troops, ordinary men who have bested their social superiors, I find I have little choice but to surrender as the chill of the summer's morn starts to torment my aching bones.

I am impotent, unable to play the part of the comforter. And I feel wretched.

My gaze falls on the man I respect more than any other in this violent and turbulent world.

Oliver Cromwell is Lieutenant-General of the Eastern Association army. He is also my friend.

Magnificent on the field of battle, Oliver now sits before me a broken man, no longer the powerful, all-conquering soldier who has just blooded a Sovereign's nose. Tonight he is closer to resigning his commission than ever before. He has been tested many times already in the turbulent months since Charles raised his standard at Nottingham. Tearful and angry, he is no longer the warrior hero his devoted men perceive him to be. The source of his distress is the double tragedy that has befallen him and his family.

In the battle that saw Prince Rupert's finest men routed as a direct result of Cromwell's strategic brilliance and bravery, Oliver's nephew, Valentine Walton, was killed.

A cannonball sliced through the young man's leg while he was leading a charge against the enemy. Despite his best efforts, the field surgeon could do nought for him, so the limb was lost, as was much of the young man's precious blood, which bathed the fields of Yorkshire in garnet gemstone red.

After the hacksaw that sliced through Valentine's bone had been wiped clean, the young man's life force quickly ebbed away, condemning him to the same fate that awaited many comrades that day – men like Major Charles Fairfax and Captains Micklethwaite and Pugh. All fought and died so bravely for the cause we all serve.

Cromwell has spent the last few hours writing a letter conveying the terrible news to his brother-in-law, the dead officer's father, a man who also carries the name of Valentine Walton.

"What say you, Francis? How does this read, is it any better than my previous inadequate attempts?" whispers Oliver, his voice barely audible as he holds the manuscript with a shaking hand. He moves a flickering candle closer, allowing its dancing flames to offer an illuminating shroud of light.

"Tell me, truthfully, friend, do my words offer the comfort and love that is intended and needed at this most terrible of times?"

Brushing aside several sheets of paper, Cromwell rises from the table and steadies himself. He turns to face me. His eyes are swollen. Deep folds of skin hang like sacks underneath his sockets. Grief has taken its toll. He pauses for a moment and then slowly starts to recount the few short sentences that will surely bring further miseries to another unsuspecting family.

"Dear Sir,

"It is our duty to sympathise in all mercies, that we may praise the Lord together, in chastisements or trials, so we may sorrow together.

"Truly England and the church of God hath had a great favour from the Lord in this great victory, given unto us such as the like never was since this war began. It had all the evidences of an absolute victory obtained by the Lord's blessing upon the godly. We never charged, but we routed the enemy. The left-wing, which I commanded, being our own horse, saving a few Scots in our rear, beat all the Prince's horse. God made them as stubble to our swords; we charged their Regiments of foot with our horse, routed all we charged. The particulars I cannot relate now, but I believe of twenty thousand, the Prince hath not four thousand left. Give glory, all the glory to God.

"Sir, God hath taken away your eldest son by a cannon shot. It broke his leg. We were necessitated to have it cut off, whereof he died.

"Sir, you know my trials this way, but the Lord supported me with this, and the Lord took him into the happiness we all pant after and live for.

"There is your precious child, full of glory, to know sin nor sorrow any more.

"He was a gallant young man, exceedingly gracious. God give you his comfort. Before his death, he was so full of comfort; it was so great above his pain. This he said to us. Indeed it was admirable. A little after, he said one thing lay upon his spirit. I asked him what that was. He told me that it was that God had not suffered him to be no more the executioner of his enemies.

"At his fall, his horse being killed with the bullet and, as I am informed, three horses more, I am told, he bid them open to the right and left, that he might see the rogues run. Truly he was exceedingly beloved in the Army of all that knew him, but few knew him, for he was a precious young man, fit for God.

"You have cause to bless the Lord. He is a glorious saint in heaven, wherein you ought exceedingly to rejoice. Let this drink up your sorrow, seeing these are not feigned words to comfort you, but the thing is so real and undoubted a truth. You may do all things by the strength of Christ. Seek that, and you shall easily bear your trial.

"Let this public mercy to the church of God make you forget your private sorrow. The Lord be your strength, so prays your truly faithful and loving brother..."

As he reaches out and puts the letter on the desk, I can clearly see the tears streaming down Oliver's reddened face, staining his doublet and the shirt beneath. His acute distress is plain to see.

"Is it suffice, dear friend?" he enquires of me. "Is it the epitaph and encourager I hope it to be?"

I nod my head in approval, saying: "Words really are inadequate at moments like these, Oliver. You know that as well as I. Yet what you have written will be a true source of comfort. They will know their son died bravely, like the martyr he is."

For the briefest of moments, a flicker of contentment flashes in Oliver's eyes. Then it is gone.

"Thank you for your forbearance, Francis," he adds. "I may make some further, minor amendments, but I think it will do. It will have to. I must write to more unfortunate people who have suffered the loss of loved ones, and there are also campaigning matters to consider."

I have never met Valentine's mother, but I am told her son was the embodiment of her. All members of the Cromwell family have the same distinctive physical features: a prominent nose and a full, strong forehead. They are also the bravest of people. Margaret, Valentine's mother, is cut from this rock. So, too, is her brother, Oliver, the rising star of the Parliamentary army.

While Valentine's fate has deeply upset Cromwell, this is only a minor part of the torment that now grips his soul at this increasingly late hour. For what has caught the Lieutenant-General off-guard and unprepared is the news he has just received about the fate of his eldest surviving child, a gallant youth also named Oliver.

Cromwell's son is a Parliamentary officer. He is based at Newport Pagnell, where he has been garrisoned for several months. The stronghold seeks to keep the peace on the Northamptonshire border, where Royalist forces violate villages and towns indiscriminately.

During his time at the garrison, young Cromwell has acquitted himself well, much to the satisfaction of his doting father. The latter, while in my company, has frequently talked about his heir affectionately and lovingly.

Just after Oliver had started to write to his brother-in-law and sister about Valentine's tragic demise, a messenger arrives at the make-do army headquarters, informing the Lieutenant-General of a most grievous personal tragedy.

According to the dispatch now resting on the floor, discarded as unrestrained grief claimed its intended target, young Oliver was struck down by Smallpox only a few days ago. Despite valiant efforts to save him, the young man slipped into the after-world painlessly, without gaining consciousness.

My friend has said nothing of note to me since reading the message. Instead, the colour has continued to drain from his face, and I have heard the occasional sob. But, such is the man's integrity; he continues to put the interests of Valentine's parents before those of his own. There is flowing movement in the quill as he makes a handful of necessary changes to the letter he read to me, which conveys the news every parent dreads receiving.

Eventually, he completes the painful task. He looks up. He is staring out of the window into the void that is the early morning of Monday, the fourth day of July. Only now is it time for Oliver to comprehend his loss.

"I am hard-pressed to believe what I have read," he says, breaking the silence, his right hand wiping away more tears. "I can scarce believe it: Oliver, my eldest son, gone? So young, so vibrant, a young man with so much to offer this world. Lost to the Pox! Francis, my heart aches in a way I never thought possible. Tell me, man, what am I to do?

"I know I can speak openly to you, my friend. I am

safe from ridicule and being patronised. You know the pain of a father who has lost a child. The agony is tangible. It is all-consuming."

I am unprepared for Oliver's stuttering, rasping words.

It is just three months and a few days since my beloved daughters, Barbara and Isable, were murdered in cold blood by a heartless Royalist mercenary, whom I will track down and dish out my own summary justice to.

Gustav Holck, an officer loyal to the princes Rupert and Maurice, is the man's name. And I will do everything in my power to hunt him down like the dog he is.

"Alas, there is nought I can say that will ease your pain, Oliver," I say rather clumsily. "Only the Lord has the power to do that. But I will pray for you, your family and the soul of young Oliver. That, I am afraid, is the extent of what I can do."

Before Saturday's great victory, I spent seven long weeks attempting to track down Holck in Newark-on-Trent and the surrounding area, aided by a loyal agent called Edmund Goodyeare.

Unfortunately, our efforts were to no avail. On the occasions we saw the Bohemian, he was in the company of other Cavaliers. To have confronted him would have meant certain death or, at the very least, capture, imprisonment and torture.

While I care little for my own life, I could not condemn Goodyeare to such a fate. He is too valuable to Parliament's cause for me to sacrifice him in pursuit of my own vendetta.

I have also pledged to my wife that I will do all in my

power to stay alive. For she, and my surviving four children, need me. And, when my heartache pains me no more, and a renewed zest grips my soul, we will most surely need each other.

Cromwell knows of my suffering. And now, alas, he can relate to the all-consuming grief I continue to experience and the utter feeling of helplessness I endure.

How I wish it weren't so.

"Oliver, my friend," I say, looking at him directly. "Words cannot express how I feel at this time. My sorrow for you is profound and sincere. I know precisely how you are feeling, for it was not so long ago I discovered the deaths of my girls and was gripped by an indescribable torment and pain. And, even after all these weeks have passed, it remains so.

"Nothing prepares you for the sense of loss, helplessness and anger that is unleashed from within, albeit we all grieve in different ways, as you will.

"At times like this, we need the support of our friends and family. And you will be no exception. But the army and Parliament also have vital needs. So there will be an expectation you are of sound mind, with few distractions, building on the resounding success you have overseen here, in this barren place. Oliver's death is tragic for Elizabeth and your children, but it is also a badge of honour for the man taming a King.

"One more victory like this, and the war will be won. But you must allow me and others who have experienced the awful loss of a child to help you through what will be a challenging time. Allow us the honour of supporting you as only brothers in Christ can."

Cromwell stares into the gathering gloom for what seems like an age. He says nothing. There is much to ponder and many things to digest. At such times words are no comfort. Eventually, his hooded and bloodstained eyes focus on me.

"Go to your mattress and sleep, my young and concerned friend," he says with a composed voice. "Pray to our Father for the souls of your daughters and ask him to continue protecting Isabel, Francis and Anne. God is good. He never fails us, and he will always seek to reward the righteous.

"Allow me the night to grieve for my son and my nephew. I will not dwell on things. But I do need to pray and reconcile myself to their losses. I also need to write a letter to Elizabeth. Her pain, the suffering of a mother, will be so much greater because I cannot console her. But I pledge I will be myself come the morn. I cannot be anything else. The King has been weakened, so I cannot allow my tragic circumstances to get in the way of everything that has been achieved."

I stand up and embrace him. For five long minutes, we hold each other as brothers in arms and faith do. Then he suddenly releases his grip, and I sense he is relaxed once again.

"Try and rest," I say. "Like Valentine, young Oliver is now at peace, sitting in the company of our Father. So there is a joy to be had as well as grief. And I will pray the torment you are suffering is short-lived."

I take my leave of the Lieutenant-General, closing the heavy oak door as quietly as I can as I seek the refuge of my makeshift quarters.

As I walk down the dimly lit hall to my chamber, loud, heart-wrenching sobs follow me into the darkness.

Now I have left his company, Oliver can stop pretending. Once again, he can be the father and husband he longs to be.

TWO

LESS THAN FIVE HOURS AFTER I left him to come to terms with his despair and inner thoughts, Cromwell is standing over me, gently shaking me by the shoulder.

His firm hands draw me out of my slumber. Temporarily my vision is blurred; I cannot make out the features of my friend and superior. I fumble for my pocket watch. I look at the dial, but for a moment, all I see are the ghostly faces of Barbara and Isable staring back. Then reality sets in, and I see the time: it is seven o'clock. My head quickly clears, helped, no doubt, by the bed lice as they continue devouring my filthy and tainted flesh.

"Come, young friend," commands Oliver as my eyes connect with his. "There is much to do and such little time. And you need to be on your way before the ninth hour of this fine summer's morn. So make haste. We breakfast in ten minutes, and we have a visitor of note who wishes to speak to you."

My limbs ache. The ague that envelops my entire body on occasion is with me once again, and I am aware of an acrid bitterness in my mouth. I take a sip from the ale tankard that I brought to my room only a few hours ago, and I instantly regret my decision. It tastes like weasel piss, and I spit out the foul liquid as quickly as I have consumed it. I rise, dress quickly and make my way to where Cromwell and his most trusted officers are being fed a concoction of pottage and The Word.

As I approach the scullery, I hear the final verses of Psalm One being read aloud by Oliver and at least twenty voices.

I recognise some of the officers present, the likes of Rossiter and Langland; their features daubed in a mixture of excitement and deep concentration.

Two men standing on either side of the solitary window basked in sunlight are the sole focus of the tightly packed room. On the left is Cromwell, his face full of vitality and vigour, with no trace of the deep emotions he displayed so vividly to me only hours earlier. If you didn't know him, you would be oblivious to his pain and suffering. Yet, while his innards may have been torn into pieces at the news of young Oliver's demise and Valentine's tragic loss, he is mastering his feelings admirably. He is a leader of men who can exercise the utmost control and self-restraint, not the weakling I am.

To Cromwell's left stands Sir Thomas Fairfax, joint overall commander of the victorious Parliamentarian army.

Although severely wounded in his arm during the fighting and having lost his brother, Charles, Sir Thomas radiates a power, confidence and humility only found in a small number of men. Cromwell is another who exudes this kind of aura, as did the late John Pym, or "King Pym" as we used to refer to him when he was among the living.

I last saw Fairfax just before my company was routed at the one-sided slaughter we now call the Battle of Adwalton Moor. That day, when I was given orders by his over-confident father, General Ferdandino Fairfax, forty-nine of my best men perished needlessly. As a result, the Fairfaxes bore the brunt of my anger and dismay. Later, when my hot head had cooled, I realised the General and his son had little choice but to engage with the enemy that fateful day when God allowed the blood of good, honest soldiers to stain the lush grasslands of Yorkshire.

It is just over a year since the events that took place at Adwalton changed the course of my destiny. And as I listen to Thomas Fairfax, I realise I am not the only one who is now embarking on a new path in life's ever-changing tapestry.

"Brothers," he proclaims. "Comrades, for that is what we are, our valiant efforts of recent days have humbled the King and brought about Parliament's greatest success of the war. Be assured, your country is grateful."

Cheering accompanies these words, but young Fairfax quickly hushes the room.

"Nay, this is not a time for self-congratulation; far from it," he says. "Friends, I am honoured to be in your presence this morning. You and your men have fought valiantly and won a mighty victory. But let us not forget that there are those among us who are bearing grievous loss. Their pain is raw. Its presence threatens to suffocate our souls, and I know what I speak of as I count myself among this number.

"But, as much as I mourn the loss of my beloved brother, as much as you do your loved ones and friends, I say we must set this pain aside and begin the next phase of this war with a speed and precision we have rarely displayed. There is so much that still needs to be accomplished if we are to win the day. The King and his armies must be defeated absolutely. There can be no let-up on our part, not until the tyrant is crushed and a new kind of peace restored to our land. And, in this endeavour, you all have critical roles to play. What say you, are you up for the fight that is to come?"

Enthusiastic cheering accompanies the rousing words. After a while, a gesture from Cromwell is all it takes to silence the appreciative audience once again, allowing Sir Thomas to continue his oratory. He leans forward, gripping a rustic chair to steady his balance, speaking slowly and deliberately.

"As you are aware, Lieutenant-General Cromwell, myself and others, are formulating plans for the creation of a new type of army, one built upon the principles that defeated our foe just two days ago. But even though we achieved remarkable success on the moorland of Marston, I do not think we have widespread support for our venture. On the contrary, there will be much opposition to the changes we are to propose, not least among the Lords. My father may even oppose our plans. But change is sorely needed, and regardless of the personal cost to myself, I am resolved to doing all in my power to make our ambition of creating a New Model Army a reality."

At that moment, Sir Thomas lets out a groan, and a red stain is visible on his doublet for the first time. He pauses. An officer standing close by eases him onto the chair at his side.

"Please accept my apologies," he chirps in a bid to

appease any anxieties that may be growing among the assembled men. As Fairfax speaks, he glances at his doublet. "As you can see, my wounds are still fresh from the fighting, and an over-excited disposition is not good for them!"

Appreciative nods and a chorus of "aye" greet this statement.

"Now, getting back to business, I urge you to go back to your men and begin preparations for what is to come," he adds. "Do not shirk from your duties, gentlemen. You must continue the quest of turning your companies and regiments into disciplined fighting units. It will take practice and vigour, and you will not be popular for taking your men to task. But take heart from knowing you will be doing the right thing for England and your God."

A ripple of approval cascades through the men standing around me when it is clear young Fairfax will say no more. Ale tankards start beating the table in unison, regardless of whether they are empty or not. The ovation, which is genuine and unprompted, lasts for several minutes. It would have lasted longer if Cromwell had not called proceedings to a halt.

"Brothers," he says. "Eat and then be about your business. There is little time and much to do. May you go with God's blessings, knowing you are fulfilling His will."

As I prepare to take my leave and return to my room to await my orders, Oliver beckons me to the window, where he and Fairfax remain.

"Sir Thomas, I think you are already acquainted with my good friend, Captain Francis Hacker," he says by way of introduction. "Francis has been an invaluable servant to Parliament's cause these past few months and a very good friend to me."

The young man's intelligent dark eyes fix on me. He says nothing for a few seconds, but an inner sixth sense tells me I meet with his approval.

"I remember you well, Captain," he says warmly. "I seem to remember you being a frustrated soul when you addressed my father and myself shortly before the Northern Association army was defeated at Adwalton. And, of course, you had every right to be dismayed. How I wish we had listened to your advice more intently that day."

As I try to recall the detail of our first meeting, Fairfax leans forward slightly and takes my hand. Like Cromwell, he has a natural, vice-like grip.

"It is an honour to be in your company once again, sir," he continues. "I have heard much about your exploits on behalf of Parliament these past few months, not least the terrible personal sacrifice you recently endured. Tell me, how is your good wife and family. Are they bearing up?"

Talk of Isabel and my beautiful surviving children disarms me. I am unprepared for the emotions that well up inside me and threaten to spill over. It has been more than two months since I left Stathern in pursuit of Holck. Since then, I have attempted to do all in my power to avoid thinking of my beloved home. My only focus has been the delivery of my own swift justice. The lure of Isabel and the children is always strong and, if I let it, plays to my natural weaknesses. Even so, I recognise I have been a negligent and selfish husband and father, deserting those dearest to me at their greatest hour of need. And if I know this to be true, others do too.

If I am brutally honest about my motives, I realise my absence from Stathern has nothing to do with seeking justice for my slain children and Peter and Marjorie Harrington, who were butchered by the hands of the same assassin. No. It is all about my inability to deal with the guilt I feel for the deaths of people I cared for deeply but could not protect. That is the nub of it.

I was warned from the outset that if I interfered in affairs of the State, I could suffer dearly. These were the prophetic words spoken at the outset that I chose to ignore. It was an inconvenient truth, something I defied because I sought the acclamation of my superiors rather than honouring the vows I made to Isabel on the day of our wedding. Now I have been caught out, and I am paying a high price, for the guilt I bear is crushing me.

I am in danger of being carried away on a wave of regret, but thankfully Cromwell brings me back to reality.

"What say you, Francis?" I hear the Lieutenant-General saying to me. "Francis, what are your thoughts on the matter?"

My vacant expression betrays the confusion and embarrassment I am feeling. I have wandered off into my own world again, something I am prone to doing, albeit usually in far less illustrious company. It appears the dullard in me has come to the fore yet again.

"I… I… I…" The words will not come. I cannot speak.

The simple truth is I do not know what is being asked of me and by whom, such are the deep emotions evoked in me when I think about my family.

My acute and obvious discomfort is eventually relieved by Oliver's comforting voice.

"You have been through a lot this past year, my young, loyal friend," he says while holding my arm and looking directly at me. "That is plain for Sir Thomas and me to see. However, you were thinking of something else when Sir Thomas asked your opinion of how we should seek to organise and recruit the Horse of the New Model Army.

"If anyone else had shown such discourtesy, I would have them horse-whipped on the spot. But not you; you have been sorely tested this past year, and, in the face of adversity, you have proven the strength of your friendship and loyalty on countless occasions.

"I know you, Francis Hacker. I can feel the inner torment and pain you are experiencing. On the one hand, you seek to serve Parliament as the committed officer you are. Yet, you also wish to protect your wife and children and lead the men you have turned into one of the finest companies of horse in the whole army. I understand these emotions very well, and that is why you will be astride Bucephalus and making your way home before the day is out. Isabel and your family need you, and you need them. Therefore, there will be no discussion on the matter."

Oliver is good to his word. I leave the camp at two o'clock in the afternoon. The sun is beating down, and a gentle breeze is blowing through the hills that surround Cromwell's temporary headquarters. I have a little more than forty miles of riding ahead of me and need to make good time to reach the outskirts of Barnsley, where I hope to find a quiet, isolated inn to rest up for the evening.

Considering the lateness of the day, I intend to complete just under half of my journey today and go at a steady pace the morrow, when a further sixty miles will need to be negotiated. The ride will be tiring, but the reward of being reunited with those dearest to me, and the men of the Leicestershire Militia, is ample recompense.

Bucephalus is eager to be on his way. My magnificent horse, named after the jet-black steed that carried Alexander the Great into battle so many times, has been incarcerated in the stables for long periods due to my relative inactivity. Understandably, he has grown frustrated at his lack of freedom. However, now he has open fields and roads ahead of him, and he is determined to make up for lost time.

Even though I don't know if he observed my departure, I count myself blessed to be trusted by a man like Cromwell. I do not know what the man sees in me, for I am acutely aware of my limitations, weaknesses, and sins. But he talks to me as if I am his equal, and he confides spiritual and worldly things in me that I cannot believe he utters to many others. He is more than a score of years older than me, yet I feel a connection and loyalty to this man that is hard to articulate. I only hope I can remain faithful to him.

Before I leave him, Cromwell talks frankly about the war effort and the critical need to keep the north of England connected to the south.

"Although you are departing for home, do not think for one minute you will have an easy time of it," he says with a sternness and seriousness to his voice. "You and the Midlands Association army have a critical role to play in keeping the likes of 'Blind' Henry Hastings and Gervase

Lucas occupied. We cannot allow them to disrupt our supply lines and wreak havoc. Parliament needs you to take the fight to these men, even though your own commander is reluctant to do so."

Talk of my superior officer forces me to think of Lord Grey of Groby, the overall commander of the Parliamentary army in Leicestershire, Nottinghamshire, Derbyshire, Rutlandshire and Northamptonshire. He is an ancestor of the nine-day queen, Lady Jane Grey, son of the Earl of Stamford, and, in my opinion, a proud, arrogant and weak man. I have little time for him, and Grey knows it. Nevertheless, he tolerates me and men like Cromwell. We are drawn from the gentry, and because we are capable soldiers, we are useful to him. If we couldn't fight, there would be no reason to acknowledge us.

"I know what you are thinking," comments Oliver while wagging his right index finger admonishingly in my direction. "My encouragement to you is banish these thoughts; I know of your loathing for Grey. It is certainly equal to that of my own, possibly greater. But let us not forget, the man controls Parliament's strength in a critical part of the country. If he is not prepared to use his forces correctly, we need him to allow you, and others, to be able to use your companies to take the fight to the enemy with his blessing.

"Do you understand what I am asking of you, Francis? You need to be the fist that holds everything together."

A curt nod of my head encourages the ever-animated Lieutenant-General to continue.

"Gain his confidence. That is what I am urging you to do, Francis. The Midlands is crucial to the success of the war. We need to keep Hastings and his Ashby hordes at bay, and we need to contain Lucas at Belvoir Castle and not allow him untroubled access to Newark. The more you can influence proceedings in these parts, and the more you can tie these two men up, the closer we will be to prevailing."

My conversation with Cromwell was more than six hours ago, and the army encampment is now far behind me.

I have almost reached my destination. Bucephalus and I are tired, and our stomachs are protesting due to a lack of sustenance. We need to find a place to rest and some food to eat.

A snort from Becaphalus helps me focus on negotiating a fast-running stream that blocks our path. It is a minor tributary feeding into the River Ouse, which flows from beyond York to the outskirts of Hull.

As we began to find a path through the water, I see, barely a hundred feet away from me on the opposite side of the bank, a family watching on. They must have been scrutinising me for several minutes, yet I have only just noticed them.

A man, a woman and what I take to be their two young urchins – I cannot identify whether they are girl or boy – have been looking at me keenly, ever since I entered the fast-flowing mud-brown waters. As I watch them, I berate myself for my lack of alertness. They could have easily been Cavaliers, and I wouldn't have known about their presence until it was too late.

"Good day to you, sir; God's blessings be upon you, madam," I say to the couple as I pass closely by, tapping the brim of my hat respectfully. "Is it not a fine day?"

The man lifts his head; his face is scarred. A blistering, vivid red wound runs diagonally across his left cheek. "And a good day to you, sir," he says, his accent cloaked with the thick lilt associated with Yorkshire folk. "That is a magnificent horse; he must be at least nineteen hands high?"

I stop and turn Bucephalus, so I am directly addressing the man and his family.

"He most certainly is," I say as I ease out of the saddle and jump onto the firm ground.

"Are you far from home?" I enquire. "Is there aught to fear in these parts for a man such as myself?"

I am tired, and my concentration is poor. At the moment, I am a liability to myself and the cause I serve. But I desperately need to know what lies ahead as there are more than three score miles to cover before I reach the safety of Stathern.

"The King's men have fled; no Cavaliers are remaining in these parts," says the man, growing in confidence. "Since the great battle, none have been sighted around here. The last ones left two days ago. If they had stayed, they would have received little comfort. Moreover, local people in these parts have no particular love for the Royalists."

My wariness starts to ease. I find the man's words reassuring.

"And you, sir," I enquire. "To be sure of whom I am addressing, to whom do you give your allegiance: Parliament or the King?"

Before he can answer, the woman I presume to be his wife steps forward. She has a confidence and grace not customarily associated with the poor.

"He fought for Lord Fairfax, sir, for the first year of the war," she says with steel in her voice. "He was a Pikeman until the defeat at Adwalton Moor. Since then, we have been near destitute, doing as best we can to eke out a living. And while not all of our neighbours take delight at Parliament's great victory, my husband and I are thanking God for His blessing on our country. For we are no lovers of Kings, their evil ways and their broken promises."

I nod my head in approval.

"Aye, mistress," I say. "And it is my good fortune to meet you this day. I know all too well of the ills that befell Parliament at that dreadful place just over a year ago. I was there myself, and I lost many a good man to the Cavalier's musket, sword and axe, but enough of the woes of the past. Pray, tell me where I am, and if there is an inn in these parts where a man such as I can rest until the morning?"

The pair turn to each other, speaking in hushed voices. As hard as I try, I am unable to hear what they are saying. Finally, after a minute or two of conversation, they appear to reach an accord.

"Sir, you are close to the villages of Crane Moor and Thurgoland," says the man. "We hail from these parts, and I am sorry to have to tell you there is no inn within ten miles that is likely to be able to offer you the lodgings you seek this evening.

"You will need to ride to Sheffield, some eighteen miles away as the crow flies, to secure comfort at a tavern or hostelry. And there is no guarantee they will have room for you at this late hour. But you are more than welcome to stay at our humble dwelling. We don't have a lot of food or space. But what we do have, we are willing to share with you."

My relief is palpable. I nod my head and smile. I am grateful to accept the generous terms offered to me by this family of Samaritans.

We travel the short distance to Crane Moor, an isolated place consisting of a few houses and surrounded by miles of open, lush countryside. A well dominates the centre of the village, and the four sails of a Mill fill the sky to the north.

Close by, Rooks are nesting in a copse brimming with Ash, Oak and Chestnut trees, and they are in full cry. So too are the sheep that are dotted around the fertile fields. Their bleating invades the stillness of an evening sky that is preparing itself to embrace the rapidly approaching dusk.

It has taken twenty minutes to travel the short journey from the stream to Crane Moor. During that time, I have learned my hosts for the night are called Josiah and Ursula Goswick. Their two children are eight-year-old Eunice and Gideon, who is eighteen months younger than his sister.

The family's humble home, a small wattle and daub construction comprising four tidy rooms and a thatched roof in need of repair, is a very welcome sanctuary. Forty miles of riding and the rigours of recent days have taken their toll on my body and mind. I am exhausted, and Becaphulus needs to recuperate, as it is several weeks since he last undertook such a journey.

After taking my bedroll to an attic room where the children usually sleep, I make my way to the kitchen and scullery. There I witness family life in full flow: Eunice and Gideon eat bread cakes and cheese and talk animatedly about my arrival. Ursula, meanwhile, is toiling over the fire, stirring what appears to be an excellent stew; its rich aroma can be smelled throughout the dwelling.

I notice a crudely crafted crucifix situated just above the doorframe of the kitchen, honouring the death and resurrection of Christ Jesus. There is one in the room I am occupying. A copy of the King James Bible is also visible. It seems I am staying with believers who can read and are able to study the Word.

The sight of the crosses and the Good Book brings a smile to my face. I am left thinking that although prayer has not featured in my daily rituals in a meaningful way since the deaths of Barbara and Isable, and the sin in my life has undoubtedly been controlling my actions for far too long, it appears the good Lord is continuing to watch over me.

"I hope you have made yourself comfortable," says Josiah when he notices me watching his family go about their business. "As you can see, we don't have much in the way of luxuries, but the rooms are dry and clean. So you should be able to get a good night's sleep before you continue your journey. And Ursula is a wonderful cook. She is just preparing our fare for the evening. So dinner will be served shortly."

My host points to the far end of the table that dominates the room. The two children are finishing their meal at one end. On occasion, I see them looking up and watching me, yet as soon as I cast a glance in their direction, they avert their gaze from the stranger in their midst. But they cannot conceal the impish grins in the corner of their mouths, which tells me all I need to know: this is a loving and caring home.

I sit at the place where Josiah has ushered me. Within a few seconds, a tankard full of ale appears and is placed before me.

"This will quench your thirst until Ursula has finished preparing the meal," he says. "And there is more should you need it."

I drink vigorously and start to relax, the sweet taste of the barley helping my body and mind gain some long overdue peace and respite.

The warmth of the hospitality I am being afforded threatens to overwhelm me. Here I am, a wealthy and relatively powerful man, being given charity by people who can scarcely afford to feed themselves. Yet here they are, freely giving their precious food to me, knowing well they may not be able to feed themselves in the days to come.

I feel hot tears welling up inside me. Shame too. Before the dam threatens to burst and my weakness comes flooding out, I seek to engage Josiah and Ursula in conversation.

"In these hard times, it is surprising to find people as generous as yourselves," I say. "I thank you warmly for your kindness and hospitality. But, pray, tell me a little about yourselves. How are you surviving, and what can be done to give you the security you and your children need?"

Josiah turns around and looks at me coolly. He focuses on the sword at my side.

"Francis," he says. "It may seem strange, but we have no fear of men like you carrying a weapon of war. On the contrary, our faith is our guide. It strengthens and emboldens us, for we take the words of Mark's Gospel literally, particularly the passage that commands us to love our neighbour as much as we love ourselves.

"We are simple people who love God. We are not ashamed to call him Saviour. In times like these, we know He will never desert us or abandon the promise He has made to us."

As I listen to Josiah's words, goosebumps appear on my arms, and I am suddenly reacquainted with a presence I have not known for many months.

Even though I have spent several weeks in the field with Cromwell and his band of priestly warriors, defeating the very best men the King could throw at us, I have been unable to be at peace with my God. I have been disobedient. I have been in the wilderness, obsessed with seeking revenge for the pain inflicted on my family. Yet now, by having a conversation with a man I do not know, I suddenly start to see things differently, and I feel humbled and wretched.

Ursula breaks the spell I am under by placing a bowl of steaming stew under my nose. A chunk of bread accompanies it.

After we give thanks for the food on the table, my hunger takes hold, and I do not raise my head until the last spoonful of gravy has been consumed. If anything, the smell of Ursula's fine cooking didn't do the meal justice. It was wonderful. God is good.

When my belly is full and my hosts are relaxed and seeking to converse, I start to tell them about the pain I have experienced in my own life. Shortly after I have finished recounting the trials and tribulations of the last two years, I feel a sense of tranquillity. And as peace starts to descend, it is not long before the tears I have fought hard to suppress all evening are finally released.

"I feel your pain," says Josiah, reaching out to grip my hand. "To lose your children under such circumstances is truly heart-breaking. The man, Holck, is consumed with evil. But you can be assured he will face his own Judgment Day before God. That is something of which you can be certain. None of us can escape this moment. But the path of revenge is not one you should be taking. Francis, I sense our Lord has other plans for you that you must heed."

The truth sometimes feels like a dagger piercing your flesh. It bites deep, and you are powerless to prevent its thrust. Tonight is one of those occasions. I should have the strength and determination to challenge these assertions. But I have none. I am impotent.

Perhaps sensing my unease, Josiah changes the subject.

He enquires: "Francis, what of your wife and your surviving children, how have they been faring these past few months? Do you know how they fare? Have you been writing to them? Have they been in your prayers? Is all good with them?"

I stop eating and put down my fork. I feel a coldness within.

"I meant no offence," Josiah says quickly, seeing my abrupt change in mood and perhaps fearing a violent reaction. "I spoke out of turn. Please forgive me."

Sitting alongside him, Ursula looks alarmed. Her right eye starts to twitch. She is tired and stressed. Thankfully the children have long since settled down for the evening in the room they will be sharing with their parents, where the black of the night provides a soothing blanket.

After a while, I unclench my fists.

"There is nothing to forgive," I say, my voice flat and detached. "You have simply brought me to my senses. I have been a reckless braggart these past months, wallowing in self-pity and forsaking my God and my family. My quest for vengeance has been a corrupting influence. It has been consuming me from within.

"Your kindness will not be forgotten. Nor will your willingness to listen to my tale of woe. You have made a new friend this day, one who will remain loyal and indebted to you."

Even as the gloom of the evening obscures our features, the relief on the faces of Josiah and Ursula is plain to see.

I reach out and clutch their hands, a motion that catches them both by surprise. As I hold their calloused fingers and palms, I close my eyes and pray aloud. Thanks to these gentle people, I am on the path of being at one with my God again and understanding my destiny. And for that, I will be forever grateful.

I awake on the morning of Tuesday, the fifth day of July, reinvigorated. It is seven o'clock, and I can hear the world is alive with the noise of activity. My head no longer feels heavy, and there is a zest coursing through my veins that I haven't experienced in a long time.

In the house, there is also a vigour I find myself longing to taste once again. I can hear the children, Eunice and Gideon, playing downstairs. Their infectious, innocent laughter is ringing throughout the house. Outside, the family's resident chickens and cockerels are making a noise that is so loud the dead buried in the nearby churchyard could soon be awoken. I smile to myself. Witnessing this uncomplicated and simple life is making me feel good.

I wash my face. Coldwater has rarely felt so refreshing. I tidy my hose, shirt and doublet. At long last, I feel ready to continue on my journey.

"Francis," comes Ursula's voice, speaking with genuine warmth. "There is food on the table. It is only pottage and oatcakes, but it will hold you in good stead until lunchtime. Come, help yourself."

I need no further encouragement.

I have almost sixty miles of riding to negotiate today; I will be passing Sheffield, following the main supply route to Nottingham. The town of Newark would be a more obvious destination, but it has been under the control of the Royalists since the outbreak of hostilities. So a detour is in order. But once I see the shimmering waters of the River Trent, I will know I am close to home.

Under normal circumstances, Stathern – and Isabel – will be less than an hour's gentle ride away when I reach this point. And right now, I can almost taste the excitement I am feeling.

After finishing my breakfast and drinking some fresh goats milk, I take my leave of Josiah, Ursula and the children. The sun is shining brightly, even at this early hour, and the omens feel good. I recite Psalm Twenty Three, the Lord's Prayer, with them as we stand in their garden, and I feel a strong and true bond.

"I thank you," I say. "In a short space of time, you have given me something very precious, something I thought was lost. Words cannot describe the gratitude I feel and the debt I owe to you both."

Josiah has ensured Bucephalus has been watered and fed, and my impatient steed is again pawing the ground where he stands, eager to be on his way. He senses that before the day is over, he will be reunited with my dear wife, his mistress, and he wants to be on his way.

Unknown to my hosts, I have left them most of the money I am carrying, except for a few shillings. It amounts to more than five pounds and a few half-crowns, enough to keep them in food for several months. It is all I have. If I could do more, I most certainly would.

I get comfortable in my saddle, wave my goodbyes to my newly found saviours and kick my stirrups gently into Bucephalus's muscular flanks. A trot becomes a canter, and a canter quickly becomes a full-blown gallop. In quick time, master and beast are a blur of motion, the pulsing sun guiding our way as we ease through the pasturelands of Yorkshire and Derbyshire and into the cattle-filled fields of north Nottinghamshire.

I have been absent from Stathern and the Vale of Belvoir for what seems like an age. God will dictate what kind of welcome awaits me, but I am now fully aware my homecoming is long overdue. My family and men need me – and I most surely need them.

The slate rooftops of Stathern, silhouetted like glistening rows of discoloured teeth by the fading rays of the summer sun, act as my compass for the last couple of miles.

The last part of my journey has taken some nine hours to negotiate and has been trouble-free. The closest I came to being ambushed was when an adventurous seagull, almost a hundred miles away from the nearest coast, attempted to steal the bread and cheese lunch I was eating beneath a large Sycamore tree, sited on the hills just outside Chesterfield. As I looked yonder, marvelling at the crooked spire of Saint Mary's Church, the impudent bird made its audacious bid. Thankfully, I was more than a match for the would-be thief, who scampered away defeated after my outstretched boot just failed to connect with its probing beak.

To see my home on the horizon, looking so peaceful and tranquil, evokes deep emotions in me that I have locked away securely these past ten weeks. How right I was. I can feel my heart beating wildly. A layer of sweat covers my brow. There is a knot in my stomach. I am happy.

Bucephalus knows these fields and lanes better even than I do, and he needs no guidance from the reins I am holding lightly in my hands. Despite riding for so many miles this day, he is revitalised when he senses the Hall is tantalisingly close. So am I.

I glance at my pocket watch. It reveals it is ten minutes past five in the evening. The children will be eating their supper. But I am not sure what Isabel will be doing or whether she will be pleased to see me. After all, even though I had her blessing when I left Stathern, I deserted her at the greatest time of need.

A couple of faces appear at windows in neighbouring cottages as I make my approach to The Hall. I wave and receive beaming smiles in return. I pass by Saint Guthlacs, silently praying I won't have the misfortune of running into William Norwich, the church's King-loving Minister and the last man I would wish to see on my return. Thankfully, he does not appear and, therefore, will not impede my progress.

I turn a corner and enter the familiar courtyard. I dismount where the slate paving slabs start, and the grass of the garden ends, and I immediately gather the reins. As I do, I hear a direct challenge barked in my direction.

"Stand still, sir, and state your business," calls a determined and robust voice. "Pray, tell me why you think you have a right to be visiting this house uninvited at this hour?"

I recognise the voice immediately.

"Abijah?" I cry. "Abijah, is that you?"

I hear footsteps to my left. Out of the dense foliage and branches of the trees emerges the finely cut figure of Abijah Swan, my oldest and dearest friend and my second in command. He is running towards me.

"Francis, is that really you?" he says as we come together and embrace. "Forgive my jest. I received word you were travelling this way less than an hour ago when a dispatch rider alerted me. So I have known for almost an hour you are heading this way. Even so, I have been unable to prepare for your return, and I haven't yet informed Isabel. I have been planning for an engagement at Wilne Ferry, which takes place the morrow."

I take a pace backwards and look at my friend. He looks well. Strong. Confident. And he is smiling.

"It is wonderful to see you," is all I can say before the shrieks of my daughter break through the serenity of the early evening.

"Papa, Papa, Papa" is shouted aloud excitedly by Anne, my surviving daughter, as she races towards the spot where Abijah and I stand. Following a few paces behind is Isabel, and by her side is Francis, my son and heir. They are holding hands, slowly approaching the spot where I stand. My wife is weeping uncontrollably, and I pray they are tears of joy.

Suddenly I feel the impact of a young body hitting my midriff. It is a joyous feeling. I bend down and run my fingers through Anne's dark hair as she grips me tightly around the waist, her head nestling on my hip bone. But as much as I love my children, I cannot take my eyes off my wife. When she is a few yards away, out of the corner of my eye, I see Abijah gently retreat a few paces. And then my Isabel is standing before me, her head encompassed by a golden orb weaved by the rays of the early evening sunshine.

"Francis, you have returned," she says, her voice trembling, struggling to contain the emotion welling up inside. "Thanks be to God. You are home."

THREE

I AWAKE TO THE GENTLE touch of Isabel running her fingers through my hair. I do not know how long my wife has been watching me, propped up by her delicate yet deceptively strong right arm. How I have missed her touch and smell.

It is dawn on Tuesday, the fifth day of July, and it is now a little more than twelve hours since I returned to my family and friends from my self-imposed exile. It is also the twelfth anniversary of my wedding. Today, the air of Stathern is fresh, untainted by the stench of human filth or rotting limbs. I feel blessed. I feel alive. And I know I am loved.

Thankfully, Isabel understands I am not yet ready to answer all her questions, so she has held back from probing too deeply about my whereabouts these past months. The only thing I have spoken about in detail is our glorious victory at Marston Moor, news of which is only now reaching parts of England outside of the north.

Her reaction is predictable and loving: she doesn't

want to know any detail about the fighting; all she seeks are assurances that I have kept myself out of harm's way. When my stilled tongue remains silent in this regard, the topic of our conversation changes.

"The fact you are here, and in one piece, is enough for the moment," she says when she is no longer able to hide her mild irritation. "I will ask no more questions and think it best that we change the subject."

And so we do.

I don't underestimate the difficulties my wife is experiencing in suppressing her natural inquisitiveness and concern; after all, she knows of my weaknesses and the unpredictable state of my mind. But she also knows I will tell her all. I always do, eventually, when the healing has started, and I am able. For between man and wife, there can be no secrets.

Isabel adopts a patient approach, choosing to inform me about everything that has transpired in these parts: how the family has adjusted to the tragic loss of Barbara and Isable; how the Militia has regrouped and taken the fight to the likes of Hastings at Ashby and the wider region; and how the ordinary folk of the surrounding villages are coping with the continuing deprivations the war is bringing to their own doorsteps.

We finish talking at seven o'clock in the morning, as the Hall comes alive once again, for my wife has much to say and even though I am weary and my body will willingly succumb to the bosom of the night, I do not do so. And this is the right thing to do, for what I have learned gives me renewed hope.

As every day goes by, Francis and Anne are gradually forgetting the terrible events of Sunday, the twelfth day of March. More than three months on, joy is starting to return to their lives. Anne, the youngest of my surviving children, is taking comfort from reading Paul the Apostle's biblical letters to the Thessalonians and Galatians and by confiding in her mother. On any day, she can be strong and brittle. But the shoots of recovery are a lot more than Isabel was expecting.

As for Francis, Isabel is unable to say how my son is faring. She suspects he is in turmoil, but she cannot be sure about anything as he refuses to speak of the events that led to the slaughtering of Barbara and Isable.

"The tragedy has affected us all in equal measure," admits my wife, when we are dressed and sitting in the kitchen that was once the domain of the traitor, Else. "We are finding ways to cope with our loss. Some days are easier than others, my love. But now you have come back to us, it will get easier. And Francis needs his Papa."

I am about to ask about my son and talk about my ill-fated attempts to find Holck when I hear urgent footsteps in the hallway. I look up as Abijah enters the room. He is wearing the clothing of a soldier, and his agitation suggests there is something important that needs to be discussed.

"Apologies," he says when Isabel has retired to spend time with the girls in their chambers. "I have got used to acting on my intuition these past few months and not being accountable to my commanding officer. So forgive me if I am not my usual self this morning."

I smile. A quality I have always admired in my friend is his ability to talk directly without mincing his words. He is a good man and will make a fine commanding officer once he embraces diplomacy and tact and learns to appreciate the freedom of tongue I afford him.

"Draw up a chair," I say, "and pour yourself a drink. I have had little time to think about Militia matters these past weeks, but you will have my fullest attention, and I will do all I can to help."

My second-in-command does as he is invited. Soon I am engrossed in the affairs of the Leicestershire Militia and the war once again.

"Lord Grey has sent a messenger requesting we muster south of the Wilne Ferry this evening," reveals Abijah. "With the King's forces now in disarray, his Lordship is eager to press home the advantage we hold. He is particularly keen to inflict a wound on Henry Hastings, who has been continuing to frustrate our forces on a near-daily basis."

Wilne Ferry can be found on the Derbyshire-Leicestershire border by a narrow crossing of the Trent. It is a small place fortified by local Royalists to keep open a line of communication between their garrisons in Leicestershire and those in north Derbyshire and South Yorkshire. Not far away is King's Mill, the traditional crossing point of the River Trent between Castle Donington and Weston-on-Trent in Derbyshire. The Mill is the farthest point that traffic from the River Humber can progress into the Midlands. Its importance is evident to all.

To free the area of Royalist influence has been a strategic objective since Hastings established the fort in October 1643. Until now, however, the momentum has always been with the enemy. We have been impotent, unable to wound him. But not anymore.

As Abijah continues to relay Lord Grey's message, it

quickly becomes apparent this will not be a small-scale skirmish. The objective is to capture the stronghold and kill, or capture, as many of the 300-strong garrison as possible, including its governor, Captain Thomas Robinson. And, for once, it sounds as though our illustrious commander means business, for he has ordered Colonel John Gell's regiment of horse from Derby to join us.

My mind recalls the odious Gell, who commands the Militia in Derby. He is a man with a high opinion of himself, whose ego is far greater than the sum total of his abilities. And I don't know anyone who would relish standing alongside this wretch in the heat of a fight.

"We are required to secure as much hay and straw as possible," continues Abijah, snapping me out of the stupor I am prone to experiencing and threatens to diminish my ability to think clearly. "Lord Grey is advocating an unconventional approach: he wants to burn the King's men out of the Ferry!

"He believes that smoking the Royalists out will result in minimal casualties on our side and expedite the speed of the enemy's capitulation. I, for one, am all for it."

Unconsciously, I begin rubbing my chin. All things considered, it sounds like a plan that actually has a great deal of merit.

"I will make a point of congratulating his Lordship on his thoroughness and imagination," I say. "Anything that reduces the suffering of our men is to be congratulated. It certainly meets with my approval. Shall we discuss the detail?"

As I speak, I sense an awkwardness welling up in Abijah.

"Is everything alright?" I enquire. "You look as

though you wish to say something but have lost the power of speech."

Abijah clears his throat before he speaks and makes a point of averting his gaze from mine.

"Lord Grey's dispatch specifically orders you to remain at home, Francis," he tells me. "Under no circumstances are you to lead the Militia this evening. You are requested to stand down until his Lordship has spoken to you directly."

The sun is at its zenith as I watch my men depart Stathern on their way to rendezvous with the fifteen cartloads of hay we have secured for the Wilne Ferry sally.

I feel an acute emptiness inside. I do not know why Thomas Grey has ordered my absence from the field this evening; I trust he has his reasons. But it is a decision that has left me feeling sorely frustrated.

Isabel is sitting next to me as I fight the temptation to succumb to self-pity.

My wife and I have ridden a couple of Piebalds to the top of Mill Hill, past the ruined cottage where Peter and Marjorie Harrington once resided, and we are now surveying vast tracts of the Vale of Belvoir's glorious, open countryside. Even though I am sore because of my rejection, the view that confronts me is breathtaking, one I never tire of seeing.

And my mood starts to thaw.

As the last of the men disappear from view, swallowed up by the large, thickset copse of Ash, Beech, Oak and Hawthorn trees that line the track to Long Clawson, situated some six miles yonder, I am struck by the size of the world we live in, its diversity and its breathtaking beauty. When I see perfection such as this, I am convinced only God can create such immensity and complexity, interlinking everything in complete harmony – with the notable exception of men.

"I know that look," says Isabel patting my arm. "What are you thinking, Francis. Are you fearful your men won't return, or do you wish you were with them, putting yourself in more danger?"

I sense my wife is spinning one of her notorious webs, one that traps me effortlessly, and I am never able to break free from. So I avoid answering her. All I offer in response is an ambiguous shake of the head, much to her frustration.

After a moment, Isabel relents and signals for us to dismount. We lead the horses down the hill towards the distinctive square tower of Saint Guthlacs; holding hands as we stroll, we watch the Swallows darting back and forth in the perfect summer sky. And as we do, I find myself opening my heart for the first time in what feels like an eternity.

"My love, the simple truth is I do not know," I say in answer to Isabel's original question. "My head is telling me one thing while my heart is demanding something altogether different. And it has been like this ever since we lost our dear girls and our home was violated. I am tormented; I have no peace, and nothing I do seems to fill the emptiness I now have inside me. Soldiering is the only thing I can turn to at these times. To start talking about my innermost feelings would lead me, I fear, into the abyss."

Isabel nods. Her intelligent eyes look at me thoughtfully. I feel her hands clasp mine, squeezing my fingers in gentle acknowledgement. She, too, is enduring the very same pain I am carrying, and, the dullard that I am, I forget the most dreadful torment and remorse haunt her also.

"Francis, it is time for us to talk earnestly," she says. "There is much to tell you still, and I sense there are many things you may wish to confide in me.

"It is time to focus on our family and the villagers who need a strong Squire. The events of March killed much more than Sergeant Farndon and the many brave souls who tried to defend Stathern that fateful night. And you and I have a responsibility to our people that we cannot discharge if we continue to seek vengeance for the wrongs done to us.

"Come. Let us use the rest of today to talk things through properly, leaving nothing unsaid. It is time for us to look forward, my love, and consign the evil of the past to its rightful place."

By the time we stop talking, it is Wednesday, the seventh day of July. It is another golden morning, the noise of the cattle and the hens the only sounds to rise above the stilled air at this early time of the day.

There has been much for Isabel and me to discuss and so many things to reconcile. But the one thing that has helped us in these times of need is our love for one another. For despite everything that has happened since the outbreak of war, we remain inseparable: as one.

For the first time in a long while, the guilt I have been carrying about my two daughters, and the family I was unable to defend, starts to lift. With my wife by my side, I realise the weight I carry is becoming bearable.

"Come," urges Isabel. "Continue walking with me in the garden before the children rise and we become embroiled in the day-to-day activities of life at the Hall."

There is a slight chill as I expose myself to the open air. The dew soaks my bare feet in seconds, and I leave a trail of haphazard footsteps from the rear of the kitchen to the orangery. It is a delightful building my Father added to the Hall's features some twenty years ago, long before they became the talk of England's gentry and aristocratic classes. He had occasion to visit Paris on business, where he received an invitation to the Palace of the Louvre. There he fell in love with such a building, and upon his return to Stathern, he commissioned the construction of one for my late mother as a 'present'. It has been a permanent feature of our garden ever since, through good times and bad.

Isabel is waiting for me by one of the mahogany tables that divide the building into neat symmetrical sections. She feels the cold but has taken steps to protect herself by wrapping a shawl around her shoulders and wearing a pair of boots on her feet.

Ignoring my unkempt appearance, she beckons me to sit next to her.

"Husband," she says when I am comfortable. "We have come a long way these past twenty-four hours. We are on the mend. Every part of me feels it. But we must continue to trust one another, and we must pray more devoutly. You have been lost to the Father, as have I. We need to seek his forgiveness for the hatred we are carrying in our hearts. It has infected everything and will continue to do so until we repent and seek His forgiveness."

So, as the Church bells ring out, signalling the eighth hour of the day, Isabel and I kneel and pray to our Maker. We seek His forgiveness and pray for the souls of the departed and the living.

When we rise an hour later, a renewed vigour is pulsing through my veins, and the words of Psalm Forty-Six are on my lips:

"God is our refuge and strength, an ever-present help in trouble. Therefore we will not fear…"

It is some twelve hours later before Abijah and the Militia return to Stathern. They are in a jubilant mood, and their presence in the village is heard and felt long before they trot down the High Street and make their way to the stabling, where food and rest await their faithful steeds.

The enemy has been beaten soundly at the Wilne Ferry. Many men, weapons and horse have been captured, and not one Parliamentarian soldier has lost his life. Prayers have indeed been answered. The Maker has looked favourably this day on the righteous.

I leave Abijah to tether his horse and go about the business of a commanding officer, but not before making arrangements to meet him later in the evening.

At nine-thirty, I make my way to his cottage. It is part of the estate's outbuildings and close enough for me to visit him. And if I am not absent for too long, there is a remote chance Isabel won't notice I am gone.

Before I can knock on his door and reveal myself, a blood-curdling bark announces my arrival. Prudence, Abijah's loyal collie, rarely misses anything, and my ascent to the top of the garden and through the woodland is something she has been monitoring for several minutes. In all the years I have been visiting my friend, I have never bested her. And, in truth, I am never likely to such is the faithfulness with which she protects her master.

With its well-used fireplace, the cottage's parlour is

just as I remember it: dimly lit and snug. Prudence is slumped on the floor, at the feet of her Lord, looking at me with those deadpan eyes. Such are the feelings of inferiority aroused by this dog that, for a fleeting moment, I am convinced she is openly mocking me.

Thankfully, Abijah comes to my rescue by beckoning me to take a seat.

"Francis, please take the weight off your feet," says my host. "I have a bottle of claret in the scullery if you would care to share a drop with me?"

Usually, I would never refuse such an invitation. Alas, tonight I must. I need to retain a clear head as I wish to learn of the fight that took place just hours before and, just as importantly, speak openly to my friend about Lord Grey.

"That was quite a victory," I say, congratulating Abijah on the action that secured a vital success for Parliament on the banks of the River Trent. "You and the men have acquitted yourselves well these past two days. It will do our morale a world of good to see Hastings' men capitulate so readily."

Abijah has just spent the last hour describing how the Royalist fortress at Wilne Ferry surrendered with only a handful of muskets fired and one enemy soldier killed.

The remarkable success came about after the men of Stathern, and the surrounding villages, joined with Lord Grey's larger force, comprising several companies of the Leicestershire Militia and Colonel Gell's Derby detachment. As one body, they marched to Castle Donington by the cover of night, taking with them some sixty cartloads of hay and other combustibles. Their plan was simple: set the hay alight and force the enemy to retreat from the fortification.

Much to the surprise of Abijah and myself, it worked magnificently.

"I have never seen a fire like it, Francis," he recalls, the excitement still evident in his voice. "I would never have believed our enemy would have given way so easily had my own eyes not witnessed it.

"Once the flames had worked their way into the thatches and trenches, there was no containing it. The smoke was suffocating. It was hard enough holding the ranks of the Militia together, such was the heat, and we were two hundred yards away from the firestorm! I can't imagine what the King's men were forced to endure before they yielded in the early hours."

We laugh aloud, giddy with the excitement coursing through our bodies. A decisive victory always tastes sweet.

"All I could hear was our men shouting 'in God's name' at the top of their voices as we watched the blaze take hold of the fortress," he continues. "It was terrifying and exhilarating in equal measure."

Before the one-sided fight, the fort's commander, Captain Robinson, had sought to negotiate with his Lordship. But his request to march out with his colours held aloft, his men fully armed and retaining two drake cannons, were not to Thomas Grey's liking. So, with no agreement reached, Wilne Ferry was consigned to its fiery fate.

In the morning, all that remained was the smouldering carcass of a building and scores of broken, bewildered enemy soldiers who had lived through Hell, believing their end to be imminent. I know from personal experience, such thoughts can grievously wound the soul of a man, even the most steadfast. And as Abijah continues to tell me of the rout, I find myself pitying the Royalists. To face your foe on the battlefield is one thing. To watch on and remain passive and indifferent as he burns is another evil this war has brought upon us all.

"We were late leaving the site because his Lordship wanted to ensure the fort could never be garrisoned by the enemy again," adds Abijah, reaching the end of his tale of triumph. "Our company destroyed the walls and outbuildings. All that now stands are ruins, fit for nothing only the nests of Starlings and Blackbirds."

I reach forward, extending my right arm and clasping my friend. As I do, Prudence lifts her head, inspecting the uninvited limb that is now gripping her master. She bears her teeth for a moment and then thinks the better of it before quickly settling once again.

"While I would not deny you glory and advancement, on this occasion, I am truly delighted you were not required to fight," I say. "His Lordship's plan seems to have been executed to perfection, which is another cause for celebration, albeit I am not confident his next strategy will have the same effect. That you have returned with no casualties means my prayers have been answered, for it is only when you are in command that you are truly aware of the weight of your responsibilities. And as you now know, there is no greater responsibility borne by any officer than ensuring the welfare and safety of his men."

Silence follows. Both of us recognise the preciousness of life, having been responsible for committing too many men and women to the grave in the two years we have been fighting our Sovereign King.

Another matter of far greater consequence than yesterday's destruction of the fort is the reason I have come to Abijah's cottage this eve. And so I begin the task of taking my right-hand man into my confidence.

"A situation is developing in the county, and I fear we must choose one side or the other," I say, gaining Abijah's attention. "Lord Grey is at odds with Arthur Haselrig, and their petty differences are now threatening the safety of Leicester and the surrounding areas. The spat has grown into a full-blown disagreement on everything and anything, and it would appear there is no middle ground for men of conscience to stand. We must take the side of one or the other."

I allow my words to sink in before continuing.

"As you know, I am no great supporter of Thomas Grey. Yesterday's success being the exception, he is an idler, someone who lets self-interest prevail, a man more concerned about the welfare of his estates than the prosperity and well-being of the country.

"I cannot find it in me to actively support such a man, even if he is my commander. But I will not force my prejudices on you, Abijah. You are free to choose where your allegiances lie. And if they differ from my own, then we need to find a way of working together that does not undermine the position of Parliament. For I fear that will be an inevitable consequence of these two men not finding common ground."

Ill feeling between Grey's officers and the Mayor and Aldermen of Leicester, who are loyal to Haselrig, one of the city's two Members of Parliament, has been simmering for several months. The breakdown led to the city's Mayor infamously being arrested by Grey, who has desperately sought to reassert his authority in recent months. And the common soldiery, the men who are the heartbeat of the Militia, are too often forced to go weeks without pay, all because their superiors squabble like infants and put their own self-interest before the needs of the country.

Several attempts have to broker peace between the sides have been made. Yet a common accord has so far eluded the peacemakers in the two camps – with Haselrig actively promoting the cause of the moderate Independent faction and Grey attaching his colours to a more radical group altogether. And while the in-fighting continues and men became more disillusioned and hungry, the enemy turns its head in our direction, for disunity breeds weakness.

"It will come as no surprise, my friend, that my loyalty is to Sir Arthur," I continue. "But do not be swayed by me. You are free to choose whatever side your conscience dictates."

Abijah rises from his chair, much to the annoyance of the sleeping Prudence. He turns to the hearth and grips the corners of the mantelpiece. The minutes tick by. My friend remains motionless, choosing to stare at the wall rather than converse.

Eventually, after almost a quarter of an hour has passed, he turns and faces me.

"Francis," he says in a voice that emanates resilience and confidence. "My mind is as yours. I cannot envisage any situation that would see me side with Lord Grey in any argument involving Arthur Haselrig. I know both men, not as well as you, but well enough. And I know of their morality and their commitment to the cause. And I am with you on this matter: I too am Haselrig's man."

Although I hoped this would be the outcome of the conversation, I was by no means certain Abijah would choose the same path as myself. He knows his own mind and frequently disagrees with me. While I was confident we would find a way to ensure any difference of allegiance would not damage the command structure of the Militia and our friendship, I am mightily relieved to hear we are in accord, and it will not come to that.

"I am obliged, my friend. You don't know how much that means to me," I confess. "To be united with you on this matter is of crucial importance. There is much to be done in the weeks and months ahead, and to be of one mind will mean the Militia is in a better position to prosecute the war effort with all necessary speed."

FOUR

AFTER THE EXCITEMENT OF EARLY July, the next few weeks of summer pass by gently and uneventfully. Being held back from leading the Militia is a blessing. It allows me to rebuild my relationship with Isabel and the children and continue my spiritual renewal.

Daily prayers have again become the norm. Every morning at six o'clock, my wife and I kneel together at the foot of our bed and speak as one to our Father. At first, there was awkwardness between us, with long silences dominating our hour-long devotionals. But within a few days, our focus has moved to the supernatural power that guides our lives, and our embarrassment is no more. Now we pray openly and intimately, in a way that has strengthened the unbreakable bond that exists between us.

But while there is peace in the village and Hall, away from Stathern, events continue to develop at a pace.

Almost three weeks after the victory at Marston Moor, the remnants of the Earl of Newcastle's Royalist army in the north have surrendered the prized city of York to Parliamentary forces, thus wiping out the King's influence beyond Newark.

I have also learned of a major falling out between Henry Hastings and Gervase Lucas, with the latter refusing to accept Lord Loughborough as his superior. Knowing the Governor of Belvoir Castle as I do, this does not surprise me. However, if the word of our informer is to be believed, it seems the dispute was only settled by the King's personal intervention, which granted Lucas semi-autonomy. I have informed Lord Grey of the matter and dispatched a messenger to Cromwell in Huntingdon, advising him of the advantageous situation. Such a very public disagreement between two of our most noted enemies can only be a blessing for Parliament.

In London, rumours abound that Charles Louis, the Elector Palatinate and elder brother of Princes Rupert and Maurice, will soon offer his allegiance again to Parliament. Reliable tongues tell me the motive for this overt display of support by the ambitious young man, who is no lover of the King, is his undiminishing desire to be nominated as Charles's successor.

It would seem Charles Louis and his supporters know nothing of the events that took place a year ago when Prince Maurice agreed to a very similar proposal, one I brokered at such a high personal cost. At the time, it was a move that had the backing of Cromwell and John Pym. But we live in unpredictable times, with the winds of politics altering their course on a near-daily basis and an agreement reached on a Monday quickly becoming null and void just forty-eight hours later. Or so it seems.

As there was ultimately no appetite twelve months ago to see one Stuart replaced by another, today the position is even more resolute: Cromwell and the likes of Sir Thomas Fairfax will never allow it to happen, thereby making Charles Louis surplus to requirements.

One positive outcome of the Elector Palatinate's reappearance is the refusal of the King to promote Prince Rupert to the position of overall commander of all Royalist forces. An announcement confirming the Prince's elevation had been expected long before the Royalist's defeat in Yorkshire. Indeed, Rupert's reputation has not suffered a jot as a result of this calamitous reversal. Yet the arrival of Charles Louis on the scene has forced the King to postpone making overdue changes to his high command. This serves the cause of those who oppose him very well indeed.

But the news is not all good.

On my own doorstep, two events are dominating conversations between Isabel, Abijah and myself: the very public disagreement between the Earl of Manchester and my friend and confidante, Cromwell, and the well-being of my brother, Rowland, who has pledged his allegiance to the King's cause.

It would appear the relationship between Manchester and Oliver has reached the point of no return. A fracturing of the tenuous bond that held the two men together for so long has occurred, and I am told they cannot bear being in the same room as each other. To complicate matters, the Earl is blissfully unaware of the secret pact among some Parliament's officers to create the New Model Army. How I wish my life and the lives of my contemporaries could be simpler, more harmonious affairs, instead of being the deceptions and fuddles they so often are.

While this news is distressing, it assumes lesser importance when I receive word on Saturday, the sixth day of August, about the welfare of my brother.

A dispatch arrives at Stathern from Leicester informing me of a skirmish on Belvoir Bridge, located just outside the city, involving a detachment of Cavalier horse, led by Rowland, and at least three companies of horse and foot from the Leicestershire Militia. During the fighting, it appears Rowland was injured. The extent of his wounds are unclear, but the author, a Captain Adinson, who was involved in the confrontation, suggests they may have been severe.

I compose myself before reaching for my quill and writing a letter to Rowland, which I send via a dispatch a rider to the home of Owen Giddersby, a mutual friend we share. Owen resides in Knipton, a small village found just two miles to the south of where my brother is now living, and I know he will ensure it will find its way to the intended recipient.

Until I can find out what has happened, I must do everything in my power not to despair.

Several days pass, and I have heard nothing about Rowland's fate.

My anxiety about my brother's injuries is always in my mind, never far below the surface, making me tetchy and argumentative. Thankfully other matters come to the fore, helping me forget about Rowland's immediate plight. Among them is the deterioration of Cromwell and Manchester's relationship, which is being played out very publicly.

An unambiguous dispatch I receive from Oliver on

Tuesday, the twenty-third day of August, leaves me in no doubt the two former allies will never again see eye to eye.

Hugh Walker, the Eastern Association rider used by Oliver to communicate his most confidential messages, delivers it to my personal safekeeping. I recognise the young Presbyterian's voice as soon as he introduces himself to the guard at the front of the Hall. I walk out and greet him, acknowledging James Ainscough, a new member of the Militia, who is positioned at the entrance. Since Holck's surprise attack in March, when so many of our men lost their lives, we no longer take any chances.

Walker and I embrace each other like long-lost brothers, for that is what we are in the eyes of the Lord. Our rank and social standing are immaterial. It is good to see his friendly face once again after all these months, and I assure him I will be finding out all I can about the affairs of State and the army from his own lips once I have absorbed Cromwell's latest musings.

"Tell me, young friend, how is Oliver?" I enquire before I seek out a quiet place to open the dispatch. "How is the Lieutenant-General in himself?"

Still covered in the dust and grime from his lengthy journey, Walker wipes some grit out of his eyes before replying. I like this man. He clearly has his wits about him and understands the real meaning of my question in an instant.

"You are one of the few men to ask," he says appreciatively. "The Lieutenant-General has naturally been distressed at the passing of young Oliver; the loss has hit him hard. But I am pleased to report he is bearing up well. The army's affairs are taking up much of his time and energy, which is a blessing. He is also consulting the Good Book every day and praying. Then, when he has a spare moment, Good Wife Elizabeth and the Cromwell brood are occupying what remains of his time and thoughts."

I am reassured. I walk into my study, leaving Walker to find refreshment in the scullery, and I open Cromwell's hastily written letter. It reads:

"Francis, my dear and esteemed friend.

"Much has happened since we last saw each other at Marston Moor, and I intend to hasten to Stathern to speak to you directly. Expect my arrival on, or about, the early evening of Thursday, the twenty-fifth day of August. At your convenience, it will be good to spend some time in your company and that of your gracious wife.

"In the meantime, I would be grateful if you resisted any requests for information that may be forthcoming from the Earl of Manchester. I will explain more when we meet in person.

"Your loyal and faithful servant, Oliver."

I let out an audible groan.

It seems the tranquillity I have started to enjoy is to soon come to an end, for when Oliver visits, there is always a task I am required to undertake on behalf of my Parliamentary masters. And now I am rested, and in good health, I fear it is likely peril may become my shadowy companion once again.

Excitement fills the air in the village on the day of Cromwell's expected arrival, some two days since Hugh Walker's surprise appearance.

The streets have been swept of dung and detritus, and a sense of anticipation is tangible among the soldiery and villagers, not least because we will all be eating out-doors tonight as Isabel has invited everyone in the locality to attend. There has been too little to cheer about in recent times, and my wife is determined to improve the mood.

Almost a hundred souls, and the bodyguard the Lieutenant-General chooses to bring with him, will feast on roasted pork and beef and drink several barrels of ale dry before the late summer sunsets once again.

Among those invited is William Norwich, Rector of Saint Guthlacs. Of all the people invited to the banquet, he is the one person I am least looking forward to exchanging pleasantries with. So I will do all I can to attach myself to others, thus avoiding an awkward conversation with the minister.

Norwich is a man my wife has taken pity upon and seeks to protect. For some reason, unbeknown to me, Isabel believes him to be a good and godly man. How she has reached this conclusion, only God knows!

I cannot see it myself. But I have pledged to treat the Rector kindly, faithfully carrying out this promise for many months. But judging by his most recent sermons, which I have borne witness to these past weeks, he is determined to test my good nature and patience. If I didn't know better, I would say William Norwich is doing everything in his power to follow in the footsteps of Archbishop Laud, who is currently on trial for High Treason and will soon be a martyr for the King's cause.

Right now, it would be wonderful to dwell on the most malicious thoughts that have entered my mind concerning the troublesome Rector. Still, as the solitary bell of Saint Guthlacs announces the arrival of midday, I am acutely aware I have more pressing matters to consider than the rebellious churchman and impending visit of Cromwell. I have much to think about concerning Lord Grey, who, three days ago, sent a dispatch requesting I attend on him at his estates in Newtown Linford, a tranquil place located close to Leicester and an invigorating hour-long ride from Stathern.

His Lordship's residence had the unfortunate distinction of being the first grand house in England to fall victim to the civil war when the villain Hastings took it upon himself to spring an opportunistic attack. That was two years ago, and, unfortunately for Parliament and the men who serve the Midlands Association, Hastings failed in his quest, for Thomas Grey was not to be found at home that day – much to the regret of many!

Since my return from the north, Lord Grey has refused all of my pleas to be allowed to return to my duties. To many, this could be seen as an act of kindness considering everything my family and I have endured while serving Parliament's cause. But I am far from sure about the sincerity of his Lordship. He has good reason to question where my loyalty lies, knowing, as he does, of my close association with Cromwell and Haselrig and the various factions they support. I suspect, in the current political climate, he is eager to see how much he can rely on me to do his bidding before he allows me to lead my men once again. Upon reflection, I suspect I would do precisely the same with any officer whose loyalty I doubted.

I care little for Lord Grey. But I am a committed Parliamentarian, which means I can prevaricate no more; respond to the man I must. So I spend the afternoon writing a dispatch to his Lordship, detailing the company's strength, describing a couple of minor skirmishes that have occurred since Wilne Ferry, and confirming I will travel to see him on Tuesday the thirtieth day of August. Five days hence.

Oliver Cromwell breezes into Stathern at four o'clock in the afternoon, galloping into the Hall's courtyard with the sun at his back and looking every inch the mighty warrior he has become.

Black Jack, his trusted and much-admired horse, is sweating heavily. So, too, are the Master and the twelve dragoons that make up the Lieutenant-General's very own Praetorian Guard. They have been riding for several hours, travelling cross-country from Lincoln, where Cromwell has been overseeing the continued strengthening of the city's defences.

Lincoln was seized a little over three months ago by the Eastern Association with minimal loss of life on both sides.

Looking at the vibrant figure sitting astride his jet-black steed, it is hard to comprehend the pressure the man is under to continue out-thinking and out-fighting the King's men. But if he is feeling the pinch, he doesn't show it.

"You are a sight for sore eyes, young Francis Hacker," he roars as he leaps out of the saddle. "I hope you have some food and ale waiting for us, my friend, for my comrades and I are thirsty and famished."

And then he is upon me, crushing my hand in his vice-like grip and patting me on the shoulder, as an uncle would greet one of his favourite nephews.

"There is much to talk to you about, Francis, and there is not a lot of time to do it," he says with a note of unmistakable urgency in his voice. "Much has happened in the weeks since I saw you last. And a great deal is likely to occur in the days ahead that will occupy my wits and those of the men closest to me. And you, my friend, are one of the confidantes I will be forced to call upon most. So let us find somewhere quiet to retire to, so I can unburden my soul and tell you of everything that has passed.

"But before we discuss these things, I would be obliged if you escorted me to your good wife. I wish to pay my respects to her and also take a look at those children of yours. I have been looking forward to reacquainting myself with your family, and, my friend, you will not deny me that pleasure."

It is not until six o'clock that we can break free from the children and Isabel, such is their contagious delight at being reacquainted with Oliver.

The village has turned out in force to enjoy the feast and entertainment laid on for them by my wife, and there is no privacy to be found at the Hall. So Cromwell and I decide to take a brisk walk to the ruins of Rose Cottage, the former home of Peter and Marjorie Harrington.

As we stroll up Mill Hill, taking in the vast and panoramic views of the Vale of Belvoir and easing past the temporarily stilled Red Lion Inn, the zest that was so evident in Oliver's face upon his arrival has been replaced with a hard and serious palour. When he speaks, I understand why.

"We are facing the most critical phase of the war," he declares when he is sure an eavesdropper cannot overhear our conversation. "The fight for the soul of our country has started, and our greatest enemy may no longer be the King."

I stop and look at him. His face is flushed; his eyes are dark, emotionless brooding pools. His jaw is set as if he has just received a harsh blow from an invisible assailant.

"Whatever are you saying, Oliver?" I ask, my surprise all too evident. "We may be in the ascendency after recent events, but Charles and his supporters surely represent the greatest threat to unity. What else can possibly be an obstacle?"

Oliver doesn't say anything immediately. Instead, he turns away and scans the landscape, following the flight of an ornately decorated Jay as it flies from branch to branch amidst a thicket of young Hazelwood trees. Eventually, after losing sight of the shy bird, he faces me again, and I feel his eyes penetrating my inner recesses. He straightens his hat before speaking.

"I am confident as I can be that the war against the King is close to being won," he announces. "The momentum is now with us. So, too, are greater pockets of the country. Although it may yet take some time, I believe the outcome is already secure as far as the King is concerned. But, my dear friend, the fight is far from over.

"The war, if that is indeed the correct choice of word, will now be fought among the victors, and it may be more brutal than what came before.

"The nobility and men of rank and status are likely to become our new adversaries. That, as much, has become abundantly clear to me in recent weeks. These men despise us and what we stand for. Unlike us, they have no piety and little regard for our nation's well-being; they are merely fighting for political and financial reward. If the wind had been blowing in a different direction two years ago, they would most certainly be our foe today, not our so-called brothers. Be of no doubt, they will do almost anything to ensure men like you and I do not prevail."

Oliver lets his words sink in. He has always had a sound grasping of the English language, and this evening his oratory skills are as compelling as ever.

"You are aware Manchester and your own commander, Lord Grey, fear the likes of you and me?" he continues, confident I will not seek to question his words. "Even though they are fighting the King, they do not truly oppose what he stands for. On the contrary, they seek his swift return to the throne, albeit they will tell you they are seeking to have his wings clipped so he can no longer wield the kind of power he enjoyed before the war started. But, alas, to the likes of you and me, there will be no noticeable difference. Charles will be the same tyrant he always has been; only the support of the nobility will, in time, enable him to emerge even stronger."

I know what Cromwell says to be true, and I am about to reply when the iron gates of the Harrington's ruined cottage appear in the corner of my vision.

It is almost six months since my dear friends were slain. Their once happy home is now a tangled mess of debris, collapsed walls and charred wooden beams left where they fell in an overgrown and weed-ridden garden.

Amid the ruins, I notice a large quantity of white and red roses have been laid at the doorway to the house. They are fresh and vibrant, most likely cut from the garden of their son, Stephen, who lives in the nearby village of Harby, and who regularly visits this hallowed place. He is another who continues to grieve for the innocent victims of this senseless and bitter feud.

I prod a darkened ember with my boot. It snaps in two, unable to resist the mild pressure I have applied.

"I know what you say to be true," I say, my voice almost a whimper. "I have sensed the unease that exists among the officers and the factions that are growing within our army. I have perceived as much with his Lordship and some of the officers who are closest to him. Of course, we fight alongside each other, but trust and respect are in short supply when we are not engaging with the enemy.

"I had hoped my fears would prove to be groundless, but your words today convince me there is more foundation to them than I had appreciated. So tell me, what is to be done, Oliver? How do we keep the peace and ensure the painful sacrifices we have all endured will count for something?"

Cromwell moves towards the gate, which like everything else in this graveyard, has been damaged beyond repair. As he reaches the entrance to the garden and the rust-encrusted structure that still bears the scorch marks of the flames that consumed the cottage, he beckons me to follow.

"Let us return to the Hall. There is nothing more to be achieved by remaining in this sad place," he says as I join him on the dirt track outside once again. "All I require you to do, my dear friend, is listen to what I have to say. I will tell you all that needs to be done, and when I have finished, I want you to accept the important role I have earmarked for you."

FIVE

I RISE FROM MY SLUMBER on the morning of Tuesday, the thirtieth day of August and prepare for my ride to Bradgate House, home of Lord Groby.

Several days have passed since the conversation I had with Cromwell, and I have used the available time to digest the details and reflect on what is required of me. And the sense of unease I am feeling is growing.

Oliver is adamant plotting among different Parliamentary factions has already started, and whatever the cost, he is determined to win the day.

"We will not be cowed into submission by our rivals," he tells me before leaving Stathern after breakfast to return to Lincolnshire. "We must prevail; we will prevail. It is of paramount importance that we turn this country of ours into a God-fearing nation once again, one that is founded on solid principles and practices, not the follies of a sop of a King. I will not be able to live with myself if we fail in this task.

"Every man with a conscience must act quickly and

decisively. That means, my dear Francis, men like you and I need to use the wits we have been blessed with. And for you, that means aligning yourself to the cause of the snake in our midst and ensuring he takes you into his confidence. Lord Groby must begin to trust you. He needs to believe you support his cause and ambitions and have turned your back on your previous associations, particularly with men like me and Sir Arthur Haselrig."

Cromwell's edict needs no interpretation.

I am to be used as a spy once again, just like I was twelve months earlier when I was tasked with snaring a Prince. Then, I was successful. This time, I must convince a man who openly despises me that I am worthy of his trust.

I can only pray I am equal to the task.

Bucephalus is in a boisterous mood as we make our way to the small village of Newtown Linford. Surrounded by a dense mass of trees, it is located on the outskirts of Leicester and is where his Lordship resides when he chooses to bless Leicestershire with his presence.

We leave at eleven o'clock. The morning sunshine is drenching the trees and fields with light and heat, and the meeting is in two hours.

Our route takes us close to Melton Mowbray, Queniborough, Leicester, and Anstey. The Royalists have no authority in these places, and relative calmness reigns. It also takes me close to Colston Bassett, where my late brother, Thomas, lived in the manor house until his untimely and tragic death almost eighteen months ago. His demise, which came about as a result of my men ambushing a group of Cavaliers, continues to haunt me.

Although I pray regularly to my Maker and seek his forgiveness, a clear conscience has not been granted to me on this matter. Nor is it likely to be.

And peace isn't a commodity I am likely to find on this late summer's day in the saddle, where my steed is sorely testing my horsemanship and patience. Thankfully, despite contending with the guilt of my memories, I am in a relatively jovial mood; otherwise, Bucephalus's belly would have felt my stirrups bite deeper more than they usually do.

The tracks are bustling with farmers, traders and fellow travellers, all eager to complete their daily business briskly and with the minimum of fuss. Bucephalus draws praise and glances from a host of well-wishers – and curses, scowls and taunts from some malcontents, including several Parliamentary soldiers who should know better.

Matters reach a critical point close to the village of Syston, when a group of men, standing in the village square and wearing the colours of a company of dragoons from his Lordship's very own regiment, enrage me by bellowing crude and caustic comments as I pass by. Angry, I turn around and confront the men directly.

"Gentlemen," I say as authoritatively as I can, "do I know you? Have we had reason to quarrel in the past, or have I, in some way, caused you some offence? Pray, tell me, for I wish to know the source of your uncouthness and agitation."

The largest member of the group, a lumbering oaf of about six feet in height, shuffles forward. He eyes me warily through the lank strands of unkempt hair that hang from his unwashed scalp. I see him glance at my two pistols and the sword that is hanging at my side. And I quickly realise the man standing before me is making his calcu-lations.

Seemingly unarmed, I can't believe this thug of twenty-something years is seriously contemplating attack-ing me for the few shillings I am carrying? Not for the first time, I underestimate an adversaries intentions.

Before I have time to prepare for an assault, he is upon me, grabbing at my thigh and seeking to rip me from the saddle. Thankfully, he is not as strong as his frame would suggest, and he is a man lacking confidence and a plan. And that is his downfall. In an instant, my right-hand draws my sword out of its scabbard, and I bring the full weight of the pommel crashing down onto my assailant's head.

I hear a dull, sickening thud as I feel the heavy metal connecting with flesh and bone. I hear a groan, and then the pressure on my leg is no more. I look down and see the wretch lying prostrate on the sun-bleached grass. I do not know whether he is dead or alive, but blood is oozing from a wound at the top of his scalp. My heart is beating wild-ly. The hunter within me has been awoken, and as I turn my attention to his stunned accomplices. I am ready for the fight, and right now, that's all I care about.

"Are any of you curs brave enough to step forward and try your luck?" I growl as a challenge. "Would you like to see if you can do better than your fallen comrade?"

The three men glance at each other, shock, fear and desperation etched on their faces. And I detect something else: a simple desire for survival!

"We didn't know he was going to do that, sir," con-fesses a youth who looks to be the youngest member of the quartet. "We meant you no harm. We are not savages and rogues. We are simply beggarly soldiers, sir, men who are near destitute and haven't eaten a proper meal for almost four days. We have received no pay from his Lordship and the Leicestershire Committee for near on a month, and I confess our tolerance is wearing thin.

"Be assured there was no plan to attack you. Our friend's desperation simply got the better of him, and he has now paid the price for his foolishness."

Another groan, louder this time, signals my attacker is still in the land of the living. I signal to the men to recover their fallen friend before the irresistible and powerful hooves of Bucephalus finish off what my sword has started.

After they have made him comfortable, I dismount in the shade of a nearby Horse Chestnut tree. From the panniers, I pull some cheese and bread and my water bottle. I was planning to eat at around midday, so I take the modest fare to the group, who tend to their unconscious companion.

When the men see what I am offering, they fall on the food like a pack of wolves. The youth was not lying: he and his accomplices truly are starving wretches.

After their bellies have benefitted from sustenance once again, and their thirst has been sated, I start talking to them, eager to understand why their circumstances are so desperate.

"You are clearly a gentleman," says the youth, in response to a question I have posted about their allegiance to Lord Grey of Groby. "And that means you are not experiencing the kind of deprivations that men like us have had to endure for months now.

"Our officers have promised us pay and food for as

long as we can remember; on the proviso we continue to serve Parliament in the fight against the King, and spill our blood whenever it is necessary to do so. In this regard, we have accepted the word of gentlemen. But their promises have been nothing less than falsehoods designed to placate the many Militia companies and not meet the need that is growing daily.

"Sir, we have had enough of the lies and deceit that comes out of the mouths of men like Thomas Grey. We neither trust him nor the gentlemen who serve him. They have no honour, and they have little empathy for the common soldier – even though their standing is nought without us.

"We are fighting an enemy that is better provisioned than us, and we are expected to continue to sacrifice all for the cause we believe in. That was fine when we were being paid and fed, and we had the strength to lift our pikes and muskets and fight the enemy. But the truth is only a few of us are fit to fight. And we will not be forced to do the bidding of Parliament anymore unless we are given what we are owed."

The young man's confidence falters, and he averts his gaze when I look directly at him.

"You speak from the heart," I say to him reassuringly. "I commend you for your honesty. But I must warn you that your officers will interpret these grievances as tantamount to cowardice and sedition. Should you refuse to fight the enemy, you will be hanged or shot. Summarily executed. Nobody will shed any tears for you. And you will bring terrible and unnecessary shame to the doorsteps of your families."

Thinking carefully about my next words, I speak

slowly and quite deliberately.

"But I can see very clearly there is a great injustice being done to you," I say. "Your actions this day are not those of men who are behaving and thinking rationally. So I will personally intervene in this matter. I will take your concerns to Lord Grey and to Lieutenant-General Cromwell and Sir Thomas Fairfax if I have to. You have my word I will do all I can to seek a fair resolution, and quickly, too.

"In return, I urge you to seek strength and encouragement from your pocket prayer book. I know it has served me well, and my men, these past few months. And I ask you to give me a week to try and restore the order you are seeking. I will do all I can in this time to try and make right the wrongs that have been done to you and the other men."

The three soldiers look at each other. I see what is tantamount to renewed hope in their eyes.

"Aye, sir," says the young leader who I learn is called Gracious Claypole. "You have my word and that of my friends. We are looking to you to assist us in this matter.

"You can find us and the rest of our company, garrisoned in Anstey. We are not difficult to locate; the stench from a hundred unwashed and unruly souls should lead you straight to our encampment, which is next to the Hare and Hounds Inn. We will do all we can to quell any unrest until we hear from you. But suppose it is longer than a week. In that case, I am afraid I can offer no guarantees after that, for discontent and thievery most surely will follow."

I nod my head in understanding and shake the hands of all three men. As I grip them, I am shocked by how weak they are. Claypole was not exaggerating; these really are men living life close to the precipice. Thankfully matters have been resolved constructively for the time being, albeit I do not underestimate the problems that will face the Parliamentary army in the Midlands if issues are not resolved to the satisfaction of these men very soon.

As I start to leave the group and continue to my rendezvous with Lord Grey, a thought occurs.

"Forgive me," I say, stopping Bucephalus before we walk less than five paces. "I haven't introduced myself..."

Claypole flashes a brief grin as he holds up his hand, cutting my words off in mid-sentence.

"Don't worry, sir, we know who you are," he says. "You are Captain Hacker. We recognised you after you had drawn your sword against us. We know of your repute, and we are honoured to make your acquaintance. But I beg of you, please don't let us down."

I remain unmolested for the remaining few miles of my journey and arrive at Bradgate House ten minutes before my meeting with his Lordship is scheduled to commence.

Set in beautiful grounds, amounting to more than three hundred acres and stocked with plentiful herds of Red and Fallow deer, Lord Grey is a member of one of the two foremost families in Leicestershire. His father is the Earl of Stamford, another limp commander whose disastrous campaigns in the southwest have led to disaster for Parliament and accusations of cowardice being levelled. A noted ancestor is Lady Jane, the tragic nine-day Queen who was outwitted by the potent Mary more than a century ago.

The Earl of Huntingdon is head of the county's

other esteemed family. His second eldest son, Lord Loughborough – or "Blind" Henry Hastings as we choose to call him – is the greatest thorn in our side. Nonetheless, he is a man who has gained our utmost respect, unlike our commander.

What I would give to fight alongside a leader like him.

Perhaps it is Thomas Grey's link to the throne of England that is responsible for the arrogance and conceit he has displayed on virtually every occasion I have been in his company? The one notable occasion when I have experienced politeness is when he and I fought shoulder to shoulder in a bid to help save the lives of two clergymen and thirty commoners held prisoner in Hinckley. On that fine day in March, Grey, the Militiamen, and I displayed great courage, besting the enemy and rescuing the hostages from the grisly end that awaited them at the end of the hangman's noose. Maybe it was the thrill of battle that thawed Lord Grey's prickly persona that day, helping him to forget his social superiority and breeding for a few moments? Whatever the reason, the moment was soon forgotten once the corpses of the enemy had been buried in a mass grave close to Saint Mary's Church, and a new crisis became the priority. Grey returned to being the aloof and incompetent commander men such as Cromwell and myself dislike and distrust when that happened.

It is now some six months since that fateful occasion, and so much has happened since then.

Today, I have been invited to his palatial home for the very first time. I have no doubt the meeting will require a great deal of contrition on my part, for it is unlikely his

Lordship will sanction my return to active service without extracting certain assurances from me, not least because of my prolonged absence from Stathern while I pursued Holck. Accept his rebukes I must, as my desire to be worthy of the trust shown in me by Oliver and Fairfax, is far greater than my pride. Yet, I do have a puzzle to solve. For I now have the added complication of seeking recompense from Lord Grey for Claypole and the many other Parliamentary soldiers who have not been paid for a considerable time.

How to achieve a fair resolution to the matter has left me with a problem I have, so far, been unable to resolve. Yet, I must.

Oh, how I wish my life was uncomplicated.

Lord Grey invites me into one of the many large, soulless rooms in abundance at Bradgate House. According to my pocket watch, it is precisely fifteen minutes past the appointed hour. Like many young members of the nobility, he is eager to assert his authority. Keeping me waiting is an excellent way to demonstrate who is Master and who is Servant.

As we walk into the room and take our seats, I study the man I have been instructed to swear allegiance to. Short in stature, he reeks of weakness and is a far cry from the warriors who are winning the war against the King, the men I admire and follow.

Close-up, his face is even more unremarkable than I remember it.

Today, his flaky-white jaw is clean-shaven. He looks more an infant than a man of twenty-one years. Where there should be a strong beard, he has chosen to grow a moustache, further emphasising a lack of gravitas and character. I am told these follies are popular among the French and Spanish nobility, dandies more concerned with wooing ignorant young women than prosecuting State affairs. Whatever the truth of the matter, it matters little: in my opinion, such abominations are not to be displayed by any Englishman who seeks to be taken seriously!

Just as my thoughts and prejudices threaten to run away with themselves, a tap on the table brings me to attention. His Lordship is signalling it is time for us to talk.

"So, Hacker, I trust you are suitably rested, and your affairs at Stathern are now in order?" he enquires, the voice seeking to conceal something I recognise as unbridled anger. "Are your good lady and children recovered from the recent tragedies that have beset you all?"

I say little other than confirm our lives have returned to a degree of normality, and we are all fit in mind and body. Although I do my best to be conversational, I remain wary and on edge.

"Good," he says drily. "So, now that question is out of the way, shall we talk openly about your conduct as a Captain of the Militia. In particular, I would like to review the events that saw you remain absent from your post without my permission for a considerable period."

For two long hours, Thomas Grey adopts the poise of a Lincolns Inn lawyer.

At every junction of our conversation, I sense he is seeking to find an objection to my conduct and testimony while probing the many flaws in my character. His interrogation – for that is what appears to be – is forensic and meticulous. If I liked the man, I would say it was reasonably impressive. He has no intention of letting me off without exerting his authority. Indeed, Gervase Lucas, my Royalist gaoler at Belvoir Castle at the end of last year, was not nearly as brutal in his questioning.

"The chain of command is based on trust, Hacker. Nothing more. Nothing less. When trust has broken down, so has the chain. And that cannot be tolerated," Lord Grey spits in my direction through that pale, pursed mouth.

"I have to tell you that I have grave reservations, particularly concerning where your loyalties lie. You are a key part of our forces in the region, yet I have it on good authority you tip your hat in the direction of Fairfax and Cromwell. Tell me plainly: can I count on you? Can Leicestershire count on you? Are you for Grey or against him?"

There is no doubt about it, His Lordship intends to win the day with me, one way or another. Contempt and distrust are etched all over his face, emphasised by a fine line of spittle that cradles on his bloodless lips that are cocked and ready to fire more uncompromising barbs in my direction.

In truth, I have some sympathy for him, for my loyalty does lie elsewhere and with good cause. But I will never admit it to this poppycock.

Up until now, I have spoken honestly, answering his Lordship's questions as fulsomely as I can. But now, I am required to deviate from the path of honesty. Just as Cromwell told me I must. It is now time to soothe Thomas Grey's concerns about where my allegiance lies.

And so the deceit begins.

"My Lord," I say, "you can count on my men and me. We are at your command and willing to do your bidding. We always have been. It is true, we do have a fond-ness and respect for Lieutenant-General Cromwell, borne out of an association spanning many years. But first and foremost, we are Leicester men. Honour dictates we call on you for our orders and direction. Nobody else."

I look up. His Lordship is listening intently, his brown eyes unblinking. May my God, the creator of the universe, hear my prayers and forgive me. And may he also permit my falsehoods to be convincing.

"The deaths of Barbara and Isable have affected me sorely," I continue. "I have not been myself for many weeks, grief and vengeance consuming my soul for far too long. But I am restored and almost back to my usual self. Of course, I still carry the pain. And I will forever, for repentance and prayer will not ease that burden. But I realise I must be the husband Isabel needs me to be. And to be that, I must be allowed to lead my men. Therefore, my Lord, you have my assurance you will never have the need to quarrel with me, sir. I am your man."

Mentioning my murdered daughters and Isabel causes my left eye to start twitching, as it is prone to do whenever I feel deep agitation or I am required to lie.

It is true, I am not the desolate figure I was some weeks ago, but I have a long way to go before I am the man, husband and father I once was. Recuperating I am. But restored? Nay, I am a long way from being able to say that. Indeed, I do not truly know if the man I once was will ever return. The Francis of yesterday is seemingly lost. I can only pray, hoping my Maker will make me wholesome again one day.

Lord Grey taps the ornate, panelled table. His expression tells me he is eager to end our meeting.

"There can be no doubting your fine abilities as an officer, Hacker," he says briskly, in a more conciliatory tone. "You have proven yourself on many occasions, not least at Hinckley when you fought courageously alongside me. We forged a strong alliance that day when we routed the enemy. And I would have it again.

"But there will be no more looking to Fairfax and Cromwell for guidance and no more following their orders. I am your commander, no one else. Should they seek your support in one of their plots, or assistance on the battlefield, you will tell me so before you do anything else. Am I understood?"

I nod my head in assent.

"What's that man?" snaps Lord Grey, rapping the table with his gilt-edged cane. "Speak up, Captain Hacker, and say it plainly. Tell me whose orders you will be following."

"Yours, my Lord," I respond, chastised like the irresponsible schoolboy I once was. "I am your man, and the Militia I command are your soldiery. There will be no need to question my loyalty. I will prove it so."

After almost two and a half hours, we have an understanding. A triumphant grin spreads across the young nobleman's face.

"Don't worry, I intend for you to demonstrate your allegiance very soon," he says triumphantly. "Our enemies are in a state of confusion since their defeat at Marston. It is time for the Midlands Association to take advantage, just as we did at the Wilne Ferry. So go back to Stathern and prepare yourself, for there is much to do."

Lord Grey looks down at a sheet of paper on his desk and makes a dismissive gesture with his left hand. He picks up a quill and starts to write. My audience has come to an abrupt end.

Yet I stay seated.

"Your Lordship," I say after an uncomfortable minute has passed. "There is another matter I must speak to you about, one that has a degree of urgency. It concerns the pay owed to a large number of your dragoons…"

"I don't have time to deal with that tittle-tattle, Hacker," he says, clearly losing his patience. "I have been petitioning the County Committee and the Mayor of Leicester on this matter for several weeks, and nothing has been forthcoming. My officers have been unable to extract one single extra Laurel from that mob of scoundrels to pay the wages of the soldiery. In truth, there is no sign of a resolution on the horizon, and I don't see how matters can be much improved. The Mayor simply refuses to release the monies we need to pay the men. Even his short imprisonment, at my behest, has done little to make him more compliant."

I look coolly at Thomas Grey. His disdain for me has turned to anger.

"My Lord, the men are close to desertion and insurrection," I say calmly. "We must find a way of paying them their dues. A great deal is owed to them, and new taxes will not recompense them fully. If we do not pay what is owed, our ambitions to take the fight to the likes of Hastings and Lucas will come to nought."

My words force Grey's patience to snap.

"Good God, man, do not tell me what I already know," he yells, awakening a Peacock that is roosting outside, close to the open window. "If you think you have it within you to do a better job, then be on your way and see to the matter. And, if you must, send the Mayor and Aldermen my esteem and regards. But, after bringing this concern to my attention, you had better succeed in getting the men their dues. Treat this as the first test of your renewed loyalty to me.

"Now, leave me alone, Hacker. I have some real business to attend to. For the avoidance of doubt, I will be confirming your reappointment as Captain of Horse within the next twenty-four hours. Do not disappoint me, and do not abuse the trust I am showing in you. Now be on your way, man."

When it is abundantly clear His Lordship will not be speaking to me again, I walk slowly out of the resplendent room, closing the heavily set oak door as quietly as I can. As I do, an immaculately dressed attendant beckons me to follow him down the hallway and to the stables. I stand and bow, admiring the delicate features of this young dandy's marvellous residence.

As I leave his Lordship to his affairs and follow the footman. As I do, and expensively dressed man of a similar age to myself walks towards me with a purposeful stride. As I observe him, I can see the faintest of limps. It isn't a recent injury. It looks as though the fellow may have broken his leg some time ago, and he now has a permanent reminder of the incident.

As he passes close to me, the attendant calls out: "Monsieur Guillaume, you will find his Lordship in the far room, where he is expecting you, sir."

The visitor raises his hand to his wide-brimmed hat in acknowledgement, and then he is gone. I think nothing more of him, for my thoughts are focused on enjoying the journey home, my obligations here completed.

Soon I am astride Bucephalus, riding through the lush fields that encircle Newtown Linford and past a vast herd of Roe Deer grazing in the local woodlands of Swithland. Soon Hose and Harby will be on the horizon, and then Stathern.

I have much to ponder as my faithful steed devours the fine Leicestershire countryside. My meeting with Lord Grey went far better than I anticipated, albeit my opinions remain the same: he is a weak and vain man. Yet hide these feelings I must if I am to succeed in my quest.

I have been put to the test – and I am determined I will not fail.

The Guildhall emerges out of the gloom on the morning of Thursday, the first day of September.

It is ten o'clock, and the streets of Leicester are already bustling with activity. It seems every man, woman, and child who lives in these parts is out in force this morn, mingling with a multitude of visitors. Stall traders are doing brisk business, serving the large influx of farmers who are making their weekly visit to the cattle market, while a host of God-fearing souls are listening intently to a young preacher calling on the Almighty to strike down the King and end the war. As his sermon reaches yet another crescendo, I find myself saying "amen" as I pass close by to the large crowd listening intently to every word coming out of the speaker's mouth.

Once I am clear of the throng, I seek out a post where I can tether Bucepahlus close to the whitewashed walls of the imposing municipal building. This is where I have agreed to meet Thomas Haselrig and Arthur Staveley.

I spy a shelter close to the walls of St Martin's, an imposing Norman church that sits alongside the Guildhall and pay a grateful stable lad a couple of pennies to feed and water my faithful horse.

"Be wary of those hind legs," I warn the young man, who looks as though he can't be much older than my own son, Francis. "He likes nothing better than to give a vicious kick to any stranger who gets close to him. Whatever you do, don't stand behind him. You will regret it if you do."

The youngster looks up, offering an impish grin and a glimpse of his double row of crooked teeth. "Aye, sir," he replies. "You can be sure I will heed your words. I have no desire to be battered by such a powerful beast."

Haselrig and Staveley are two of the score and ten of men who sit with me on the Leicester Committee, and when it comes to the affairs of the city, both have my utmost respect and trust. Like me, they were captured by the Royalists at Melton Mowbray last November. That particular adventure cost us our liberty for two and a half long months. But it cemented the bond that now exists between us, and for that, I am thankful.

Today will be the first time I have been with both men since our release, and the memory sends a dull ache pulsing down my spine.

"Francis! Francis Hacker!"

I hear the voice of Thomas Haselrig long before I see him emerge from the Recorder's chamber on the first floor of the building.

"My goodness, man, you are a sight for sore eyes," he says enthusiastically. "How good it is to see you again."

Like the friends we are, we embrace, ignoring the scowls of a large group of rotund clergymen who have just emerged from one of the rooms adjoining the narrow hall-way where we are standing.

"I was delighted to receive your dispatch of yester-day," continues Thomas, as we sidestep the onrushing priestly congregation. "I have to confess, your note left me intrigued. Tell me, friend, what is the urgent matter you referred to?"

I guide the younger brother of Sir Arthur, one of Leicester's two Members of Parliament and a long-time irritant to the King, to the far corner of the cavernous chamber. When I am convinced we cannot be overheard, I spend the next fifteen minutes telling Thomas about the altercation I recently had with Lord Grey's dragoons, as well as everything else I know about the deteriorating morale of large parts of the Leicestershire Militia. As I speak, I sense he wishes to say something. But, blessed with impeccable manners, Thomas bites on his tongue until I finish.

"Arthur will certainly have a view on this matter," he says after a moment of contemplation. "It is essential he endorses whatever we agree the next steps should be, for he is close to the Mayor. But be of no doubt, the Aldermen are feeling a growing sense of unease and hostility towards his Lordship and the Militia officers closest to him.

"Ever since the outbreak of the war, we have sought Lord Grey's assistance in strengthening Leicester's defences and ensuring the Militia is adequately trained, so it can repulse a siege. Francis, you know as well as I that our pleas have fallen on deaf ears. His Lordship has done nothing to aid the town or the people who depend on his protection. He has sought to relieve the Mayor of whatever monies he has at his disposal without taking responsibility for anything. And the people have had enough of it. There is widespread outrage.

"The situation is so urgent that the Mayor is actively seeking to engage Parliament in the matter. A petition has been drawn up and signed by as many as two thousand souls, including myself and Arthur. It is scheduled to be dispatched to London on the morrow. When it reaches Parliament and becomes common knowledge, the matter is certain to cause Lord Grey significant embarrassment."

I am about to ask Thomas some highly pertinent questions when the friendly and familiar face of Staveley comes into view.

"Please accept my apologies," he says, bounding across the room like a hound pursuing a lame rabbit. "I was detained outside listening to the most remarkable preacher. A large crowd was blocking my way, and I had to wait for them to disperse. But I am here now. I hope I haven't put either of you to any inconvenience?"

I reach out and clutch Arthur, who is taken aback at my overt display of friendliness. When he has adjusted the shirt and doublet my man-hug has displaced, he enquires: "So, tell me, why the need for such a clandestine and urgent meeting?"

I clear my throat, glancing at Thomas as I do. He gives an encouraging smile. It's all I need. And so I begin to tell Arthur Staveley why it is vitally important Mayor of Leicester releases one hundred pounds of the city's reserves to make good my promise to Gracious Claypole and his impoverished comrades.

Within the hour, the three of us have reached an accord. Arthur and Thomas will do all they can to ensure the funds are forthcoming. I will set about the task of examining the city's defences once again and getting the most essential repair work to Leicester's weakened walls underway.

I re-emerge onto the streets of the city after midday, just as the autumnal sun breaks through the protective shrouds of mist that have been cloaking the heaving pavements.

Bucephalus has been well looked after by the young stable hand, so I give him an extra penny for his troubles, much to his delight.

When I have swapped a few pleasantries with passers-by, I lead Bucephalus by the reins down High Cross, making my way towards North Gate. As I do, my senses are assaulted by the overpowering smell of shit and piss. My nose wrinkles as torrents of brown fluid gush down the middle of the cobbled street on their way to the all-cleansing waters of the River Soar.

Yet even the stench of fetid decay is incapable of dampening my spirits. For I remain as positive as anyone can be under the circumstances. There is still work to be done to ensure Claypole and the men will receive their pay. But with Arthur and Thomas taking responsibility for the matter at hand, I feel confident a resolution is not far away. And that means I am on course to pass Lord Grey's all-important first test.

SIX

GOOD TO THEIR WORD, ARTHUR and Thomas somehow persuade the Mayor to release the necessary funds from Leicester's Treasury that prevents an uprising by several hundred of Lord Grey's dragoons.

I receive a concise confirmatory letter, written in the eloquent hand of Staveley, at midday on Monday, the fifth day of September. It simply says:

"My dearest friend,

"The Mayor was not willing to listen to the representations Thomas and I made to him. But do not despair. I can confirm the monies due to the soldiery will be paid by Thursday of this week. Five Committee members, the quorum we need for decisions to be made, have instructed the Treasury to pay one hundred pounds to the Militia's Quarter Master. He will see to it all affected men receive the monies owed to them. We are hopeful this gesture on the part of the city will convey our good faith to Lord Grey and demonstrates our willingness to work together for the common good.

"Be aware, however. There are moves afoot, brought about by the Mayor, to force Lord Grey to deliver the support the city requires. I am afraid we have been unable to discover what this entails, only that it may undermine somewhat the efforts you are making to placate his Lordship. Either Thomas or I will write again when we have more details.

"I remain your obedient servant, Arthur."

Unsure of precisely what the latter part of the letter means, but assuming it refers to the Petition Thomas warned me about, I choose to focus on the positive outcome engineered by my two friends.

Now, with the matter of the unpaid militiamen put to rest for the foreseeable future, I can turn my attention to affairs closer to home. I do this by preparing to spend the next few weeks rebuilding my relationship with Abijah and the men – and supporting Isabel and the children as we seek to continue healing the terrible wounds associated with the first half of the year.

Apart from the occasional light skirmish with the enemy, the war does not intrude on our daily lives even though the nearest Royalist garrison is located less than five miles away from Stathern, at the imposing stronghold of Belvoir Castle. This is a blessing for all concerned. While death is a tragic consequence of this bloody conflict, there is no satisfaction in knowing I am responsible for extinguishing the life of any man, particularly one in his prime. So any lull in the fighting is one I will willingly embrace.

The warm days of late summer and early autumn allow me to spend time with the children. Francis, in particular, needs my affection, for I have neglected his needs for far too long. Indeed there is some urgency, as my son is about to start attending school in Coventry, where he will reside for long periods.

I remember the moment when my own father and mother dispatched me to the very same school, which was founded by King Henry the Eighth some eighty years ago. During my first few weeks, I felt lost, alone and inadequate. Being introduced to a highly disciplined and rigorous learning environment, which required real application to understand subjects like Latin, Greek and Mathematics had a deeply profound impact on my own self-worth.

It is this very world Isabel and I have decided our eldest child must join.

"Papa, why are you forcing me to go?" asks Francis one Saturday afternoon as we are preparing for the autumn harvest. "I don't want to leave you, Mother and my sisters. Can I not stay here instead and help you with the Militia? Can I not become a Cornet in your Company?"

I look up from the desk where I am writing my latest dispatch to Lord Grey. I say nothing. Instead, I scrutinise my son in a way I have not done for a long time, and what I see makes me realise Francis is a lot more mature and perceptive than either Isabel or myself appreciate. He is growing into a mature young man and is no longer the whelp he was just a few months ago.

"Francis," I say, "very few things in life are as important as a classical education. At the moment, I am sure you will not really understand what I am saying. I certainly didn't when I was required to leave home when I was just eleven. I felt resentment. Like you, I also felt as though my Papa and Mother were abandoning me. But as time passed and I grew used to my fellow scholars and the Masters, even liking a few of them after a while, I discovered the truth to be very different to how I initially perceived it to be.

"The single most important thing I learned when I went to Coventry was how to live an independent life. Yes, I read my Homer and Plato; I got to grips with Latin; and long into the evening, I would read about Romulus and Remus, the founding fathers of Rome. But the education I received was much more valuable than simply absorbing information: it gave me sobriety and self-confidence. These traits have enabled me to be a Squire of some note and a Gentleman at a time when virtues like chivalry are hastily being abandoned. For education offers these things and so much more."

Talking about my formative years in such animated fashion takes me back to before I was introduced to Isabel, to a time long before I was even allowed to fire a musket. King Charles had recently succeeded his father as our monarch, and there was optimism in the country that has been lost these past fifteen years.

In truth, my childhood is a period I associate with deep unhappiness, not least because my mother died shortly after I started attending the school. Within a year, my father remarried a woman I could never take to. It wasn't her fault. Indeed, her failure was trying too hard to replace the mother I had lost.

As I reminisce, I realise Francis is quite right to speak his mind about his very valid concerns and anxieties in a way I never did.

"Papa," asserts my son when it is clear I have finished speaking. "Why can I not go to a school closer to home, somewhere like Melton? That way, I could be at home more often and see you and Mother a lot more."

I look at him, my eyes betraying all.

"Son, I am sorry, but the decision has been made," I say. "For many reasons, not least your own long-term well being, your mother and I believe it is in your best interests to attend the school we have chosen for you. And it really is futile discussing the subject further.

"In time, you will grow to like the place. And while there, you will prosper in a way I never did, for you have been blessed with your mother's brains and tongue. So, for the next few days, let us enjoy the time we have together and not indulge in any quarrelling or bickering. What say you?"

Francis glares at me, his lips remaining tightly closed as a watery film covers his dulled blue eyes. No words are forthcoming from the son I love with all my heart. As the tears start to run down his cheeks, he turns around and walks out of the room.

I don't see him for the next two days.

A message arrives at the Hall in the early afternoon of Sunday the eleventh day of September, written by my good friend, Haselrig.

Isabel, the children and myself have just returned from our weekly trial with William Norwich at Saint Guthlacs when the flushed and weary rider arrives. He is flecked with mud after riding hard for the last hour, and he and his horse look as though they require some rest.

After he is escorted to a scullery used by the farm-workers, I take a seat in the parlour and read Haselrig's note, hoping it will improve my spirits, for I am feeling sour.

Today, with William Laud, the despised Archbishop of Canterbury locked in the Tower after being charged with Treason, I have been forced to listen to my very own Minister speak out on the matter, telling his congregation that Laud's imprisonment is neither just or legal.

Such was the anger I felt; Isabel had to physically restrain me on two occasions from walking out of the church. As it was, those villagers close to me could have no doubts about my reaction to the Reverend Norwich's blatant appeal to Royalist sympathisers, of which there are still some in the congregation.

Shortly before the deaths of my daughters, I promised Isabel I would turn a blind eye to Norwich's conduct as long as he behaved himself. Yet, judging by the evidence of today and other recent incidents, this vow has been well and truly broken. I can prevaricate no more. But before I turn my attention to the Minister, there is the small matter that has just been presented to me by Haselrig – the submission of a petition to Parliament by the Mayor, Aldermen and inhabitants of Leicester about the conduct of Lord Grey and his officers in recent months. Critically, the document I have before me seeks to call his Lordship back to the county from his London home, so that differences between the two sides can be resolved speedily and amicably.

I look down at the distinctive hand of Thomas Haselrig, who writes:

"My dear friend, Francis.

"It is indeed a blessing to have you back in our midst. I thank God for your safe return and fear your services will be sorely needed in the days ahead, and not just as an administrator of the affairs of Leicester.

"I promised I would alert you about any significant developments, and there is one I need to draw to your attention.

"After seeking to address a problem that has been escalating for more than a year now, The Mayor has today sent a petition to the House of Commons demanding the return of Lord Grey of Groby to the county. There is widespread concern among many Committee members that Leicester's state of readiness is woeful should we be attacked. Many do not believe the defences have been strengthened since Prince Rupert last entered the city two years ago. Understandably they are demanding the situation is addressed as an immediate priority.

"The Mayor is determined to act while there is still time. He has asked me to send you notice of his intentions on behalf of the Committee and hopes he has your support in the matter. As do I.

"Your obedient and devoted servant, Thomas."

Alas, I fear I will have to disappoint Thomas and the Committee, and it may be the first of many times I do so.

As I contemplate how I should respond to the dispatch, a rueful smile finds its way onto my face. If I had received such correspondence a few weeks ago, I would have been delighted to give my full backing to the venture. But I have given my word to Lord Grey that I am his man, which means remaining loyal regardless of the circumstances. I am honour-bound to show him solidarity, and even though it pains me to do so, I have also pledged I will do all I can to win the young noble's trust to none other than Cromwell. ¬So I find myself unable to publicly stand alongside the Committee on this matter, even though my heart wishes it could be so.

I reach for my quill and inkpot. The Lieutenant-General is overdue a dispatch from me. I have been silent for too long. It is time to inform him of the disquiet that is forming in this part of England.

But first, I must write to Lord Grey, assuring him of my steadfast support in the matter and offering to intercede on his behalf, should he need me to…

With relative tranquillity descending on Stahern once again, a surprise visitor arrives at the Hall three weeks later.

It is Saturday, the first day of October, and my brother Rowland, the scourge of the Parliamentarian garrison in Nottingham, is in rude health as he strides across the spacious room with arms outstretched.

"Brother, it has been too long," he says, the warmth of his smile as infectious and heartening as it always is. "It is good to see you. Apologies for the lateness of the hour and for not giving you, or Isabel, warning of my visit."

Surprised, I let out a burst of spontaneous laughter. It masks the relief that is coursing through my veins at the sight of my youngest sibling.

The last thing I heard about Rowland suggested he had been badly wounded during a skirmish on Belvoir Bridge, on the outskirts of Leicester. That was almost two months ago. Despite my best attempts to find out details about the incident and my brother's well being, my enquiries have drawn a blank.

Until now.

"You rogue," I say jokingly to the handsome, dark-haired figure that stands before me. "Your manners deserted you many years ago, just hours after you were born, I seem to recall. Nonetheless, it is good to see you. Despite your irreverence and appalling lack of judgment, we are family, and nothing will break our bond.

"I have been worried about you, brother. I have been making discreet enquiries about the state of your health for several weeks, ever since I heard about the scrap you got yourself into just outside Leicester. I was told you received a serious wound. Yet here you stand, looking every inch a well and healthy soul. It seems my worries were unfounded?"

Mention of the altercation sees Rowland noticeably adopt a more reserved demeanour. His smile is gone. I recognise the pain that fills his eyes.

"I was lucky that day," he says eventually. "Some of my men were less fortunate, falling to the lead shot of the muskets of Captains Adinson, Grey and Tapper. Ten of my company died that fateful day. I received a flesh wound to the same arm that I injured just over a year ago. But it is now healed. However, I am carrying the scars in my mind. And it will be a long time before they stop hurting."

Rowland need say no more. I, too, know what it is like to lead men to their deaths. It is the cross an officer bears and something that preys on our conscience until the day we meet our Maker.

I gesture to my younger brother to take a seat by the window. The scullery's shutters are closed, so we cannot be observed from outside, and I have just opened a fine bottle of claret, which I know Rowland will have the greatest of difficulty in declining.

As he sits down, I walk over to the door that leads to the hallway.

"Isabel! Isabel!" I call into the rapidly deteriorating light. "Come, my love, I have quite a surprise for you."

It is time to raise our spirits.

My wife is overjoyed when she recognises who the visitor is. Quickly regaining her composure, Isabel joins Rowland and me, sitting at the large table that dominates the room.

"My goodness, Rowland!" she says. "I didn't realise you were coming here tonight. Is everything okay? Are you well? Has something untoward happened?"

The alarm in Isabel's voice is apparent from the very moment she starts speaking.

My brother looks at her. He reaches out and grasps her hand.

"My dear Isabel, you have the uncanny knack of looking radiant whenever I see you," he says reassuringly. "I promise, there is nothing to worry about. I just felt it was time I visited my nearest and dearest. Too many months have passed since I was in your good company. And, as I was passing close by, it would have been impolite to have not heeded the call of Stathern and the chance to see you both."

Isabel lets out a throaty roar. It is good to hear my wife laugh so fulsomely once again. It has been a long time since I have seen her relax.

"You are a cad and a flatterer, Rowland Hacker," chuckles Isabel. "You always have been, and I am sure you always will be. We love you for it, and even though you continue to ride for the King, and it brings Francis and myself much-needed cheer to see you again."

As she finishes the sentence, another laugh escapes.

"Indeed, when you are an old man, I am sure you

will still be making flirtatious comments to innocent young ladies," she adds. "Alas, I cannot stay. Nor am I sure you would wish me to do so, for you both have some catching up to do.

"I must attend to the needs of the children. Anne is feeling unwell and needs comforting. And she must not realise you are here. So, as much as I would like to spend the rest of the evening with you and Francis, I am afraid my duties lie elsewhere."

With that, Isabel rises, bends down and gives Rowland a gentle kiss on the cheek. As she does, she looks over to me, and I give her hand an encouraging squeeze.

Straightening herself, she wags her forefinger at me reprovingly, saying: "And no retiring to our chamber at four o'clock in the morning, Francis Hacker. We have Church in the morning, a busy day ahead – and you need to have a clear head."

As Isabel departs, I pick up my glass and raise it in my brother's direction. He reciprocates. The time is ten-thirty.

"May our Lord continue to protect you, brother," I say. "And may we have many more opportunities to spend a night in each other's company, away from scrutinising eyes.

"Now, tell me why you have really made your journey this evening, for I certainly don't believe your story about being in the vicinity of the Hall? Something is troubling you. I know it, for you only come here when something is agitating you. So free your burden and tell me what it is, and let's see what can be done about it."

Three hours later, cold anger has replaced the joy I experienced at being in the company of my brother after so many months of separation.

The source of my trouble is the news Rowland has brought with him.

"Are you sure you don't know why he has returned or what his plans are?" I ask of my brother. "I need to know more. You must tell me everything you know on the matter. So much depends on it."

Rowland's expression remains set and is as sombre as my own.

"Francis," he says, "If I knew more, I would tell you so. You must believe me when I tell you I am lucky to be able to say anything at all. It is clear my superiors do not trust me and are unwilling to tell me anything about this venture. I know discussions have been held at Newark and Belvoir Castle, but I am not privy to the detail. Nor am I likely to be.

"What I have discovered is the result of overhearing some loose tongues. But I have been unable to ask questions for fear of raising suspicions.

"It will not surprise you to learn I am suspected of warning you about our affairs earlier in the year. I was questioned when Else was caught and exposed as a spy. Prince Rupert was not happy when he found out the web he had helped to create was unravelled. Thankfully, I persuaded his men that I had no involvement in alerting Parliament about her treachery. But I will not be believed a second time."

I rub my forehead. My temple is throbbing. The pulsing ache feels as if the backs of my eyeballs are being held in a vice, and the pain is quite acute. It is little wonder, for I am reeling from a revelation I was not expecting.

"I need to think about what you have told me, and I need to make some urgent plans," I say, my words slightly slurred, my head made light by Rowland's disclosure. "By all means, please stay the evening. We have ample room, and we can talk again before you leave in the morn."

Rowland nods his head in appreciation.

"You know where to go," I say. "You can bed down in the chamber above the study. It is comfortable and will ensure you get a good night's sleep, albeit there are only a few hours before the dawn chorus intercedes."

My brother rises and walks the few steps to where I am now standing. He wraps his arms around my shoulders and holds me tightly.

"If I could spare you this pain, I most surely would," he whispers. "But it is important you found out from me. I could not help you when you lost Isable and Barbara, which I will never forgive myself for. But I can help now. And you have my word I will do all in my power to see my nieces avenged."

When Rowland is gone, raw emotion overcomes me. Anger, pain, loss, a need for retribution; all these things batter my skull from within.

I look at the scars on my fingers. The wounds are less than a year old. In the cold, the welts where the pliers set about their work are clearly visible. Right now, they are a livid red. As I look at them, I recall the agony I endured as my nails were ripped from my hands and then my toes.

Stinging tears force me to close my eyes. As I do, I see the innocent faces of my murdered daughters, two infants killed in cold blood.

I blink away a salt-laced droplet. The vision of my girls disappears into the void. Their beautiful faces have been replaced by the dark, menacing features of Gustav Holck, the assassin who kills to satisfy his lust for blood.

The Bohemian is the only man I have hated. One day I will kill him. I have vowed it will be so, and I believe God will be by my side when I do so.

Thanks to the information my brother has shared with me, I may now get my chance. For Rowland had told me the mercenary, a trusted part of the inner circle of princes Rupert and Maurice, is to return to the Vale of Belvoir on a secret mission.

I do not know how and when he plans to execute his plans. But I do know he is plotting to kill a leading member of the Parliamentarian cause.

Rowland is unaware of the identity of the intended victim, and right now, there are many potential targets, all of them causing the King's men a great deal of discomfort as the war progresses. But he has promised to try and discover the name without putting himself in harm's way.

As I stand alone at two o'clock in the morning, I feel bitterness in my heart that I thought repentance and prayer had banished. I was wrong; it is still there. So I close my eyes again. As I do, a deep sigh forces its way out of my mouth. Fatigue is starting to claim me.

My life has taken another twist, one I cannot control, and I realise I will not be able to rest until the child-killer I have vowed to kill has taken his last breath.

It is time to start planning my revenge.

SEVEN

THE CALMNESS OF AUGUST AND September shows no signs of abating as we prepare to enter the final months of the year.

Keen to maintain the mood of optimism that prevails, I have decided not to tell Isabel about Rowland's revelation.

My wife has suffered enough. For her to discover Holck will soon be residing a little more than four miles away is something I am not prepared to share with her. Doing so would inflict more pain on the woman I love – not least because I would be forced to confess my true intentions, and I would have to confirm my own life is again in mortal danger.

I stay silent, preferring instead to focus my efforts on helping Isabel and the children rebuild their fragile lives.

For weeks now, my wife and I have been holding a daily prayer vigil, seeking the Holy Spirit's healing and restorative powers. While communing with the Lord has positively affected my good wife, I am conscious there is a barrier between my Maker and myself. I am in no doubt it has come about because I am playing a game with deceit at its heart. Yet, I am not prepared to yield; such is my obsession.

At the Hall, we both spend time with the girls, who no longer have the comforting influence of their elder brother to call upon.

Francis has left Stathern, reluctantly succumbing to the collegiate life Isabel and I have chosen for him.

Since the end of September, he has been pursuing an education in Coventry. However, he was full of resentment at the time of his departure, which manifested itself in the form of increasingly hostile disagreements and growing belligerence.

I understand why he was upset, and it grieved me to see him so distraught in the days before he left for pastures new. Nonetheless, I am confident it will lead to a world of opportunity, knowledge and privilege that he is far better equipped to handle than I ever was.

Thankfully, we visited him two weeks ago, during the third week of the Michaelmas term. We were delighted to see his spirits had improved considerably. He greeted us warmly and seemed genuinely pleased to see his mother, who bore the brunt of his anger in the days that preceded the beginning of this new chapter.

There are only five more weeks to go before he returns to the Hall to celebrate Christmas. And when he does come home, I am sure we will see more signs of the new influences increasingly shaping and defining his young and precious life.

As the days pass by, I find myself thinking of my son often.

He has left another hole in the family. The truth is you only really miss someone when they are not alongside you. And in the first few weeks, the pain I feel at Francis's absence affects my mood terribly. But thoughts of his welfare and happiness are set to one side on the morn of Wednesday, the twelfth day of October when Isabel enters my study abruptly at nine o'clock in the morning.

As soon as my good wife fixes her calm and determined eyes on me, I know there is a problem. What I don't know is if I am the cause of her agitation and distress?

"Whatever is the matter?" I say as calmly as I can, shaken by Isabel's sudden appearance. "My dear, I beg you, tell me what the problem is?"

Isabel walks to my desk, where I am surrounded by recent dispatches from Lord Grey and the Leicester Committee and while composing my first response of the day. As she approaches, I can see the concern on her face. She is rattled, no longer the assured figure that effortlessly helps me deal with many military and estate-related problems and conundrums.

She sits opposite me, her face flushed. Her movements are deliberate and precise. I know what Isabel is doing: she is regaining her poise before speaking.

"We have some visitors," she announces eventually, her voice faltering. As she speaks again, Isabel looks out of the window towards the woodlands where a host of evergreens compete for attention some four hundred feet away from the Hall.

I can see her eyes are bloodshot.

"They are known to you," she continues. "And what has befallen these poor people is as great a tragedy as the one that afflicted our own family less than six months ago."

Isabel reaches out and clasps my hands, her fingers lacing between my own. Instantly I understand what she is referring to. And I feel her pain as it surfaces once more.

My wife then proceeds to tell me of the terrible events that have afflicted the Goswick family of Crane Moor, the kindly people who gave me shelter in July, shortly after the glorious victory at Marston Moor.

When she is finished, and there are no more words to come, I am left feeling bereft and empty. My face may be unmarked, but it feels as though a powerful force has struck, leaving me dazed and uncertain.

"Are you sure this is true?" I enquire after her words start to sink in. "Can this really be so?"

My wife says nothing. Her face is white. The slightest of nods is sufficient to confirm everything.

Yet another chill pulses through my body. I shudder involuntarily.

"May God have mercy on those poor wretches," I say, staring at the crucifix positioned atop the hearth. "I pray our Maker is with this good family at such a tragic time."

Taking her cue, Isabel rises and leaves the room. She returns within a couple of minutes. At her side are the broken, filthy and malnourished figures of Josiah and Ursula.

Eight-year-old Eunice and her younger brother, Gideon, are not at their sides. But, thanks to Isabel's forewarning, I know why they are not accompanying their loving parents, and I can refrain from asking crass and insensitive questions.

As I look at these two helpless souls, I suddenly sense the intense hatred that is alive in me.

For what seems like an eternity, no words are spoken.

It has been so throughout my life; when I am required to say something to soothe or inspire, I am often found wanting.

Finally, with despair threatening to close in, I find my tongue stilled no more.

"My dearest Ursula and Josiah, I thank our God that He has guided you here, where you are most welcome," I say to them both with as much compassion as I can summon. "Please stay here as long as you wish. What is ours is yours."

Before I can finish speaking, Ursula starts sobbing uncontrollably, her head resting on the broad shoulders of her husband as her slight body crumples. Josiah wraps his powerful right arm around his wife, steadying her while attempting to say some tender and soothing words.

As they attempt to regain a semblance of composure, I realise the couple standing before me present a very different picture to the one I recall so vividly from our fortuitous encounter a few months ago.

Eventually, when the crying has started to subside, the man who fought at Adwalton Moor for Parliament's routed Northern Association army looks directly at me.

The red scar on his cheek is alive, and there is a fire in his eyes.

"We had no-one to turn to, other than your good selves," he says. "Our neighbours were either killed or wounded when the Cavaliers came and set the village ablaze, as was anyone who had offered hospitality or support to men such as yourself. Plenty of folk were prepared to tell all and point their fingers at others, so they could escape scrutiny and the harshest of punishments.

"The soldiers didn't care who they harmed. They

were like wild, base animals, slashing their swords and cleavers at anyone and anything that moved. All they wanted to do was bring destruction and death to Crane Moor.

"Those that did the accusing gave an undertaking they would offer no help to the likes of us. They were told that if they were found to have offered assistance of any kind, they would suffer the same fate that befell us."

I draw in my breath and reach for a fresh quill. I am buying time, allowing every one of Josiah's words to register.

Thankfully, Isabel understands my struggles and her kind, unspoken encouragement offers me the reassurance I need, for I am struggling to find words of comfort and assurance to say to our desperate guests. Despite my best efforts, I cannot fully comprehend everything that is unravelling, so I embrace the nearest emotional crutch I can find. As I toil with the stylus, I urge Josiah to tell me as much as he can about what happened.

"I remember it as if it were yesterday," he recounts in a monotone. "It was the Popist Feast Day of Saint Bartholomew the Apostle. It was the late afternoon, just before supper, and we were all searching for eggs in the long grass. I could hear the children. They were happy, as were Ursula and I. Our laughter filled the air.

"All of a sudden, chaos descended on us, and then everything happened so fast. One minute, we were tending the birds, the next, we were being assaulted by the King's men, and we were powerless to resist."

Tears are running down Josiah's cheeks as he relives the tragic events of late August.

Ordinarily, I would seek to comfort someone

expressing such torment. But my visitor needs to speak: he needs to release some of the pain that is torturing his soul, and Josiah can only do this by talking to people who have suffered similar agonies, people like Isabel and myself, who know what it is to experience the same unbearable and excruciating loss.

"They showed the children no mercy," reveals Josiah through clenched teeth as he relives the attack on his home. "They simply cut them down where they stood. My beautiful children: one minute, they were alive and full of excitement; the next, they were lying in pools of their own blood, slaughtered like animals.

"I was too far away from them to offer any protection. By the time I reached them, nought could be done for them. They were gone. So, too, were the killers."

I close my eyes, recalling the infectiousness of Eunice and Gideon's laughter on that glorious summer's evening when the family opened the doors of their humble home and showed me such tenderness. The two children, as much as Josiah and Ursula, were responsible for mending my hardened soul. Now they are fading memories, like so many other innocents. Yet, at the same time, the perpetrators are free to roam and commit atrocity after atrocity in the name of the tyrant they serve.

I dry my own tears with the back of my hand, blinking away the pools before they threaten to steal what is left of my composure.

"Friends," I say as warmly as I can. "I am honoured you chose to come here. I remember telling you I would gladly reciprocate the hospitality you showed me in my hour of need. Little did I know we would meet again under such terrible circumstances? How I wish it wasn't so.

"Know you are among people who will do all they can to help you overcome this dreadful burden. Allow us to care for you. And for as long as you desire, you must stay among us and rebuild your lives. We can accommodate you for as long as you wish."

Isabel reaches out tenderly and touches the shoulders of Josiah and Eunice. Then, when we all realise there is nothing more to say, she ushers them towards the door. Her gentleness leads to more necessary outpourings. The children may have been killed six weeks ago, but the pain is still very raw and alive.

It will take a lifetime before it starts to fade.

I don't see Josiah and Ursula for the rest of the day.

Isabel takes the couple to the only vacant cottage we have on the estate. The building looks resplendent after being recently refurbished and whitewashed, ready to welcome its new occupants. It has been empty since the late Spring, when Else, our cook of almost twenty years, was exposed as a traitor.

The cottage was ripped apart by the Militia as I sought evidence of her complicity in the murders of Peter and Marjorie Harrington. The thoroughness of my men ensured we discovered everything: details of her spymaster, the network she belonged to, and the extent of her cold-hearted betrayal.

Even after so many months, I am still finding it hard to understand how we suspected nothing of the viper in our midst.

Else still lives, but only just. Gone is the smile that would light up a room. It will never return.

Lord Grey's torturers have done their work thoroughly on her. After telling all, she is now a broken woman spiritually and physically. The fists of his Lordship's men have been thorough, mutilating Else's womanly features. Now she awaits the gallows and her own judgment day. And, for those of us in Stathern who suffered because of her treachery, her demise cannot come soon enough.

For the rest of us, life must go on. It is a futile exercise living in the past. Hoping. Wishing. Regretting. Nothing we do will alter the course of history, so look forwards we must.

And as I refocus and seek some inner peace, I take a small degree of comfort, knowing we have somewhere to house Josiah and Ursula, even if it was once the home of the vilest of conspirators.

Being in my own company for too long can bring on the Black Dog – feelings of despair that consume me from within. I am prone to it and have been most of my life. So I am relieved when I hear Abijah's brisk footsteps echoing off the slates in the hallway as he approaches for our daily discussion about military affairs. It is the distraction I am seeking.

"Francis," he says as he walks into the room. "Whatever is going on? I have just seen Isabel escorting a young couple away from the Hall. They appear to be in a terrible state. So, too, is your good wife."

I am unable to concentrate on the letters I need to write. So I push the paper to one side and tell Abijah the whole tragic story.

Once I have talked to my friend for an hour and delegated some minor Militia matters to him, I am exhausted. And it is not even midday. After he departs, I give orders to be left alone. I need time to myself. My emotions are drained.

The nature of the Goswick's arrival at the Hall has deeply unsettled me, not least because it has come so quickly after Rowland's revelations about the new Royalist plot.

With Josiah and Ursula now living at Stathern, and their woes consuming my thoughts, I struggle to focus on anything other than vengeance and wrath.

I am acutely aware this is not how followers of Christ Jesus should behave. So I attempt to pray. But I am distracted, and nothing of any substance comes to me.

I lean forward and put my head in my hands. As I do, sunshine drenches the room. To my shame, I realise I have been sliding from the path of righteousness for far too many days. So I reach for my Bible and immediately turn to Psalm Three, reading aloud the words of King David that have always given me reassurance at times of fear and turbulence. And, as I do, my strength starts to return.

> *O Lord, how many are my foes!*
> *How many rise up against me!*
> *Many are saying of me, "God will not deliver him."*
> *But you are a shield around me, O Lord; you bestow glory on me and lift up my head.*
> *To the Lord I cry aloud, and he answers me from his holy hill.*
> *I lie down and sleep; I wake again, because the Lord sustains me.*
> *I will not fear the tens of thousands drawn up against me on every side.*
> *Arise, O Lord! Deliver me, O my God!*

Strike all my enemies on the jaw; break the teeth of the wicked.
From the Lord comes deliverance.
May your blessing be on your people.

For the next couple of hours, I ask for restoration. The price I am required to pay is repentance. Utter and total.

At four o'clock in the afternoon, there is a knock on the door. It is Isabel. She is carrying a tray laden with cheeses, bread and ham. I beckon her in, and as the intoxicating aroma gets ever closer, I realise just how hungry I am.

"You must be famished?" she says. "You didn't eat breakfast, and, as far as I can tell, you haven't left this room all day?"

I shrug my shoulders. As usual, my good wife is right. Thank goodness she is not only the love of my life but the guardian of my stomach and overall wellbeing.

"Thank you, my dearest," I say appreciatively. "Where would I be without you, a woman of such intellect and beauty? How you have steered me onto the right path so many times and ensured I am sustained to meet the challenges of the day."

On other occasions, my remarks would have extracted a laugh or even a playful prod from an index finger. But not today; cheerfulness will not be emerging from the gloom for a while yet, I fear.

"How have Josiah and Ursula settled into the cottage?" I enquire. "I hope they will be comfortable enough there."

For a minute, Isabel just stares at me. Then, when

she speaks, her undisguised scorn catches me off-guard.

"Husband, you forget too much too quickly," she says. "Mercifully, our girls were not killed before our very eyes. We were spared that barbarity. Nonetheless, the last six months have left us scarred in a way neither of us can truly comprehend.

"For Ursula and Josiah, that pain is certainly more acute because they were within a few feet of their children when the killers struck, and they could do nothing to save them. Imagine what that is like for a moment? Then, think hard about how that would affect you?

"That horrific image will be with them until their dying day. It will influence everything they do and say, just as it does with us.

"So before you open your mouth and say something stupid and insensitive, remember what we have been forced to endure. Asking a foolhardy question about whether they have settled into a cottage that last housed a heinous traitor is going to cause nothing other than distress.

"Feeling truly comfortable again maybe something that eludes them for the rest of their lives. But right now, at least they are around people who understand what they are going through. And because we understand, we need to make sure we make a special and concerted effort."

I look at Isabel. Her rebuke has struck home, and she is right.

Over the years, I have thought on many occasion I am undeserving of such a woman. And today, I think so again.

She has cut me to the bone. Yet she has done so lovingly, with no desire to cause me distress or pain. Instead, she wishes to see me grow a trait that eludes many men: sensitivity!

Before I can process everything I am thinking, Isabel speaks again.

"Now, Francis, kneel with me and give thanks to our Maker for all He has blessed us with. And when we are done, eat the food I have brought you."

Needing no further encouragement, I do as I am told. And for the second time in the day, I begin a period of deep soul-searching and atonement with my Creator.

EIGHT

FOR SEVERAL DAYS, A DEEP peace claims me.

Riders arrive at the Hall carrying blunt missives from Lord Grey, seeking information about the enemy's strength and movements. Terse and to the point, these communiqués fail to provoke me in the way they once did. Instead of responding in my usual blunt style, I find myself writing fulsome reports at every opportunity, enthusiastically displaying the newly found esteem I have for my superior – just as Lieutenant-General Cromwell has instructed me to do.

And the more I write, the easier the deception gets.

My fawning letters seem to be convincing His Lordship that I may have indeed turned an important corner, and my loyalties are no longer questionable. At least, that is what I and others are hoping.

As is often the case at the end of the campaigning season, little is happening on the military front, and I am grateful for the welcome respite.

The lull in hostilities enables me to see Josiah and

Ursula many times as they start the process of settling into life at Stathern and getting to know some of the wonderful people that make this a blessed place to live. While grief continues to envelop them at every opportunity, I am pleased to note they are noticeably making an effort to integrate with other villagers. I have certainly learned from experience this is an essential step in the healing process.

Isabel has been a wonderful source of support for Ursula during her period of mourning, spending as much time as she can afford with the distraught newcomer.

A bond is developing, borne out of mutual grief, understanding and faithfulness. And this pleases me greatly, not least because my wife, who has herself struggled to come to terms with our own losses, has now found a new lease of life and something positive to focus on.

It is a mild Wednesday for the time of the year, and I am in the stables spending some precious moments with Bucephalus when Abijah finds me. His agitation is apparent long before he starts speaking.

"A messenger has arrived from Lieutenant-General Cromwell," he says in a clipped and formal tone, all too aware of the dangerous game I am playing with Lord Grey. "It's the usual fellow, and he carries a message that he is unwilling to give to anyone other than yourself."

I pat my stallion affectionately and point a carrot in his direction as my final offering of the day, which he takes out of my hand with the utmost care and precision. As he chews, Bucephalus looks at me with superiority in his eyes. He then turns around and walks away, swishing his tail from side to side as he does. This is his way of informing me our time together is at an end.

"Lead the way," I say to Abijah, with as much cheerfulness I can muster. "I am always eager to read any words of wisdom Oliver has to offer."

Hugh Walker is drinking a tankard of beer when I enter the study. He stands to attention as I enter the room and looks slightly embarrassed as some of the contents of his jar spill onto the floor, such is the haste in which he seeks to greet me.

"Sit still and continue to refresh yourself," I say to the tired young man, one of Cromwell's loyal band of Ironsides and a Presbyterian who hails from a village close to Ely. "Knowing you as I do, I am sure you will have covered many a mile this day?"

Before he can answer, I extend my hand, beckoning him to pass over the package, the reason for his visitation.

"Let me have it, man," I urge. "Let me see what is occupying the Lieutenant-General's thoughts so much that he sees fit to send you here at this late hour."

My voice is half-joking, half-serious.

Walker, who in reality is just a couple of years younger than me, hands over an envelope. It bears the unmistakable seal of Cromwell.

I notice he still has a plate of bread and cheese to finish. So I encourage him to retire to the kitchen he knows so well before finding a comfortable chair for myself by the large window in the parlour. When I am settled, I proceed to read the dispatch written in Oliver's distinctive hand.

"Warm greetings, my courageous and beloved friend.

"It seems like an eternity since we last saw each other. I trust you, Isabel, and the children are well and, God willing, your position in the Midlands Association

is more secure due to the decisive actions you have taken?

"As you may be aware, relations between myself and the Earl of Manchester continue to deteriorate. We have sought to reconcile matters, but we can find little common ground between us. I am reconciled to being unable to find a compromise that will agree with either of us. I fear our difficulties can only assist the enemy. While we dither and disagree, our soldiers cannot make the progress Parliament needs in the East as we take the fight to Crowland.

"Intelligence has reached me this very day that the King's men are preparing to take advantage of the situation and our perceived weakness. In this regard, it would seem Belvoir Castle is likely to be the point from where an attack is expected to take place, in all probability by the end of the month.

"My friend, we stand on the brink of a great victory against the armies of Charles. Nothing must prevent us from prevailing. But if the Eastern Association was to be defeated in battle, the setback will be immense. Indeed, it could once again tip the balance of the war in favour of the King. Therefore, I find myself in need of your help.

"With the utmost urgency and discretion, I urge you to find out as much as you can about the whereabouts of Sir Richard Byron. I am told he is mobilising his forces at Newark and intends to join up with the Royalist garrisons of Belvoir Castle and Wereton House. Any information you can uncover on this matter will benefit me and the fight we are jointly engaged in.

"Be assured, I would not ask this of you if it was

not of importance.
    "Your faithful brother in Christ, Oliver."

I look at the date at the top of the letter. It was written on Monday, the seventeenth day of October, and it has taken more than two days to reach me.

I have less than two weeks to get the information Oliver needs.

"Why is it always you that gets thrown to the Lions?" asks Abijah, who is clearly angry by Cromwell's latest demands of me. "We will need the luck of the Devil to uncover Byron's intentions between now and the end of the month. It is nigh on an impossible task, and the Lieutenant-General knows it to be so."

I don't respond to the challenge. Instead, I feel a warmth generated from the knowledge that I continue to be trusted by one of the most influential and powerful men in the land, a man who calls me his friend.

Under such circumstances, I would also be seeking the aid of the men I can rely on most in this turbulent world.

My second-in-command and I retire to the cottage he shares with Prudence, the faithful hound that has no love of me. It is now past ten o'clock in the evening. The Tawny Owls are out in force, hooting what appears to be coded messages to one another as Abijah and I set about formulating a plan that will serve our purposes and that of Cromwell.

Like so many, I need time to collect my thoughts when presented with a surprise. Now I have digested the contents of Oliver's dispatch and bidden Hugh Walker farewell, I feel sharp once again, my vigour returning.

"We need to mobilise our agents as discreetly as possible," says Abijah, thinking aloud. "If they ask too many direct questions, they will be exposed and arrested. And once that happens, our chances of discovering the King's intentions and neutralising Byron's force will be almost impossible, and the damage to our intelligence-gathering network will be irreparable."

I sip slowly from the glass I have been holding for the last few minutes. In the candlelight, the claret resembles black tar. Thankfully its taste is somewhat more pleasant, and I am pleased to say the alcohol actively stimulates my thinking.

"We have an agent who resides close to Newark, whose services we can call upon immediately," I say, recalling the times I have been forced to rely on the guile and ingenuity of Edmund Goodyeare, a loyal and cunning Parliamentary spy.

"He has a proven stable of reliable people that have never been exposed, including men and women who are active in the castle. I am sure he would be willing to assist given the urgency of Cromwell's letter."

Abijah raises his glass. The gesture confirms he is happy with my suggestion.

"What about getting our hands on information relating to matters closer to home?" he enquires. "The castle is just twenty minutes away from here. On a clear day, it can be clearly seen on the skyline. We know plenty of folks who can tell us things about the Governor's intentions and the coming and going of troops. Do you want me to start making some enquiries?"

I nod my head in affirmation.

"That's a very good idea," I say. "The more who are

feeding us tidbits, the better chance we will have in finding out what is going on. We have an uphill mountain to climb, my friend. But the more trusted souls we can rely on, the better our chances. It really is as simple as that."

One piece of information I deliberately choose not to share with my best friend is my intention to engage the services of another informant, one who has been very useful in recent months. His name is Rowland, and he is my Royalist brother.

For the next four days, Abijah and I work tirelessly. We rise early in the morning and don't succumb to fatigue and the pull of the night until the early hours; such is the sheer volume of secretive work we have to undertake.

After setting specific actions in motion, we do our best to stay on top of the fact-finding, logging as much detail as possible and ensuring we do not get distracted by tasty morsels that, on other occasions, would result in us mobilising the entire eighty-strong company. One such opportunity that we must forego will present itself in the next few days at Copt Oak, a small outpost just outside Coalville. Abijah's agents have told us 'Blind' Henry Hastings is planning to attack the small Parliamentary garrison that overlooks Leicestershire and Nottinghamshire from its lofty perch.

It is one of the hardest decisions I have made in recent times, but make it I must. So I forward the information with as much haste as I can muster to Copt Oak's commander. He needs as much time as possible to prepare his defences and seek support from the Leicester Committee and officers, such as the very able and diligent Captain Thomas Babington.

As for me, I do my best to forget about Hastings for a few days at least. For I am sure our paths will cross again when the time is right.

Right now, we have a job to do and very limited time in which to achieve it.

Eight days after Cromwell penned his letter to me, we get the first of two significant strokes of luck.

It is the twenty-seventh day of the month. There is dampness in the morning air as autumn prepares itself for the harsh realities of winter, and a cold draught has awoken me from my disturbed slumber.

Isabel is still soundly asleep; her gentle, rhythmic breathing is the only sound that breaks the silence of the early morning.

I look at my pocket watch. I can just make out its face and numerals in the gloom. I rub away the sleep from the corners of my eyes and see it is ten minutes to six, an unearthly hour for any mortal to be awake. But I cannot sleep. I am thinking about too many things.

I roll over to the side of the mattress, sit upright and shake my head a few times to clear away the remnants of the brain fog that has claimed me for the last few hours. I then dress as quickly, eager not to rouse my good wife from her precious slumber.

As I leave the chamber and start to descend the stairway, the sound of a horse can be heard. At first, it is only faint, but it is distinctive nonetheless. Within seconds I realise a rider has arrived at the Hall, so I ease my way to the foot of the stairwell, gripping the rail tightly as I can in a bid to ensure the poor visibility does not result in me toppling over. I then make my way to the front door, guided by the light of the early morning dawn breaking through the dark cloak of nightfall.

I open the door to the world and walk out into the square at the front of the house. I move forward just a few yards, the chilled air taking me by surprise, when I am confronted with the sight of a large Chestnut mare, carrying a well-built male, that is blocking my path. The rider looms over me. His face and upper body are wrapped in a heavy cloak protecting him from the bitterly cold autumnal breeze. On his head is a wide-brimmed hat, popular with men of a particular class. At his side is the kind of sword carried by an officer.

The man waves enthusiastically and, in a blur of motion, dismounts from his steed.

As soon as the horse is tethered, the visitor pulls the cloak from his face, and I recognise him in an instant. It is my errant brother.

"What in blazes are you doing here, and at this time?" I bellow. "Good grief, man. Do you know what time it is? What about our understanding?"

If Rowland is offended by my unfriendly and tetchy greeting, he doesn't show it. Instead, he strides over to me, taking in the familiar surroundings. When he is close enough, I feel his crushing and affectionate embrace.

"And it is good to see you too, brother," he whispers in my ear shortly before kissing me on the cheek. "I appreciate the hour is early. But by the time I leave, you will be very grateful for this small disruption to your day. Of that, I promise."

Without saying another word, Rowland takes a firm hold of my left elbow and guides me into the Hall. When he has taken a seat in the main kitchen and helped himself to the remnants of the evening stew, he proceeds to spend the next hour telling me about what he has learned about two key events that have enormous implications for Parliament.

And my visitor is right.

When he leaves my company and the relative security of Stathern an hour and a half later, I am as grateful as any brother could be to his rebel sibling.

I have lost track of time mulling over everything Rowland has told me when Abijah knocks on the door of the study. I look at my watch: it is just after nine o'clock. My second-in-command is early for our daily briefing.

I ate breakfast on my own an hour earlier, and, ever since, I have been coming to terms with the information my gallant younger sibling has presented to me.

Thankfully, Abijah brings me to my senses.

"You need to read this," he barks, desperately attempting to conceal his excitement as he hands me a dispatch I recognise is written by the precise hand of Lord Grey. "The Melton garrison captured a courier last night as he was attempting to get through to Gervase Lucas at Belvoir Castle.

"Thankfully, Colonel Rossiter's pickets caught him long before he got near the stronghold. And when they searched his possessions, he was carrying some very important and revealing instructions. It sets out everything in detail. We have them."

I look down at the crumpled paper Abijah has handed me. My deputy has clearly opened it.

"It wasn't addressed specifically to you," explains Swan, understanding my thoughts in an instant. "It looks as though we could be seeing some action in the next few days. It confirms everything Cromwell told you; Byron is seeking to lead a large detachment from Newark and attack the Eastern Association, where he perceives its weakest point. Grey's letter confirms everything.

"We are to join forces with the Derby and Nottingham Militias and confront the King's men long before they get near Lincolnshire."

I say nothing. Instead, I place the dispatch on the table without looking at it and attempt to conceal the large grin that is spreading across my face.

"Francis, have you heard what I have said?" asks an incredulous Abijah, surprised I am not scrutinising Lord Grey's orders with the utmost urgency. "We are being presented with an almighty opportunity to crush the enemy – and you are to be given an important command by a man, who until recently distrusted you. I thought you might have something to say on the matter?"

The minor rebuke forces me to show the Commander-in-Chief's letter the respect it deserves. I open it and consume the content of the two pages, which are a mixture of intelligence and instruction. It is just as Abijah has said: the men and I are to form part of the force that will engage with Sir Richard Byron. And I am to lead the left-wing, one of the three most senior command positions in the expedition.

Lord Groby's public display of confidence in my capabilities comes as a delightful surprise. But, in truth, I already knew about Byron's intentions as far as the impending military action is concerned.

Rowland had exposed the Royalist plot. It was one of two reasons he chose to risk compromising his own position by riding at full gallop from Newark Castle to Stathern in the early hours.

Two days ago, he attended a meeting hosted by Byron. Many of the King's principal officers from the area, including Gervase Lucas and Holck, were in attendance. It seems both men are heavily involved in planning the attack on the Eastern Association.

My brother is to play a part in the venture and will be required to lead a company of dragoons from the Newark garrison.

Thankfully, I will not be required to betray Rowland's confidences. The captured courier's crudely coded message has seen to that, for which I feel a huge sense of relief. Not only that but the knowledge I now possess means I can also do my utmost to ensure Rowland's company is not dealt with harshly in the heat of battle. He will do likewise as far as my own well-being is concerned. This is something we pledged to one another in the aftermath of the slaying of our brother, Thomas, some eighteen months ago.

Of the other matter my brother and I discussed, I find myself greatly vexed. For Rowland also shared with me a piece of altogether far more critical information: he revealed the identity of the Parliamentarian Holck is seeking to kill.

NINE

IT IS A SATURDAY, A very wet and windy twenty-ninth day of October, in the year of our Lord, 1644.

Beating rain is pulsing through what is left of the early morning mist and, as its tentacles penetrate the gloom, myself and fifteen hundred other Parliamentarian troops take a backward step in a bid to conceal our presence. We are hiding in dense woodlands, eagerly waiting for the signal that will turn the chilled air into a fog of cordite and bring Hell to the doorsteps of the villages of Woolsthorpe-by-Belvoir and Denton.

Since early dawn, we have been waiting for our Royalist quarry, praying we will be victorious on a day still remembered for the execution of the great adventurer and rebel, Sir Walter Raleigh – beheaded by James the First, father to the current tyrant King, some twenty-six years ago.

My own ancestors were well acquainted with Sir Walter and knew him to be a good, loyal servant. For many, his execution remains a stain on the honour of the

Stuarts – and the anniversary of his death is something I have mourned many times throughout my lifetime. Today is another one of those occasions. For since we left our bed-chambers just after midnight, I have been chilled to the bone, ravenous and desperate to focus my mind on the task at hand. But I have failed miserably.

Ever since first light, our eyes have been turned westward and up the sloping hill, towards the towering citadel that is Belvoir Castle. Its braziers are still aglow, resistant to the downpour and silhouetted against those imposing grey walls. Several turrets dominate the landscape, making it look impenetrable and foreboding. Yet, at the same time, for men such as myself, deemed to be traitors and notorious rebels, it is a place of despair and dread.

Less than four miles away as the crow flies, it looms large over Stathern and everything I care most about in this ravaged and unjust world.

Every day I look to the horizon, the castle's dark, brooding presence acts as a permanent reminder of the imprisonment I experienced only ten months ago and the agonies I suffered.

Thankfully, the excruciating physical pain I experienced is long gone, but, alas, the memories endure, the scars on my fingers and feet a fitting testament to the Bohemian's expert handiwork.

But this morning, I am required to suppress all such thoughts.

I am involved in a mission that will hopefully teach Sir Richard Byron, one of King Charles's principal dogs of war, a lesson he will never forget, and I cannot allow personal enmity to get in the way of achieving this goal.

Far too much depends on it.

Sir Thomas Fairfax's small force has been besieging the garrison at Crowland for several weeks, with the King's men digging themselves into the small and inhospitable Lincolnshire Abbey and holding out admirably against considerable odds.

Keen to record a morale-boosting victory and ease some of the pressure that has been building in the east of the country, the King has ordered Byron to ride to the aid of the three hundred stricken wretches who are desperately defending what remains of the recently slighted Benedictine monastery.

The Governor of Newark, a man with a formidable battlefield reputation, hopes to surprise Fairfax, whose force numbers twice that of his own.

At the moment, Byron is camped some forty miles away. But bolstered by two other garrisons, he plans to use the elements of surprise and speed to his advantage, thereby relieving the beleaguered Royalist forces.

Under normal circumstances, he may well have an excellent opportunity to descend undetected on Fairfax unmolested. But, alas, the cat is already out of the bag! The Royalist courier captured several days ago carried such a wealth of information that very little planning is actually required. Everything Parliament needs to know about the proposed venture was found in the secret communiqué sewn into the hapless rider's doublet.

For Byron's force to be routed, all that is needed is patience – and for every God-fearing Parliamentarian soul to do what is required of them this foul morn.

As we wait in the stillness, I sense Abijah, sitting atop a fine-looking chestnut stallion and standing next to me, wishes to speak. So I turn and face him, giving him the opportunity he needs.

Mixed emotions are etched across his rugged features. He attempts to make conversation on two occasions but falters, and then silence descends. My friend clearly has something on his mind but cannot find the words to articulate what he is thinking.

"Is all in order?" I enquire. "If you wish to speak, do so; say whatever needs to be said. All I ask is you say it quietly. We don't want to alert our enemies!"

Abijah's embarrassment is acute, my attempt at humour unable to improve his mood. His eyes look away momentarily before he fixes me in his sights for the third time and readies himself.

"Francis, I have been having some bad dreams of late," he says, his voice only just audible, barely above the whisper I have requested. "I have been contemplating unspeakable things that are now causing me some anxiety. Last night is the worst it has been… I am now having premonitions about my own demise!"

At that exact moment, a strong gust whips up the branches of the trees. The horses stir. Up and down the line, I hear men muttering to their steeds, seeking to calm them with soothing words and the odd tasty morsel of food.

My own horse is unmoved by the commotion; he stands imperiously like a jet-black rock, surveying all before him. I take Bucephalus's reins in one hand and reach out with my other, firmly gripping my friend's wrist.

"What kind of drama and nonsense is this, Abijah?" I say, seeking to convey my understanding. "What is this of death I am hearing? You are indestructible, my friend.

Believe it as I, and the men, do. You will never die, not while I, your most needy and demanding comrade, is alive and well."

I look directly at Abijah. There is no reaction; my words appear to be impotent. So I try again.

"My friend, I promise, you have nothing to fear," I continue, my white knuckles emphasising the pressure I am now applying on Abijah's arm. "Our men will protect you with their lives, as will I. That should give you some confidence, particularly when you have the likes of Smith, an expert with cleaver, sword and musket, watching your back.

"Let us get the day done; we can then discuss this matter for as long as you wish. Then, of course, I will seek to aid you in whatever way I can. But, before then, I need you to be at your most attentive and diligent. So, too, do our men."

I look once again at my friend, scrutinising his features. For a fleeting moment, I see the hand of fear distorting his good looks. Then, as he contemplates the sincerity of my reassurances, I visibly see him relax and become the man I recognise.

I smile, acutely aware of the relief I am feeling. As I do, our horses snort simultaneously, plumes of steam cannoning out of their flared nostrils. Then, instinctively, I let out a nervous laugh. In such situations, my old Latin Master would often say to me "noli timere". And even though he sincerely believed what he was saying, the truth is fear is often contagious!

After a while, with the only audible noises coming from the rustle of branches and leaves that are bending to the rhythm of the winds, Abijah reaches into his doublet and pulls out an envelope. He looks at it long and hard, then extends his arm, indicating he wishes me to take it.

"This is for your eyes only," he says deliberately. "Keep it safe. Should I fall, please read it. It says all that needs to be said."

I look at the crudely sealed packet. It is small, comprising no more than a few sheaves. What it says, I can only guess.

"Of course," I confirm. "You have my word; it will be safe with me. I vouch I will return it to you as soon as the reason we are assembled here today is settled. And I guarantee I will, for nothing is going to happen to you."

At ten o'clock, the telltale noises of a large column can be heard clearly above the drum roll of rain and the increasingly feisty winds.

All commanders wish their men could travel in absolute silence. It is a worthy notion, one that is an absolute impossibility to put into practice. But, this morning, I am grateful it is so.

With two thousand men snaking their way down the hill, their pendants and banners flapping vigorously as the gales catch hold of them, Parliament's hidden force has little difficulty in identifying the various companies of men that make up Byron's army as they march in close formation towards their doom, oblivious to what awaits.

I desperately look for Rowland's colours, eager to protect my brother from the carnage I know is about to come. Thankfully, I find him and his men located towards the rear of the long line of humanity and horses that are proceeding down the hill and are now at least a quarter of a mile away from the protection of the castle walls.

All around me, I hear Parliamentarian troops and officers preparing for the fight: prayers are being said, and bladders and bowels are being emptied. It has always been thus, for, before the fighting, fear grips a man as he contemplates making peace with his Maker and repenting for a lifetime of sin.

I hear the rider approaching long before I see him.

He is a messenger sent by Colonel Edward Rossiter, governor of Melton Mowbray and, like me, one of the joint commanders of the small Parliamentary army I am a part of.

"Captain Hacker, the Colonel sends you his warmest regards and esteem," says the sharp-eyed rider as he draws up alongside. "The attack will commence when the enemy has cleared the castle and are sufficiently far enough away they cannot be reinforced. This dispatch sets out Colonel Rossiter's requirements of you and the men under your command."

I take the sodden message from the dragoon and quickly scan its contents. It instructs me to take four companies and encircle the Royalists, so they are cut off and unable to retreat.

On the enemy's left flank, Colonel Gell and the Derby Militia will carry out the very same manoeuvre, joining us at the top of the hill and forming a compact line, before charging the rear of Byron's force while their main body remains fully engaged with the bulk of Rossiter's units.

"The Colonel wishes you God's speed," adds the rider as he prepares to depart. "He wants you to know he is looking forward to celebrating a resounding victory with you and Sir John this evening."

The voice trails off; the messenger's job is done.

I lean forward and grip the young man's wrist, as so many soldiers seem to do before the heat of battle consumes them. I just have time to wish him well before he is gone, no doubt off to relay the very same instructions to Gell, a man despised by many because of his outrageous conceit, arrogance and utter selfishness.

At ten minutes past the appointed hour, Rossiter unleashes his main phalanx on our unsuspecting foe.

To my left, some three hundred yards away from where I am concealed, all along a dense thicket of trees, hundreds of men wearing the recognisable lobster helmet favoured by the Parliamentarian army emerge from their hiding places. Behind them comes the cavalry, led by Rossiter and his Cornet, a dark-haired youth proudly holding aloft the regiment's black and white flag. It features a bold armoured arm holding a sword aloft.

As the young officer violently waves the flag from left to right, signalling to our troops it is time to engage with Byron's shocked Royalists, I make out the words "For the Cause of the Lord I draw my Sword" embroidered into the huge pennant.

How very appropriate. In acknowledgement, I hear myself saying "amen" to whoever will listen.

Taking my lead from the standard-bearer and ensuring a grim-faced Abijah is close by at my side, I dig my heels into the flanks of Bucephalus and begin the task of making the ascent to the brow of Barrowby Hill. At all times, I remain wary of stray branches and tree trunks that have the power to unseat a careless horseman – and I am also conscious of the need to conceal our approach for as long as possible.

It takes what seems like an age to climb the sloping hillside. Oaks, Sycamores and Chestnut trees bar our way at every juncture. But, thankfully, the two main bodies of troops are now locked in combat and making enough noise to drown out the movements the men and I are making as we race through the bracken and branches as quickly as we dare, all the time acutely aware Byron's men have recovered their wits and courage.

Eventually, we reach the agreed assembly point where we have decided to join up with our Derby comrades and complete the ensnarement of the King's men.

I pull on the reins and, as one, Bucephalus and I veer to the left, towards the vast expanse of open ground. Just yonder are the ruins of the Church of Saint James. As the trees start to become less dense and give way, all I can see is the vast mass of horses and bodies pressed closely together. Desperate men from both sides are engaged in hand-to-hand combat, and blood drips from the blades of hundreds of axes, cleavers and swords that are hacking the life out of those souls unfortunate to be barring their way.

Where can my Maker be at times such as these?

Time stands still. I find myself racing across the brow of the hill, searching for Gell's force. Bucephalus is excited. His ears are erect, and he is snorting the war cry he always exalts when he knows it is time to ready himself for battle.

And all the time, the incessant deluge continues to bounce off our bodies, and more and more steam, emitted from thousands of men and beasts, starts to rise and form a fog over this wretched field of death.

On the opposite bank, no more than two hundred yards away, the Derby Militia emerges. They are in an imperious and confident voice, crying "In God's name" as loudly as they can. Their arrival clearly has an impact on the enemy line, with more than a few of the troops at the rear of the Royalist column unnerved by the sudden and unexpected appearance of more Parliamentarian horsemen.

I quickly look behind me to see how close we are to the stronghold, estimating it to be now almost three-quarters of a mile, much more than we need to be safe from the garrison's raking guns and cannons – and too far away for reinforcements to bolster their hapless comrades.

Part of me wonders fleetingly if the likes of Lucas and Holck, if they are still resident within, will be enjoying grandstand views of the carnage unfolding below them?

As I dwell on events that may, or may not, be occurring within the magnificent castle, a sudden burst of melancholy threatens to overwhelm me. The blackness is all-consuming until I suddenly become aware of Abijah's grip on my arm as he shakes me violently.

"Francis. Francis," he is shouting as loudly as he can in a bid to be heard above the melee. "They are regrouping. We need to act quickly if we are not to be bested this day."

I shake my head, clearing the stupor instantly. Abijah is pointing animatedly at the enemy, who are a lot closer than I initially perceived. As I watch, at least three companies of Cavalier dragoons hastily dismount from their horses and start preparing their cumbersome muskets for action. They appear rushed and disorganised, unable to control the fear pulsing through their bodies. Their curses and blasphemies fill the air as they ready themselves to repel our imminent assault, just as their match fizzles and belches out acrid plumes of suffocating smoke.

Then I see him.

My brother is a lone figure standing tall while many men around him cower and seek shelter behind the nearest human shield. Undaunted, Rowland is all motion, oblivious to the perils and mortal dangers that threaten him.

Even though he is my avowed enemy on the battlefield, a sense of pride fills my heart as I watch him mould his men into a disciplined fighting unit. He is the one Cavalier who looks as though he knows what he is doing. While the other companies are struggling, he and his men have already formed up into two well-drilled rows, and they have a look of deliberate intent.

I wipe my brow as the agonising cries of men in the final throes of life pierce the air. I am sodden. I am nervous. Yet, I am desperate to enter the fray.

"Are you and the men ready?" I bark at Abijah breathlessly. "It is critical we hit the column before they have time to get off the first volley. If they do, it will be carnage, and our momentum will be lost. So we must not fail."

Whatever words my friend chooses to say are lost in the noise of battle. But I see the dutiful nod of his head and the flash of an impish and confident grin, and that is all I need.

It is time to go to war.

Thankfully Gell's men have now fallen in alongside us. In total, it has taken less than two minutes for almost six hundred battle-hardened killers to create the required formation. We are now ready to be unleashed on our hapless foe.

"Hacker. Captain Hacker, where are you?" a voice calls out.

I know who it is without needing to see the face of its owner. It is Gell, trying to sound every bit the General he will never be.

"I am here, Colonel," I say coolly. "We are prepared. Are you and your men ready?"

An elegant white mare, carrying the distinctively red-faced and portly figure of John Gell, edges forward. Cocking his head slightly to the left, he searches me out. I can see he is clearly as impatient as I am to commit to the fight.

"For goodness sake, man, what are we waiting for?" he yells. "Every second counts."

And then the line explodes as we begin our bloody assault.

Words cannot describe what it sounds like when hundreds of warhorses collide with scores of fragile bodies. 'Terrible.' 'Horrific.' 'Sickening.' None is sufficient. The truth is no adjective can capture the enormity of death and destruction on such a grand scale.

Yet when you are responsible for the carnage, and it is being committed against men who would do the same to you if they had the opportunity, it is exhilarating – until the aftermath and your God-fearing conscience forces you to comprehend the slaughter and barbarity you have inflicted on another human being.

I am yet to reach that moment. The lust has a firm hold of me and my steed, and we will not be done until our thirst has been sated.

Bucephalus weighs twelve hundred pounds. When he is excited, he kills indiscriminately for fun. Three of the enemy have already met their doom, crushed under his powerful and deadly hooves as he tears through the rows of condemned dragoons, the rain dowsing the cord of their muskets and flooding the firing pans, thereby rendering their weapons useless.

Once our advance has been halted by the sheer press of bodies ahead, we begin to work as organised units, hacking away at anyone we believe to be a Cavalier.

This is no place for the pistol or gunpowder. Sharp blades are the proven and trusted tools of the trade; when men are so tightly packed, you can smell what they ate for breakfast as they squeal their death rattles.

All along the line, I see Parliament's forces making short shrift of the enemy.

Some have already thrown down their arms. But many others fight on.

Byron's men have sought to rally. Alas, the speed at which we have carried out the ambush, and our superior strategic position, makes it almost impossible for them to form an effective defensive line. The mud also plays its part, as the King's troops lose control of their bodies on a slippery slope, quickly becoming a passage to the afterlife.

I am watching Abijah fend off a half-hearted sword swipe from one of the few Cavaliers who still has some fight in him when I feel a stinging sensation in my right leg. I look down. Blood is spouting from my thigh, the result of a wound inflicted by an enemy rider who has gone unnoticed until this moment.

There is no pain. Not yet. All I feel is the sharp sting-ing sensation as cold steel is wrenched from my punctured flesh.

I reach for my sword. As my hand clasps the hilt, my left shoulder spasms as cold steel pierces muscle and sinew. The Cavalier has had more success, and I let out an almighty groan and my vision starts to blur.

Suddenly the pain is excruciating. I lose control of everything, and I am thrown from Bucephalus. A mist descends. Once again, my world slows down. Where, just seconds ago, I had a full view of the battle, all I can now see are the feet of the living and the lifeless eyes of the dead. There is nothing more. Even the noise of the fight-ing has been silenced.

Then I become aware of strong hands taking hold of my shoulders. The agony I feel down my left side is numb-ing. I cannot speak. All I know is I am being pulled back-wards. Urgently. Towards safety.

"Francis. Hold on," yells a voice I recognise, but I am unable to put a name to. "I have you now, and you will soon be safe. Stay with me, my brother."

And then the blackness takes hold.

When my eyes open, the killing is over. Calmness has descended. Parliament has won a decisive victory.

Almost a hundred of the enemy have been slain. Among the dead are some of their finest officers. Scores of men have been badly wounded, and a further three hun-dred have been taken prisoner. In addition, a great many horses and muskets have also been seized.

And, somehow, I am among the living.

Abijah stands over me, shielding me from the torrential, stinging rain that continues to hammer the grasslands and trees of the Vale of Belvoir. His face is spattered with blood and filth, but his perfectly aligned teeth are a brilliant white. I rarely see them, only when he is smiling. And right now is one of those welcome occasions.

"You have given us all a fair fright, Francis," he says reproachfully. "Smith saw you go down, and we thought you were done for. By the time he and some men had cut through to where Bucephalus was standing, you were gone. And for a full ten minutes, we could not find you."

I allow his words to sink in. As I do, I become aware of the resurgent pain in my thigh and shoulder. I grimace and let out another muted groan. But, alas, I am not strong enough to pretend I am not suffering.

"You have taken two deep sword thrusts, but you will live," adds Abijah. "However, I fear you may incur the wrath of your good wife, Isabel, as I am sure will I when we return to Stathern."

I attempt to laugh, but I am forced to stop abruptly when my convulsions inflame my shoulder, leaving me feeling like a red-hot poker is being twisted deep within the wound.

I wait a moment for my senses to clear, so I can regain my composure. When I am restored enough to reopen my eyes and talk, I become aware of my surroundings. I am propped against the trunk of a tree. The battlefield is empty. A handful of our men are checking bodies for signs of life and stripping the dead for any valuables they are carrying.

As I comprehend what I am witnessing, the bile within my stomach rises. Of course, at times such as these, the victor is always allowed to enjoy the fruits of his labours. But watching the men go about the gruesome business makes me want to puke.

"How did I get here?" I enquire, shifting my gaze away from the grotesque sights that lie prostrate on the battlefield and focusing my attention on Abijah and my men. "Forgive me, but I remember very little after I fell from the saddle."

Abijah crouches down.

"Now, there is a question that requires an answer," responds my second in command as he scratches the new growth of stubble that is blossoming at the base of his chin.

"I am afraid I cannot tell you anything about how you were transported to safety other than it would seem the Lord has been watching over you once again."

My confusion must be evident to everyone who is surrounding me.

"I don't know for certain who came to your rescue," continues Abijah. "All I can tell you is the description of the man who pulled you out of harm's way is remarkably similar to that of your brother, Rowland."

Abijah lets his words sink in before continuing.

"It certainly wasn't one of our men," he says, seemingly sure of the facts. "If it was, they would have come forward by now. You are dear to their hearts, and they are loyal to you, and they would take great pride in being the one who came to your aid.

"None of our men were killed in the fighting, and everyone has been questioned. However, three of the company were wounded, with you the most sorely hurt of all. So the identity of your saviour remains a mystery. But, whoever he is, I thank God for placing him next to you this day."

I close my eyes and recite the first three verses of Psalm Twenty-Five, words written by King David thousands of years ago that have resonated with me throughout my life:

"To you O Lord, I lift up my soul; in you I trust, O my God.

"Do not let me be put to shame, nor let my enemies triumph over me.

"No-one whose hope is in you will ever be put to shame, but they will put to shame who are treacherous without excuse."

I often recite Holy Scripture when praying. And right now, it seems very appropriate to do so, for I again realise just how blessed and unworthy I am to receive such heavenly grace.

"Be assured, I am thankful too, my friend," I say after a short while, holding out my uninjured right arm and beckoning Smith and another of the men to help me stand.

"Now enough of the idling. Our business here is done. It's high time you got me home so I can be with the woman and children I love."

TEN

I SPEND THE REST Of the year recovering from my wounds, forced to be an impotent and muted bystander as radical and necessary changes begin to sweep through the corridors of power.

November and December have seen me isolated once again, albeit I reside at the Hall where no enemy chains bind me to a cold granite wall, unlike a year ago when the Melton Mowbray garrison's capitulation to the Royalists led to my protracted incarceration and torture.

The recent injuries I received while fighting at Woolsthorpe by Belvoir have proven more problematic than anyone anticipated. The sword wound I suffered to the shoulder is the biggest concern.

It became infected shortly after I returned to Stathern. After putting up a futile fight for several painful days in a bid to ward off the ill humours, I eventually succumbed to the poison. I was forced to endure almost three weeks of fever and delirium, drifting in and out of consciousness while drained of strength, purpose and hope.

And throughout, Isabel has been by my side. She has ensured I follow the physician's instructions – and do not give in to the dark moods that seek to consume me at every opportunity. Her faithfulness and love, which has led her to take sole responsibility for treating and dressing my wounds, checking my bile and attending daily to my every need, ensures I do not yield.

I remember very little about my bed-ridden state during those perilous few weeks. But I do have an enduring memory of my wife kneeling at the foot of my mattress, her head bowed, and her hands clasped together, reciting the Lord's Prayer. It is the image of the guardian I sense is so often by my side, and I will treasure the thought until the day I meet my Maker when I go down on my own knees and thank Him for blessing me with his protection and grace.

When I am through the worst, Isabel tells me she has regularly prayed for my life. There were concerns the injury was contaminated; it was feared gangrene would set in, and the rot is nigh on impossible to contain. Many men leave the world in such a way, their lives eaten away by this putrid and agonising condition that devours the flesh as much as it consumes the soul. And I thank God for not allowing me to be claimed by this cruellest of fates.

My good wife also discloses Josiah and Ursula have been praying for me vigilantly. Even Abijah, who is known for resisting the call of faith as much as he can, has lit candles for me and called on our glorious Father to intercede.

Thankfully, the fears of my family and friends have not come to pass. The wound is now healing, and my strength is returning.

I have no doubt the Lord heard the urgent and

heartfelt pleadings of the people who care about me. Although my recovery has taken considerably longer than expected, I am now well and truly on the mend with a renewed zest for life – and I find myself indebted and thankful beyond measure.

It is now the bitterly cold eighth day of January, in the year of our Lord, 1645.

Today is a Sunday.

Isabel, the children, and most of the household are taking communion at Saint Guthlacs in the presence of the Reverend William Norwich, a minister whom I am determined to deal with when my mind and body is fit enough to do so. I have ignored his vocal and spiritual allegiance to our tyrant King for far too long. But I can do so no more; I must act decisively against the man, even though that will incur the wrath of my wife. To continue to condone his actions and religious practices seriously undermines my position as a Leicester Committee Member. For the sakes of Cromwell, Fairfax and Parliament, I cannot afford that.

My family's temporary absence from the Hall enables me to catch up with local tittle-tattle by reading the weekly estate reports prepared by my most trusted workers. Once satisfied I know all that is required, I turn my attention to news of more national significance.

Of keenest interest to me are the dispatches informing me of the valiant attempts being made to curb the malignant influence of the nobility who fight in support of Parliament's cause on England's bloody battlefields.

I read several of Oliver's letters that explain, in detail, how things are proceeding. They give me enormous encouragement, for it seems there has been considerable progress in holding the likes of the Earl of Manchester to account.

While I have lain in my bed recovering, the Lieutenant-General has bloodied the Earl's nose in the House of Commons by successfully challenging his authority and right to lead an army.

In recent months, the relationship between the two men has disintegrated, as they have become deeply distrustful of one another. Oliver's main objections are that he believes Manchester is weak, lacks strategic vision, and is a poor tactician and leader. The Earl, meanwhile, sees his deputy as an over-ambitious and disrespectful zealot who doesn't know his place.

If they did not jointly command the Eastern Association army, the most successful and revered of Parliament's forces, the bickering and fallout would not be of the importance it is. But the enemy is acutely aware of the situation and is actively seeking to exploit the scale of discord that exists. Its spies learn more every day as the feud escalates, and Parliament's ability to win this cursed conflict is further compromised.

Come to an end, it must; there can be no other way. There can only be a clear winner and loser. And everyone who knows what is at stake has been praying for the right outcome: a decisive victory for Cromwell.

Just two days before the last of my last dispatches was sent to me from London, an investigation into the many accusations and counterclaims of both men found in Cromwell's favour. The result means Parliament will reorganise its stretched and ill-disciplined military resources, and many nobles will be purged from its ranks.

The nub of Oliver's argument, which I am well acquainted with after spending many an hour talking through its merits with him, is that no Member of Parliament or the House of Lords should be allowed to hold an army or naval command. He believes there is an absolute need for focus, discipline, and professionalism. Having feet in both camps dilutes everything, which often means the difference between victory and defeat on the battlefield.

Of course, there is one notable exception to this rule: Oliver himself!

The wily fox has been using his growing influence to ensure he will be the one man to be exempt from this draconian ruling. And on Wednesday, the sixth day of January in the year of our Lord, 1645, just two days ago, Oliver's grand vision became a reality.

I spend much of the morning comprehending the developments in London, allowing their significance to sink in. While there is much to digest, one thing is absolutely sure: much is about to change, and for the better.

My overactive imagination ensures three hours quickly slip by. A lust for knowledge consumes me, and I am so grateful for my intimate window into the outside world.

Midday arrives, and Isabel and the children return. Even though the Hall is spacious, the noise of family life invades every nook and cranny. The distraction forces me to refocus my efforts, banishing thoughts of the war and politics so I can concentrate on becoming a dutiful husband and father once again.

I have just put the last of the papers I have been reading on the desk adjacent to where I am resting when there is a gentle knock on the door of my chamber.

"Come in," I say as conversationally as I can, expecting to see the figure of Isabel emerge from the anonymity of the hallway.

But it is not my wife who greets me.

Instead, to my absolute surprise, Thomas Babington, a Captain of the Leicester Militia and a man with whom I am well acquainted, walks in.

The last time we saw each other was in May of last year. Thomas was the officer who alerted me to a clash he and his men had experienced with a small party of Cavaliers. Unbeknown to the hapless and innocent Babington, this skirmish would lead to my two youngest daughters losing their lives.

I do not blame the man standing before me for the cruel loss inflicted on my family. Thomas simply did what any committed Parliamentarian would do given the opportunity: he challenged the enemy and loosed off a volley of muskets. He was not to know what was at stake when he confronted Holck, the ruthless and cold-hearted killer.

I would have done the same.

But Holck, who had taken my daughters hostage after failing in a desperate attack on Stathern, promised they would perish if he was molested on his journey from the Hall to Newark.

And he was good to his word.

Despite the torment and anguish I feel due to my inability to resolve these past tragedies, I do my best to try to sweep aside the most painful memories as I now look at the statuesque Babington. He is a man of similar years to myself, and I have to admit he is a fine soldier and committed rebel.

"Francis, it is good to see you looking so well," he says as he strides over to where I am resting and extends his right hand in greeting. "It has been far too long."

I grip Thomas tightly, just in time. My emotions are threatening to overwhelm me.

"It is good to be reacquainted with you, Captain," I splutter as coherently as I can. "Unfortunately, you find me recuperating and not at my best, but I will endeavour to be at your service. Are you here at the behest of the Committee, or Lord Grey?"

Babington doesn't answer the question immediately. Instead, he pulls up the nearest chair, his gaze never leaving my face.

When he is sitting comfortably, he gets down to business.

"The Committee has asked me to apprise you of several things, matters that are of concern and require you to play a part in progressing," continues my visitor, who has adopted a sombre tone.

Opening the satchel he is carrying, Babbington hands me several official-looking documents, all of them bearing the large red seal of the Committee.

"These papers relate to a host of routine matters," he explains. "The one exception is the document relating to Archbishop Laud. As you will be aware, the cleric has been found guilty of High Treason, and the sentence is due to be passed at any time.

"As a former Minister of a church in the county, the

Committee feels it is important a letter is sent to Parliament affirming support for the legal process that has brought Laud to justice. We feel such a letter will send an important signal to all those other Ministers within Leicestershire who continue to support the King's illegitimate religious views and promote the use of the calamitous Book of Common Prayer. Therefore, I would be grateful if you signed this document now, so I can take it away with me."

I haven't thought of Laud for several months. He is a man I have met on numerous occasions, albeit the last time was a few years ago when he was just about to leave the Parish of Ibstock after being recalled to London.

He seemed an amiable enough fellow until the subject turned to religion. Only then did I realise that he and his kind practice a very different type of faith to the one I know.

"Pray, pass me the quill and my seal," I say to Babbington, pointing in the direction of my table. "Although it gives me no pleasure to see a man condemned to death for his faith, some heresies cannot be tolerated. Therefore, you find me a willing signatory."

It takes me ten minutes to read the declaration, for that is what it is, and only a few seconds to add my own name to those of the twenty others who have endorsed it. When the ink is dry, I find myself feeling no remorse for a man who will soon lose his head for the role he played in dividing our broken nation.

Nonetheless, I pray silently for Laud, asking our Lord to show compassion to his soul, should it be allowed to enter the eternal afterlife that awaits all good and faithful servants.

With the document safely tucked away in his tan satchel and the time getting close to one o'clock, Thomas turns his attention to discussing the main reason he has ridden some twenty miles from Rothley on this cold winter's day.

"Of paramount concern once again is the increasingly strained relationship the city enjoys with Lord Grey and many of his officers," he states, his voice laced with concern. "Despite repeated representations, the difficulties that existed months ago remain to this day. And many of us are now so concerned about the predicament we have decided we must do all we can to reach a settlement with the man before it is too late."

I nod my head, appreciating everything Babington is saying. I have had the same thoughts myself for a considerable time.

For some unknown reason, his Lordship refuses to cooperate with the people of Leicester. As a result, the city's weakened defences will be unable to resist anything other than the timidest of assaults. In addition, too few trained men are available to hold the walls, should the King and Prince Rupert come calling, as they most certainly will in the not too distant future.

The matter has already been the subject of the petition sent by the Mayor and Aldermen of Leicester to Parliament, which was read in the House of Commons on the sixth day of November. Thomas Haselrig, a good friend of mine and, like myself, a Committee Member, consulted me at the beginning of autumn on this very subject. More than a year earlier, we had formally reviewed the city's defences and concluded there was a need for urgent reconciliation between the two sides. Yet our attempts to bring the two parties together failed miserably, mainly because Lord Grey has steadfastly refused to compromise.

Now, after almost half of the city's total population have signed the petition, Grey continues to turn his attentions elsewhere, deaf to the pleas and desperation of one of the key cities he serves.

What an obstinate and infuriating man he can be.

"The Committee is aware your own relations with Lord Grey are strong, and he now looks on you extremely favourably," continues Thomas. "So there is hope you will be willing to present our grievances to him and seek a resolution that suits all parties?"

I let out an incredulous chuckle, humoured by this level of optimism.

"I am hardly in his favour, my friend," I say, not wishing to dampen Thomas's spirits. "It is true, relations between us have improved, but I am a long way from being a part of his trusted inner circle!

"I do not share the Committee's belief that I am the man to break the impasse and get his Lordship to see sense. I have tried before in this matter and failed. I have no reason to believe a renewed attempt on my part to make Lord Grey do the right thing will be any more successful than the first time I tried.

"But I will go to him once again and plead for him to see sense. You have my word. I have some important business with his Lordship that cannot wait much longer. Be assured that this matter will be discussed when I am fit enough to ride and see him. I will do all I can to bring about the reasoned resolution the Committee is seeking. I can guarantee nothing other than I will try my best."

Babbington visibly relaxes. He has secured the outcome he sought. For a moment, a deafening silence echoes around the room. Neither of us knows what to say now the formalities have been concluded. Eventually, I puncture the air by addressing the matter we are both avoiding.

"You know, there is no reason for you to shun me," I say. "Before the girls died, you were someone I saw regularly. Our families are connected socially, and our good wives are firm friends. Yet, neither Isabel nor myself have heard from you since the day of the funerals."

Thomas lowers his gaze. He cannot look at me.

"I want you to know we don't hold you responsible in any way for what happened to Barbara and Isable," I continue. "The good Lord has called them home, that is all. We would have wished it differently, but it is not for us to challenge our Maker's wishes, no matter how painful it may be.

"If memory serves me right, you were returning from Newark when you challenged the Royalist party, as you had a duty to do. When they failed to stop, you fired at them. Any officer would have ordered a similar course of action. I would undoubtedly have done so.

"I have thought about these events a lot in recent months, and I can tell you I would most certainly have done as you did. So feel no guilt. There is no need for awkwardness between us. Let us be reunited this day, putting past events where they need to be – behind us. What say you?"

My words clearly affect Babbington, who looks out of the window for several minutes. When he is in control of his emotions, he says: "You are a fine man, Francis. To know I have your forgiveness means everything. You have lifted an almighty burden I have been carrying these past months.

"I thank you for being so understanding. If I had lost two of my beloved children under such circumstances, I may not be showing you the same kind of compassion you are offering to me. So please accept my most sincere thanks."

Thomas stands and prepares to take his leave of me. Gratitude and relief are imprinted on his face.

I sit up, swing my legs out of the bed and rise. I am not yet accustomed to standing as the infection has left my body wracked with weakness.

Although my legs feel as though they may buckle at any moment, I manage to walk over to where Thomas is standing and put my hand on his shoulder, slowly guiding him to the door from where he can return to his Militia duties.

"I am glad we have been able to talk about things," I say. "This conversation is long overdue. Like you, I am heartened that we have at last addressed the matter. If the truth be known, I also feel relieved."

No more words are necessary.

We embrace in the doorway as two soldiers who have witnessed and perpetrated far too much horror and destruction. Remembering and honouring the fallen.

As I watch Thomas walk down the hallway, my mood suddenly feels better than it has in weeks. It is as if someone, or something, has slotted another piece of my restoration firmly into place.

It is apt we are at the beginning of a New Year. For the first time in a long while, I sense that I am ready for whatever is to come.

ELEVEN

A MAN ARRIVES AT THE Hall on Monday, the eighteenth day of January. He brings with him the dusk of the night and more sombre tidings.

I recognise the unexpected visitor as Campion, my father's faithful assistant of more than thirty-five years. His tonsured pate, stooped shoulders, and towering frame ensure he is easily identifiable long before he is close enough to speak to.

As I walk down the hallway to greet him, he looks towards me. His eyes are dead, and I instinctively prepare myself for the worst.

"Francis," he says before I have a chance to welcome him. "I am here at the behest of your father, who is gravely ill. He has asked me to call upon you and tell you he is not long for this world. The plague is upon him, and he wishes to make his peace with you before he meets our glorious Maker."

My father, who was also named Francis at birth, lives in East Bridgford, a mere dozen or so, miles away from

Stathern. On the occasions I made the journey, it took me less than forty minutes to ride to his home and share a glass of claret while relaying tales of the comings and goings-on in Stathern and the wider county.

But it is a long time since my father and I shared anything that can be remotely regarded as happiness.

Since my mother died when I was a young child, the relationship I have enjoyed with him has been strained. We have rarely seen eye to eye. And I know not why.

Of course, the simple and most obvious answer could be that we are two opinionated men who have radically different views of the world, one that leads to quarrelling and rancour rather than love, unity and peace. We are similar in so many ways: we worship the same God, and we enjoy many of the same things. Yet, we can no longer abide to be in the company of one another.

Whatever the reason for our long-standing discord, which has become more pronounced since the war started, it now appears there will be permanence to our estrangement, for it is unlikely my father would send word of his illness unless he knew for sure his time was short.

I sense Campion scrutinising my face for visible signs of my reaction to the news. Alas, I struggle to feel anything other than an inner coldness and aloofness for my own flesh and blood, whose estates and fortune I stand to inherit.

"Allow me to get my hat and cloak," I say flatly as Campion visibly becomes agitated by my lack of urgency. "I need to let my wife know where I am going, so go ahead without me. I know the road to my father's house. I will join you within the hour."

Campion, a man who has shown me respect for as

long as I can remember, bows his head and says: "As you wish, Francis. I will tell your father you are on your way. But make haste. He does not have long."

East Bridgford, a village close to Nottingham, is where I spent my early years.

As much as I can remember it after all this time, my childhood home was a happy place where my brothers and I could play freely, our loving mother always close by. It sat atop a high hill, from where panoramic views of the Vale of Belvoir were available to the observer.

From her chair in the populous garden, mother would keep an ever-watchful eye over Thomas, Rowland and me, ensuring we enjoyed as much freedom as she could afford yet were as safe as three energetic boys could be. Abijah would visit me regularly, and it is from here we forged a friendship that has lasted a lifetime.

The picturesque village is where I first met Isabel, where I enjoyed my first kiss with my wife to be, where I got married – and it is where I witnessed my mother, Mary, being laid to rest in the chapel of St Peter's Church, when I was just nine-years-old.

I loved her dearly. And life changed dramatically after her tragic and unexpected passing.

My father felt her loss most grievously. But he quick-ly found another home for his affections in the form of a young, fertile girl whom he quickly became infatuated with and married in the year of our Lord, 1617. From that moment, my relationship with him started to disintegrate.

By the time I was married to Isabel, my father and I had become estranged. And for the last thirteen years, it has been ever thus. And the outbreak of war has done little to draw us closer. I am a staunch Parliamentarian, with little time for those who espouse popery and the autocratic rights of Kings. Yet my father and two brothers openly support the cause of the House of Stuart. We have argued more times than I care to remember about the rights and wrongs of both sides, never finding a middle ground, only a more entrenched and polarised position on everything we have discussed. It seems there can be no compromise on either side.

To my eternal shame, one of these heated arguments led me to threaten to pistol-whip Rowland because he refused to yield my point of view. This moment of weakness is widely known and now used by my enemies to condemn my character. These foolhardy words were said in the heat of the moment, designed to hurt the mind rather than the body. Alas, for many, my reputation is now demonised and set in stone.

How I wish I could learn to think before I speak!

As I watch Campion's silhouetted shape leave the grounds of the Hall, many things come flooding back into my consciousness, not least the realisation my family is indeed at war with itself.

My optimism of recent days is crushed, for it seems that only in death is a lasting peace ever likely to be found.

Isabel kisses me affectionately when I tell her about the urgency of the hour and my need to ride to East Bridgford. She promises to pray for my father and Margaret, the wife that took the place of my mother all those years ago.

With my wife's help, I am on my way within fifteen minutes. Bucephalus is always eager to please and, at a good canter, he makes excellent time to my father's house, which dominates the outskirts of the village where he has lived all his life.

Campion is waiting anxiously for me, holding a flaming torch aloft at the gates to the manor. His horse, sweating heavily, is tied to a post close by. As soon as he sees me approaching, he beckons me over to where he is standing by one of the large granite pillars that proclaim the entrance to the estate.

"Francis. Francis," he calls out. "Come. I must speak with you before you enter the house."

I guide Bucephalus to where the sixty-year-old is standing and dismount.

"What is so important we can't discuss it inside?" I enquire rather more brusquely than I intend. As if I needed punishing for my caustic comment, a painful twinge in my recently wounded shoulder momentarily forces me to reach out to my saddle for support.

No words are spoken, but I sense my weakness hasn't gone unnoticed.

"The plague is taking your father from us," reveals Campion, his voice calm and empty. "He is in a sore state. The Last Rites have been administered this evening. I fear he will not see the new dawn.

"I know you have your difficulties with each other. But, for his sake, can you please make a supreme effort to ensure he passes into the afterlife as peacefully as he can.

"He has been a good Master to my family and me. He is not the man you think he is. So please help him on his journey. But be sure to keep your distance. It would be a double tragedy if you were to also catch the cursed disease."

I have always held Campion in high esteem. And

tonight, the high regard I have for this dignified and loyal man grows even more. Loyalty is a virtue I respect beyond any other quality. And this man displays devotion beyond the call of duty.

"Aye," I say. "You have my word. I will do everything I can to make my peace with the man, and I will only go as close as is necessary."

On cue, the wind intensifies, prompting Bucephalus to let out a startled snort. Campion's steed is also unsettled. As the gale starts to blow and the trees bend and sway, men and beasts are ushered towards the safety of the Hall and a final farewell.

I am no stranger to the smell of death.

On the battlefield, it is everywhere. Its stench can stay in your nostrils for days, leading men to drink themselves to a stupor when the guns have stopped harvesting their gore and blunted swords have been sharpened and returned to their scabbards.

But nothing prepares you for the stink of a man being eaten alive by the plague, which is the sight that confronts me when I enter my father's darkened chamber a little after six o'clock in the evening.

I can feel the bile rising from my stomach long before I see the ashen, living corpse that is propped up by three fat pillows on the large mattress located in the corner of the room. An array of scented candles are lit, and incense is burning. Peeled onions are scattered liberally around the room in a valiant bid to absorb the infection that is draining my father of his life. Yet, despite these efforts to purify the space, the corrupted smell of decay is all-consuming.

"Francis, is that you?" The voice is weak, barely audible. Yet, it is undoubtedly that of my father. "Francis, I cannot see you. My sight has been taken from me. I beseech you, if you are in my presence, please speak to me."

I edge forward, a mixture of morbid curiosity and a desire to be a faithful son fighting for internal supremacy.

In the gloom, the hand of a broken man reaches out, seeking contact and reassurance.

"Father, it is I, Francis. I am with you," I say eventually, all the time consciously refraining from touching the skeletal fingers that continue to probe the semi-darkness. "Do not distress yourself. I came as soon as I found out. I am here as your humble son and obedient servant."

A rasping cough sends my father into a spasm. As I move forward and try and aid him, I see for myself the extent of the disease's destructive force.

Campion had warned me what to expect. But his description is nothing like what confronts me.

Livid red blisters cover my father's face and hands. Blood and mucus are everywhere. His lips are purple, and the sheets are speckled with the stains of vomit.

"Draw up a chair," says the shell of a man who lies stricken before me.

There is a paternal kindness in his voice I cannot recall ever hearing before. I am struck by his warmth and do as I am instructed without saying a word.

When he is ready, he starts to speak.

"Forgive me, Francis. I have not been the father you deserved or needed," he confesses between ragged breaths. There is no small talk. Time is against him.

"I wish it were not so. But it is what it is. None of

what has passed between us, the harsh words and the estrangement, can be undone. Not now.

"But you can forgive my many sins and transgressions against you. A father and a son should always be united, never at odds with one another. So please grant me this last wish."

The window frames rattle as the harsh winter winds intensify, and the candle flames flicker as the draught of the night entices them to perform yet another lurid dance. Despite Campion's warning, I cannot stop myself from reaching out and taking my father's outstretched hand.

"Can we pray together?" I ask. "Can we recite Psalm Twenty-Three, the words of King David you taught me as a boy?"

A flicker of a smile passes across my father's face.

"I remember it well, son," he says. "We were happy then when your mother was alive. How I have missed her these past years. Let us do it." Together, we recite:

"The Lord is my shepherd, I shall not be in want.

"He makes me lie down in green pastures, he leads me beside quiet waters, he restores my soul.

"He guides me in paths of righteousness for his name's sake.

"Even though I walk through the valley of the shadow of death, I will fear no evil, for you are with me; your rod and staff, they comfort me.

"You prepare a table before me in the presence of my enemies.

"You anoint my head with oil, my cup overflows.

"Surely goodness and love will follow me all the days of my life, and I will dwell in the house of the Lord forever."

As we finish the psalm, my father grips my hand tightly. For a fleeting moment, I sense the power and vibrancy of the old man returning.

Then it is gone, bone and flesh claimed by the all-consuming embrace of death.

I look at him, his dark, unruly hair matted against his still perspiring brow, his mouth open, and his blinded eyes staring aimlessly ahead. He has said his final farewells to the world.

I lean forward and kiss his forehead. I don't think about it; it is a natural gesture.

While praying, I forgave him for all the ills that blighted our troubled relationship, and I genuinely hope he has now ascended to the paradise all Christians are promised for living a faithful life.

Just four of us attend my father's funeral at St Peter's: the Minister, Campion, Rowland and myself.

The brief service is held just before midnight on the nineteenth day of January. The chapel is cold and damp, which might account for the minister's mood and his very obvious desire to get proceedings completed as quickly as possible. It is common for plague victims to be buried at such times. There is little need for ceremony; just a few short prayers are deemed suffice, thereby condensing fifty-four years of life into ten minutes of solemn remembrance.

The tomb already contains the earthly remains of my mother, who, despite my father's remarriage, appears to have never left him.

Farewell, Francis Hacker. My Father. Until we meet again.

The lateness of the hour serves the selfish purposes of my brother and me. Not only can we mourn together, but we can retire to the manor house and talk openly about the events that are shaping and defining our worlds.

There is much to say.

It takes us fifteen minutes to walk back to the estate, the full moon acting as our guide. We say little as we walk at a brisk pace, both of us contemplating another life lost and our own mortality.

Unlike me, Rowland enjoyed a closer relationship with our father. His personality is not like mine; he is far less obstinate and challenging. This meant his childhood was a lot more fulfilling than my own. There were moments when he had major disagreements with my father, usually over his many dalliances with young women in the locality, but these were not regular occurrences. This ensured he continued to be a regular visitor to East Bridgford, never turning his back on our family.

We talk of these things and much more after we have retired to a quiet spot in the house, taking with us a bottle of port, my father's favourite drink and the source of the painful gout that afflicted his latter years.

"May the old bugger rest in peace," I say as I hold my glass aloft. "I pray he is reunited with our mother in heaven and is a more contented man in death than he was during the last ten, or so, years of his life."

Rowland stands and lifts his own glass, which is filled to the brim.

"May it be so," he says. "May the Heavenly Father welcome him into the Kingdom, where I pray he will find the peace he has sought for so long."

We look at each other, staring and saying nothing, just reflecting on our memories. The only sound that can be heard is the occasional sip of the intoxicating red liquid we both hold close to our chests.

"Byron has been replaced as Governor," says my brother after a while, breaking the respectful silence and forcing me to turn my thoughts to the war. "The disaster at Woolsthorpe-by-Belvoir was the last straw for the King. Sir Richard's position was untenable after we were routed so badly. He has been replaced by Sir Richard Willis, a roguish character with no known association to the town or the county.

"He has already taken over the Governor's House in the Market Square and has made himself unpopular with everyone who has made his acquaintance – with the exception of one man…"

My interest has been piqued, and my brother finds himself the focus of my undivided attention.

"I am fascinated by this development, which is great-ly encouraging for Parliament," I say. "But before we talk about these events, tell me, where you my saviour at Woolsthorpe?"

I have been eager to ask Rowland this question all evening, but there has not been an appropriate moment to do so. I press him further.

"I recall little about the battle, but I do remember my rescuer referring to me as 'brother' – and when I asked my men about who had come to my aid, nobody stepped forward to receive my heartfelt thanks," I say. "When I spoke to Abijah about my rescuer, he suggested the man was likely to be you.

"I know you were close to where I was fighting, and

with nobody coming forward from my own ranks, I can only deduce I am indebted to you. If that is the case, please accept my sincerest and most heartfelt thanks."

Rowland stares at the fire. Flames lick at the walls as the crackle of the logs punctures the air, and the surrounding walls are enveloped with an orange glow. My brother kicks forward his right leg, catching a lump of coal with his boot. When he is comfortable, he leans forward, a frown appearing on his brow.

"I sensed that something would go wrong that day," he says. "Because we had agreed to a specific course of action between ourselves, I was confident my men and I would be relatively safe when the fighting started. But when I saw you line up on the hill and then unleash your undisciplined assault on Byron's men, I feared the worst would happen. And it so nearly did.

"Thankfully, I was able to disengage myself and reach where you had fallen, stopping the man who had caught you off-guard from running you through a third time. He thought I was claiming you for ransom or to safeguard my own skin. Little did he know I was returning you to your own people and asking for nothing in compensation.

"Once I had you, it was simple enough to take you to safety. And here you are, fit again and ready for whatever lies ahead. And I thank God for this being so."

A tear forms in the corner of my eye. I quickly brush it aside.

On the night Rowland and I have laid our father to rest, I find myself thanking my Maker yet again for the protection he continues to offer me. I seem to be blessed beyond measure. Why I do not know. All I know is his protective arm is locked firmly around me.

With the mystery of Woolsthorpe now solved, Rowland and I return to discussing the plot to kill Cromwell.

"Holck would appear to be a confidante of the new Governor, the man, it is said, who was more responsible than anyone else for Byron's dismissal. It would not surprise me to discover they are long-standing acquaintances, such as the manner they adopt when they are together.

"On two occasions, I have seen them at the Wild Hart Inn locked in deep discussion. I heard Cromwell's name mentioned several times, and both times I came away convinced they were talking about the plan to assassinate him."

I quickly digest what Rowland is telling me.

"What are you saying, brother?" I ask. "Do I need to alert the Lieutenant-General and warn him of the danger?"

Before answering, Rowland reaches for the poker and prods the large, smouldering Oak logs that fill the large fireplace. They need little encouragement to spark into life once again.

"I don't really know what I am saying, Francis, if the truth is known," he admits cautiously. "But I tell you this, they are up to no good. I know it. And I am as sure as I can be that Cromwell is the focus of their attention."

We look at one another, communicating without saying a word. We raise our glasses and drink vigorously.

My injury at the end of last year has meant my attempts to find out about the plot to kill Cromwell have not progressed very far. I have relied on Rowland to spy on his Royalist comrades, putting him at an unacceptable level of risk.

"And another thing," he says with some urgency. "I am sure I overheard them mention the name an Earl's man. I cannot remember the name of the fellow; all I know is it sounded foreign. But I am sure they have a traitor in their employ.

"I will try to find out more, but my opportunity to do so will be limited. Now Byron has gone, I am distrusted because of my links to you. I am sure they are looking for evidence they can use against me. They've admitted as much."

I have heard enough.

"Brother," I say. "You will not put yourself in harm's way. Not any more. From now on, there cannot be any hints of suspicion directed towards you. Your loyalty must not be questioned, not by the likes of Holck."

To emphasise the point I am making, I flex my fingers. Rowland looks at my disfigured hands, which were the handiwork of the Bohemian some fifteen months ago. It doesn't take long for him to understand what I am saying.

"I am fit again, and I am more than capable of taking on the task of foiling the plotters," I continue. "I have a very reliable and diligent man I can call upon. He has served Parliament well these past months, and I know he will do whatever he can to aid our cause. Allow me to use him in this endeavour. As for yourself, I suggest you get yourself back to Newark before breakfast is served, so you don't give Willis and Holck any reason to ask about your whereabouts. We need to be very careful.

"Should I need to speak to you, my man will find a way of contacting you."

Rowland takes off his hat and runs his hand through his thick copse of dark hair. Eventually, when he has finished rearranging his locks, he nods his head in assent.

"You speak wisely, Francis," he confers. "I agree. We need to tread carefully. I have no desire to find myself dangling at the end of the hangman's noose. But tell me, what is the name of your man? How will I know he is your agent?"

Before I answer, I reach for the port and refill our glasses.

"His name is Edmund Goodyeare," I say. "I spent several weeks with him in the summer. He is most reliable. He will use the password 'the fifth of July, 1632'. You may recall this is the day Isabel and I were wed?"

Remembering the day well enough, Rowland smiles. Aged just ten, it was the first time he succumbed to the notorious powers of the famed ale of the Vale of Belvoir.

He laughs aloud, and I join him. It was indeed a happy day.

With everything agreed and dawn rapidly approaching, I bid my farewell to my beloved brother and retire to the numbing coldness of my chamber. I don't know when I will see him again, so we embrace and wish each other well. I know he is one person I can count on in a world where uncertainty and fragility reign supreme.

Rowland is my rock in the lair of the foe, and I must do all I can to protect him.

I climb the stairs to my room. As I do, I realise how tired I am; my legs are leaden, and my eyes are sore – yet there is still so much to ponder.

It is unlikely I will get any sleep tonight, so I make

myself comfortable and ensure the room is well lit. I need to make an accurate record of everything Rowland has told me, not least what he has revealed about Holck and Willis openly talking about the assistance they are receiving from an officer who has pledged his loyalty to Parliament.

The threat to Cromwell is obvious and significant, and I need to think about how I can stop the assassins before they have a chance to pull off their coup.

Time is of the essence. I can be impotent no longer.

TWELVE

WITH MY HEALTH RESTORED AND the fighting season getting ever closer, I have some pressing matters to deal with, not least seeking an audience with Lord Grey and then turning my attention to outwitting the Royalist plotters.

I write a letter to the Lieutenant-General, informing him of developments. However, after much deliberation, I choose not to disclose the potential involvement of a Parliamentary officer in the plot to assassinate him.

Something doesn't sit comfortably with me concerning this claim, which Rowland has brought to my attention. While I do not have a liking for all my fellow officers, I know many of them to be loyal, God-fearing souls, and I cannot name one that I would suspect of such duplicity and treachery.

At all times, I must be discerning in the way I process information; I have a responsibility not to raise the alarm unnecessarily. Cromwell has too much on his plate to be preoccupied with reports based on speculation and rumour rather than cold and irrefutable facts. So I decide to bide my time. When I have proof, I will reveal my hand. Not before. In the meantime, I won't be resting on my laurels.

In an attempt to make quick progress, I take Abijah further into my confidence.

He is already overseeing efforts in the Vale to keep track of the movements of Holck and the Royalist garrisons at Belvoir and Newark and is enjoying some success. I will tell him everything I know, thereby helping him see the bigger picture and play to his biggest strengths: thoroughness, determination, and free-thinking. All three are essential at times like this.

But that can wait for a few hours. Right now, as a priority, I must make arrangements to meet Lord Grey. I promised Thomas Babington I would do all in my power to have an audience with his Lordship and seek to reach a reconciliation with the Mayor and Aldermen of Leicester.

The latest intelligence reports circulated by Leon Watson, the Eastern Association's highly regarded Scoutmaster-General, suggest the King is actively looking to revitalise his faltering war effort by securing the scalp of a Parliamentarian stronghold. Watson is the best of the dozen, or so, scoutmasters overseeing a web of spy networks throughout the land. If he says the King is seeking a Lamb for the slaughter, then I believe him. And Leicester and its crumbling walls fit the bill perfectly.

If I can persuade Lord Grey to at last devote men and resources to the city, Charles may be forced to think long and hard about launching an assault. Already, it may be too late to achieve such an outcome, particularly after such a lengthy impasse. Still, I have to try, and if it requires me to speak out on the matter, then so be it.

I reach for my quill and start writing.

His Lordship responds to my letter with a suitable degree of urgency.

I receive his dispatch in the afternoon of Sunday, the twenty-second day of January, just two days after my original letter was sent. As usual, he is terse and to-the-point.

"Dear Captain Hacker.

"I acknowledge receipt of your dispatch of the twentieth day of January. Your points are duly noted.

"Can you please present yourself at Bradgate House on Wednesday the twenty-fourth day of January at one o'clock? I will happily discuss these matters with you directly.

"There is something else of importance I wish to discuss with you. It pertains to a change in your status.

"Please be punctual.

"Yours, Thomas Grey.

I have two days to prepare myself for what I know will be a stressful and potentially frustrating meeting.

Abijah comes to my study at ten o'clock on the morn of the following day.

My second-in-command and I have not seen a lot of each other in recent weeks. He has been in Nottingham supporting Colonel John Hutchinson, who commands the garrison keeping the Royalists at bay north of the River Soar.

It has been a relatively uneventful time for my friend and confidante, and he is pleased to be back home with Prudence, his faithful hound, by his side once again.

"So what is the urgency?" he enquires after making himself comfortable in the largest chair in the room. "We don't normally meet at this time on a Saturday. I assume you have called me here early because there is something of importance that can't wait until our normal debrief?"

Abijah is noted for his perceptive abilities, and it will take a man far more intelligent than me to stand a chance of pulling the wool over his eyes. So I don't try.

"You are quite right, my friend. There is something we need to talk about," I say. "It's Holck; it seems things are starting to happen. And to complicate matters, there is a possibility one of our own officers may be involved. But, I stress, this is conjecture at the present time. I have no evidence to back up this claim."

My words have an immediate impact.

"My God!" he explodes. "Are you telling me we have more traitors in our midst, men of rank who are aiding and abetting the enemy?"

Abijah's words are more of a statement than a question.

"I am afraid that could be the case," I reply, as calmly as I am able. "I am told Holck has resurfaced in Newark and has ingratiated himself to the town's new governor. They were overheard devising their sordid little plot while they got drunk on the local Trent ale.

"Our difficulty is establishing when they are planning to make their move and where an attack will take place.

"And that's where you come into the equation, faithful friend. I need you to go to Newark and spend some time with one of our agents. His name is Goodyeare, and he needs to become our eyes and ears. I don't care what it takes: we need to know what is going on, by any means."

Abijah's face remains neutral, but there is a glint in his eye that wasn't there when he entered the room. It usually only surfaces when his excitement has been aroused.

"You can count on me, Francis. I will be as discreet as I can be. Am I to ride for Newark immediately?"

I nod my head in affirmation.

"I have an uneasy feeling about all of this," I say to the man I trust as much as anyone. "Holck is a wily bastard. He will do all he can to triumph and has already proven he has the intellect to outfox us. So you and I need to remain vigilant and on our guard. He will surprise us; we just don't where or when."

Abijah flashes one of his brilliant smiles. He is more than equal to the task.

"Don't become complacent," I warn. "Make sure you are on your guard at all times.

"Now be off with you. Have a safe journey to Newark. Goodyeare can be found residing in a small hamlet called Coddington, just a couple of miles outside the town. You'll discover he is a well-known local figure who has a high opinion of himself.

"I am sure you won't encounter any problems while you are there. But make haste, and don't fall foul of the local hostelries. The ale is dreadful and the company even worse. I don't want you away from here any longer than you have to be."

On cue, we both stand. Abijah gives me a confident smile, and we embrace as brothers.

"God bless you," I say. "I look forward to our reunion in three or four days. Until then, may our Redeemer King keep you safe. "

Lord Grey's country home, set amid the lush grasslands and forests surrounding Newtown Linford, looks impressive as I arrive for our meeting on Monday afternoon.

It is another cold day. The ride has been refreshing and a good outing for Bucephalus, who doesn't get out as much as he would like during the winter months. As I am instructed, I arrive punctually. Indeed, I note I am at least ten minutes early.

A herd of red deer grazes near the stables. The stags stand a good foot taller than the does, guarding the perimeter of the large group. A guttural noise is emitted from at least three males keen to assert their masculine authority on their competitors within the herd. I watch for a minute, appreciating their exquisite physiques and sheer beauty. Yet again, I find myself praising the creator who made all of this possible.

My appreciation is shattered when one of Lord Grey's footmen bellows my name. I have been spotted. The deer scatter; I shrug my shoulders and continue walking to the house. His Lordship clearly doesn't want me enjoying myself.

"To the point quickly, Hacker, I am a busy man, and I do not need you cluttering up my day."

Thomas Grey is his usual self: brusque; arrogant; all the while bordering on the incompetent. He seeks to disguise these weaknesses and ugly traits by shouting at his subordinates and, when he can do so, bullying and intimidating them, so his edicts go unchallenged.

In September, my last meeting was typical of the man: lots of bluffs, a great deal of posturing, and the exertion of his authority, using intimidation rather than persuasion. That I am not visibly frightened only adds to Grey's attempts to crush my independence of spirit.

"I promise I will be as brief as I can be, your Lordship," I say. "I am sure you will have some interest in what I have to report."

Grey tilts his hand towards a chair. I am being invited to sit. Once I am comfortable, I explain the dire position Leicester now finds itself in – and the need for military and financial support from the Militia. For precisely three minutes, I am allowed to speak. Then Lord Grey explodes.

"Hacker, what did you misunderstand when you agreed to be my man?" he shouts at me, the contempt in his voice undeniable. "Let me say this plainly, man. You are to do my bidding while you sit on the Committee. Your role is not to be a peacemaker. It is to persuade the dullards who control the city that my demands are reasonable and, when appropriate, equitable. Is that clear?"

I sit, stunned by the tongue-lashing I have just received. I thought my relationship with Lord Grey was improving after I had placated several mutinous companies in the latter part of last year and brought some honour to the county with the resounding victory at Woolsthorpe-by-Belvoir. How I have underestimated my commanding officer.

"Sir, I appreciate your position as far as the Mayor and Aldermen are concerned," I say, seeking to control my emotions at all times and play the part of the diplomat. "But what I am talking about goes way beyond any enmity that may exist between you and the city. The plain facts are Leicester is defenceless. It is ripe for the taking.

"In recent days, I have received intelligence suggesting the King will be seeking a morale-boosting victory come the Spring. Having seen the woeful state of the walls and the readiness of the men charged with repulsing an assault, my considered view is you are behaving negligently by ignoring the city's pleas for help."

I have gone too far. I know it. So, too, does Lord Grey, and he is eager to exploit his advantage.

"Listen to me, you worthless upstart," shouts my superior. "You are in danger of causing me great offence and testing my patience sorely. I have tolerated your disloyalty for far too long. You answer to me and no one else; not Cromwell, not Fairfax, not anyone. I am your superior, and you will do my bidding.

"I thought we had established where your loyalties should be directed in the Autumn? But it appears you still have some lessons to learn. And you will."

Grey stands up and turns his back to me. He looks at a flattering portrait of his father, the Earl of Stamford, a senior member of this less than illustrious family. All the time, he pats the top of his right thigh with his hand. The man is clearly frustrated.

After some time for contemplation, Grey spins round, catching me off-guard.

"The matter you have brought to my attention most crudely will not be addressed by myself or any member of this household," he spits through his pursed mouth. "I have no desire to offer any support whatsoever to the cretins that have responsibility for managing Leicester's affairs. They are on their own. I hope I make myself clear?

"The city has made its views about me well known. The Petition that was sent to Parliament has caused some mild embarrassment, nothing more. However, its publication has not endeared me to the men responsible for drafting it. Some of them are acquaintances and friends of yours. So go back to the Guildhall and tell the Mayor there will be no help forthcoming from the Midlands Association or myself. As far as I am concerned, it can fend for itself. I hope I make myself clear?"

His Lordship clearly sees the shock on my face and revels in my discomfort.

"You weren't expecting that, were you Hacker?" he says after he has seated himself once again. "You thought you would be able to persuade me to do something I am totally opposed to doing. Well, sir, you and your would-be meddling have been undone. You now have the pleasure of being the bearer of some sad and unexpected tidings.

"But before you get out of my sight, I have some more news for your ears. It is my desire for you to join the garrison at Kirby Bellars in six days. You are to stay there as the fort's governor, protecting the southern flanks of Melton Mowbray for the foreseeable future. So make haste in tidying up your affairs.

"You will learn that interfering in my business comes at a price, and that means it is time you did some serious soldiering once again. So be off with you before your insolence forces me to give you the punishment you deserve."

I am conscious the colour has drained from my face. The meeting has been a complete disaster, and the outcome could not have been any worse than it is. Becoming the Kirby Bellars garrison commander on the first day of February, a Wednesday, if I am not mistaken, was not something I foresaw before the meeting started.

I have been caught off-guard. What a dullard I am.

Rather than continue to earn the trust and esteem of Lord Grey, I have offended him and destroyed the bridge I have been building in recent months. This has put Leicester in grave peril and doesn't bode well for the work I have promised to undertake for Cromwell.

As I stand in this hostile place, I hear the raised and impatient voice firing barbs in my direction. My mind is wandering, and I am quickly forced to refocus.

"Get out, Hacker," yells Lord Grey as I stand numbed by the severity of his verbal assault. "Get out of my sight, and start to do your duty."

The ride back to Stathern and the security of the Vale of Belvoir is one of the most uncomfortable I have ever been forced to endure.

I barely notice the rain splashing off my cloak as Bucephalus and I pick our way back through the bracken and long grasses of the verdant Leicestershire countryside. Usually alert, I am a danger to myself and my steed, for I cannot concentrate. I am preoccupied with my thoughts and anxieties: how could I have misjudged things so badly, and how could I allow my relationship with Lord Grey to deteriorate so quickly?

Try as hard as I can, I can think of nothing I have done that could have possibly aroused Grey suspicions. Every time he has put me to the test, I have triumphed – and I have been meticulous in concealing my ongoing links to Oliver.

Correspondence has continued to flow between the Lieutenant-General and me, as was agreed when I first embarked on the venture to become a trusted member of Grey's entourage. Nothing has been intercepted or compromised, and I can recall no noticeable mistakes that have been made. And there are only three souls involved in the subterfuge, and I can vouch for all three.

No. There is something more to today's extraordinary proceedings. There has to be.

I barely notice a branch that connects with my shoulder as Bucephalus wanders off the well-worn track due to my lack of control of the reins. Its sting clears the fog in my head, and I quickly refocus and get him back on to the path that leads to home. As he settles once again into his stride, I feel wronged and angry, completely unable to comprehend the sense of the matter.

An hour after leaving Newtown Linford, I see several plumes of smoke rising from an assortment of chimneys into the grey skies as I approach Stathern. I am wet, cold and feeling utterly sorry for myself.

As I start my descent from the crest of Mill Hill, the village laid completely bare before me, a pair of Jackdaws, braving the atrocious weather in the rotting embers of Marjorie and Peter's former home, call out to me.

This once happy place was the scene of the notorious and gruesome murders of the Harringtons nearly a year ago. Then, as of now, there were too many unanswered questions about events that were too big and complicated for anyone to fully comprehend.

The truth eventually made itself known, with tragic consequences for so many of us.

Since then, I have learned to listen.

Hearing the harsh cries of the carrion, I sense the return of a feeling that has deserted me in recent months. The Lord is upon me, and I know instinctively He is imploring me to look into the affairs of Lord Grey.

It is a tangible feeling, usually only felt by those of us who believe in Him, and it is a call I cannot ignore.

Within a few seconds, I know what to do; I must obey Grey's order to join the Kirby Bellars garrison, based in the fortified country manor of a notorious Royalist sympathiser. But my isolation will not prevent me from seeking answers about Grey's conduct.

I grit my teeth; I will be deemed to be behaving recklessly by some, not least Isabel, who will not be happy with the news when I break it to her. Thankfully, I am confident Abijah will have made good progress in extracting the information we need from Goodyeare in Newark. So at least I will be spared his remonstrations upon my return.

But I know my Maker is by my side once again, and that is all that matters. And with His help, a plan is already forming…

THIRTEEN

I AM BUSY IN MY study, organising my papers and making my final preparations for my journey to Kirby Bellars when a man arrives at the Hall with news that will affect the rest of my life.

A commotion in the hallway draws my attention to his arrival. I am bored, and the raised voices have left me intrigued, so I rise from my desk and walk towards the sound, keen to discover what all the fuss and excitement is about.

As I approach the main door, I see Guy Goodman, a new recruit to the Militia. He is doing his best to restore some peace and decorum to a rapidly deteriorating situation. A man of mature years is remonstrating with the young soldier, and he is becoming increasingly agitated and vocal.

"Calm yourself, man," says Goodman, his hand never leaving the sword by his side as he talks to the visitor whose arms are flapping wildly and whose face is flushed. "If you have something of importance to tell Captain

Hacker, I will ensure he is informed with the utmost haste. So speak plainly and tell me what the source of your distress is."

I look on, only a few feet away from the rumpus, hidden in the shadows. I am impressed with the way young Goodman is conducting himself on this, his ninth day of duty.

"Young man, I have come from Newark with grave tidings," says the man, who is distressed and frustrated. "My name is Oswald Honeyman, and I am in the employ of Captain Hacker's brother. I am here because Rowland Hacker has been betrayed. So, too, has a man called Abijah Swan. They are both imprisoned in the dungeons of Newark Castle, where they are condemned as spies and traitors."

Honeyman's words leave me stunned. I reach behind me and clutch the coarse wall. My head starts to spin, and I suddenly feel myself falling backwards as the gravity of the situation becomes clear. Thankfully, the cold brickwork comes to my aid and props me up. Gradually, I start to regain my composure. When I look up, two sets of eyes are staring directly at me.

"Captain, I didn't realise you were there," says Goodman, attempting to hide his embarrassment and concern. "This man has…"

I hold my hand up, indicating the need for silence. I must think before I speak.

I allow a couple of minutes to lapse. When I am sure my mind has exercised some semblance of control over my frail emotions, I look at my visitor and say: "Master Honeyman, speak plainly, sir and tell me how dire the news you bring about my brother and Abijah is, and please leave nothing unsaid."

As soon as Oswald Honeyman starts to tell me everything that has transpired in the last three days in the town that lies seventeen miles away from Stathern, darkness takes a firm hold of me. For, although this stranger may use kind, encouraging words and seek to remain optimistic, it would appear I have been directly responsible for the extreme difficulties my brother and best friend now find themselves in.

By two o'clock in the afternoon, I know enough.

"Master Honeyman," I say. "I cannot thank you enough for coming here as quickly as you have and telling me as much as you know. You have put yourself and your family at grave risk, and I will not forget the loyalty you have shown this day."

My words prompt the older man to let out a grunt in protest.

"I have not known your brother for very long, sir," he tells me. "But in a little over eighteen months, I have grown to respect and trust him deeply. Master Rowland is a man of integrity. He has shown me the utmost respect and courtesy at all times. And he trusts me. How can I not do the right thing in his time of need?"

I nod my head in agreement. At a time of utmost brutality and selfishness, it is reassuring to know there are still people who believe honour and integrity are essential values. Honeyman is one such soul.

"Whatever happens, I want you to know I am deeply grateful for everything you have told me about these dreadful events," I say directly. "And I want you to know that Stathern will always be a place you and your family will be welcomed."

Honeyman rises. He has an hour-long ride to negotiate on this mild winter's day, and he has a story to con-
coct, for it is critical the Royalists believe he is innocent of
any of the charges levelled against Rowland and Abijah.

So much depends on it.

Isabel sits on the side of the mattress in the bed-chamber
we share as she attempts to comprehend everything I have
told her.

"How is this possible?" asks my steadfast wife, who is
shaken to the core by the devastating news. "Who is the
snake who has betrayed us all?"

I take a deep intake of breath.

"It is a man who has been trusted by Parliament
since the outset of the war," I tell her. "There has never
been any reason to suspect he was anything other than a
loyal agent. His intelligence has always been reliable. He
even provided me with a safe refuge in the summer when
I went to Newark.

"Something must have happened in recent weeks
that has forced him to swap sides. He must have been
coerced, threatened or blackmailed. There can be no
other explanation. The man I know was as true as I am
when I last saw him."

Isabel isn't listening. She is far away, looking through
the window and into the trees that line the garden.

"Your brother and your closest friend; caught and
now helpless. What kind of fate will befall them?" asks my
wife, knowing exactly what the future holds for a man condemned as a traitor. "Francis, you have to do something.
You must try to rescue them. There has to be hope…"

By six o'clock in the evening on Thursday, the twen-ty-sixth day of January in the year of our Lord, 1645, my bag is packed. I have shaved my beard, and my hair is now shorn of the long locks that have been a source of great pride for many years.

As I look in the mirror, the man standing before me is someone I do not recognise. I pray my enemies will be fooled and do not recognise me as the country squire and man of privilege I have been for these past twenty-seven years. For it is my desire to be an invisible figure when I venture into the Royalist stronghold, one of the most secure in all of England.

I bid my farewells.

As has been so often the case in recent times, Isabel is weeping as I leave her, distress and concern etched on her face. But my wonderful wife, the woman I love with all my heart, is as adamant I must go into the lair of the enemy and attempt to rescue two of the people I care most about in this world. They cannot be allowed to face their fate on their own. Nothing else matters: the garrison at Kirby Bellars can wait, and Lord Grey can go to hell. My brother and my best friend are the only things of impor-tance right now, and I will do everything in my power to save them.

Newark is the second largest town in the county of Nottingham. Nestled alongside the Trent, it is crossing point over the river before it reaches the Humber estuary. It lies astride the Great North Road, which links York and Newcastle with the capital, and it is also linked to the old Roman Fosse Way, which traverses the country from east to west.

Its importance as a centre for trade and commerce is recognised by both sides.

Two attempts to take the town have been mounted by Parliament. On both occasions, its garrison has held firm and beaten off the attackers.

If all the towns in this realm were as loyal to the King as Newark, the result of this bloody conflict would be a foregone conclusion.

It is to this fortress that I travel on this sad and gloomy night. The moonlight is sparse, the fields heavy with mud, and a deep foreboding threatens to engulf any zest for life and wit I may still retain.

My senses have been numbed by the news of the last few hours. And I am blind, not knowing what awaits me. For I have had no time to make any detailed plans or receive the assurances I normally secure before making such a hazardous journey.

My own fate, and that of the others, is indeed held firmly in the palms of God's hands.

A messenger left Stathern three hours before my departure, seeking out another agent, who is as trusted as anyone can be at the present time. I pray the rider will find the man I will be calling upon, one Benjamin Beasely. He is an established fellow in the locality who needs to be made aware of my needs and the quest I am undertaking.

I will not know whether my rider has been successful until I arrive. And for all I know, by then, a trap may already have been set for me.

As the cold night's air whips across my naked and clean-shaven face, I have plenty of time to ponder my actions and prepare for what is to come – and reconcile myself with the terrible rage welling up within. And there is something else I recognise… it is fear, an emotion I rarely experience, yet it has a firm grip on me this night.

Farndon, a small village less than a couple of miles away from Newark, is where I make for first.

It would be folly to enter the lion's den without discovering what awaits me. So I visit an inn, where locals still bend their knees to Charles. Here I buy some food and ale and attempt to avoid drawing unnecessary attention to myself.

The place is a hovel, but a large fire emits plenty of heat and liberally sprays out sparks and smoke from the immature logs that were lit long before I arrived.

As I sup on my lukewarm ale, which tastes as though rats have pissed in it, I catch the innkeeper and his wife looking in my direction. They are eyeing me suspiciously. I look away, desperate for the shadows to consume me.

The next time I dare glance in their direction, the publican, an obese fellow with a ruddy complexion and lank, greasy hair, is jabbing his finger towards me. He is talking animatedly to a group of villagers, who take it in turns to gaze towards me, wariness written all over their ugly features.

Strangers clearly aren't welcome in these parts. It is time to leave.

The streets of Newark are unusually quiet as Bucephalus and I pick our way over the pockmarked cobbles being assaulted by the unrelenting rain.

Clouds of steam rise from the back of my steed and out of his flared nostrils. His ears are pricked. He is alert, just as I need to be.

It has taken less than twenty minutes to get from Farndon to Millgate, on the east side of the town. It is almost eleven o'clock. The place is tightly packed with timber-framed houses that are so typical of places like Newark. And woe betides me if I misplace my feet, for running down the centre of the street is the channel carrying away the foul-smelling detritus that has been ejected from the bowels of hundreds of townsfolk.

As I edge forward, seeking to find my bearings, I hear people going about their business. The munitions and weapons businesses that supply the Royalist army are all located in this area, and their doorways are illuminated by a combination of torches and lamps.

I grimace. Even at this late hour, it seems the devil's work needs to be done.

Thankfully, my destination is not far away. As I negotiate the last four hundred yards, I find myself praying all will be well when I arrive at the house of Benjamin Beasely, which is conveniently tucked away in the quietest part of Ironmonger Lane.

Beasely is clearly nervous and wary when he ushers me into the unassuming house he shares with his dour wife, Kathleen.

"I won't pretend," he says to me after taking my cloak. "This is an irregular visit, one I was not expecting. I have not had time to prepare. The risks right now are significant, so I would ask you to state your business and be on your way."

I am sitting at a table in the parlour at the back of the house. A draught from the windows is toying with the three candles working tirelessly to illuminate the room.

In front of me sits the diminutive figure of one of the three Parliamentary agents that have continued to operate in Newark since hostilities started more than two and a half years ago.

I regularly benefit from the information contained in Beasely's intelligence reports that have proven to be invaluable. This is the first time I have met the author, and the reception I am being afforded is less than impressive.

"I need to know if you have heard anything about the whereabouts of a man called Abijah Swan," I say as calmly as I can. "I have been told he has been arrested by the town's governor on suspicion of being a spy. If this is the case, I need to know where he is."

Beasely scratches the back of his neck. He is nervous and clearly thinking about how he should answer my question.

Before he has time to speak, I add: "I also need to know what fate has befallen my brother, a Royalist officer called Rowland Hacker. He, too, is being held somewhere in the castle, accused of committing treason. What say you, can you assist me?"

After mopping his damp brow, Beasely starts to shake his head.

"My God, Captain Hacker, do you really think you can ride to the aid of these men?" asks my host, his voice unnaturally hawkish. "The man they call Swan is condemned as a Parliamentarian and is set to hang the morrow. Right now, he is incarcerated in the dungeons of the castle. There is nothing you, or I, can do to save him other than pray for his poor, wretched soul.

"He was tried and convicted two days since. He will

die in the morning, hung on the gallows they have built on the Great North Road. They lie about half a mile outside the fortified walls.

"As for the whereabouts and fate of your Royalist brother, I am afraid I know nothing. I suspect he is in chains in the bowels of the castle. But that is conjecture, not knowledge."

The news leaves me reeling. I am breathless. My head is spinning.

I tell myself it cannot be so; Beasely must be wrong. My best friend, the man who has saved my life on more occasions than I care to remember, cannot be about to meet his Maker. He is untouchable, a man of integrity and honour, not someone to be hanged like a common thief.

"Are you sure?" I ask, more in hope than expectation. "Is there any chance you may have been misinformed?"

Beasely's patience is close to snapping.

"My good Captain, I make it my business to know what is going on in this town," he retorts. "There is no mistake. I witnessed the trial myself and was there when the sentence was passed. Your man is to die. Nothing can be done to spare him.

"It is why the town is quiet tonight. Many will be getting up early, for he is to be hanged in the morning – when the sun rises."

I cannot sleep for much of the evening in the small room provided to me. When I do finally succumb to the slumber, nightmares ravage my mind, tormenting me in a way I could never imagine. Abijah features in all of them, taunting me as he vents his fears and anger.

At last, signs of life break through the dimness of the early dawn: a stray dog barks, and someone belches loudly as they pass by close to the house.

I reach for my pocket watch, a gift from Isabel in happier times. I move my wrist close to the burning candle, which illuminates the dial and tells me it is six o'clock in the morning. I have barely slept.

Outside it is dry and cold. Soon the rays of a new winter's morn will break through the gloom. And when the full glare of the sun is upon us, it will be time for Abijah to depart this world.

Tears fill my eyes. I am powerless and alone, and I must bear responsibility for sending my most loyal and devout friend to his death. How will I ever be capable of forgiving myself?

I get dressed. My clothes are still wet from the night before, but I don't care. My discomfort is nothing to that being experienced by Abijah and Rowland. What they would give to enjoy the freedoms I have.

He says little. I leave the house an hour after I have risen. It is clear Master Beasely is relieved to see the back of me, as is his wife.

Spying can be a very profitable business. But it is a dangerous game, particularly when one of your paymaster's turns up on the doorstep. The risks then start to outweigh the benefits. And I suspect my presence has left Benjamin and Katherine Beasely actively considering their futures as Parliament's eyes and ears in these parts.

Right now, their future does not concern me. All that matters is I make my way undetected to the Great North Road and try to get as close to Abijah as he sets out on his final journey. I must see him and, if I can, help him make his peace with the Lord.

I have been standing alongside hundreds of folk from the town for what seems like an age, whereas in reality, it is probably no more than thirty long, torturous minutes.

The crowd has swelled, attracted by the lure of seeing a Parliamentarian pay the ultimate price for all the suffering Newark has been forced to endure.

Although tightly pressed, I do have the fortune of being as close to the scaffold as I dare be. I will be able to see my friend and, from my vantage point, I will share the agony of his cruel fate. He may even see me and hear my prayers.

I thank God that his pain will be fleeting. Rightly so, mine will last a lifetime.

At precisely eight o'clock, on the morning of Sunday, the twenty-ninth day of January, a deathly silence comes over the crowd. As one, their heads turn. They are looking towards the town at a small procession weaving its way down the long, winding road.

A lone kettledrum is beating a slow lament. There can be no doubting where the chained prisoner, standing motionless in a wooden cart drawn by a single horse, is heading.

The scaffold beckons. It is time.

Abijah passes within a few feet of where I am standing. His clothes hang off his bruised body by threads. He is drenched in blood.

The procession is travelling at an excruciating pace, allowing onlookers to get their fill of the condemned man.

As it passes by, I clearly see the vivid welts and wounds that have been inflicted on my second-in-command. At least one of his shoulders is broken, and there are many telltale signs of bloody trauma around the stumps that were once fingers.

Yet, despite the agonies he is suffering, Abijah stands tall. Ready; defiant; broken in body – but certainly not in spirit.

Eventually, the nag that is dragging my friend to his doom reaches its destination. As it does, my anger rises. Yet, I can do nothing. The odds are overwhelming. I am impotent once again, and my lust for the blood of my friend's captors must remain stilled.

Out of the corner of my eye, next to the steps of the scaffold, stands a man I recognise. It is Holck, and he is wearing the smile of a killer.

I grip my sword and try to move forward. As I do, the man in front of me turns around and yells a stream of curses, ordering me to stand still. He wants to preserve his unrivalled view of the kill.

If I want to live, I have no choice; I must do as I am told.

I look closer at my nemesis, a man I have sworn to kill, and my heart starts to beat wildly. I bite the corner of my mouth and draw blood. I can't stand what is unfolding before my very eyes, so pain becomes my salvation.

Two men climb aboard the cart and throw Abijah to the ground. He flails momentarily before rough hands drag him up crudely erected steps. And all the while, he remains silent, proud, and defiant.

It is more than I can bear. In a bid to quell my inner demons, I look anywhere other than the scaffold.

As I do, I see him. Standing right behind the Bohemian assassin is someone I am acquainted with – the well-dressed and smiling figure of Edmund Goodyeare.

"The man before you stands condemned of the foulest of treasons," barks Holck in his brutish, Germanic accent, standing some six feet above the assembled throng and radiating in the prolonged suffering of his victim. "The retribution he will face this morning will ensure he will never be able to plot against the King again."

Cheers ripple through the crowd. Those present, and there are many, are clearly looking forward to their post-breakfast entertainment. To add some macabre colour to proceedings, a bombardment of eggs and rotten vegetables rains down on Abijah, who looks on unperturbed.

"Let this man's death be a warning to our enemies that anyone who seeks to defy the King will suffer a quick, harsh and painful punishment," continues Holck. "There will be no mercy shown to spies who seek to undermine everything we stand for."

Turning to one of the men on the dais, Holck adds in his native tongue: "Mal sehen, wie mutig dieser Abschaum mit einer Schlinge um den Hals ist und wie das Leben aus ihm herausgedrückt wird. Er wird sich bald wünschen, er hä tte gesprochen."

Translation: "Let's see how brave this scum is with a noose around his neck and the life being squeezed out of him. He will soon wish he had talked."

Holck makes a hand signal to the executioner. This stocky, bare-chested, balding man revels in being in the limelight even on this cold day. He steps forward and grabs

Abijah by the shoulders, positioning him on a short, raised platform. Shortly it will be kicked away, leaving Abijah to hang by the neck until he is breathing no more.

Holck punches Abijah maliciously in the chest, laughing cruelly as the defenceless prisoner lets out an audible groan. He does it again and again. Each time, my friend grunts as pain racks his broken shell. It's this kind of sport the crowd has eagerly been waiting to see.

More degradations and humiliations follow, and through them all, Abijah stands tall, taking everything these savages can throw at him. Watching on, I am proud and humbled to call this warrior my friend.

"Let the Roundhead rot in hell," shrieks the man in front, phlegm and spittle showering the heads of those standing directly in front of him. "Make him suffer before he goes to meet Lucifer."

Holck raises his hands, signalling it is time for the executioner to regain control of proceedings.

With his hands tied securely behind his back, Abijah remains motionless as his head is guided through the thick, coiled rope that will soon be his passage to the afterlife. The crowd hushes. They are ready for what is about to come. As they wait, all that can be heard are the cries of a couple of inquisitive Magpies, who have chosen this very moment to emerge from the nearby copse.

Then time stands still. Everything slows down. My body feels numb; the voices around me become incomprehensible and slurred, and then sunlight breaks through, blinding one and all.

After a moment, I become conscious of a jubilant roar puncturing the frigid air. The rope is taut as it bears the weight of the condemned. Then the crowd finds its voice. I hear vile curses shouted, drowning out the cacophony of noise; they mock and slander the bravest man I know.

In front of me, no more than twenty feet away, Abijah's feet kick frantically, seeking to find purchase where there is none. As my friend struggles and fights for life, the noose strengthens its vice-like grip. Getting ever tighter. Sadly, this battle will soon be over. It is a contest this great man cannot win.

And so it proves to be.

After ten minutes of resilience, Abijah's body spasms and his tongue probes for oxygen one last time. Then he is gone.

His body swings silently. The pain is no more.

Sorrow and regret are heavy stones to carry, and I am sorely weighed down as I make my way back to Newark.

My eyes are red from weeping. My throat is hoarse. A deep hatred rages within.

Abijah left his world alone, not realising I was there, and I will never be able to forgive myself for condemning him to the loneliest of deaths.

But there is a time to mourn, and this is not it.

The fate of my brother is still unknown, so I must do all I can to establish where Rowland is and what can be done to assist him.

And then there is the matter of Edmund Goodyeare. His appearance, alongside Holck at the scaffold, can only mean it is he who is the rat in the nest. There can be no other explanation.

As I ponder my next move, I become acutely aware

I only have one viable option: interrogating the cur, Goodyeare, and discovering the extent of his betrayal.

Everything else depends on what I uncover.

FOURTEEN

WITH ABIJAH'S BODY NOT YET cold, I begin the task of tracking down the man who will be the first the feel my wrath.

Edmund Goodyeare lives on his own in the humble hamlet of Coddington, located some three miles to the east of Newark. He has resided here all his adult life, or so he told me when I spent several weeks at his home following Holck's brutal slaying of Barbara and Isable.

At the time, I had no reason to believe Goodyeare was anything other than loyal to the Parliamentary cause. He was spoken highly of by the likes of Cromwell. There has never been a reason to distrust him.

But all men are weak, and it matters little whether they are enticed to the dark side by the promise of money, the seduction of a beautiful enchantress, or simply forced to submit. Betrayal amounts to the same thing, regardless of the reason. And it is unforgivable.

I return to the stables where Bucephalus has spent the last

twenty-four hours. I pay the simple young lad the agreed penny for his services and then take my leave, ever mindful of the large number of Royalist troops garrisoned in and around the town's impregnable walls.

By eleven o'clock, I can breathe easier, and Bucephalus can at last stretch his legs on Beacon Hill, albeit we both need to be alert to the many deserted earthworks that are dotted around this vast area of open space. Their presence is a reminder of the previous attempts by Parliament's armies to conquer the region.

With the immediate danger now behind me, the grief I have been forced to suppress finally overwhelms me.

I have known the torment of torture, but what I feel right now is despair and hurt as grievous as I have ever experienced, equalling that of the deaths of my mother and my beloved daughters.

With my chest tight and my emotions running high, I bring Bucephalus to a halt on the brow of the hill. I shake my head and look to the skies. As I do, I make a solemn vow to the memory of my departed friend: as God is my witness, I will not rest until I have righted the wrongs of this damnable day.

The cottage I am seeking is located on the lane stretching directly between Coddington and Balderton. It stands in the distant shadows of a windmill constructed some years yonder, built to aid the immediate area with the drawing of water and to offset the effects of repeated droughts.

Smoke, a sure sign someone is at home, climbs out of the red brick chimney that dominates the neatly thatched roof.

It seems a fire is ablaze. If I have my way, flames will soon be engulfing the whole building – but only after I have sated my thirst for revenge on the man inside.

I take my time approaching the dwelling. Only a fool rushes in, and it is always good to check a few things, particularly when I don't know how many people are at home.

My caution is my salvation.

No sooner have I tethered Bucephalus to a post attached to a large, mature Oak tree and skirted my way to a vantage point overlooking the front of the house, when the door opens, and three men in jovial spirits depart. One of them is Holck.

"Wir müssen schnell sein," he says, clearly within earshot of where I am hiding. "Es gibt noch viel zu tun."

Translation: "We need to be quick. There is much that still needs to be done."

The bitter taste of bile rises from the depths of my stomach as the Bohemian's words ring in my ears. It takes all my self-control to stop myself from rising from my cover and challenging my avowed enemy. But, thankfully, sense prevails this day. As I curse under my breath, I am more determined than ever before to have my vengeance. But I must bide my time.

After a couple of minutes, with my bloodlust fading, I hear the clatter of hooves as three mounted horses appear from the side of the building. Holck and the other two riders are in a hurry; in unison, their whips are used on exposed equine flesh, the sting of the lash encouraging the steeds to gallop as fast as they dare.

I wait, biding my time, as the thunderous noise of the beasts and their masters' fades into the distance.

Nothing moves for the next twenty minutes. Finally,

with no visible signs of activity to suggest there may be other visitors inside the cottage, and with my courage emboldened, I walk nonchalantly to the front door.

My shaved face, short hair and unimaginative, plain clothing mean I am unlikely to be recognised from a distance by anyone looking out of one of the building's small windows. So I make sure of my approach, rap on the door assertively and wait for Goodyeare to make himself known.

I am not disappointed. It takes the weasel inside but a few seconds to issue a challenge.

"Who is it, and what do you want with me?" enquires a voice I know to be that of my prey. "State your business. I haven't got all afternoon."

I cough, seeking to disguise my own voice for fear of Goodyeare identifying me and barring my entry.

"I have a message for the Master," I state, putting a heavy accent on my words as I spit them out. "I have explicit instructions to hand it to Edmund Goodyeare in person and to no one else. Are you he?"

Silence greets my declaration.

A minute passes, perhaps two. I become worried that Goodyeare has indeed recognised my voice and is making good his escape. But just as the first threads of panic pulse through me, I hear a reassuring noise on the other side of the stud-encrusted door: the iron levers are being pulled back. My crude ruse has worked.

Quietly, I pull my sword from its scabbard; I stand ready, gripping the hilt tightly, all set to knock Goodyeare senseless.

As the last of the bolts makes a loud rasping noise as it is pulled backwards, I know I have only one chance to time my assault correctly. Surprise is everything, and I must not waste the opportunity.

I have little time to react when Goodyear's face, his cheeks reddened and his eyes probing, stares back at me from the slit that has suddenly appeared in the doorway.

No words are spoken; they are not needed. The moment he looks into my eyes, he knows who I am. It is time to strike.

With the speed of a viper, the pommel of my sword hits Goodyeare flush on the bridge of his nose, spraying blood, snot and cartilage in all directions.

Even in the heat of battle, I always try to avoid destroying another human being's face. It is a rule I have always adhered to. Yet, I am aware of a sadistic pleasure that has taken hold of me as I set about mutilating this man.

Goodyeare's flailing hands seek to shield him from the destructive blows that rain down on him. But it is too late. Before he hits the floor, his face is a bloody mess.

"Nay, nay," he sobs. "Francis! Please, please spare me. I can explain everything."

It is too late. There will be no concessions granted this day. So I push my way into the homestead and continue to strike out; indiscriminately, as powerfully as my strength and anger will allow.

After a while, I stand back, wiping my sword on a cloak hanging close to a large crucifix featuring the body of a nailed Jesus. This Catholic icon was not in the house when I stayed in the summer; it's another secret that adds to my rage.

My breathing is ragged; such has been my exertion

in the moments it has taken to knock the resistance and spirit out of Goodyeare.

My surprise has been complete, and my quarry lies semiconscious on the floor, continuing to plead for his worthless life.

I will hear what Goodyeare has to say, for I still need to aid my brother. But the man at my feet will be lucky to see the rise of the moon.

For the next two hours, Edmund Goodyeare proceeds to tell me precisely how Abijah and Rowland became snared in the Royalist trap he helped to set.

"I had no choice," he pleads, wiping blood from his face as several of the wounds I have inflicted on his scalp weep uncontrollably. "Holck's agents discovered my presence, and I was arrested not long after you left in the summer. I was betrayed. They tortured me for almost a week, and ultimately I was powerless to resist. I swear, nobody could withstand the pain they inflicted on my body.

"I did all I could to stay loyal, but in the end, I could stand it no more. The pain was too excruciating."

I look at the man I have now bound tightly to an ornately decorated chair. As I do, I feel only contempt and loathing. I will never understand how values, honour, comrades and faith itself can be so easily sacrificed.

Goodyeare can sense I am repulsed by his protestations. Nonetheless, he continues to plead for his life, and as he does, his cries force me to recall once again my own ordeal at the hands of Holck.

It was November, in the year of our Lord, 1643, and I was held prisoner at the grand castle of Belvoir. I had been neither spy nor felon. If anything, I had been an ally.

Yet, it was perceived I could do great harm. So my fingers and toes were mutilated one at a time. I was tested to see if, in my weakness, I would reveal Prince Maurice's great secret: that he had been willing to accept the crown of England and become the puppet of Parliament.

During the ordeal, I experienced pain, the like of which I never wish to taste again. The severe shoulder wound I suffered just before Christmas was a scratch in comparison. Death itself would be a mercy compared to the torment meted out to my body by Holck's practised hands.

But suffer the agonies I did. And I betrayed nobody, even though I was most sorely tempted.

Scotland's decision to join the war on the side of Parliament prevented the plotters – men like Cromwell, the late John Pym and me – from making a King out of Maurice. The over-ambitious Prince, a younger brother to Rupert, was dismayed. He was also terrified his uncle, Charles the First, would learn of his deceit. So, I needed to be tested to see if I was complicit in any wrongdoing and could be trusted to keep my mouth shut.

That I am alive today is testimony enough.

These memories flash across my mind as Goodyeare spills his guts. When I am satisfied, I sit back and stare at the broken man whose body I have ruined. From what I have just learned, the extent of Goodyeare's treachery is overwhelming.

He has confessed to being a double agent for the last six months. During that time, every bit of intelligence he has fed Parliament has been laced with half-truths and lies. The information has had some value for Lord Grey's scoutmaster. But the greatest value has been to the Royalists, who have used Goodyeare to mislead the Midlands and Eastern Association armies.

Holck and his cronies appear to know almost everything after Goodyeare offered up all he knew to save his scrawny, worthless neck. My enemies are now aware of the scale of Leicester's defensive weaknesses. They possess important details about the troop movements of Lord Grey's regiments, and they also know when Oliver is scheduled to be in London. They may even know where he is planning to reside.

As I have questioned the traitor, one thing has become very clear: the betrayal clearly involves more than just one man. A sophisticated network is at play, and it is committed to compromising those opposed to bringing the King to heel.

Unfortunately, the pawn I have in my custody can shed no light on the identities of the others. If Goodyeare did, he would have blurted out their names, such as the violence I have been forced to use. But knowing conspirators are actively plotting against us tells me they fear something. Whatever it is, I will do my utmost to uncover it.

As far as Rowland's immediate prospects are concerned, the news is also less than favourable: Holck knows my brother and I have met.

Goodyeare himself followed Rowland to East Bridgford when he attended my father's funeral. He admitted reporting everything to Holck. If there is one, the saving grace is that Goodyeare didn't hear anything that incriminated Rowland. If he had, my brother would have already suffered Abijah's cruel fate.

Many permutations and scenarios race through my

mind as I struggle to understand everything I have learned. But I won't get the answers I am seeking from this place.

It is time to tidy things up.

"Your treachery will not go unpunished," I say. "And I intend to be your judge and jury this very day.

"You can make life easier for yourself by telling me anything else you feel you may have omitted thus far. What say you? Is there anything you have been holding back that your traitor's conscience would like to inform me about?"

An inaudible babble comes out of Goodyear's mouth. I can neither hear it nor comprehend it.

"Louder, man, louder," I shout, lashing out at one of Goodyeare's unprotected groin with my boot. "Speak up and tell me plainly, so I do not misunderstand any of the words that come out of your vile cesspit of a mouth."

The prisoner howls as a fresh wave of agony causes him to bend over and retch. I give him less than a minute to recover before prodding him with a heavy iron poker I have found hanging on a hook by the hearth.

He looks up, and there is genuine fear in his eyes. Despite his injuries, Goodyeare struggles with the bonds I have tied and tries to break free. To no avail, they are securely fastened. There will be no escape.

"There is one thing more," he says, spluttering violently, such is his desire for self-preservation. "I will reveal it to you if you promise to spare my life."

I sigh and nod my head. "Continue," I demand. "But hurry. My patience is wearing thin."

Thirty minutes later, as the night starts to descend, Goodyeare has offered up the identity of one of the

Parliamentarian traitors. I am astride Bucephalus, making my way back to the house of Benjamin Beasely. He will not be pleased when he sees me on his doorstep once again, but I need a place to sleep and think for the next twelve hours, and Ironmonger Lane is the only place where I can hide and make my plans.

Behind me, less than half a mile away, an inferno engulfs Goodyeare's home.

I hear the timbers crackle as flames bring purification to the wicked. The unmistakable sound of brickwork crashing down is drowned out by the noise of the roof collapsing. Soon only ashes and the odd charred beam will remain. It is as I intended.

Bucephalus and I stop to watch the spectacle as the destruction takes hold.

I eye the scene with morbid fascination as the blue, yellow, and orange tongues caress the darkening skies. The blaze will be clearly visible from Newark's bulwarks and fortified walls, and it won't be long before my handiwork is discovered. So hasten my departure, I must.

Strangely, I feel an overwhelming sense of satisfaction. I have defied my Maker. I have killed in cold blood. But I am comforted knowing at least one traitor can betray no more.

FIFTEEN

Revulsion and hatred consume me for the next few hours. For many, powerful emotions such as these crush and destroy the spirit and attack the soul. Yet, perversely, I find such feelings driving me on at a time of the sincerest grief. They help me believe Rowland's dire situation is far from helpless and ensure the responsibility I feel for Abijah's death is stored in an appropriate place.

After the traumatic events on the Great North Road, I have made my way to the home of the Beaselys once again and persuaded them to give me refuge for another night. Their reluctance is plain to see in their pinched and withdrawn faces. Still, they voice no objections, preferring instead to curse inwardly at the enhanced dangers I have again brought to their door.

There is barely enough space to spread my mattress in the threadbare room, where I conceal myself for a second, cramped night until daybreak. Then, with nothing to occupy my time, and nobody to talk to, I think about Goodyeare and how I misjudged the man so badly.

As I mull over things, I remember Else, the cook and friend who brought tragedy to Stathern not so long ago. I see her smiling face; it haunts me. I hear her mocking voice, taunting my family. Isabel and I trusted her implicitly, yet she betrayed us most grievously.

How we forget things too quickly. How we want to trust, and how we suffer most terribly when that trust is misplaced.

I shake my head, eager to disentangle the past from the present, for all that matters is what I do next.

But one thing I am sure of is my actions; they have left me damned. Of that, I am sure. The eyes of the Lord may still be upon me, but where there was once love, I am convinced there will now be only loathing and contempt. I am no King David, who sinned and was forgiven by the Maker.

I am now just another remorseless, cold-hearted killer who is unwilling to repent.

Before his remains succumbed to the flames, Goodyeare revealed three things of importance.

He told me all he knew about the plot to kill Cromwell, his role in 'fixing' certain things for Holck and his clutch of cutthroats – and he also gave me a name I will divulge only to the Lieutenant-general. I will think more about things as I return to Stathern, which I intend to do sometime this evening.

Before then, and of much greater immediate importance, is the snippet of information I hold about the man responsible for overseeing Newark Castle's rat-infested gaol: a certain Ambrose Crump.

It would appear Crump has a weakness for cards

that have left him indebted to some of the town's most notorious criminals. If his superiors knew of his vice and the extent of his problems, it would be a serious cause for concern, leaving the gaoler open to blackmail and bribery.

Goodyeare told me, as he begged for mercy, that he had passed money to Crump on several occasions in return for prisoners receiving vital messages. I was told the going rate for such a service is somewhere in the region of five Laurels, a considerable sum of money by any standards.

Thankfully, I am carrying more than double that in coinage, so I will be able to grease the palms of the greediest collaborator and ensure very few questions are asked.

With limited time at my disposal, bribing the rogue Crump appears to be my only feasible course of action. The risks are high. If I am caught, I, too, will face the gallows. But that matters not; I do not fear death.

At all costs, my brother must be saved, even if I am sacrificed in the endeavour.

To live with Abijah's death on my conscience is something I must, and will, come to terms with. I have been carrying such guilt since the demise of my other sibling, Thomas, who also fought for the King and died at Colston Bassett, cut down by my own men.

These are grievous weights to carry, and one day there will be a reckoning. But knowing I am responsible for Rowland's death will be too much to bear.

I must find a way of prevailing.

The knock is light, but it is more than sufficient to wake me from my troubled slumber.

"Master Hacker, I have the items you requested."

The voice is unmistakable. It is that of Kathleen Beasely, and it pierces the stillness of the night, catching me by surprise and forcing me to forget my memories, such as the stealth in which she has climbed the stairs.

It is the first time the mistress of the house has spoken to me with anything close to a hint of warmness. Her soft lilt is pleasing to the ear, but there is undeniable steel lurking underneath. I also sense fear. If it's as I believe, it is little wonder. Goodwife Beasely will face the noose if the subterfuge she is engaged in on behalf of Parliament should ever be exposed. For her husband, it will altogether be a far more unpleasant experience.

"I am coming, mistress," I confirm, "I will be with you in just a moment. But, first, allow me to light the candle."

I rise from the mattress, where I have lain these past eight hours, sleeping fitfully for less than half of them. Then, finally, I am awake, my mind and body alert and ready for whatever the day confronts me with.

When I am composed, I open the door. As I do, a wooden tray is thrust through the gap. On it is a box containing three hens' eggs, a bowl filled to the brim with vinegar, several sheaves of paper, a quill, an inkpot and an ornate knife with a razor-sharp edge.

It seems my instructions have been followed to the letter.

"These will do perfectly," I say. "I thank you most sincerely for your assistance and forbearance, Good Wife Beasely. Be sure I will be leaving shortly. And I will not be returning."

Kathleen lifts her head and looks directly at me. Her eyes are the colour of the sky, and there is an honesty and integrity within them I have not appreciated until now.

"Do not think harshly of us, Master Hacker," she implores. "Our loyalty will never waiver; you can be sure of that. But we have grown accustomed to the simplicity of our lives and the minimal dangers we are exposed to.

"The events of recent days have reminded us of the sacrifice we will both be required to make, should our true purpose here ever be exposed."

I smile ruefully, understanding the lady's concerns. But, unfortunately, these are the gravest and most dangerous of times.

I reach out and rest my hand on hers, seeking to reassure.

"Fear not," I say. "Your secret is mine alone. Only I and two other people know of your existence. And none of us will compromise you. So be assured, you are safe."

My comforting words appear to work. Kathleen grips my hand momentarily and flashes a smile, which transforms her features. Finally, she bows her head, and then she is on her way, returning downstairs to her wifely duties.

I now have just over four hours to complete the critical part of the plan I have formulated overnight: devising the means to communicate with Rowland.

Lady Lucy Hay, a woman who shares her bed and the secrets of the State with whomever she deems fit, is someone who has not been in my thoughts for a long time.

I made her acquaintance when I was seeking to persuade the princes Rupert and Maurice to accept the English throne and become de facto allies of Parliament.

Over several months, we formed a bond that served

both sides well. During one notable occasion at Banbury Castle, Lady Lucy revealed to me some of the arts and ways of spying, including how she hides secret communiqués from prying eyes.

The conversation was fascinating and illuminating, albeit I never thought for one moment that it would ever come in useful.

Today, however, is when I will put this knowledge to the test. For I intend to send my brother a message of hope that I will conceal in a raw egg, a technique refined by Lady Lucy and frequently used to her profit.

By ten o'clock in the morning, I am ready to begin. I have allowed the three eggs to be soaked in vinegar for the last couple of hours. The effect has been quite startling: the shell has softened significantly without breaking, just as Lady Lucy told me it would.

Holding one of them as delicately as possible, I take the knife and press the blade into the shell. Instantly it yields, and some of the egg white oozes out of the incision. It is through this opening I will insert a message for Rowland.

I put the egg down gently on the tray and reach for the paper. I will only need a small amount of velum to write my instructions, which will be brief and to the point.

As I extend my hand, my cuff clips the tray, sending the contents crashing loudly to the floor. The commotion forces Kathleen to call upstairs to enquire whether I am in difficulty. I quickly reassure her I am fine and then set about the business of recovering the eggs and the tools that will serve me this day.

I look to the floor and see the crushed shells of at

least two of the eggs. I groan aloud and hit the table with my fist. It would seem my clumsiness has jinxed the whole venture. I get down on my knees in the confined space and look closer. There is little light, the room cast in near-permanent semi-darkness.

After a few seconds, I find the third egg. It is undamaged, having rolled away and nestling under a nearby table. I examine it quickly, seeking signs of breakage. But I am in luck as it appears to be undamaged and in near-perfect condition.

Once again, I take the knife in my right hand and hold it against the bright white shell. It's time to try again, all the while being acutely aware I don't have a second chance. I will either succeed or fail.

After a few seconds of the utmost concentration and with sweat pouring off my forehead, the knife has done its work. A perfect aperture has been cut into the egg's supple shell.

It's now time to insert the message for the eyes of my beloved brother.

As the feather of the quill dances to the tune of a forgettable melody, I drill out the words I formulated in the early hours…

"Forgive me, brother, for any part I may have played in your misfortune. Be assured, I intend to find a way to make good your rescue this evening, at seven o'clock. Remain vigilant and pass on any knowledge you wish to share to the bearer of this message. He will ensure I receive it. Francis."

I have done my best to write the script legibly, but as small as I can, ensuring the width of the communiqué is no bigger than the tip of my little finger, while its overall length will fit snugly into the chamber of the egg. To protect it, I have wrapped the sheaf with another page of vellum.

Only when I am happy with everything do I insert it into the neatly formed cut, applying pressure as carefully and skillfully as I can.

Once the paper is safely inside the shell, I place the egg into the tankard located by the post of my bed. The cold water erases the evidence of my manipulation and interference by closing the slit in the shell almost perfectly. Now, should anyone take an interest in the egg, it will almost be impossible for the naked eye to detect any signs of tampering. It will appear to be nothing more than a simple egg. Or at least that is my hope.

After a few minutes, and with my self-doubts intensifying, I start to have concerns about the validity and sense of the whole exercise.

I stand and walk over to the table, where I pick up the egg and take it to a candle that is flickering wildly as the draught from the door breathes life into its golden flame. I check it thoroughly once again for any apparent signs of trauma. To my utter amazement, I can find none.

By three o'clock in the afternoon, I have made myself scarce from Ironmonger Lane and the home of the Beaselys. I am now waiting for the first sight of the man who fits the description of Ambrose Crump.

I am standing on the pavement opposite The Saracen's Head Inn, located in Newark's bustling Market Place, when a bald-headed man of a score and ten years, and wearing the distinctive uniform of a gaoler, staggers out of the hostelry and takes off in the direction of the castle. I allow him to get a start on me before setting off in pursuit, all the while doing my best to use the shop fronts and houses to safeguard the anonymity I crave.

As we walk up the deserted Kirk Gate, and the spire of the church of Saint Mary Magdalene casts its dark shadow across the thoroughfare, it is time to make my move.

"Master Crump," I call as discreetly as I can while crossing the street. "Master Crump, I have some urgent business I need to discuss with you."

The gaoler stops suddenly as he hears my cries. He looks startled. His hand moves quickly to his side. There is no sword, but as I get closer, I detect a small dagger tucked into a pocket close to my quarry's midriff.

"Who are you? How do you know me?" asks an alarmed Crump, drawing the knife and running his left forefinger down its razor-sharp blade.

"Do not be alarmed," I say as soothingly as I can. "A mutual friend has given me your name and suggested you may be willing to provide an important service if the price is right?"

Crump's face stays stony, but I detect a flash of interest in his eyes.

"Before you say any more, is there anything our friend told you to say to me to confirm he sent you my way?" enquires the gaoler. "You could simply be seeking to entrap a loyal King's man. So be on your way, sir, unless you can give me the reassurance I need."

I have no way of knowing whether Goodyeare's information is accurate or merely words designed to bring an end to the suffering I had been inflicting on him. But I have no option; I am being put to the test.

"My friend told me you are a man of words," I say as boldly as I can. "And he says Chaucer's great Tales of Canterbury is a favourite book of yours, particularly the verse "If gold rusts, what then can iron do?"

Crump stands still for a moment, processing what he has just heard.

A minute passes. Suddenly the bells of the church ring out, calling believers to its early evening service. When the world is gripped in war, the need for the Lord is as great as ever. I look at my pocket watch: it is now three-thirty in the afternoon.

"Follow me," barks Crump as he tucks the knife away. "Edmund Goodyeare is a man I trust. If he has sent you, I will be happy to listen to what you have to say."

We walk to the church graveyard, from where I can see the towering walls of the castle. Earth has been disturbed in many places, such is the number of people who have been claimed by a resurgence in Typhus and the plague. The diseases have infected Newark ever since the garrison expanded to its current size.

There will be many more to bury in this hallowed place before this bloody and senseless conflict is ended.

Crump knows where he is going. He leads me along a well-trodden path to a burial mound in the far corner. It is set away from the rest. And it is a place that clearly has some meaning to him.

"This is where my wife has been laid to rest," he explains. "She was taken from me in the summer by the plague. It was merciless, ravaging her fine features and reducing her to a shell of a woman in just a few days.

"She was the dearest of wives. I miss her terribly."

I nod sympathetically. Whatever I feel about Crump, I understand pain when I see it. And this man is suffering.

"I am sorry for your loss," I say. "Fate can be a cruel princess. I know it to be so. But I am afraid I must talk to you about business, for I am told you may be able to get a message to a man held prisoner in the castle. Is this so?"

The gaoler looks at me appraisingly before speaking. Then, after seemingly deciding he can trust me, he says: "That would most certainly be possible, but it is a danger-ous task, even for me. If I were to be caught, I would be in serious trouble. It is likely I would be hanged. However, suppose you are willing to pay a generous price. In that case, I am open to being persuaded the opportunity out-weighs the risk."

Speaking like the experienced negotiator he is, Crump waits for his words to sink in. When they have, he gestures with his hand, making it clear he is awaiting my answer.

"I can pay you five Laurels, not a shilling more," I state. "In return, I need to get a message to a prisoner who means a lot to me and who needs to know he is not alone in this world. Nothing more. Can you do that?"

My would-be accomplice laughs aloud. I have clear-ly humoured him.

"Anything is possible, my dear sir," he responds. "But my fee is double what you are offering. So, I am at your service for ten Laurels, as would be the new governor, if he had the opportunity. If you offer anything less, I will be bidding you a good day."

I am momentarily stunned. I wasn't expecting Crump to demand such a large sum.

"Whatever message you wish to pass on, it must be

important," he continues. "So show me your money; ten Laurels, nothing less. Prove you can pay."

It seems I have no choice. I must concede with no ability to get the terms I am seeking and time of the essence. I wait a few minutes for a couple to pass. They walk through the church grounds and look at Crump and me as we seek to be as inconspicuous as possible. When they are out of sight, I reach for my purse. It is kept close to my own dagger, on the opposite side of my body, where my scabbard is belted into place.

Crump edges forward when he sees the bulging bag, the metallic clink of coinage drawing his attention. He leans forward, eager to see my true worth.

"Back off," I bark. "Stand your ground, and I will show you the money I have promised for this endeavour. Come another inch forward, and you will find my sword at your throat."

My warning has the desired effect. Crump keeps his distance. I quickly withdraw ten large coins. They are heavy, made of gold and emblazoned with the portrait of Charles, the tyrant King.

"These are yours if you do my bidding," I confirm. "I will give you three of them as an advance; the remaining seven will be yours when you return and tell me all you have learned. Agreed?"

The gaoler looks disappointed.

"I was hoping you might be a little more generous, considering the risks involved," he protests, testing my resolve. "What say you we make this an equal division: five gold coins now, five when we meet again?"

I think about the proposition and quickly decide it is not to my advantage.

"That is out of the question, Master Crump," I say with as much gravitas and authority as I can muster. "You have my terms; it's three or nothing. You decide."

Crump's greedy hand, a rich tapestry of tattoos and tobacco stains, reaches out and takes the first instalment. It is the equivalent of three months' pay. Once he has pocketed the gold, he extends his feral paw again.

"Shake it," he commands. "I want your word you will not go back on our agreement."

I am getting tired of the ridiculous game we are playing. Nonetheless, I do as Crump asks, gripping his sweaty, weak hand. Eventually, he is satisfied.

"So who do you wish me to speak to on your behalf?" enquires Crump nonchalantly.

We have been rooted to the same spot in the graveyard for almost fifteen minutes while the drama has been played out. More and more people are walking through the thoroughfare that runs alongside the church. I decide it is time to move on.

As I walk, Crump moves alongside me.

"I want you to get something into the hands of Captain Rowland Hacker, who I believe is languishing in one of your cells," I tell my accomplice. "I then want you to relay to me exactly what he says to you. That should be easy enough, even for a man like you."

Crump starts to cough; it is as though he has been taken by surprise and punched in the stomach.

"My God, are you insane man," he splutters when he recovers his poise. "It can't be done. Rowland Hacker is being guarded around the clock. He is sure to die. They suspect him of betraying the King and undermining the garrison for two years or more. If I am caught passing him messages, I am done for."

I stop abruptly and turn to face Crump. My expression is as dark as the night will soon be. I see the fear on the man's face; his cockiness has deserted him.

"You have accepted payment from me," I say. " A contract has been entered into. If you want to live, you will not dare break it."

Reaching into my pocket, I pull out the hen's egg, which I have wrapped in paper and protective towelling. All my hopes depend on this Trojan Horse doing its job.

"Make sure you give the good Captain this egg," I instruct, handing the small parcel to Crump. He looks at it warily before securing it in a small box that is quickly secreted in an inner pocket in his stained jerkin.

"It doesn't matter how you achieve the task I have set you. Do it, you must. Tell Rowland to break the egg gently, for there is more than a good yolk inside the shell that will be of interest to him. And make sure you remember everything he tells you. So much depends on it."

For the next five hours, I amuse myself in the taverns of Newark, never staying too long in one place to arouse suspicion but long enough to pick up important pieces of intelligence.

After spending the best part of an hour in The Angel, located in Mill Gate, I make my way back to the centre of the town and the popular White Hart Inn. Here I mix with cavaliers and locals alike, as the hostelry is one of the places where Royalist army's officers have taken up lodgings.

On my travels, I hear Rowland's name mentioned frequently. It is no secret he has been arrested. However, the apparent reasons for his incarceration are as wild as they are misinformed and highly speculative. I have heard the gossip-mongers cite murder and theft several times and everything in between. If only they knew the truth!

By the time I reach The Ram, I have less than thirty minutes to wait for Crump. I have agreed to meet him in the dilapidated coaching inn, conveniently situated in Castle Gate and just a short walk from the misery of the dungeons he polices for governor Willis.

Apart from a couple of drunkards propping up the ramshackle bar, the inn appears to be deserted, which means it is perfect for my purposes.

I order a tankard of foul-smelling ale, giving the appreciative innkeeper a penny and a smile for her troubles.

After exchanging the briefest of pleasantries with her, I seek out a convenient spot at the rear of the hostelry. Here I will pass the time and keep a watchful eye on the entrance.

At precisely eight-thirty, the unkempt figure of Crump walks in. He is clearly nervous. By the time he has stumbled from the entrance to where I am sitting, he has looked over his shoulder at least three times.

"Has it been a tough day?" I ask mischievously. "I hope you have been able to fulfil your part of our arrangement?"

Before Crump has time to answer, the woman behind the bar appears at the side of the table we are sitting at. She is keen to ply us with beer and fatten our bellies.

"Will your friend be joining you in having a drink, sir?" she enquires. "I can recommend the eel pie and the rabbit stew if either of you are hungry?"

Trying to conceal my impatience, I order two plates of the eel concoction, a dish Isabel introduced me to several years ago. It is one of my favourites. I also buy a tankard of ale for Crump. It is a necessary expense, as I need to loosen his tongue and glean every bit of information my ten Laurels will buy.

"Are you sure you are not exaggerating?" I ask Crump when he has finished telling me all he knows.

"I swear on the life of my late wife and on everything holy, Captain Hacker," he retorts. "Your brother does not wish you to rescue him. He told me to tell you such and that he considers any bid to secrete him away to be unnecessary. He believes it will put everything you have both been working towards at risk.

"He urged me to seek your earliest return to Stathern. He is confident he will convince the governor of his loyalty and believes the grievous injury he has already suffered has planted doubts in the minds of his interrogators.

"He will soon be a free man again, of that he is sure. But he is adamant he does not want you to stay in Newark any longer than you have to. He wants you gone by midnight and asked me to impress that upon you most urgently."

While the news is better than I anticipated, one aspect of Crump's tidings has left me reeling.

His casual reference to Rowland experiencing a severe injury is the first I have heard about it. It leaves me feeling nauseous, angry and deeply concerned.

Crump goes on to explain my brother has lost his

right hand. It was cut off by Holck and one of his Bohemians when the questioning was at its most savage and Rowland at his least cooperative.

"It happened four days yonder," adds Crump, who shows no signs of merriment at my obvious distress, now he has discovered who I am. "Your brother lost quite a bit of blood, sir. He is weakened by his injury, and his spirits are at a low ebb. Still, he also believes he has paid the fullest of prices and will be allowed to regain his liberty in due course.

"He is adamant there is no evidence that can be used against him, and he will be a free man again before the end of February. They were his exact words.

"He told me the surgeon has made good his stump, at least as well as can be expected, and you are to worry no more. He vows to get in touch when it is safe to do so."

I look away into the gloom, unable to control my wayward emotions. Sorrow is stalking me this night.

I stay silent for a long time, thinking things through and regretting everything that has happened that has put my family and friends in such peril.

As I mull over my thoughts, Crump watches me keenly, waiting to press his claim for the payment he has been promised. It doesn't take long for the opportunity to arise.

"It is getting late, Captain Hacker, time for you to be on your way and for me to return home," he says, his voice snapping me out of my light-headedness. "I have kept my side of the bargain, putting myself at considerable risk on your behalf. Will you now settle what is owed?"

From the moment I first saw Crump, I didn't like

him. I perceived him to be nothing more than a profiteer, exploiting the misery of others, and this he has certainly proven to be. But I find myself having a begrudging respect for this uncouth and violent urchin, a man who walks with a pronounced limp and shares a table with me. He is clearly terrified at the prospect of being found to have taken a bribe from a notorious rebel. And so he should be.

I know many men who would have turned me in by now in return for a pardon, the desire for life greater than their promises. Yet Crump hasn't done so. Instead, he has stayed true to his word. These days that is a rarity.

The gaoler is an avowed enemy, someone I should feel bitterness and anger towards. But I don't. I feel nothing more than a sense of gratitude, even though the information I now possess has been bought for a high price. So I fish out my purse and lay seven more Laurels on the table. Even in the gloom of the dimly lit inn, the brightness of the gold lights up the room.

"These are yours," I say. "A fair day's pay for an honest day's work. I thank you most graciously, Ambrose, for all you have done. It is a shame we are on opposing sides in this barbarous conflict. But I am reassured you will be keeping a watchful eye on Rowland.

"Should anything change, and my brother is not released, make sure you send word to me as quickly as you can. My home can be easily found, and you will find me most generous."

When there is clearly nothing more to say, I reach out and grip Clump's limp and damp fingers once again, unintentionally half crushing them. He winces, stutters a couple of inadequate sentences, confirming he will do as I request, then Crump is gone. I watch him leave. He is as nervous as he was when he first arrived.

My tankard is empty, so I reach for my pocket watch. I can just make out the Roman numerals on the ornate dial. It is almost eleven o'clock. It is time to leave this cursed place and start grieving for the dear friend I have lost.

SIXTEEN

KIRBY BELLARS IS A HAMLET some three miles from Melton Mowbray. It comprises a few houses, a church with a towering spire, an inn – and the manor house of a notorious Royalist, where fifty-five Parliamentarian soldiers are now garrisoned.

Following Lord Grey's instructions, I arrive at my new outpost on Wednesday, the first day of February. Whereas most properties house impoverished families, the manor is set in a large country estate, comprising almost two thousand acres of fertile farming land. It was acquired by the unpopular Erasmus de la Fontaine more than forty years ago, long before the King and his people had cause to engage in a bitter and bloody struggle for freedom.

If we were not involved in such conflict, it would indeed be a pleasure to pass my time in these comfortable surroundings, which, before the reformation years, were home to twelve Augustinian Canons and a portly Prior.

It was among the first priories in England to face King Henry's anger. It was sold off to the highest bidder, eventually ending up in the hands of the acquisitive de la Fontaine, whose first act was to clear thirteen families from his new lands, consigning them to destitution and poverty. Locals still talk of his malign presence and are grateful he has long fled these parts. If he had remained, there might have been long-overdue retribution for many of the injustices suffered by locals at his hands.

I learn all of this, and much more, as I take in my new surroundings, a place where I am determined I will not become an idler, regardless of the distance his Lordship seeks to put between me and the nub of the action.

I start my assignment, as all officers should, by learning as much as I can about my comrades and the challenges they face, and within a couple of hours, there is no more to uncover. I seem to know it all.

What I learn in that short amount of time reflects well on Stathern and less so on my new Company, for the men of Kirby Bellars are poorly trained, lack adequate weaponry, are angry because they haven't been paid for months – and have seemingly lost the desire to fight.

I realise I have a job on my hands if I am to get them cut into half-decent fighting men before the war reignites, which it soon will, as sure as night follows day.

It is little wonder Lord Grey has consigned me to this place. While here, I am a threat to nobody.

To be away from my home and family arouses a mixed web of raw emotion. It is a wrench to be parted from Isabel and the children, but Abijah's death, and the seriousness of Rowland's situation, of which I have learned no more, cast a dark shadow over Stathern for three long days after my return from Newark. My wife was inconsolable when I broke the news to her, and she wept for a full day. She said some harsh words to me in her anger, many of them biting deeper than a musket ball. The pain was all the harder to bear because I know much of what she said, as her grief for the passing of our dear friend poured out, was true. Even so, it will take time for the wounds to heal.

The children have been spared. Isabel will tell them long before the tongues of the gossips and estate workers reach their ears, but not before. And when they hear the news, they too will be distraught.

Abijah was like a brother to me – and a favourite uncle to them.

We had been the best of friends since childhood. I trusted him with my life. He was also a loyal friend to my good lady, helping her manage the estate when I was absent and talking to her about things I was incapable of reconciling. The deaths of Barbara and Isable are an episode that scarred us both, and Abijah played a significant part in helping us both come to terms with their tragic loss.

Over the years, there have been many other things that have seen him play an important role in our lives, all the time being understated, reassuring and giving his all.

I am now aware of the enormous hole his passing leaves in my life and that of Isabel. Yet, strangely, it is only in death, when nothing can be done or said, that the extent of loss hits home the hardest.

I felt nothing like this when my father departed this world a few weeks ago. Then, of course, there was remorse, some guilt too. But nothing like the aching pain and deep regret that now grips my heart, squeezing it so tightly it feels ready to burst. I have taken so much for granted. And now Abijah is no longer standing next to me or able to guard Isabel and my family. I don't know how I will cope. But find a way, I must.

I am forced to banish my thoughts when a sharp rap at my door interrupts my self-pity and brings me back to reality.

"Captain, I have important news for you," says Clement Needham, a fresh-faced and eager-to-please young Cornet. "A messenger is waiting for you downstairs. He refuses to give his name, but he is adamant you know him and will want to speak to him."

I stare at the junior officer, taking in what he has said while tapping my desk impatiently.

"Is that it?" I enquire brusquely. "You come to me, Master Needham, with not even the vaguest hint of what this man has to discuss, only a diktat. And you expect me to drop everything and follow you?

"Cornet Needham, this really isn't good enough."

Although deeply embarrassed, my subordinate stands his ground.

"Captain Hacker, I asked the man to state his business, and he refused outright to say anything to me other than he was here to discuss an urgent matter with you," responds an unyielding Needham. "I tried my best, sir."

I wave my hand irritably, indicating I will attend to the visitor.

"Tell him I am on my way," I say. "And be sure to mention I don't tolerate time-wasters."

My anger turns to delight when I recognise the man waiting for me at the manor house entrance is Hugh Walker,

Cromwell's trusted messenger. He stands and smiles as he watches me descend the ornate stairs.

"I apologise for not revealing my name and intentions to your officer," he says when he can do so unobserved. "I thought it best to be discreet. I hope my furtiveness has not caused you any difficulties, Captain?"

I laugh aloud, the first time I have done so in days.

"Hugh, you are a welcome surprise," I say. "It is good to see you. I trust all is well with you and the Lieutenant-General?"

Before he has time to answer, I beckon young Walker to follow me back up the stairs to the large room that is my quarters for the foreseeable future. We don't say anything else until I have closed the heavy, oak-panelled door behind me and offered my guest a glass of half-decent port, which he gratefully accepts.

"I cannot be sure of the men I command," I explain. "I arrived here yesterday, and I only know a few of their names. So far, I have been unimpressed by what I have seen. Therefore, we should talk privately, for Lord Grey has put me in this place for a reason. It would not surprise me to discover he has spies in this place, reporting everything I do, and everyone who visits me, to Bradgate House."

Walker nods. He has seen enough of the war and the factions at odds with each other to know discretion is an essential commodity.

"It is best to be wary," he agrees. "For what it is worth, I think it is a very sensible precaution. Is there anything you wish me to report on the matter to the Lieutenant-General?"

I think for a moment before shaking my head. I

would like to say much about the conduct of Lord Grey, but Cromwell does not need to know of my petty squabbles with my commander. Not yet.

"Considering everything Cromwell and I agreed the last time we met at Stathern, something must have happened that I need to know about," I say to Walker after the port has ignited a warm fire in the pits of our bellies. "So what is it? Tell me plainly, Hugh."

The messenger reaches into his bag and reveals a sealed letter, written in Oliver's own, very distinctive hand and addressed simply to "FH". The sender's bold, red wax seal leaves the recipient in no doubt about the originator's identity.

"He was adamant I hand this to you in person," reveals Walker. "And he urged me to impress on you the importance of its content. Then, when you have digested everything, the Lieutenant-General would appreciate it if you burned the letter. He doesn't want anyone other than you reading it."

I am intrigued.

"Of course, Hugh, you have my word," I confirm. "Please, retire to the scullery and find yourself some food and refreshment. One of the soldiers on guard will assist you. I will make myself available in due course."

As the stairs creak once again as they bear the weight of Hugh taking his leave of me, I turn my attention to the matter at hand. I haven't heard from Cromwell for several weeks. For him to have gone to such obvious trouble means something is urgent and needs attending to.

I reach for my knife and open the seal. Within moments, I am reading the contents of the brief dispatch.

"My dear Francis.

"I trust you are well and settled at your new posting, news of which I only learned of a few days ago?

"I would be grateful if you would ride forthwith to Northampton. My men and I will be in the town for two nights, and I need to apprise you of an urgent matter that has come to my attention in recent days that has left me much vexed.

"Be sure to tell nobody of your intentions.

"Hugh will act as your escort. Please come immediately. It is of the utmost importance that I see you as soon as possible.

"Your loving brother in Christ, Oliver Cromwell."

I put the letter down and draw a deep breath. Oliver is worried, and if he is prepared to express his concerns so openly, then there is indeed a problem to deal with.

As the crow flies, the town of Northampton, which has remained fiercely loyal to Parliament since the outbreak of hostilities, is a little under forty miles away.

Close by is the village of Great Houghton.

It is a small place, of no great note; near enough to be afforded the protection of the town's garrison and far enough away to be rid of the eavesdroppers whose prying and mischief is the prime source of much rumour-mongering and misinformation.

Situated in this place is an impressive inn, The Cherry Tree. Its ales, fine stews and discretion commend it to visitors and locals alike. It is to here Hugh and I travel on Thursday, the second day of February. A thick layer of ice-encrusted snow greets us on many of the roads we ride along, emphasising just how cold the winter months are.

Yet, despite the frostbite attacking my fingers and outer bodily extremities, it feels good to be free of the claustrophobic manor house, and the bitterness within that has started to consume me.

Hugh races ahead on his glistening Chestnut mare, making good speed. I canter alongside him, chatting occasionally and enjoying the power and grace of Bucephalus as his long legs eat up the lush fields of Leicestershire and Northamptonshire.

By four o'clock in the afternoon, almost three hours after I left the Kirby Bellars garrison in the custody of young Needham, and with sweat streaming off the flanks of both horses, Hugh and I arrive at the inn.

The surrounding fields are full of tents and soldiers. It would seem the mighty Ironsides are in attendance. Several cheerful guards guide us to our destination with their braziers aglow and cooking pots filled to the brim.

At the doorway of the hostelry stands a familiar figure. He is waving, anticipating our reunion. It is Cromwell, and it is time to discover his intentions.

"As God is my witness, you have had a rare old time of it, Francis," says Oliver, as he paces across the wooden boards of the inn's main room. "Abijah was the bravest of men. You could not have wished for a better deputy and friend. He deserved a more befitting end than the hangman's noose. May he know the peace of our Heavenly Father.

"And the betrayal of Rowland and your position with Lord Grey being undermined so grievously? A bad odour accompanies these, too. I fear something is not right here.

"It's time we investigated these matters thoroughly.

And I must also tell you about some intrigues I have stumbled across myself, so we can start piecing together this tapestry of events that seem to be unconnected yet, in reality, I suspect are more interlinked than we dare imagine."

Cromwell and I swap pleasantries for more than two hours, which is a considerable time for the Lieutenant-General to tolerate small-talk for anyone, not least a subordinate. But that is precisely what happens, and I am grateful to him for the courtesy, respect and friendship he shows me this day.

By the time he is ready to get down to business, I am prepared for whatever is to come.

"What say you if I told you my men have captured two couriers in recent weeks, riding southwards to London. Both men were carrying coded messages to a known Royalist spy?" enquires Oliver, with controlled anger in his voice.

"In their satchels were found the colours and insignias of the Earl of Manchester. The messages they were attempting to secrete into London referred to 'the event', which, it would seem, is due to be carried out just before the Ordinance confirming the creation of the New Model Army is ratified.

"When questioned about the treasonous contents of the dispatches they were carrying, both couriers told my men they had been sent by a senior Eastern Association officer. The man they named was brought to their cells, where he identified himself. Yet neither man recognised him. His name and status were the same, but he was unknown to them both.

"During their interrogations, both claimed to have

been handed their satchels by this man who bore the Earl's colours. And I believe them: I am sure the man did exactly as they said. But he was not acting with the Earl's authority, of that I am sure.

"This leads me to one conclusion, my dear Francis. The man who did this is an imposter prepared to risk his own life to create a powerful and convincing illusion."

Cromwell lets his words sink in before continuing.

"As you know, there are many things the Earl and I disagree on, not least the way the army is run by men like him. But he is no traitor. In my heart, I know this to be so. In his own way, he is as loyal to Parliament as I am. He just believes the passage to victory can be achieved differently to the way I advocate.

"Nonetheless, I have no hesitation in vouching for his honour. Manchester is no John Hotham, I am sure of it. And, if I am right, then it beggars the question, why is somebody, or some persons unknown, trying to lead us a merry dance?"

Suddenly, Oliver stops speaking and looks directly at me. Known for his quickness of wit, Cromwell is capable of talking and thinking at a phenomenal pace. He has a lawyer's mind, which is a throwback to his days at Cambridge, and he is one of the most demanding people I have ever met.

"Francis, are you alright?" he barks, sensing my growing unease. "You look as though you have seen a ghost. Talk to me. Tell me, have you been listening and following all I have said?"

For the last few minutes, I have heard everything Cromwell has uttered, but I also recall many of the things Rowland has told me in recent months – particularly the conversation he overheard in Newark some weeks ago between Holck and Willis. On that occasion, the two King's men openly discussed their plans to collude with a Parliamentarian officer. His name is the same as that cited by Cromwell: Peter Worthington. I tell Oliver of this, and he lets out a loud and rare curse.

"I knew it, Francis," he bellows. "Those scoundrels are up to no good. I can always detect when the biggest of turds is emitting the foulest of smells. And right now, the stink from this particular cesspit is threatening to overcome us both.

"My friend, I think the time has come for you to tell me all you know. Leave nothing unsaid. Much will depend on what you tell me and what we do now."

So I reveal all I know: my suspicions, the intelligence I have been collating secretly for several months, and what I have discovered in recent days from the mouths of Edmund Goodyeare and Ambrose Crump. I leave nothing unsaid.

By nine o'clock in the evening, Cromwell and I have dissected every last morsel of information and cross-referenced every bit of knowledge we jointly possess. Or so I believe. There has been a lot to digest.

"See, my friend, what a long way we have come in such a short space of time?" says Oliver, pleased with the progress we have seemingly made. "So many little things, on their own, appear innocuous and don't add up, yet piece them together, like we have done this day, and they form quite a remarkable and disturbing picture."

I am exhausted, unable to stay focused.

"The mistake on the part of the enemy has been to

be too obvious in trying to steer Parliament down a certain road," continues the Lieutenant-General, speaking more to himself than me. "Out-thinking your enemy is the key. It always is, particularly when you are engaged in a grisly, heinous war. You are trying to manipulate different factions, so they do the dirty work for you.

"I am not saying, for one minute, the Earl of Manchester is not plotting against me. Of course, he is. I know it as much as the next man. It's just I believe him to be conspiring against me politically. He wishes to eliminate me as opposition, that is all. He certainly has no desire to see me dead, for he is a fair-minded, God-fearing man.

"What advantage is there to him if I were to die? In reality, rather than positively affect his position, I suspect it would be quite the reverse. Fingers would be pointed in his direction. He would be the man the back-stabbers and gossipers would target and accuse. Life would become intolerable for him."

Cromwell's rapier-like eyes flash in my direction. I indicate I am keeping in step, and I concur.

"No. Francis, I fear we need to look more deeply into this matter," he continues. "I am in no doubt whatsoever, a conspiracy is being played out, and we are its unwilling participants. Yet to find the man's identity, or men, who are betraying us and engaging in this unholy alliance, we need to ask the question: who stands to gain the most from my downfall?

"When we have the answer, that's when we will have found our conspirators."

Oliver and I continue to talk animatedly for another hour, making detailed preparations. Finally, when we are done for the day, satisfied we have covered as much as possible, there is a loud rap on the door.

A young man I recognise enters the room. It is Guy Goodman, one of the most recent batches of new recruits at Stathern.

Putting his glass of claret down on the table, Oliver gets up and strides over to the visitor, who seems slightly overawed by his surroundings.

The candlelight gives Oliver an ethereal glow, exaggerating the power and confidence that emanates from his energetic body. It is little wonder Goodman is intimidated. I am too.

"I understand you and young Guy are already acquainted," states Cromwell, with a mischievous and knowing grin chiselled onto his face as he slaps the youngster on the shoulders.

"Come forward, lad," the Lieutenant-General calls to the newcomer. "Join us."

When Guy is standing by the large table, Cromwell pours him a goblet of wine and adds: "This remarkable young man has agreed to be my eyes and ears in Stathern while you are occupied elsewhere, Francis. He will also be a bodyguard for Isabel and the children, not that I expect them to experience any difficulties. But I want you to feel as secure as you can."

I say nothing. I don't need to; my surprise is clearly evident.

"Guy's father is a distant cousin of mine," explains Cromwell in a matter-of-fact way. "And when I heard he was contemplating joining the cause, I had a little word in his ear. Although young, Guy is loyal to me and will help both of us as we continue to combat the forces pitted against Parliament, including some of the men deemed to be our brothers in arms.

"I will receive weekly intelligence reports from Guy, and he will keep a watchful eye on the locality. Things seem to be hotting up all around us, and we don't want to get caught with our trousers down, do we? When you return home, he will report directly to you. But, for the foreseeable future, only the three of us must know about this arrangement."

I nod in agreement as I examine young Goodman for the first time since I saw him handle the surprise visit of Oswald Honeyman, my brother's personal attendant. He impressed me that day with his maturity and authority, as he is doing again right now.

"Just keep them safe," I say to him quietly. "I will ask nothing more of you than that one simple thing."

I awake the following morning to the delicious smell of smoked kippers. Cromwell is renowned for starting the day early with a lively reading of the Good Book and a hearty breakfast. I glance at my pocket watch. As the cloak of nightfall lingers as long as it can, I can just make out the time: it is six-thirty.

I rise from my mattress and push open the shutters. Shards of grey light illuminate the small room. As my eyes refocus, I see hundreds of the Eastern Association's finest men going about their business in the fields behind the inn.

For as far as I can see, the long grasses of Great Houghton appear to be in the grip of yet another winter's morn frost. Icicles hang from several large trees, fires crackle, cauldrons bubble away, and steam fills the air as an army gets to work.

Then I hear a melodious sound rising, and it gets louder. As it does, I can feel a smile erupting across my face as the Ironsides, men known for their piety and commitment to Christ, sing psalms and praise God as loudly as their larynxes will allow them. It is a sight to behold.

"Good morning, Francis," cries Oliver as I make my way into the large hall. "Is it not a joy to be alive? There is smoked fish for breakfast or some eel pie, if you prefer? Come. Join me. Let us give thanks to the Lord and eat."

Oliver's ebullient welcome catches me unprepared. Only hours before, we were both in a sombre mood, discussing death and the damning and damaging consequences of betrayal. The conversation left me subdued.

"I sense some confusion, Francis?" probes my host. "Does my enthusiastic disposition unsettle you?"

I let out a chuckle, and then another. My laughter becomes infectious, and soon a belly laugh has been forced out of the Lieutenant-General. Then another.

"We must live every day, my friend; that is what the Good Lord has taught me," he says jovially after we have settled ourselves. "But just because you see me laughing and smiling does not mean I am not suffering the deepest of torments.

"You have seen me at my lowest point. At Marston Moor, you witnessed my reaction to the death of Valentine, my nephew, and then my outpouring of grief when the news of young Oliver's demise reached me. Not many men have seen me brought so low. And not many will ever do so again, not if I can help it.

"You, too, have been tormented while in my company, not least when you lost your dear girls. These mutually shared experiences have created a bond between you and me, Francis, that is hard to ignore. Our rank is immaterial. As men, we have seen each other come as close to despair and destruction as any mortal can get.

"We helped each other overcome some desperate situations. Today, I know you as a brother in Christ. My equal. Whatever else that affords, it also means I trust you.

"So trust me when I encourage you to smile and live a little. How we start the day influences how we finish it. Enjoy the good food and, as you do so, allow me to bask in your company."

By eleven o'clock, it is time for me to return to my Militia duties at Kirby Bellars. I have spent the morning agreeing a plan with Oliver, one we both believe can end this unfolding drama satisfactorily. But, alas, there are no guarantees. All we can do is try our best.

As we shake hands and say our farewells, I realise this may be the last time I will see Cromwell alive, should matters take a turn for the worse. The prospect of such an eventuality shocks my senses, and I am unable to conceal it.

"I know what you are thinking," he says perceptively as he hands me a letter I am to give to Lord Grey. "I am also having those very same thoughts and anxieties. Who wouldn't? There is much still to uncover and many things that may not go our way.

"But stay faithful, Francis, and draw your encouragement and strength from the father. Put your trust in Him, and all will be well. Of that, I am certain."

I leave Oliver dictating another letter to Sir Thomas

Fairfax, who will shortly take overall command of the New Model Army.

Soon he, and the six companies that have shielded him for the last two nights will make their way to Huntingdon, where they will stay briefly. Then London beckons, and Oliver will remain in the capital for the rest of the month.

The Ordinance decreeing the formation of England's very first professional fighting force is set to be read in Parliament in just over a fortnight. When it is passed, Cromwell will become Fairfax's second-in-command.

For men like me, there is only one man to look to for leadership. But for Cromwell's position to be secure, the Royalist plan must be thwarted and the traitors exposed.

As Bucephalus and I pick our way along the icy roads, plodding our way towards the town of Market Harborough and whatever awaits us beyond, I am acutely aware of how much I must do and how little time there is to achieve it.

Oliver and I now believe the assassins will mount their audacious bid within the next fourteen days. And by the seventeenth day of the month, Cromwell will either be still among the living – or the dead.

SEVENTEEN

SPENDING TIME WITH CROMWELL HAS a cathartic effect: I now feel renewed, refocused and ready for the hardship and danger that lies ahead.

The man is extraordinary, asking nothing of others that he isn't prepared to commit to himself. Generosity, kindness and forgiveness are qualities he possesses in abundance. There is self-sacrifice and humility too, far more than his detractors are willing to give him credit for. To his enemies, he is a merciless religious zealot prepared to crush all opposition in the name of the Lord he serves. Indeed, some Parliamentary factions also perceive Oliver to be this kind of man, particularly those who clash with him on matters of principle. Yet I know it isn't so.

While much of the world sees a different Cromwell to the man I have come to know and trust, I thank God for the life of Oliver, even though I doubt whether the Father is listening to my pleas at the present time. Guided by the Lord, he has achieved great things already, and I sense there is so much more to come.

That's why I will follow him obediently and why I will now do my utmost to protect him during these most important of times.

With less than two weeks to root out the plotters, Cromwell has decreed we are to deal with the weakest link first: a Royalist spy in London who has been under observation for several months.

By any stretch of the imagination, Bulstrode Whitlocke is an unremarkable man at first glance. Balding, overweight, in his latter years, and clearly a writer, not a fighter, the native of Southwark has seemingly led a peaceful existence as a lawyer's clerk at Gray's Inn for as long as anyone can remember.

He has few vices and is regarded as a pious man, albeit he is known to have some Catholic sympathies. That aside, the worst his neighbours can say of him is that he occasionally enjoys the company of a particular woman he has known for several years and drinks some of London's most putrid ales at The Bear at Bridge-Foot and the Bell Sauvage, two well-known inns located close to the great River Thames.

Yet underneath the surface, there is another side to the gentle and unassuming Master Whitlocke, one that is only known to a few: he provides intelligence to Henry Jermyn, one of the King's principal aides and a man reputed to have once held the affections of Queen Henrietta Maria.

Parliamentary agents suspect information has been supplied by Whitlocke to the Royalists since war broke out. The clerk is well placed to pass on information he comes across during his day-to-day duties. Much of it is sensitive and, in the wrong hands, very damaging. We can't be certain of everything we believe to be true. Still, a system seems to be in place between the Master and his servant, one that is well-oiled and tested and delivers up damning barbs that undermine everything Parliament stands for.

According to Cromwell's sources, Whitlocke is working with Willis and Holck to spirit the assassins into London securely and then make good their escape.

As agreed with the Lieutenant-General, my objectives are to ensure he fails, and everything he knows is revealed long before the assassins make their attempt. I am also to find a French mercenary and ensure he is captured alive – and identify Holck, for it appears I am the only man who knows what he looks like.

Cromwell has picked a select group of men from the Eastern Association to take care of everything else.

Before I can travel to London, I must take leave of my new Company at Kirby Bellars.

Cromwell's letter to Lord Grey, dated the third day of February, in the year of our Lord, 1645, gives the commander of the Midlands Association no room to manoeuvre or decline his wishes. To ensure I am prepared for any backlash, he gave me a copy. It reads:

"Dear Lord Grey.

"With immediate effect, the commanders of the New Model Army require the support of Captain Francis Hacker for a period of no less, or greater, than three weeks.

"As you know, the force will not be effective until later this month, once the Ordinance has been formally ratified by Parliament. However, we have a special dis-

*pensation from Parliament to appoint officers for specif-
ic and critical tasks to make ready the new army. A
copy of our Warrant in this regard is enclosed.*

*"We thank you for your gracious support in this
most important of matters and trust it will not inconvenience the affairs of the Midlands Association too
greatly."*

Ordinarily, Cromwell would have simply signed the
communiqué in his own hand. But not on this occasion;
knowing Lord Grey's propensity to raise objections whenever he can, Cromwell has used his heavy wax seal to make
the document as official as it can be.

There can be no mistaking the gravity of the instruction. And, for good measure, the Lieutenant-General has
added a second seal – that of Sir Thomas Fairfax. Grey
would be foolish to do anything other than accede to the
request.

I have twenty-four hours to make my preparations and
begin the long journey to London. Rather than travel
directly to the Kirby Bellars garrison, where I intend to
place Cornet Needham in temporary command, I make a
detour and go to Newtown Linford. From Northampton,
it takes a good two hours to reach the small Leicestershire
village. Upon arrival, I am greeted by a furious Lord Grey,
who is with one of his hounds on the steps of Bradgate
House.

His Lordship is preparing to travel to London to be
present at the Palace of Whitehall to celebrate the founding of the New Model Army when it officially comes into
being. While he may have significant grievances about his
failure to secure a senior post within Fairfax's new force,

Thomas Grey is forever the all-consuming diplomat and politician, a man who rarely allows his mask to slip.

Today proves to be an exception.

"What the hell are you doing here, Hacker," he shouts as I approach. "You have strict orders to remain with your men, not be gallivanting around playing the county gentleman and officer.

"You had better have good reason to be here, man. I am not in the mood to pretend I am pleased to see you. So speak up, and make it quick."

I say nothing, maintaining a neutral expression as long as I can. When I am close enough, I dismount from Bucephalus, reach into my panniers and hand him Cromwell's order.

"This is for you, sir," I say a bit too smugly for my own good. "It is effective immediately."

No sooner has Lord Grey snatched it from me than the seal is ripped open and the contents greedily devoured. Grey's pale face takes on a purple colour within seconds, and his thin lips turn blue. He clearly is not happy to read Oliver's diktat.

"How dare this upstart tell me what I must do," he rages as the note is crushed and thrown at me. "Who in blazes does Cromwell think he is?"

For the next few minutes, a stream of curses and blasphemies come out of the ignoble Lord Grey until his fuse is spent.

"You have crossed me for the last time, Hacker," he hisses breathlessly, realising there is nought he can do to rescind the order. "I see you for what you are, and you had better pray your friend, Cromwell, is going to be able to look after you when this is all over. For I am going to see you regret the day you chose to double-cross me."

I shrug my shoulders. I can say nothing to alter Lord Grey's opinion, so I tip my hat in a sign of farewell. My act of respect is interpreted as defiance, and more shouts and protestations echo around the compact, red-bricked court-yard. With Grey's shrill voice ringing in my ears, I mount Bucephalus once again and lead him away from this wretched place. It is time to regain my focus. I now have much bigger fish to fry.

I smell London long before I can see the sprawling metropolis. Smoke and the stench of life that emanates from the great city combine to form a fog wall a little more than four miles away from the place almost a quarter of a million people eke out a daily living, many of them in abject poverty.

As buildings, monuments and people pass by, excite-ment pulses through my veins, replacing the fatigue, hunger and saddle soreness that not so long ago was dulling my senses.

I attempt to take in my surroundings, but I find it is an impossible task. There is too much to comprehend in this architectural and cosmopolitan wonderland. In the end, after seeing Westminster Abbey in the far distance and using it to get my bearings, I estimate I will arrive in Clerkenwell Green, where my modest lodgings are locat-ed, within the hour.

It has taken a full day and night to travel here. How welcome it will feel to be able to lie down and savour some long-overdue rest.

The White Horse Tavern in Lumbarde Street is bustling

with diners and drinkers alike, all fresh from warming the pews of the many churches that form an imposing part of London's skyline.

It is midday on Sunday, the fifth day of February, and, after sleeping for almost eleven hours, I have walked from my lodgings as I seek to make the acquaintance of Cromwell's most trusted man in the city.

Hercules Sowerby is a lawyer. From his chambers at Lincoln's Inn, he has represented the Lieutenant-General for twenty years or more. He practices the dubious art of commercial law and litigation.

I have heard Oliver refer to Hercules as his friend and confidante on several occasions. I am intrigued to meet him, and I am looking forward to the occasion, albeit I am apprehensive about discussing the whereabouts of plotters and the intricacies of conspiracies so openly.

Cromwell assures me being in such a visible place is the best possible location for such a rendezvous and discussions. With the time being ten minutes to one, I don't have long to wait before I will be able to put a face to a name – and Oliver's theory to the test in the draughty recesses of the inn.

As I take a sip of claret from my glass and start to relax, a dark shadow looms over the table where I am sitting, blocking out what little light there is.

"I presume by your appearance you must be the Captain Hacker I am here to meet?" enquires a refined accent.

I look up. Standing close to the table is a man some twenty-five years, or so, my senior. He is tall, standing well above six feet, broad-shouldered and clean-shaven. He is immaculately dressed. But the most memorable thing about Hercules Sowerby are his eyes; they are the purest blue I have ever seen, and they have the power to penetrate your very soul.

I stand and extend my hand in greeting.

"Master Sowerby, it is a pleasure," I say, shaking my visitor's shovel of a paw as firmly as I am able. "Allow me to pour you a glass of this fine wine. It will help to take the chill out of your bones."

Hercules takes off his cloak and pulls up a chair. Nearby, the fire belches comforting sparks and puffs of smoke. Soon the warmth, and the alcohol, work their magic, and we start to talk.

It is only after a couple of hours have passed, and I begin to process everything that has been said, that I realise Sowerby is a font of knowledge and much more than an average lawman.

"Forgive me for enquiring," I say, "but where did you meet Oliver and how long have you had an association with the man?"

Sowerby laughs for the first time. It is a deep roar that sounds more like it comes from the throat of a lion than a man.

"Now that is a question," he says evasively. "Where do I start?"

My fingers start tapping the table, adding to his discomfort. Ordinarily, I would stay silent and allow my behaviour to be cordial and respectful. But today, I believe Sowerby has a story to tell, and I want to hear it, so my usually impeccable manners are sacrificed.

"We were undergraduates at Cambridge together," he admits eventually. "Oliver and I studied law at Sidney

Sussex College, and we also worked briefly together at Lincoln's Inn, before other distractions closer to home claimed him.

"We have been firm friends since those halcyon days when we both committed ourselves to changing the world.

"In Oliver's case, he has started to make good that pledge. A significant spiritual awakening has helped him in this regard. As for myself, I am afraid I am nothing more than a huge disappointment. The world of tortes and litigation has claimed me, turning me into a pale shadow of the idealistic firebrand I once was."

I suspect Sowerby is jesting with me, but I also believe there is an element of regret in his words, so I press him further.

"Come, Master Sowerby," I say provocatively, "I do not believe your friendship with the Lieutenant-General would have lasted so long if it was as you say. Oliver is a man of vitality, passion and great wit. I am sure you are too?"

Before the last words leave my mouth, I regret what I have said.

No further discussion is forthcoming from the man sitting opposite. He simply sips from his wine glass, studies me and tilts his head occasionally in response to my continued probing.

Sowerby's stoic expression and silence are unnerving, and after five minutes, I can bear it no more.

"Forgive me, Master Sowerby," I say. "I did not mean to pry. I hold Cromwell in very high esteem if the truth is known, and I merely wished to find out more about him. Nothing more. Please accept my apologies if I overstepped the mark."

My assurances seem to do the trick.

"Captain Hacker, we are here to discuss the present, not my past or that of Oliver," says Sowerby. "I would be grateful if we could keep our conversation related to the likes of Bulstrode Whitlocke. You will find me more than happy to talk about him and what he and some of his associates have been up to. And I am willing to do so all evening, if necessary."

I raise my glass and point it in the direction of Sowerby. "Thank you," I say appreciatively, my relief plain to see. "Please tell me all you think I need to know." For several more hours, Hercules Sowerby does precisely that.

It is late on Sunday evening when I return to the house in Clerkenwell Green, where Cromwell has arranged for me to stay for the next two weeks.

The area is up-and-coming, a good two miles away from Whitehall, which is perfect for my purposes. My refuge is comfortable, functional, and rather cold as the hour creeps closer to midnight. Such is the chill; I decide to keep my greatcoat on while I light three candles, close the shutters in the parlour and set about lighting the fire.

It takes twenty long minutes before yellow and blue flames start to consume the beech logs and provide me with enough heat to permit me to disrobe and relax on the hearthside rug.

As I unwind from the rigours of the day, sipping from my goblet and thinking of Isabel, the children and Abijah, I realise I am far more confused than I dare admit.

There is much to mull over after my conversation with Hercules Sowerby, who is as much power-broker as he is a lawyer.

Sowerby has told me a ring of Royalist spies at work in the capital has become increasingly active in recent weeks. Five men and a woman have been identified. All are being closely monitored. There have been no arrests, nor will there be, for the time being.

At least two, Whitlocke and a French mercenary who goes by the name of de la Croix, are known to be working directly with Holck.

Since before the New Year, Whitlocke's communications have been regularly intercepted and decoded before being allowed to reach their ultimate destination of Newark Castle.

A lot of effort has been committed to watching Whitlocke. So far, it has proven to be of nominal value. Until recently, the clerk has also been very easy to track. On more than one occasion during our conversation, Sowerby remarked he was "becoming too easy to follow".

Intriguingly, during the last four weeks, the clerk has changed his routine.

On a Wednesday, Sowerby disclosed he now takes a very different route to his Gray's Inn chambers, going to a smart house in Farringdon before breakfast. The owner, who was unknown to Cromwell's scoutmasters, breeds pigeons. And shortly after Whitlocke has left the premises, the owner has been observed releasing a bird into the sky. This has happened every week since the eleventh day of January.

Unfortunately, despite several attempts, none of the messages have been intercepted. Yet, it is vital we now start to obtain them.

Little is known about the Frenchman, who is reputed to be the bastard of Henry Jermyn. Sowerby is coy about the man but believes he came to England with Queen Henrietta almost two years ago, when she brought arms, money and troops from her brother, the French King, to support her husband's cause. He is reputed to have stayed in England, fighting alongside the princes Rupert and Maurice, when the Queen again fled to her home country in the summer.

After the Queen's flight to France, nothing was heard of de la Croix for several months. After a while, it was generally thought he, too, had somehow crossed the English Channel and returned to his homeland. However, in November, his name surfaced again after he was recognised during a fight at an inn in Cheapside. According to the local Constable, tempers became frayed over a scullery maid's 'honour', a local boatman was stabbed, and de la Croix fled the scene.

Since then, two more sightings have occurred in the Southwark area, but he is as slippery as a Thames eel, and he got clean away on both occasions.

It is de la Croix who intrigues me greatly, far more so than the likes of Whitlocke.

For some inexplicable reason, I feel he could be a key player in everything that is unwinding, albeit my view is based entirely on instinct rather than knowledge, for I have scant information on the man.

As I think over everything I now know and have discussed, my head starts to throb. I have been aware from the outset that I am involved in something I cannot control and have little influence over. But now I realise nothing is as it seems, and I will have to have my wits about me if I am going to stand any chance of fulfilling my duty.

By two o'clock in the morning, I am done. My body and mind are exhausted. I am in desperate need of sleep. As the blackness of the night quickly starts to overwhelm me, a recollection from the past is pulled out of the recesses of my mind. I know not why, but my subconscious thoughts are forcing me to focus on something that happened several months ago, which, at the time, appeared totally innocuous, yet in the context of everything that is happening right now, could be of vital importance.

I reopen my tired eyes and reach for my robe. The red glow from the fire continues to illuminate the room and, as I stand and start moving sluggishly forward, I am able to pick out the path I should take.

Within a few seconds, I am sitting at the table. Two candles have been lit, and I have a quill in my hand. I take a deep breath and attempt to concentrate. It is time to write down everything I remember from that eventful day.

In the morning, when I look at my statement, there is every chance I will consign my incoherent babblings to the fire and curse my imagination for running amok and keeping me awake.

But at this moment, I sense what I witnessed could be material to everything that is happening. Where it fits, I do not know. But I am sure it is one of the keys I need to unlock the door of this unfolding mystery.

My stylus flows freely as I push my hair off my brow. It is time to recall as much as I can about a man I saw briefly when I made a visit to Lord Grey's residence in Leicestershire at the end of August, some five months hence.

EIGHTEEN

FOUR LONG DAYS OF TOIL and agonising frustration pass before the first meaningful breakthrough is achieved.

Cromwell's agents have been scouring the streets of London for the men we believe are actively aiding Holck's assassination attempt. So far, they have found only vagabonds and a couple of cutpurses, who will now face long-overdue justice.

Of Holck and his Bohemians, there is no trace.

Sowerby and I have met on two occasions to review the progress of our enquiries. And both times, our concerns multiplied.

Even though we have little information, what we do know would typically lead to progress of some kind. Somebody would be willing to talk; there would be evidence somewhere. But not in this instance; so far, our quarry has covered its tracks exceptionally well, as all professional killers are expected to do.

Even the owner of the carrier pigeons, who has welcomed Whitlocke every Wednesday in recent weeks, is blissfully unaware of why his services have been retained. All he knows is he has been paid the sum of one pound to look after seven birds, one of which must be released every week, as soon as he receives the specific one-word communiqué Whitlocke brings to his home.

If we have no luck in the next forty-eight hours, Hercules and I will be forced to tell Oliver that we are failing him. After everything we have invested in this enterprise, the prospect of making such an admission is something neither of us is looking forward to.

It is Friday, the tenth day of February, and Whitlocke is known to frequent The Mitre Tavern in Hatton Garden at the end of every week. The inn is a short walk from his chambers at Gray's Inn. Recently he has been observed arriving at this dank hole in the early evening and spending the rest of the night with like-minded sympathisers of the King.

With time passing by at an alarming rate, I decide to seek out our quarry first hand rather than rely on the information contained in the increasingly desperate reports of other men. So after a late lunch at the Adam and Eve Tea Gardens in Tottenham Court Road, I enjoy a thoughtful mile and a half walk to Holborn, and I nestle myself away in the corner of the Mitre, hiding in the shadows from inquisitive eyes while ensuring I am close enough to see everyone who comes and goes.

Crucially, where I have chosen to sit also enables me to hear almost every word uttered in the room. What I learn is quite revealing. Tradesmen and workers from the eastern side of the city appear to be regulars, talking to each other freely as if they know one another for an age.

Everyone has a view on the progress of the war, and several men, those that should know better, are openly discussing where they intend to go whoring in a few hours.

From my vantage point, having stopped listening to the gossipers, I observe jewellers, butchers from Smithfield and a smattering of well-dressed individuals, who look as though most of their waking hours are spent toying with litigious contractual disputes and points of law. All appear to be enjoying a traditional English ale, the type brewed in London for almost a century, rather than the new Dutch, hops-flavoured alternative now finding favour with so many.

There isn't much that I like about his place, but I do find myself approving of the regulars' choice of drink.

With time to kill, I read the latest edition of Mercurius Civicus, which I bought yesterday for a penny. Then, when I have digested all it has to offer, I turn to my bible, for I am sorely in need of the healing and restorative powers of scripture.

Many times these past days, I have found myself dwelling on my actions in Coddington, where I rejoiced at Goodyeare's torment and demise.

I felt the Lord's ire wash over me the moment I committed the evil deed and broke one of the sacred Commandments. I knew it would be so, but in the heat of my desire for revenge, it mattered little. To my eternal shame, I was determined one of the men responsible for putting the noose around Abijah's neck would taste the bitterness of my enmity.

Somehow, I thought the act would cleanse me; I thought I would be healed, and my guilt would start to fade when one of the executioners met his end. But I was wrong. And yet, while I freely accept I am a sinner in need of God's grace, I am also aware I must perpetrate more evil before I can ask for the Creator's forgiveness.

A reckoning is coming, and nothing will stand in my way as I go about exacting my revenge. For me, there can be little hope of redemption, not while my lust for the blood of my enemy continues to define my every thought and deed.

I am in danger of allowing my mood to overwhelm me when a man fitting Whitlock's description walks into the bar. It is almost six o'clock.

If anything, he is even more unimpressive than Sowerby's unflattering description.

Up close, he looks the type of man who would steal a blind beggar's last crust, such is his awkwardness and appearance. Yet he doesn't look capable of offering any resistance in a fight, which beggars the question: why pick an urchin like this for such an important task?

I can only think the man I am here to observe has qualities not apparent to the naked eye, so I had best remain on my guard.

Whitlocke sits at a large table diagonally opposite where I have positioned myself. The man is so close I can smell the rancid odour commonly found on all traitors.

Shortly after the liquid contents of his tankard have been eagerly consumed, two men join him at the table. Like the clerk, they appear to be older individuals, men in their late forties, who are equally unaccustomed to carrying their guilt around with them.

Like the corrupt Ambrose Crump in Newark, these men wear the uniforms of prison gaolers. Neither orders a drink. They simply exchange a few pleasantries, pass Whitlocke a copy of the same Parliamentarian newssheet I have in my possession, and then depart.

"Wednesday, it is," calls Whitlocke as they leave. "And make sure you keep your wits about you."

The meeting has lasted less than ten minutes, with the majority of the conversation conducted in muted, hushed tones. Nevertheless, I make a mental note of both men. Sowerby and Cromwell will want a full description, particularly the insignia identifying the gaols where they serve.

The minutes tick by slowly. After almost an hour, with the time thirty minutes past seven o'clock, monotony is close to setting in. I will be of little use this evening if it does, for I can feel the tiredness and fatigue in my bones.

In a bid to stay alert, I lift my head and lookup. It is a conscious effort to ensure Whitlocke is still where I know him to be. I glance around the room, making sure I am still the hunter, not the hunted. Such is the anxiety I feel; I am in need of constant reassurance.

At eight o'clock, another man sits down beside Whitlocke. He is younger than the two previous visitors, more stylishly dressed – and, although I cannot make out his face due to the dimness of the room, there is something familiar about him. He speaks excellent, heavily accented English. I can't identify the country; it could be the Palatinate, the Netherlands or France; and there is an intensity to the conversation that wasn't there when Whitlocke met the two gaolers.

Everything tells me I need to be ready. Therefore, what is being discussed is important.

By the time the two plotters have finished their conversation, the night is late, and the inn doors are close to being barred.

London is shrouded in darkness with only the occasional lantern ablaze to guide travellers. So I decide to act decisively: I will leave the inn and wait for the foreigner outside the entrance. It is a risk but a calculated one. If I were to follow the man immediately after he left, and he were to spot me, his suspicions would be aroused. Of that, there can be no doubt. This way, I have a fighting chance of finding out where he resides while remaining invisible.

I barely make it to the other side of the Hatton Garden thoroughfare before I see him. He emerges with Whitlocke less than a couple of minutes after I have risen. His distinctive cloak and a defect in his right leg that gives him a pronounced limp mean he is clearly recognisable, even in the black of the night.

The two men continue their animated conversation as they walk toward Holborn. Then, as the street meets Charterhouse and Fetter Lane, they grip one another's hands and clasp shoulders. It is a parting of ways. It is what a soldier does when he fears he may never see his comrade again.

I catch the name "Guillaume" as Whitlocke addresses his companion. And then I hear a voice that is without a doubt that of a Frenchman.

"Merci, mon ami," he says at their parting. "May God be with you in these darkest of times."

For thirty more minutes, I continue pursuing my prey as he makes his way down Fleet Street, through Ludgate and onto the river, where he walks eastwards, towards the imposing and illuminated structure of London Bridge. All the time, I am conscious he could become aware of my presence at any time. So I seek the company of the shadows at every opportunity – and attempt to be as quiet as possible.

As we approach the crossing, I see a glow on the far bank of the Thames. A large fire is raging, and many people seem to be standing in huddles watching the inferno destroy a sizeable pyre.

Only as I get closer do I recall this being the site of The Globe, home to the theatre company favoured by James the First. It was demolished just a few months ago in the wake of Parliament banning the performance and exploitation of all theatrical activities.

At least some fortunate souls are benefitting from its ruination by using the timbers to keep warm on this cold winter's eve.

Two guards look at me suspiciously as I pass them on the bridge. One is about to say something to me when a piercing shriek distracts him.

By the time the soldier takes his position once more, I am long gone, continuing to track the man I know only as "Guillaume".

My heart is beating heavily after the exertions of the last hour. I have made my way from the centre of the city to Borough, one area of London the gentry is advised to stay away from after nightfall. After the excitement on the bridge, I have lost my bearings – and sight of the Frenchman.

For several minutes I look into the gloom for the slightest indication of movement or any hint of a sound that may betray his whereabouts. Then, finally, I move forward slowly, forcing my back against a brick wall, edging my way towards a large building less than fifty yards ahead.

Alas, I am unable to react quickly enough to prevent the knife from splitting my skull.

I have just turned the corner into a place I later learn is called Angel Place, when I catch the glint of the blade arcing towards my throat. Instinctively, I attempt to move my body away from the danger, but while I escape the full force of the blade, the backward trajectory of my assailant's arm punches the pommel of his weapon into my temple.

The impact leaves me stunned. I slump to the floor, falling awkwardly, the air knocked out of my lungs.

Within seconds, someone is standing over me, ready to strike.

"Who are you? Why are you following me?" says my attacker in his guttural and heavily accented English. "Who is your Master?"

Suddenly there are shouts, and I hear rushed footsteps. My head starts spinning, and then I remember nothing more.

When I come to, a bright light illuminates everything before me. Eventually, I see two blurred and bewildered faces staring down at me.

"You are a lucky sod," says a man who introduces himself as Jonas Whiteman, the Parish Constable. "You'd be a goner if we hadn't stumbled across you. That thug would have had your wallet and stuck you with his knife.

"Hasn't anyone told you it is not safe to wander the streets around here after dark? You are one of several unfortunates to have been robbed tonight."

I have been unconscious and incoherent for thirty minutes, during which time my saviours have dragged me into the nearest house and brought me back to my senses.

"Why are you here at this time of night, sir?" asks Whiteman. "What business have you in these parts?"

I sit up, recollecting my thoughts. I rub my head, feeling the warm trickle of blood oozing from the fresh wound. The pain is intense, and it helps me start thinking clearly once again. When I feel stronger, I stand. It is a mistake. My legs are weak. My stomach spasms, and then I puke. It comes on quickly, and I cannot control it. My rescuers are not impressed.

Before they have opportunity to berate me, I say: "I was following a man of whom I need to ask some questions. I am an officer in the Parliamentarian army, reporting directly to Lieutenant-General Cromwell. It is his business I am attending to this evening."

The two men look at each other, unsure of what to say.

"The man I was following, and the urchin responsible for attacking me, is now long gone," I continue. "But there is every chance he may be living in the area."

I describe the Frenchman as accurately as I can, but I can see from their faces, my description is vague and unhelpful.

"If it was prisoners you were seeking, there would be an abundance of them," responds the other man, who I notice is wearing the uniform of a prison guard. And it is just like those of two men who met with Whitlocke earlier in the evening.

Looking at his sleeve, I recognise the insignia: a

mace and a pair of cuffs. It is the same mark as that adorning the arm of one of Whitlocke's visitors.

"Tell me," I say, as I seek to comprehend everything that has happened this evening. "Where do you serve?"

A toothless smile flashes across the fellow's mouth.

"Why it's the debtors' gaol," he replies. "You may not be aware, but you are standing virtually next door to it."

The King's Bench Prison stands on the corner of Blackman Street and Borough High Street, from where the hovel is a stinking home to more than four hundred men, who, between them, owe almost a million pounds. It is a sobering sum by any standards.

The goal is a sour place to whittle away your time if you are unfortunate enough to be unable to meet your obligations to your creditors, for the King's Bench Prison, even under the control and watchful eye of Parliament, is known for its cruelty, extortion, promiscuity and drunkenness.

"Francis, are you sure the man meeting Whitlocke was wearing the same uniform as one of your rescuers?"

The voice is that of Cromwell. I am with him and Sowerby at a hastily arranged meeting at Leicester House, the magnificent home of the second Earl of Leicester located in the aptly named Leicester Fields. Oliver has been invited to stay here until the New Model Army Ordinance is approved by Parliament in just seven days.

I sent a messenger to Hercules at six o'clock in the morning, informing him about the events of last night. Within two hours, I had been summoned to a breakfast meeting, at which Oliver demanded to hear about everything I was able to garner before I was knocked senseless.

"Try to remember as best you can, Francis, and take your time," encourages the Lieutenant-General. "Whatever you can recall could be of the utmost importance."

So I do my duty and tell it all.

Cromwell and Sowerby sit silently, listening intently to everything I say. When I am done, Oliver darts a look at his friend, who in turn nods in confirmation.

"I knew it, I damn well knew it," explodes the man who will soon become the only Member of Parliament allowed to maintain a senior leadership position in the army. "By God, they are playing us for fools. While I have men looking for them all over London, they are holed up in at least one of our prisons, hiding away like the vermin they are. That's why we haven't been able to find them. But thanks to you, my dear Francis, they will soon be priced out of their sanctuaries and face the summary justice they deserve."

Sowerby raises his hand in a bid to silence Cromwell, and eventually there is calm in the room.

"I believe you are owed an explanation," says Hercules, restoring some calmness to proceedings. "Oliver is telling you things we only suspected until now. But your enquiries have given us information that is key to getting to the bottom of things once and for all.

"But let me start by apologising, for we haven't told you everything. Indeed, we have been reluctant to do so. But, taking everything into consideration, it is only right you are now informed about certain matters that we have been aware of for some time."

I look at both men, feeling once again I have been played for a fool. Cromwell extends his hand, indicating he wishes his friend to continue, so Sowerby tells me everything that has been uncovered these past weeks. And when he is done, I realise how little I am trusted by the men in power.

"You look as though a stray dog has just pissed on your leg," barks Cromwell. "I understand your frustrations, my friend, but please understand, telling you everything would have only endangered you.

"The truth is, I have been aware of the intentions of the King since shortly after Marston Moor. I know they mistakenly believe if I die, their fortunes will miraculously improve. And I have known about the recruitment of Holck – and the treachery of one of our own side – long before you brought it to my attention.

"Information is coming into our possession every day, more so since the great battle, revealing the King's intentions on many fronts.

"As far as my own safety is concerned, I know I am at risk. As are many of our other generals. But there is a delicacy to my situation that has complicated things and meant the plot could not have been discussed as openly as I would have wished.

"Please believe me when I say I value everything you have done on my behalf. The personal sacrifice you have endured and the many risks you have faced are things I will never forget, and you have my esteem, trust and thanks for all you have been prepared to go through. You are a rare breed of friend. But all of that changes nothing. I would still have been forced to tell you only a small amount of what I know."

I sense the anger rising within. I start rubbing my bruised temple, attempting to use the pain to control my temper. But the more I hear Oliver's voice justifying his actions, the more combustible I become. Eventually, I can bear it no more.

"For the love of Christ, will you please be quiet, Oliver," I shout, my emotions taking over. "I should have known all along you were playing me; that I am expendable. Absolutely nothing has changed. When you approached me all those months ago and asked for my help in convincing the King's nephew to collude in one of your schemes, I did so willingly. For my efforts, my reward was the taking of two of my daughters.

"Now, as I seek to help you avoid the knife, bullet or poison of an assassin, I have been forced to watch my best friend be hanged because I asked him to find out information that would be useful to you.

"Can you understand why I might not be overjoyed to learn of your duplicity in this matter?"

My conduct is totally unbecoming of a subordinate. I know it, but I don't care. At this moment, my pain is flooding out and I am powerless to hold it back.

Oliver and Hercules know I have overstepped the mark quite significantly. Under normal circumstances, such an outburst from a junior officer would result in the immediate arrest of the offender, a period of imprisonment, and his total disgrace.

But instead of calling the guard and having me led away, Oliver stands and walks over to the chair where I am sitting.

"How I wish all of those things had not been inflicted on you, Francis," he says solemnly and sincerely. "If I had it in my power to undo everything that has been done, I would do so in an instant. As God is my witness, please believe me when I say withholding vital information did not play any part in these evil deeds being perpetrated. The moment you aligned yourself to Parliament, you were in line to suffer tragedy.

"My friend, I ask you for your forgiveness for any ills you feel I have been responsible for you and your family experiencing. It grieves me to think you believe I could conspire against you and contribute to your suffering. It is not so."

As I sit in my chair, my rage stirred, a golden ray of sunshine cascades through the large window, basking Cromwell in a golden glow. It is as if the Almighty has chosen this very moment to anoint the man who is the subject of my vitriol.

"Just tell me why you cannot trust me?" I ask. "I need to know."

Sowerby rises and joins Oliver. He puts his hand on the Lieutenant-General's shoulder as he is about to speak again, stilling his tongue immediately.

"Allow me to tell Francis what he needs to know, Oliver," says the lawyer. "It is right to tell him. No harm can come of it."

Cromwell walks back to his own chair and sits down, leaning forward and resting his head on the knuckles of both hands.

"To have told you everything would have put you in an impossible position," intervenes Sowerby. "It would have meant telling you what we know about your commander, a man Oliver specifically asked you to gain the trust of several months ago.

"If we have told you all we knew or suspected, that task would have proven impossible. As it was, for several months, you provided invaluable information that you would not have been able to access under normal circumstances. This has enabled us to monitor the individual quietly, without compromising you in any way. Be assured, what we have learned will serve Parliament well."

I look at both men questioningly. I am struggling to comprehend what I am being told.

"What has Lord Grey of Groby got to do with any of this?" I ask tamely, taken aback by Sowerby's declaration. "He is nothing more than a weakling who has been fortunate to have been born into a noble family. We have a mutual self-loathing for each other, and I am unfortunate to be his subordinate officer. There is nothing more."

For several moments nothing more is said. Then, a large, decorative clock on the far wall signals midday. It is a welcome distraction. We have been talking for two long hours, and I feel exhausted.

Eventually, Oliver lifts his head and talks directly to me. "Francis," he says. "Be aware, your commanding officer is the traitor in our midst. It was never Manchester. That was a rouse to confuse us, and I freely admit it did so for a short while. But Thomas Grey is the man who has betrayed us all. His ambition knows no bounds, and we are now aware he is prepared to do almost anything to get what he desires.

"We know this to be true. And with your help, we will now be able to prove it and end his traitorous ways for good."

NINETEEN

AS I STAND IN THE shadows of the cloisters of the once-mighty Bermondsey Abbey, I feel a dull ache in my fingers and toes as they surrender to the chill of the early morning frost.

Less than a hundred years ago, monastic life would have been in full flow at this time of day, with monks scurrying between the buildings that were once home to the Benedictine Order.

King Henry's sweeping religious reforms ended more than four hundred years of monastic worship at this imposing place. It no longer bears its Catholic iconography but still stands tall and defiant, dominating the landscape of Southwark as far as the eye can see.

This morning, it's unlikely any of the twenty Ironsides who have accompanied me on the two-mile march from their billet at Durham House in The Strand will care much for their surroundings. These men, faithful Protestant servants who Cromwell counts among his most trusted comrades, are here to do a job at the behest of their commander. Nothing more.

In fifteen minutes, when the early dawn has awoken sufficiently so we can all recognise the distinctive dark plumage of the resident Ravens, I will lead Oliver's fearsome warriors as they take Bulstrode Whitlocke into custody. It will be a brutal business executed quite simply. The men are aware the man we seek is a spy, and such traitors receive little consideration when they are dragged from their bed mattresses half-awake in the early hours begging for mercy.

At this moment, my only priority is ensuring there is enough of him still alive for what is to come when he is handed over to Cromwell's inquisitors.

Across London, two other raids are to be carried out. As my men set about kicking down Whitlocke's door and subjecting him to terror, a larger force, comprising a Company of Foot and overseen by Sowerby, will enter the King's Bench Prison, close to where I was attacked.

As I wait for the agreed time to be upon us, I think of those men making their final preparations to seal off all exits and search the cells where we believe Holck, up to six of his men, and the Frenchman, Guillaume de la Croix, will be found hiding in the barred cells.

How I wish I was in Borough at this very moment. I would give almost anything to be the man to put Holck in chains, see his expression as he recognises me, and then quickly slice open his throat. Alas, it will not be so. Cromwell and Sowerby have other plans for my talents.

Suppose Oliver's deductions are accurate and our informants have told the truth. In that case, the prison will prove to have been the enemy's sanctuary for several days.

Should things go according to plan, its confines will seal their doom.

A third and final raid will occur once we have snared all the main perpetrators — when we force one scheming man to face the justice he deserves. And I must be satisfied with that.

In less than twenty-four hours, things have moved at a pace I would not have thought possible unless I had not personally borne witness to Cromwell's agility of mind, decisiveness and strategic brilliance.

I have always been in awe of him, even when was he just an ordinary backbench Parliamentarian. But after seeing the way he works first-hand, I now have a far better understanding of why he is the man he is and why I, and many others, look up to him.

At the behest of the Lieutenant-General, and at breakneck speed, all the available evidence concerning the plotters has been collated and reviewed. Several prominent people have been spoken to, and a broader picture has been fully developed. Added to this, Sowerby, who is no slouch himself, has meticulously reviewed all the intelligence amassed in recent months by loyal agents working to Oliver's command, cross-referencing statements and reports with everything we now know.

It has been an incredible spectacle to witness, watching these two friends and allies unpick a web of imperfect knowledge, and reach intelligent, precise conclusions while working under the most intense pressure.

As I reflect on this unfolding chapter, and the cold air bites at my fingers and toes once again, I remember my late father describing such men to me. He had just returned to Stathern from one of his trips to the Continent, and we were having one of our many philosophical conversations in the days when we could talk to each other.

"They are precious and the rarest of thoroughbreds," he said to me. "They take the ordinary and make it extraordinary; they have sight when all around them are blind."

Having seen a Master at work, I now know what he meant all those years ago.

At precisely forty-five minutes past the hour of six o'clock, I order two of the Ironsides to break down Whitlocke's front door. Two kicks are all it takes for entry to be gained to the humble dwelling by twenty of the most feared soldiers in the Parliamentarian army. They do so with relish and precision. Amid the grunts of men searching the premises, a sudden cry from upstairs is extinguished by the sound of the butt of a musket hitting what I imagine to be the pale, terrified skull of the man we have come to get.

Then all is as it was. Quiet order and efficiency descend once again.

By the time we leave ten minutes later, the street is alive: its dogs are barking, hens and geese can be heard at the rear of several houses, and we see at least two of the menfolk going about their chores as we march past their homesteads. They look up. Their interest has been aroused by the clinking and jangling of muskets and swords, which drown out the whimpers of Whitlocke, as his limp body is dragged by two of the biggest and meanest looking brutes I have ever seen.

The prisoner's hands and feet are in chains, blood

has matted in what is left of his thinning hair, and I notice painful red welts hanging below two haunted eyes.

Knowing Cromwell's men as I do, it appears the clerk has got off lightly this morning, for if these faithful servants had known what Whitlocke's true intentions were, there is every chance I would be looking at a corpse right now, not a man still capable of breathing.

As he passes where I stand, the clerk calls out pleadingly: "I am a peaceful man. I have no quarrel with anyone, so why are you taking me away in chains? Of what am I accused?"

Before I can respond, one of the guards kicks out at the prisoner viciously, shouting: "You will find out soon enough cur, once the rack has stretched you a little and the heated tongs have warmed your innards."

Whitlocke looks terrified and recoils. Without hesitation, I decide it is time to increase his worries. I stop the column and address him directly.

"Master Whitlocke, you are suspected of taking part in treasonous activities designed to undermine Parliament and threaten the life of one of its most revered figures," I say tonelessly. "Evidence is in our possession linking you to several other suspects who we know are involved in these foulest of plots.

"We have dispensation to take you to a secure destination, where you will be interrogated until you have told us all you know. And be sure you will.

"My advice, sir, is tell us the truth as quickly as you are able. Looking at the state of your body, you do not have the strength to withstand the pain that will be inflicted on you. The longer you lie to us, the more broken you will be."

My words have the desired effect. At the prospect of torture, Whitlocke's legs buckle. If there was any doubt beforehand, he now knows precisely what awaits. As he ponders his fate, his limp body has to be supported all the way back to The Strand by the two guards, who do not appreciate the task assigned to them.

Not so long ago, I would have abhorred the use of torture. Indeed, I have reprimanded and rebuked men who have jested about such sufferings and abuses. But these are far from normal times, and my values and principles are not what they once were.

Walking directly behind Whitlocke, two Ironsides carry boxes of papers that have been removed from his house. Nestling on top of one of the wooden crates is the latest edition of Mercurius Civicus. It would appear to be the very newssheet I saw handed to him in The Mitre last night.

Out of curiosity, I reach for the paper. As I do, I notice fear and hostility growing in the prisoner's guilty eyes.

"What is it?" I say to him. "Is there something in here you don't want me to see?"

Whitlocke starts to shake and emit a high-pitched keening noise. I concentrate, listening to the feral sound that's more akin to a fox than a man.

"What are you telling me?" I demand of the terrified plotter, shaking his arm violently in a bid to help him become coherent once again. "Are you still telling me you are an innocent man who has been wrongly arrested? Is that what you are saying? Or is it something else, something to do with this?"

I indicate to the nearest guard that I want the paper. It is quickly handed over, and on page five, I see a handwritten word that catches my eye. It takes a few seconds to adjust my sight before reading the simple black script printed deliberately in the margin.

"Whatever does Zarnikh mean?" I ask of Whitlocke after deciphering the unrefined writing.

Before he can answer, I suddenly recall my classical education at the King Henry school in Coventry, where my son is now studying.

"Zarnikh is the Persian word for arsenic," I say to nobody in particular, "and it's the very poison that killed Alexander the Great."

"He's told us everything he knows: names, places, the method and the proposed time," confirms Sowerby as I greet him at the entrance to Newgate gaol.

It is late afternoon, some seven hours since the raids were carried out, and I have just arrived at the most notorious of all of London's prisons. Whitlocke is being questioned and will no doubt meet his doom once his usefulness comes to an end.

With the exception of Hercules, Newgate's governor, who is a trusted friend of the Lieutenant-General, the soldiers who completed the two raids, and myself, nobody is aware of what happened this morning. And Oliver has ordered it to be kept this way indefinitely.

I disagree with the decision, but Oliver will not be persuaded by my arguments. He has made his mind up and will not tolerate my dissent. I have no choice but to believe everything is being done for the best of reasons.

Sowerby takes me to an isolated room deep in the

bowels of the gaol, close to where those condemned to hang at Tyburn are held until their time is nigh.

The stench is nauseating; the evidence of dampness, decay and death are everywhere.

Two bare-chested men rise as we enter the cell, which is lit by three blazing torches. They are glistening with sweat, having been meaningfully employed for several hours on the flesh of their latest victim. They seem pleased with their work.

I look to where Bulstrode Whilocke's inert body hangs suspended by chains in the centre of the cell. He looks more dead than alive. His face is unrecognisable, no longer featuring the hawkish nose, prominent cheeks and remarkably white teeth. All that stares back at me is a broken, bloody mass.

"They intended to kill Oliver using a concoction of arsenic and deadly wild mushrooms," continues Sowerby, as we both shiver at the sight that confronts us. "Holck's orders were to try and make it look like an accident and not the hand of one of his enemies, lest too many questions and suspicions are aroused.

"They don't want anyone thinking there has been collusion in this matter."

I shrug my shoulders and openly look upwards into the darkness. "Thank the Lord," I say. "In the end, after all these weeks of seeking to uncover the truth, matters have unravelled so quickly. It's hard to believe it is all over, and the man I fear the most in this world is now under lock and key."

Sowerby freezes momentarily. I look at him, sensing his unease. He coughs to disguise his acute discomfort and regain some semblance of composure.

"I am afraid not everything went according to plan, Francis," he confesses, looking pensive and drawn. "We have most of them. But I am afraid we don't have Holck. He was nowhere to be found.

"It was only after we discovered two of our men were missing that the alarm was sounded. Shortly afterwards, we found their bodies in a closed-cell. It seems Holck was ready for us. He attacked our men, killing them before stealing some of their clothing and slipping through our net. But be assured we are looking for him and he will be found. He is on foot and can't get far."

I let out an anguished snort and punch the wall with all my might.

Right now, I feel the pain of disappointment as much as any sword thrust or musket ball wound. Such is my frustration and disappointment; I don't feel two of my fingers snapping as they surrender to the solidity of the granite wall.

"What incompetence is this?" I shout at Sowerby as light-headedness threatens to topple me over, and I start to feel a stabbing sensation in my left hand. "How is it possible for Holck to escape from a prison with a hundred of the best troops searching for him? Tell me, Hercules, how can this happen?"

Sowerby ushers me to a quiet spot. He shakes his head. He, too, is distraught at the outcome.

"The prison's governor is notorious for taking bribes," he whispers. "We have already discovered he was paid a small fortune by one of the gaolers you saw at The Mitre Tavern to accommodate the assassins. In return, he provided three cells in a secluded part of the prison where Holck and his men came and went as they pleased.

293

"The six gaolers working in that section of the prison were all in on it. It's the biggest reason our enquiries turned up nought. Holck was already enjoying life behind bars at the very time we were seeking to put him there. If Oliver's life wasn't in peril, and the matter wasn't so serious, I would have to admit it was an ingenious plan, for it is the very last place anyone would have thought to look for them."

I look away. My rage is threatening to best me.

"When the Ironsides entered the prison, they were denied entry for a couple of minutes," continues Sowerby, sounding ever more like the assimilator of information he is. "It wasn't long, but it was enough time for Holck to be warned of our presence and make good his escape.

"Surprise was always going to be key. We lost it, and he is wily enough to know what to do when he is trapped. I am truly sorry, Francis. I thought we had him."

I look up. Tears are running down my cheeks. The well is indeed sprung, as it has many times in recent months. I pull my handkerchief from my jerkin and dab the moisture out of my sockets, seeking to conceal yet another moment of weakness.

"You do realise," I say as my emotions start to settle once again, "Oliver is not safe until we have dealt decisively with Holck? The man will keep going until he finds a way of carrying out his orders. He is a killer, and he will never accept failure."

Sowerby bows his head.

"I know," he says. "Believe me when I say I also share your concerns. And that's why Oliver's personal bodyguard has today been tripled in number."

After a broken night of sleep, I awake on a bright Sunday morning. In more peaceful times, it would be deemed a day of rest.

But I already know it will be far from that.

I have returned to the mews house at Clerkenwell Green, where I reflect on everything that has happened during the time I have been in London.

Unlike recent days, it is warm. The winter sunshine is at its glorious best, so I decide to clear my head by going to Church and attempting to make my peace with the father. After the turbulence of recent weeks, it is time to sit in a pew and reflect on the sin in my life.

The Church of Saint James, an old Catholic nunnery dating back to the Twelfth Century, is less than twenty minutes away on foot, and I have certainly felt its impressive three-storey tower calling me ever since I arrived in these parts. Consciously, I have forced myself to ignore these feelings, as I have been all too aware of my unpredictable emotions and my current state of unfaithfulness.

This fine morning, however, I can hold out no longer. I must start the process of regaining the Creator's trust and forgiveness.

As I approach the large open doors of the main church building, a warm and endearing voice calls out: "Good morning, stranger. Welcome to these parts and our humble sanctuary."

Realising the speaker is talking to me, I smile and guide my hand into the firm clutch of Aloysius Wainwright, the man charged with overseeing the large flock of devout puritans who are assembling this morning to give praise.

"You look troubled, my friend," he says perceptively as he continues to grip my hand tightly. "I couldn't help notice as you walked down the path. Forgive me for saying so, but you seem very alone this fine Winter's morning."

Before I can reply, he adds: "Allow me to encourage you to open your heart to Christ Jesus, who will willingly take away your pain. How say you, friend, does that sound appealing?"

I am shocked by the frankness and directness of the Minister. And I am deeply grateful. I allow myself to be led into the Church, where I am guided to a firm, wooden seat positioned close to the pulpit. The sun's bright rays pierce the stained glass windows of Saint James, basking many rows of believers in light as they wait expectantly for Aloysius to deliver his sermon.

"Talk to the Father," he says encouragingly, immune to the impatience of his congregation for the service to start promptly. "Tell Him your troubles, brother. Tell Him you love him, and let Him bless you with the power of his restorative powers."

I do as I am instructed, and a little over an hour later, I emerge into daylight for what seems the first time in an age.

As the church bells signal three o'clock in the afternoon, I continue to think of the charismatic and godly Minister I have had the good fortune to meet. The events of the morning have had a significant impact on me. It is a long time since I heard a churchman talk about Faith with such conviction and purpose. To my shame, I am rarely in the mood to listen to William Norwich when I enter the chancellery of my own beloved Saint Guthlacs.

Aloysius Wainwright is a different breed of rector altogether, much more in tune with the God and protestant religion I subscribe to. As Bucephalus and I ride onto the open fields, known as the Liberties of Westminster, I decide I will try and spend more time talking to Him if He will entertain me while I am here.

The words of the Lord, spoken through this good and faithful servant, have already helped me reconcile the disappointments of yesterday. Who was I deceiving? Did I really believe the raid on the prison would be the end of my eighteen-month ordeal?

If I am truthful, I know the answer is one I do not wish to acknowledge.

I laugh aloud, my foolishness and arrogance on display for only the Maker to hear.

"Forgive me, Father," I shout into the early afternoon sunlight. "I beg you to allow me to know your love and grace once again. As you are my witness, I will not let my anger consume me and lead me away from you."

I clutch the Bible I carry at all times and say a silent prayer, remembering Isabel, the children, and my many fallen friends and family.

When I am finished, I prod Bucephalus in the flanks with my spurs and turn him in the direction of the town. It is time to refocus and hold Lord Grey of Groby to account.

TWENTY

IT IS THE DARK OF the night, and an eerie silence accompanies me as I pass the Palace of Whitehall, the former residence of the King. I stop and look at the building as it stands tall and proud. Even though Charles fled London more than three years ago, his residence still exudes power, pomp and majesty.

I wonder for the briefest of moments what might have been if the King had listened to his subjects all those years ago, heeding their needs and concerns? As my thoughts wander, I quickly decide it is time to push on towards Wallingford House, where my accomplices await my presence. I need to have my wits about me; releasing long-buried emotions and thoughts will be of little assistance this evening.

I left Clerkenwell a good hour ago, riding Bucephalus as far as The Embankment, where I left him with a reliable hand who, for the price of sixpence, will tether and feed my horse to his heart's content.

With my horse safely stabled until the morning, I

travel the remaining mile on foot, with the great river on my left, until I reach the Abbey of Westminster and Parliament. The silhouetted shapes of these two great buildings are usually enough to inspire awe and wonder. But neither evokes the kind of feelings in me that are aroused by the sight of Whitehall.

As I walk the last few yards to my destination, I find myself continuing to think of the many opportunities to unite the realm that were lost – and all the potential within the country that will never be bear fruit.

The rain falls steadily, shimmering radiantly as it bounces off the cobbles. Tonight, the streets of the capital have been emptied. The hour is late, just past eleven, and I am wet through to the skin. The unrelenting storm has found a way to conquer my protective oilskin. Yet, as cold droplets run down my spine, I have a feeling my discomfort is an omen for everything that is about to come.

Such is the apprehension I feel, it takes all my energy and determination to complete the journey. When I finally arrive, the guards are conspicuous by their absence, preferring the warmth of their braziers and the shelter of the grand doorway that adorns this finest of citadels to performing the simple sentry duties that pay them a weekly pittance.

Unfortunately, I have nowhere to hide, having received instructions to meet Cromwell and Sowerby at eleven o'clock in the evening and to tell nobody of my whereabouts or the purpose of my business.

Until recently, Wallingford House was the residence of the Duke of Buckingham, the detested lover of the late King James and, until his much-celebrated execution, a key adviser to Charles. Commandeered by Parliament in the years since his death, it is now a very convenient place for covert meetings like the one I am about to attend.

As I approach the entrance, a deep voice calls out: "State your business, sir. And do not come any further until you are told to do so."

Out of the blackness steps a figure I assume to be a dragoon, his hand clutching the hilt of his sword. He looks every inch the warrior he is, someone worthy of being handpicked to protect the architect of the King's defeat at Marston Moor. Lurking a few feet behind, two others eye me warily, and at least one of them is holding a musket in a manner suggesting he is keen to use it.

"I am here at the request of Lieutenant-General Cromwell," I say as assertively as I can, as my teeth chatter wildly and the icy rain bites at my skin. "My name is Captain Francis Hacker."

Without further ado, the soldier stands back, an indication that I am expected. He opens one of the large doors and proceeds to escort me through an elegant, twisting hallway to some stairs, which we descend. Within a few moments, the dimly lit bowels of the house take me into an underworld I am not familiar with.

The guard leads me in semi-darkness for several minutes until I see a bright light escaping through a doorframe and hear muffled voices in the far-off distance. As we get closer, and the shouting intensifies, I pass a man quietly sitting at a table. He doesn't look up.

Suddenly the door swings open, and I witness the scene being played out by two combatants engaged in a bitter and heated argument.

"I would say things are looking extremely bleak for

you right now," yells Cromwell as I enter the chamber. "You have been exposed for the traitor you are. There is no sense in denying it. We have all the evidence we need to condemn you. It's time you started telling the truth, or my patience may just run out."

The door makes a loud creaking noise as it closes behind me. The sound forces Oliver to cease his verbal assault on Thomas Grey and glare in my direction.

"I am glad you could join us, Francis," he says tetchily. "I have just been telling your commanding officer all we know of the games he has been playing these past few months. So far, he has been a little bit bashful and refused to cooperate. But now you are here, perhaps he will become a more enthusiastic participant!"

I look around the sparse room, seeking to regain my composure. I do not know what role I am to play at this meeting, which appears to bear the hallmark of a violent inquisition rather than anything else.

Five of us are crammed into the small area: Oliver is in his shirt-sleeves, on his feet, and sweating heavily; Sowerby is sat furthest away and appears to be taking meticulous notes, his sight aided by a torch burning brightly overhead; Lord Grey is seated in the centre of the room, his legs shackled to a crudely constructed stool; and I have been offered a chair closest to Cromwell. Meanwhile, a guard I do not recognise stands close by, alert to every move made by the man subjected to the questioning.

"Now we are all here, let's get back to the detail," roars Cromwell. "Lord Grey, it is important you know that we have been watching you closely for many months. You have been suspected of treachery almost since the outbreak of the war. Since the summer, those suspicions have grown significantly. The doubts about your loyalty have forced me, and Parliament, to go to extraordinary lengths to establish the truth. What say you, sir, do you think we are right to suspect you?"

For the first time since my arrival, Grey lifts his head.

I scrutinise the features of the weakling sitting before me, trying to remain levelheaded as I look upon a face that fills my heart with disgust and loathing. In the darkness, I can see crusts of blood around his nose and mouth and a mass of swelling around his left eye. There is no doubt he is here under duress, yet I feel no pity. He has earned his suffering.

"Do your worst, Cromwell," he says defiantly, spraying the room with bloody spittle as he shouts out his challenge. "Let's hear the malicious libels you have created to ruin me. But I must warn you, sir, there will be the severest of recriminations for you and everyone here when you are forced to release me. You have gone too far, and nothing will save you when I am free. I will make sure of it."

Oliver strides over to where Grey is struggling with his chains. Then, unexpectedly, he strikes him with the back of his hand. It is a blow that sends the prisoner crashing to the floor.

"Have you gone crazy?" shouts Grey when he has come to his senses. "I am the commander of the Midlands Association forces and a Lord of this kingdom while you are nothing more than a commoner who has risen above his station in life. You have no right to mistreat me this way and no evidence to back up your vague and spurious claims."

With the speed of a viper, Oliver bends down to within a couple of inches of Grey's mottled face. The nobleman looks terrified and does all he can to pull away. But his back is now pinned against the wall, and he has no way of escaping the scrutiny of the enraged Lieutenant-General.

"You miserable, traitorous coward," shouts Cromwell. "Do you really think I would go to all this trouble on a whim simply because I hold you in low esteem?"

The accuser doesn't wait for an answer.

"No, sir," he continues. "The reason we are here tonight is because you have been consorting with the Devil and collaborating with the King's men. We know it all.

"You have been plotting with them in a bid to kill me and undermine Parliament's overall fight against the tyrant. None of this has been in the pursuit of a noble cause. Far from it, for we know it has been for your own ends, for your own ambition and personal advancement.

"I can prove everything I say, and with such over-whelming evidence against you, I have no doubt that tonight you will confess to your crimes and beg for Parliament's mercy. And when you do, when that moment arrives and these men witness your confession, I alone will decide the precise nature of the justice you will face."

For the next three hours, Cromwell sets out everything he knows about the complicity of Thomas Grey in the series of events that have exposed and undermined Parliament – and directly led to Abijah's demise and my brother's imprisonment and torture.

Before the war, Cromwell and Grey received legal training. The events of this evening demonstrate they haven't forgotten the art of meticulously framing an argument and a counterclaim. As the night wears on, and despite his most valiant efforts, Grey cannot get the better of Cromwell, for the truth will always see the light.

By five o'clock, some six hours after the 'trial' began, the extent of Grey's treachery and betrayal to the cause he claims to serve has been laid bare. His Lordship's willingness to speak to the plotters and agree to their scandalous proposals is proven beyond doubt, as is his involvement in attempts to fabricate evidence against the Earl of Manchester. And his active participation in aiding Holck and his killers as they have set about their business in recent days is evidenced in the clearest possible terms.

There is nowhere for Lord Grey of Groby to hide.

"In summary," concludes Cromwell, "you are guilty of the greatest Treason. Of this, there can be no doubt. The only thing that matters now is how we reconcile these matters and whether your fate is decided at the gallows or the executioner's block."

As I look on, awaiting Grey's response, I see what is tantamount to a smile pass across his mouth as he weighs up everything that has been levelled against him.

"As always, Master Cromwell, you are the most wonderful of storytellers," he says, thick traces of contemptuous denial evident in every word as he makes one last stand. "But where is the absolute proof you need to condemn me? You have no eyewitnesses, none at all. Everything you have said is coincidental and conjecture, as you well know, sir. Therefore do yourself a favour and release me now. If you do, you have my word; I will be lenient."

Grey has overstepped the mark. In two strides, Oliver is upon him, and three heavy blows rain down, putting him on the floor once again. The sudden violence shocks me. I have never seen Cromwell so angry and agitated in all the years I have known him. And I have never seen him resort to violence.

"I do not negotiate with bastards like you," he states, doing his utmost to control his temper. "Nor do I waste my time, so enough of this folly. If you want proof, I will give it to you."

Cromwell spins around and marches to the door. He grabs the two black bars holding it securely against the wall and releases them. Soon light from the hallway illuminates the room.

I see a pair of legs stretched out only a few feet away from the entrance; the expensive boots suggest the owner is a man of status. Presumably, he is one of the men I passed several hours ago when I first arrived at this place?

"On your feet, my friend," calls Cromwell into the darkness. "His Lordship needs some convincing. Please join us and tell him, and us, all you know of the matters under consideration this evening?"

A few seconds later, a sixth man enters the fray. He is limping. And he is someone I recognise.

Guillaume de la Croix is tall for a Frenchman, standing at well over six feet. He is forced to stoop in the cramped conditions, leaning to the left to prevent his frame from buckling. Yet, even in such awkward circumstances, he retains a dignity and a presence few men hold. Such is the luck and swagger of the Gaul.

At first, I am stunned to see the Royalist agent looking in such rude health. My understanding was he had been apprehended, some two days since, during the raid on the King's Bench Prison in Borough. If indeed I had any, my expectations were that his fine features would be rearranged courtesy of the fists of Cromwell's torturers, just like those of the unfortunate Whitlocke.

Not so. From where I am sitting, this rogue appears to be untouched.

I make to rise when I suddenly feel Cromwell's hand on my shoulder exerting downward pressure.

"Sit tight, Francis," he urges. "You will soon have all the facts."

As the Lieutenant-General moves away, I look towards Grey. His body has tightened; his face is bleached; no words are forthcoming. He is just staring at the Frenchman, his mouth wide open.

"Allow me to welcome Monsieur Guillaume de la Croix, the son of Sir Henry Jermyn, one of the King's most loyal servants," announces Cromwell.

Mention of the Frenchman's name brings a string of obscenities and curses out of the bruised mouth of Grey.

"How much have they paid you, Judas?" he cries. "When word of your betrayal gets out, and it will, you won't live long enough to enjoy the thirty pieces of silver they have offered you this day."

Another powerful punch from Cromwell stuns the prisoner. He slumps and is still on the stool. When order has returned to the room, the Lieutenant-General turns to Sowerby. "My friend," he says. "It has been the longest of nights, but I still need your services for a while longer. Can you please make an accurate note of everything the witness is about to say? Evidentially, it will be an important statement of fact."

Sowerby nods his head in compliance. He dips the

quill's nib in an inkpot, indicating he is ready to continue playing the role of the dutiful scribe.

"Monsieur, the floor is yours," says Cromwell, bidding de la Croix to stand. "In your own time and words, please tell us everything you know about the complicated and confused affairs of the prisoner, Lord Grey of Groby."

Initially, de la Croix looks bewildered and unsure of how he should proceed. But soon, after some vocal encouragement from Cromwell, he starts to tell a fascinating story I would have scare believed a few days ago0.

"Monsieurs," he says. "While I have seemingly been a Royalist spy for many months, the truth is I have been working on behalf of Parliament, firstly in France and then in England."

Silence greets the bold statement. Even Grey seems fascinated by the revelations.

"Almost two years ago, at the instigation of Master Cromwell, with whom I have enjoyed a long and productive collaboration, I met Parliament's representative in Paris. I was eager to serve Parliament in some way, and embedding myself with the enemy seemed an opportunity too good to miss.

"It was Master Cromwell who suggested I should introduce myself to the French court and make my exploits in Bohemia known, where I fought against the Catholic aggressors. He was convinced this would make me an interesting prospect, albeit I was asked to conceal my Puritanism, which I did. The situation is so confused on the Continent; people are eager to believe whatever you tell them, providing you can back up some of your claims with a degree of evidence. And I was able to do this.

"I was quickly accepted at court and invited to join

several circles, one of which was very supportive of Queen Henrietta Maria. I made sure I made the right noises in this group about my opposition to Parliament and my desire to fight the Roundheads, which significantly increased my popularity.

"When the Queen visited France in 1643, I was introduced to her as someone willing to fight for her husband. She took me under her wing, and when she returned to these shores in July of that year, I was part of her retinue."

As de la Croix pauses momentarily to drink some water, I find myself scarcely believing what my ears are hearing. I feel compelled to break the spell we are all under by speaking my thoughts.

"Are you telling us you have been working for Parliament all along, monsieur?" I enquire as calmly as I am able. "You are asserting you are one of us and always have been?"

Guillaume de la Croix looks at me directly for the first time since nearly splitting my skull in two.

"That is exactly what I am telling you," he states, without giving any indication he recognises me. "I have been working to the instructions of Lieutenant-General Cromwell for almost two years. Everything I have done has been at his command and with his utmost knowledge."

Out of the corner of my eye, I see Grey wringing his hands. I look at his Lordship. His arrogance is gone. He knows a storm is coming, and he will be unable to resist.

With the scene set, de la Croix spends more than an hour describing the betrayal of Lord Grey of Groby in detail. He tells of clandestine meetings in London with Whitlocke, treasonous correspondence with the King's men in Newark, and a desire to see Cromwell usurped and ultimately killed. All because his insatiable appetite for power knows no bounds.

"In my estimation," states de la Croix, "Thomas Grey is a man without conscience; someone who believes the end justifies the means. There can be no other explanation for his actions.

"He has had many opportunities to stop colluding with the enemy, yet he has chosen to plough on regardless. I know because I have been privy to many of the conversations that have taken place. I have also put him to the test, asking him on several occasions whether the prize he seeks is worth the risk he is exposing himself and his family to. On every occasion, without fail, he has told me he wishes to proceed with the venture.

"Most recently, I was with Lord Grey when he met Holck and Whitlocke in Southwark and agreed the plan that would have resulted in the Lieutenant-General being poisoned, had the plot not been foiled. If my memory is not mistaken, I seem to remember the two men sharing a jest about Captain Hacker, which his Lordship found particularly amusing."

Mention of my name provokes a sudden explosion from Cromwell.

"And my young friend," shouts Oliver across the room. "Would you care to tell us what these two men found so amusing at the expense of Captain Hacker?"

The Frenchman's confidence seems to evaporate at this moment. His eyes look downwards, and his voice becomes almost a whisper.

"His Lordship seemed to find the death of Swan, the Captain's close associate, something to celebrate," he says.

"He said many vile things about the good Captain and his family, and he also boasted he was delighted to have played a part in depriving Captain Hacker of his most-trusted man."

I feel the eyes of everyone in the room upon me, waiting for my reaction. Inwardly, I am seething, but I refuse to be the source of anyone's entertainment or pity. Not today, and certainly not when Abijah's name is mentioned.

But there will be a holding to account, for there are now two figures for my hatred to consume, and no matter what happens in the future, I will have my vengeance. That I vow.

By the time the young Frenchman has finished speaking, it is almost seven o'clock in the morning. He is spent. So, too, are the rest of us. It has been an exhausting eight hours. Lord Grey has been condemned and convicted. The arrogant young nobleman's name will be forever known as that of a turncoat and traitor, as a man who put his own ambitions before those of his men and country. Infamy now beckons.

Die he must, for there can be no clemency shown to selfish, disloyal and cowardly men such as him. Inwardly, I rejoice at the prospect and doubt whether anyone will shed tears at his passing, such is the contempt he has displayed towards his fellow humanity, not least the good citizens of Leicester, who he has treated with scorn and neglect for far too long.

"Have you anything you wish to say?" asks Cromwell, looking directly at Grey. "Is there something I should take into consideration before I pass judgment?"

Grey looks to the ceiling and closes his eyes. Seconds seem like minutes before he focuses on Cromwell and speaks very slowly and deliberately.

"I wish to talk," he says. "But to you only, and alone. All the others must leave."

Triumph is etched on Oliver's face as he dismisses Sowerby, de la Croix and myself. Only Grey and the mute guard are permitted to remain.

"Go upstairs," he says as we make our hasty exit. "Find the kitchen. There is a hearty breakfast to be had. I will come to you in due course."

More than an hour passes. The three of us sit in silence in the sparsely furnished kitchen. We have eaten what bread and cheese we can find and sipped from the jug of luke-warm water left on a large table. During this time, not a word has been spoken. But we are all troubled men.

I reach for my Bible. The pages are damp, having fallen victim to the heavy rains of last night. Nonetheless, I thumb through the Good Book and find Two Corinthians, where I read about the troubles faced by the disciples, Paul and Timothy, as they travelled through Asia in their quest to tell the world of the wonders of Christ Jesus. In recent weeks, I have neglected scripture, my all-consuming troubles making me selfish and disobedient. Now, as I absorb these holy words, I am reminded once again of God's amazing grace, patience and forgiveness – and my own deep desire to honour Him.

And as I continue to read Paul's second letter to the church in Corinth, little do I realise my own faith is about to be sorely put to the test by the man I look up to more than any other in this turbulent world.

At almost nine o'clock, the sound of heavy boots echoing down the hall can be heard. Someone is clearly in a hurry as there is a briskness and urgency as the steps gather pace.

Suddenly Cromwell is among us once again. Gone is the tiredness that afflicted him earlier; he now bears the look of a conqueror.

"It is done," he says, looking in the direction of Sowerby. "He has admitted everything. We have him exactly where we want him. It is what we hoped for."

Oliver's long-time friend rises and walks to where the Lieutenant-General is standing. He is smiling, and his hands are outstretched, partly in celebration, partly in greeting.

"He had no choice," he says thoughtfully as he embraces Cromwell. "Not to have confessed would have been catastrophic for him and his family. We suspected he was not the kind of man willing to sacrifice everything for his principles. And we have been proven right."

I look in the direction of de la Croix. He, like me, seems surprised at the conversation. He coughs, clearing his throat. I suspect he may be about to say something, but I get there first.

"Oliver," I say. "Can you please explain to me what in blazes is going on?"

Stepping forward so he doesn't need to raise his voice to be heard, Cromwell starts to reveal all.

"I have today reached an understanding with Lord Grey," he confides. "In return for a full confession, apology and his ongoing support in the house and on the field of battle, I have agreed to overlook his recent indiscretions.

"Hercules will obtain the necessary signed statement before the morning is out. The good news is Lord Grey is no longer a threat to the vital work Parliament is undertaking. From now on, he will do my bidding, and mine alone, when I tell him to do so. And he is fully aware of the consequences if he fails me in any regard."

I am stunned, struggling to comprehend the meaning of those two short sentences.

For a moment, I lose the power to speak. I was expecting Cromwell to tell me the traitor had been dragged away to The Tower, there to await his doom. So I am unprepared for the vastly different outcome Oliver now presents.

To hear him rejoicing about reaching a compromise with Grey leaves me breathing heavily and with my heart beating fast. This is not justice. This is not what is meant to happen to a traitor. Worse still, talk of Grey remaining a free man leaves me feeling violated. My head is spinning, and I can taste the bile of my stomach as it rises.

I say nothing for ten minutes, choosing to keep my eyes closed as Oliver continues to speak. All the while, I am conscious of the animated conversation that is taking place all around me while people leave the room. As I struggle to come to terms with everything I have just heard, I sense the presence of my late friend, Abijah Swan, whose loyalty and friendship I have greatly missed. How I wish he were standing alongside me right now. He would know how to react to the situation. The regret I feel for sending him to Newark on such a feckless, misguided and fatal mission knows no bounds.

I am brought back to something akin to reality by Oliver's strong hands as they grip my shoulders. As I feel his iron touch, I open my eyes and find myself staring directly into the optical pools of the Lieutenant-General.

"Young, loyal friend," he says. "Of all the men I care about, I owe you a frank explanation about the events of today, for I know what has happened here will cause you distress for many days to come.

"Please believe me when I tell you this is the best possible outcome for Parliament and everyone in this room that believes the King must be brought to heel.

"Killing Grey, and making his treason known publicly, would be disastrous for our cause. It would play into the hands of Charles and lead to disaffection among those nobles who continue to stand by us.

"Thomas Grey and his family are senior members of the nobility. To strike against him now could result in a far bigger price being paid than the one you, and others, have had to bear. I have thought long and hard on the matter, Francis, and I cannot, and will not, allow this to happen.

"At the end of this week, the Ordinance for the creation of the New Model Army will be passed by Parliament. You and I know this will change the course of the war. With Grey now my prisoner, even though he seemingly walks free, we have our biggest opportunity to bring the different factions together. I tell you in all sincerity, this would not be possible if Grey was to be exposed and receive the fate he deserves.

"I have allowed him to remain in command of the Midlands Association forces for as long as it is useful to Parliament. As far as the world is concerned, the events of the past few months never occurred. The Royalists will not wish it to be known they failed and were duped, while I deliberately informed only a small number of men I trust about these matters, one of whom is you. Believe me when

I tell you it is in the interests of everyone to say nothing and continue as normal."

Cromwell pauses for a moment, scrutinising my face. When he is satisfied, he continues.

"You, Francis, are the man who has lost most as a result of your involvement. I have asked you to do many things for me, and you have always carried out my instructions to the letter, and this loyalty has cost you dear. So forgive me, my friend, for all I have inflicted on you, your family and your friends. If there had been any other way, I would have gladly taken it.

"Now, I am asking you to support me further by not opposing what has been done this day. In time, I believe you will recognise this for what it is – a pragmatic act done in the best interests of the cause we serve. But I do understand you may not believe that will be possible at this moment in time.

"I would like nothing better than to see Grey executed for his crimes. But keeping him in place, at the head of the army in the Midlands, means he will be controlled. You will be able to return to Stathern, with immediate effect if you wish it to be so. And, going forward, you will not have anything to do with Lord Grey. I will ensure it. Your orders will come directly from Fairfax or me. Nobody else.

"What do you say, Francis? Are you with me still?"

It is hard to describe what I feel at this moment. On the battlefield, I have experienced the agony of a sword being thrust into my shoulder and thigh and an enemy warrior twisting the weapon viciously to inflict as much bodily damage as possible. And although I have been scarred, the suffering has gradually faded, so the wounds no longer trouble me.

What has happened this morning is altogether more savage. To feel the pain and torment associated with a betrayal takes a man's trauma to a different level. From experience, I know it stays with you, hurting for a lifetime.

In truth, I cannot look at the man who has wounded me so grievously this day. Yet I must speak to him. A stilled tongue will not suffice.

"And what of Holck?" I enquire, my voice hoarse and filled with aggression. "What are we doing about finding him before he escapes our clutches?"

Cromwell lifts his hands from my shoulder. He paces about the now empty room, exhaling loudly while thinking carefully about what he is about to say.

"I have decided to let Holck leave London," he replies evenly without looking at me. "After much prayer and thought, I have decided it serves our purposes much better if he is able to return to the Midlands. Moreover, allowing him his freedom indicates to the enemy their network has not been compromised, even though the mission has been unsuccessful. Therefore, I have ordered the searches to be called off.

"For Grey to be able to function credibly, and for this arrangement to remain secret, it is imperative Holck is allowed to report to his superiors in Newark that the mission was unsuccessful because of Whitlocke's capture and subsequent confession, not because the commander of the Midlands Association decided to tell all.

"It is also important to me that Lord Grey continues to have a direct line to the King's most feared troops. As a result, he can feed them misinformation and, when it is right to do so, we can use Holck to set a trap of our own for him and many others."

I attempt to speak, but Oliver raises a fist to silence any dissent.

"It is also my intention to protect de la Croix," he continues. "As far as Willis and Holck are concerned, he remains loyal to the King and continues to be at large. But, when it serves our purposes, Guillaume will contact the Royalists once again once a sufficient period has lapsed. Hence, it looks as though he has been in hiding.

"Like Grey, he will be able to give Parliament access to vital information and feed our enemies falsehoods that will put them at a serious disadvantage. These are more important priorities in my assessment of things than settling a personal vendetta, no matter how valid and important it is to you, my dearest Francis. The State's needs must come first.

"I know this is hard to take, so I beg you to continue trusting in me. In time, you will see I am right."

I don't speak to Cromwell again. My bags are packed by two o'clock in the afternoon, and I am making what will prove to be my last visit to Aloysius Wainwright, the sage Minister I have befriended at the Church of Saint James.

The churchman has had a profound effect on me in a few short days, such is the sincerity with which he has greeted me and the purity of his words. If only all ministers could be cut from the same rock as Aloysius.

"My goodness, Francis, you look as though you have been to Hell and back," he says as he grasps my arm and pulls me into the vestry. "Come and join me. I have some chicken soup I am more than willing to share with you."

After I sit at the table, we break bread, say a prayer, and devour the food. It doesn't take long before I start to relax and feel compelled to tell this devoted disciple my worldly troubles.

He listens intently, patience clearly being one of his many virtues. When I am done, he collects up the bowls and removes them from the large expanse of oak we are sitting at. A crystal glass is placed in front of me, filled to the brim from the cask that contains the church's communion wine.

"Don't tell anyone," admits Aloysius as he attempts to suppress a smile. "I make sure only the best wine is used to honour Christ. And it seems quite apt that we should share a glass on this most solemn of days."

The priest picks up his goblet, raises it to the ceiling, and then takes a long sip. When he is done, it is empty.

"It is a good job I don't entertain guests every day," he jests before quickly returning to the role of confidante and counsellor.

"Francis, you have some difficult thinking to do and hard decisions to make," he says. "Only you, and the Father, can reconcile these things. They are deeply felt and with good reason. And although I have only made your acquaintance recently, I sense you to be a man of integrity, someone who is seeking to serve the Lord obediently and faithfully.

"These feelings you have towards the men, Grey, Holck and now Cromwell, they will weigh you down. Be warned, your anger will consume you, eating away at you from within. You will find yourself separated from our God. And when that happens, the Devil is ready to march in.

"My encouragement, for that is all I can offer, is you

spend the next few days praying deeply and seeking the Father's intercession in these matters. As I have told you before, only He can heal; only He can give you the restoration you need to move on."

I give Aloysius a rueful smile.

"I wish I had your strength and conviction," I confess, meaning every word. "I know the path I should be taking, yet I feel pulled in another direction. I feel powerless. I want to do the right things, I really do. But such is the injustice I feel; I fear it may be beyond me."

The Minister barks out a laugh. The outburst takes me by surprise.

"Good God, man, do you not think we all have those kinds of trials?" he says fiercely. "Staying on the path that leads to salvation is not an easy task, but we must strive to stay true. And I believe you will. There is a strength in you I do not think you know you have, and I suspect the next few weeks will be as much about discovering yourself as it will be about helping to win this damnable war."

TWENTY-ONE

IT WILL TAKE ME THE best part of two days to return to Kirby Bellars. The roads heading north from London are badly affected by snow and ice, so progress is frustratingly slow, thus giving me a lot of time to think about everything that has happened.

Midway through my journey, I decide to visit Stathern to see Isabel and the children. It has been several weeks since I felt the loving touch of my wife and heard the joyous sound of the girls' voices. I have missed them dearly, and I need a welcome distraction.

Considering everything that has unfolded since the start of the New Year, the thought of enjoying the small things that I have taken for granted for more than a dozen years proves therapeutic. It is the best tonic I can take for my dual ailments of acute bewilderment and grievous loss. Now, with Lord Grey no longer a threat to my position, or life, I have no reason to feel guilt or remorse for putting my own needs before those of Parliament. For a few hours, at least.

I don't stay long at the Hall, less than twelve hours in total. But it is long enough to be reunited with the people I love the most – and for my body to feel reinvigorated after such a long and hazardous journey.

After eating a delicious Coney stew with my wife and telling her all I can in the precious time afforded us, Isabel's face becomes flushed. She rises from the table, utters something I cannot comprehend, and departs. I don't say anything; I just stare at the space where she was sitting moments earlier. Then, as the fog and confusion that has been caused by the abruptness of Isabel's departure start to lift from my head, my beautiful wife returns, clutching an envelope. I recognise it immediately.

"We found this," she says with raw emotion and sorrow in her voice as she hands me the folds of creased and mud-spattered paper. "It was discovered when Abijah's cottage was being cleared of his belongings. It is addressed to you, Francis. I haven't opened it. But I expect you may want some time to digest its contents?

"And there is something else you should know: a man came to the Hall some days ago with news he claimed you would be very grateful to receive. He said you would know what he meant by the words 'all is well in Newark'.

"At first, I couldn't believe he had any association with you, such was his appearance and demeanour. But then he explained how you had met and told me how he had aided you. He was unwilling to tell me specifically what his message meant, but I presumed he was referring to Rowland's perilous state, and that is the reason I paid him the three Laurels he demanded."

The news my dear wife has provided about Rowland's condition is a relief indeed, for I instructed

Ambrose Crump to inform me when my brother's life was no longer in danger. I lived in hope rather than expectation that the man would do as he promised once he had word of my brother's fate. It has taken weeks for this to occur, and it has been a thorn in my side ever since I left him locked in Newark Castle's dungeons to meet his doom on his own. But Crump has kept his word, and for that, I say a silent prayer to my Maker. In these dark times, it is a reason to rejoice.

I am silent for several minutes, lost in my thoughts. I forget about Isabel, who waits patiently for me to say something. But my tongue remains stilled. Realising I will be offering nothing for the foreseeable future, my wife leans forward and gently kisses my forehead. Then she is gone, leaving me alone with the letter Abijah handed me for safekeeping just before the heated fighting at Woolsthorpe-by-Belvoir at the end of last year.

With everything that has happened in recent weeks, I had forgotten all about my friend's words, scribbled down after he had experienced dreams that foretold his imminent death. I feel an unusual dryness in my throat as I press the precious paper to my chest, for the words within are all that remains of my dear friend.

I pour a glass of claret, reach for the candle, placing it close by so I can see clearly, and start to read Abijah's last recorded earthly thoughts…

"My dearest Francis.

"If you are reading these words, I am no more. Gone, I hope, to a better place.

"Do not grieve for me, dear friend. Instead, remember me when the sun rises; remember me when you lift a tankard of ale to your lips and taste the fresh hops;

remember me when you are astride Bucephalus, leading our men to glory; and remember me when you are on your own, in need of a guardian angel, for I will be there, watching, guiding and protecting you. Always.

"We may not have grown together in the same flesh, but know this: you are my brother. And as brothers, we have lived rich lives; we have shared much joy and pain, and we have overseen great victories and suffered agonising defeats. These experiences have honed us, forging the links that have ensured we will be inseparable friends for eternity. How lucky we are.

"For everything you have given to me – trust, respect, loyalty, friendship and love – I give you heartfelt thanks. No man could have asked more from a brother.

"You are blessed with a loving family. Do all you can to ensure they know your love and feel your protective arm wrapped around them. Keep them safe, and do not sacrifice yourself recklessly for the cause you serve. Isabel and the children need you to survive this bloodiest of wars.

"I ask of you one just two things: on the anniversary of my demise, think of me and all the other souls who have fallen while defying our tyrant King. Toast us as the sun rises, and seek out the men of the Militia, and persuade them to sing one last lament. We will hear you and respond with our own heavenly voices. What a joyous sound it will make. And please find a loving home for Prudence, my faithful hound. Give her to souls who need a loyal dog and who will tend for her needs, as I did.

"Until we meet again in the better place we are all

called to, I wish you a long, happy and prosperous life.
"Your loving brother, Abijah."

It is some time before I can retire to the chamber I share with Isabel. Abijah's words have stirred many emotions and memories, obscuring the joy I feel about Rowland.

When I eventually climb the stairs and reach our room, my wife is sitting upright, waiting patiently for me as the candlewicks that illuminate her loving face visibly tire.

"Your eyes betray you," she says kindly as I sit on the bedding before I have a chance to utter a word. "There is a sadness in them I haven't seen since the passing of the girls."

I ease onto the mattress, stretching my legs and reaching out and holding my wife's delicate and refined hands. As usual, we interlink our fingers, emphasising the love we share and the continued strength of our unbroken bond.

"Like me, he was a man of few words. But when he did speak, it mattered," I tell her. "It seemed strange to be reading the letter. All the time, I could hear him talking to me. It was as though he was in the room."

I take the envelope out of my pocket and attempt to give it to Isabel. Immediately, she pulls her hand away.

"No, Francis," she says. "Abijah wrote that letter for you, and you alone. It would not be appropriate for me to look at it. Not now. Not ever. So, please, keep it somewhere safe and read it as often as you must, but do not reveal its contents to me.

"He was the bravest of men and a wonderful friend to our family. But it is time to move on, and for you, that means coming to terms with his passing and forgiving yourself. Abijah would not wish you to suffer in any way. He didn't blame others for the misfortunes he experienced and would not have blamed you for sending him to Newark, even when he was standing on the scaffold, and the end was near. What happened was tragic. But it's the sort of terrible thing that happens when men set about killing themselves."

No sooner has she stopped speaking than Isabel's strength deserts her slender frame, and she crumples onto the mattress and starts sobbing.

"When is all the senseless killing going to stop?" she rasps as grief takes hold of her. "Why, Lord? Why?"

I move closer and cradle her head in my hands.

"Fear not, my love," I say as soothingly as I can. "We must endure for a while longer, but the omens are good. We have experienced the worst, of that I am sure. But, better times are not far away. And Abijah's sacrifice will not have been in vain."

As my good wife closes her eyes once again and tears dampen the sheets, I gaze into the blackness of the night, hoping and praying my words are prophetic. Little do I realise, more dark days must follow before the gathering rays of hope have sufficient energy to break through the shroud of misery and death that has consumed our land and our very own house.

The morning of Wednesday, the fifteenth day of February, in the year of our Lord 1645, sees me rise early, eager to confront the rigours of garrison life with my new Company, and prepared to start the process of healing, as Isabel has wished.

By ten o'clock, I am breakfasted, have spent a good

hour or so with my adorable daughter and had time to enjoy a lengthy and lively conversation with Josiah and Ursula Goswick. The couple are still scarred by recent events, but they have made solid progress, not least because they are surrounded by loving and caring people who know what it is like to suffer such extreme loss.

As they leave, I cough before asking: "My friends, Abijah's dog needs a new home. I would bring her here in a heartbeat, but Prudence is not fond of me, and she has made that plain ever since she was a pup. I know not why this is, but it is so. Therefore, I wondered if you may wish to have her? I know Abijah's last wish was for her to reside with people who will care for her, as he did. And I know you to be such people."

Without consulting her husband, Ursula says: "We would be delighted, and honoured, to take the dog into our care. We are stronger now these months have passed. And Josiah needs some exercise; the comforts of Stathern have not been a friend to his stomach, which has grown beyond measure."

Jollity fills the kitchen as man and wife laugh aloud. Happiness is once again etched on their pinched faces. And then they are gone, with my good wishes ringing in their ears as they continue their daily chores around the estate.

I leave the Hall a few minutes later to a chorus of voices from the many wellwishers who have assembled to bid me farewell. Under normal circumstances, I would feel embarrassed and uncomfortable by such a turnout, but not today. This morning, their optimism, humour and graciousness have put me in a good heart. It is gratifying to reacquaint myself with so many familiar faces as I make my way from the Hall up to Mill Hill and beyond.

There is a numbing chill in the air as Bucephalus and I make our way towards Melton Mowbray and my new charges. What awaits me, I do not know. I can only pray Cornet Needham has kept the men in good shape and heart during my prolonged absence.

While the tide of war may have changed its course these past few months, there is no doubt the Royalists will put up the fight of their lives to protect their autocratic King. Much blood is still to be spilt before the peace can be reclaimed, and I vow I will do all in my power to ensure the people for whom I have ultimate responsibility will suffer as little as possible.

As the shrublands of Stathern and Harby give way to the pastures of Rutlandshire and, eventually, the distinctive tower and slate roof of the church of Saint Thomas of Canterbury in Frisby on the Wreake, I realise I have a great deal to ponder if I am to make this worthy ambition a reality.

TWENTY-TWO

THE SKY IS CLEAR AND dark as I rise early on the morning of the twenty-fifth day of February and go on a brisk walk around the grounds of the old priory, marvelling at the wonders of Creation.

It is over a week since I returned to my men and military life. Since I resumed command of the Kirby Bellars garrison, I have been pleased with the speed in which I have readjusted to living the solitary life of a soldier. Knowing Rowland is alive and the threat of execution has been lifted is a huge source of comfort.

When I return to my chambers, I barely have time to take my coat off before there is a sharp rap on the door. Such is the impatience of my visitor; I don't have time to respond before the door opens and Needham strides in. His face carries the appearance of a man weighed down by fatigue, worry and fear.

"Captain, forgive me for this untimely intrusion, but we have just received new orders from Colonel Rossiter," he says as he enters. "It seems the enemy is on the move and heading in our direction."

I look at the young Cornet, my irritation at his curt and official manner quickly replaced with curiosity and a significant degree of alarm. I extend my right hand, gesturing for Needham to surrender Rossiter's dispatch.

"Quick, man," I bark, as Needham hesitates, unnerved by my agitation and directness. "Let me see it for myself."

When I have read the hastily written note, I can see why Needham correctly thought it important I was made aware of the facts as soon as possible. For it seems Sir Marmaduke Langdale, one of the King's most celebrated commanders, has departed Oxford and is now making his way northward via Market Harborough and Melton Mowbray. With him is the Northern Horse, a force comprising almost three thousand fighting men.

Langdale has been ordered by the King to relieve Pontefract Castle in his home county of Yorkshire. Rossiter's assessment is that after leaving Charles two days ago, the enemy could be in Leicestershire in less than twenty-four hours.

Reacting quickly and effectively to the challenge posed by this large force is clearly of the essence as Parliament may only have one opportunity to stop the Royalists before they reach their destination and attempt to relieve Pontefract's besieged garrison.

"The Colonel makes it sound as though he is keen to engage with Langdale," adds Needham, referring directly to Rossiter's command to muster the men and prepare for action. "But do we really have enough time to assemble a credible force to halt them and gain a valuable and morale-boosting victory?"

It is a good question, and I inform Needham so. I also tell the young man I think it highly unlikely we will be able to call on the services of more than a thousand Parliamentarians from the combined Leicester, Melton, Grantham, Stamford and Derby militias, so any force we are able to put in the field against the Royalists is likely to be heavily outnumbered.

"You do the calculation, my friend," I say seriously. "I am all for fighting when the odds are more equal, but it may prove a folly in the extreme to seek combat with a much larger group of capable and dangerous men."

With nothing more to discuss and my mood becoming sombre, I dismiss Needham, who clearly has a lot to contemplate as he prepares for his first taste of serious action. Before he leaves my company, I ask him: "Tell me, young friend, do you believe in the power of prayer?"

Confused by the bluntness of my question, the young man struggles to reply. So I try again: "It is simple enough, Needham," I say. "Either you do, or you don't. So what is it to be?"

Seeking to avoid direct eye contact, Needham replies awkwardly: "I certainly do, sir, although I find it hard to find the time to pray as regularly as I would like. Why do you ask?"

Shaking my head, I laugh aloud as I respond.

"That's very good, Needham. I am delighted to hear it," I say, my sarcasm all too evident. Looking directly at the young officer, I add: "I suspect we will all be in need of our God come tomorrow evening. May I suggest that before you take to your bed tonight, you make haste to the chapel and get down on your bended knees, for the more men like us call on our Maker to intercede, the more likely some of us will be allowed to live through the madness of the next forty-eight hours."

Once Needham has left me, I sit down and devour the content of Rossiter's hastily written order.

I tried to make light of my concerns in front of Needham, failing miserably in the process, for with just cause, I have reservations about the wisdom of the Colonel's intentions.

I move closer to the window and candles, so Rossiter's words are more legible. As the flickering light illuminates the vellum, I make out the following words:

"My esteemed Captain Hacker.

"I have today received news that will raise the spirits of any Parliamentarian who is keen to bring about an early resolution to this terrible war.

"It is our good fortune to be able to deal the King's forces a crushing blow in the coming hours. You and I have waited many long months to avenge that dark day in November 1643, when Melton's garrison was surprised by Gervase Lucas, an event that led to our unfortunate imprisonment. But God is good, and the morrow, we will have an opportunity to seek our long-awaited revenge.

"Sir Marmaduke Langdale and the Northern Horse are riding towards us as I write. I intend to challenge them on favourable ground after they have departed Market Harborough, thereby bringing about their demise.

"I have sent word to Colonel Gell in Derby, summoning him to a general muster at Belton. I ask you to bring your Company of Horse to the same rendezvous.

Be there by ten o'clock in the morning. When all are assembled, we will seek to confront the enemy and end their plans to relieve Pontefract Castle. May God be with you and your men."

Such has been Rossiter's haste in writing out his communiqué the Colonel has forgotten to put his signature to his words. Should I wish to, I have the right to ignore the command, claiming its provenance to be, at best, uncertain. However, I clearly recognise the author's hand and know it to be genuine. Rossiter is also a friend, and I will not turn my back on him, regardless of the foolhardiness of the edict.

At eight-thirty in the morning, fifty largely untried and untested men are ready to meet whatever fate our Father decrees. Like me, they have slept fitfully, saying prayers and making their peace during the early hours, and knowing this morning's dawn chorus may be the last they ever hear. For some, it will be so – unless the almighty is smiling favourably on us this day.

In the short time I have been their commander, I have tried to instil discipline and pride in my new Company, not to mention a sense of belief in the cause we are upholding. A few weeks is not long enough to mould the hearts of men who, for much of this war, have been forgotten by the likes of Lord Grey and consigned to a remote outpost that is of little consequence. But the period has been long enough for me to get to know their character. And what I have sampled so far fills me with hope.

I leave the comfort and warmth of the priory behind me as I walk out of the ornately decorated front door. I have breakfasted and devoted thirty minutes to prayer, and

I am now as ready for war as I ever will be.

Standing in lines of ten, the men look up and snap to attention as they sense my presence. I smile. It is evident Needham has worked them hard while I have been in London; their newly found discipline and cohesion are clear for me to see.

Bucephalus patiently waits. He is pawing at the glue-like mud just a few feet away from where I stand. My steed has a sixth sense, always knowing when mortal danger awaits. Unlike every man I know, he seems to revel in the excitement. The greater the threat, the more animated he becomes.

I pat his muscular neck and he whinnies in appreciation, as he always does before I put my left foot in the stirrup and hoist myself into the saddle. When I am settled, I gaze at the lines before me, experiencing an equal measure of pride and unease as I look into the eyes of my men. This is the first time I will have fought alongside my Company. Can I trust this band of unproven believers? Can Needham ever cover my back like Abijah once did?

I quickly dismiss my questions and negative thoughts. I shake my head, letting the cold air of the morning envelop my head, and look directly at my subordinates and tell them what fate has in store for them this autumnal morn.

"Today, we have been summoned to bring glory to the Lord God and our Parliament," I say, my strong voice not betraying the deep unease I feel. "We are to confront the King's Northern Association Horse on the road to Harborough, and I have every confidence we will win the day.

"Colonels Rossiter and Gell await us with a large

force of men drawn from Melton Mowbray, Derby and other garrisons. Together, we will defeat the enemy and send them back to Oxford, from whence they came."

Nervous excitement ripples up and down the lines. Talk of valour and the prospect of hand-to-hand fighting consumes the men as they anticipate what it feels like to be involved in a pitched battle. They may have experienced the exhilaration of an occasional chase, which resulted in a volley being loosed off against fleeing enemy horsemen, but nothing prepares a man for the all-consuming fear that takes hold when a mass of bodies are pressed together, hacking and cleaving indiscriminately.

At such times, all men think of their own mortality and the loved ones they will leave behind, should they be struck down and their lives ended. I know, for I feel it every time I draw my sword. And this is what now confronts the men of Kirby Bellars.

"Be assured, we will have surprise, and our Maker will be on our side this morn," I continue, exuding as much false bravado as I can muster. "I am proud to be your commander. You have all come a long way in the short time we have been together, and I am sure you will not let yourselves or Parliament down this day as we set about besting our enemies one more time.

"Now dismount from your horses, and make your peace with the Lord. We ride in fifteen minutes."

The mist that has cloaked the fields and hills surrounding Melton Mowbray in thick plumes of white and grey cloud starts to rise as the hour passes two o'clock in the afternoon.

A couple of hours earlier, one of Rossiter's scouts

stumbled across the enemy column some twenty miles away from Market Harborough. They have caught us by surprise, making better time than we expected. Thankfully, Langdale has stopped to cook lunch and allow his men to feed their ravenous horses on the brow of a large hill overlooking Melton and giving them a clear view of the tower of Saint Mary's Church. To their left are the banks of the River Eye, a natural obstacle preventing both bodies of men and horse from utilising the full expanse of the lush fields that are a hallmark of this corner of England.

From their vantage point, smoke from the fires used to heat the cooking pots of thousands of ravenous souls rises into the air, filling the void vacated by the rapidly fading mist. The smell of roasted meats wafts in our direction, making me acutely aware of my own empty belly. Yet all my men and I can do is wait and pray.

As boredom threatens to set in after I have digested the first twenty-six psalms from the Book of Psalms, shouting pierces the tranquil air.

"Captain Hacker! Captain Hacker!"

The voice conveys a degree of urgency.

I look up and see several men pointing in my direction as a dragoon races towards me on a gasping Chestnut mare. The horseman's face is flushed, and he is wearing Rossiter's distinctive colours.

When he locates me a minute or so later, and he has regained a modicum of composure, he gasps: "Captain, your presence is requested at a command meeting. If you would care to follow me."

Without uttering a further word, the young man turns his horse around and proceeds to make for a thicket dominated by a large Beech tree. It is situated about half a mile away. As I look on, I see Rossiter's standard fluttering in the breeze, as is Gell's. It is time to discuss battle tactics. "Edward, it would be suicide to do as you suggest." The voice is that of Gell, the man who commands the Derby Horse, and someone I last saw at Woolsthorpe-by Belvoir. I rarely agree with him, knowing him to be something of a braggart and a thoughtless oaf. But today proves to be an exception.

"We cannot launch a frontal assault on Langdale," continues Gell, unable to hide the scorn he has for Rossiter's bold suggestion. "Our men will be annihilated."

Gell is seeking to persuade Rossiter to pursue a more cautious approach than the one he advocated a few minutes ago, which was to race up the hill while Langdale and his men rested and seek to catch them by surprise.

"They will be ready for us before we get more than a hundred yards, and then they will hold all the advantages," adds Gell, trying to get Edward to listen and focus. "The hill is steep, and their muskets will have plenty of time to loose off two rounds before we reach the brow. I am all for taking a calculated risk. But, my friend, you must see this plan is doomed to fail?"

Rossiter is clearly agitated by this challenge to his authority. He puts his hand inside his jerkin and pulls out a pouch, from which a lump of tobacco is extracted. He rips off a strip of the dry, brown leaves and proceeds to chew with vigour, then turns away from the group for a few minutes. Eventually, after sating his needs and collecting his thoughts, Edward spits out the tobacco residue and returns to the debate with renewed concentration.

Just five men are privy to the conversation that will dictate the strategy we adopt to halt the Royalist's

Northern Horse. And, with Captain Mallam's voice peter-ing out inconclusively, it appears everyone has now spo-ken; except me. All eyes turn in my direction, with Rossiter seemingly pleading with me to back his assertions. As I look at the desperation on his face, I find myself recalling the dispatch I received from him a day earlier, referring to the calamitous defeat the Melton garrison suffered in November 1643. On that day, myself and three hundred men were captured and imprisoned.

It was a day of infamy for Parliament and Rossiter, and I cannot believe that stain is not influencing the reck-lessness of the proposals we are considering this day.

I cough, clearing my throat and buying a moment. Then I speak as forcefully as I can in a bid to influence the situation and a man I have known and respected for many years.

"In all conscience, Colonel Rossiter," I say as diplo-matically as I can, "I do not believe we can be victorious if we engage the enemy in a direct fight. They outnumber us by almost two thousand men, and all the natural advan-tages are with them. Too many of our men would be cut down before they had a chance to fight.

"Like you, I desire the opportunity to take on Langdale and send him and his men back to Oxford as a broken band. But, sir, I am at a loss to see how this can be achieved if we proceed with your plan as it stands?"

Silence greets my words, but I know I have the sup-port of three of the other men, including Gell. Rossiter, his face reddened, takes my words as well as can be expected.

"Fine, we must find another way," he concedes even-tually. "But we have little time, and all the time we prevar-icate, we leave ourselves exposed to an enemy assault. We must decide on our approach, and we must agree on it quickly."

If our resistance has embarrassed or angered him, Rossiter doesn't show it. He simply turns his back on us for a moment, staring at the trunk of the Oak tree before seemingly reaching a decision.

"I accept I may have made a miscalculation," he says as he turns to face us once again. "Allow me to reflect on your words a moment and discuss tactics with Colonel Gell. When we concur on the approach we are to take, your orders will be issued. Now go back to your men and get them ready for the fight. They will not have long to wait. I bid you a good day, gentlemen."

Forty-five minutes later, I receive my instructions from Colonel Rossiter. They have been counter-signed by Gell. I am to lead the left flank and support our main body, drawn from the Leicester and Derby militias, as they engage the main force of Langdale's army.

Incredibly, nothing has changed; Rossiter has some-how got his foolhardy way, and I feel wretched, knowing the blood of scores of brave Parliamentarians will soon start to flow.

At precisely three o'clock in the afternoon, a little more than eleven hundred mounted men make their ascent up a rise that will forever be known as Ankle Hill in recognition of the calamity about to befall Parliament. Of this num-ber, a little over fifty are the contingent from Kirby Bellars.

We approach the enemy after making our way through the town and onto the lush grasslands. The ground underfoot isn't as firm as we had hoped. It ham-pers our ability to climb the slope at the pace we need to cause the maximum damage to the front ranks of Langdale's force. Now, rather than rush the enemy, we are limited to proceeding at a ponderous pace, giving our foe all the time he needs to unleash his cannon on our unprotected flesh and rake our lines with deadly leaden shot.

My Company hugs the left-wing of the phalanx, doing all it can to protect itself and those of the main body closest to us as we close in on the enemy's position. Needham is by my side. His face is chalk white, as are those of many a gallant young man. The young Cornet now realises he will be lucky to survive the carnage, and his grim expression tells me all I need to know about his thoughts at the present time.

"Prepare yourself," I caution him, as the first musket volley resounds and several men in the front rank of Rossiter's force fall to the ground, their crimson blood staining the countryside. "Do nothing foolish and let none of the men seek to become martyrs. I want you living at the end of this debacle, not joining the long list of heroes we will soon be mourning."

Needham blinks and then simply nods in agreement. He has lost his voice momentarily, as many do when they are confronted with the grim realisation of what warfare really is. Thankfully, my words have a positive impact, and I visibly see him relax as he barks an order at Johnson, his wingman. And as he does, more of Parlimanet's men are butchered as the foe set about enjoying their sport.

Swords clash, muskets are fired intermittently, and the acrid smell of gunsmoke fills the air. Above everything else, one noise can be heard above every other: the sound of men having their lives cut short. Brutally. Painfully. With no quarter offered or taken.

All the while the slaughtering takes place, I keep my men under a tight rein, for I will not be responsible for committing their souls to the afterlife. I already have much on my conscience, and I will be damned if I will carry the burden of knowing I have led these men to their deaths in this most unequal of contests. So I look on, as alert as I have ever been. And I choose to do as little as possible.

To my right, I see Rossiter and Gell making ground as they clash with Langdale's most formidable and most battle-hardened troops. Their swords are all motion, glinting in the fading sunlight as the two leading Parliamentarians attempt to slash and cut their way through the numerous and well-marshalled lines arraigned against them.

Eventually, as more and more of our men are killed and maimed, the futility of our ill-judged assault becomes evident. And at that moment, the emphasis changes from pursuing victory to saving as many lives as possible.

Even Rossiter knows when he is a beaten man. And, with the colour drained from his face as he realises the futility of his endeavours, he draws his surviving men around him and desperately seeks an escape route.

As I prepare to issue orders to return to Kirby Bellars, a Parliamentarian officer breaks through the main body and rides towards us. When he is clear of the main throng, I realise it is Samuel Collinson who captains a Company of dragoons attached to Rossiter's garrison.

"Hacker," he bellows when he is some fifty yards away. "Get away from here, man. Flee as quickly as you can. All is lost. We are disengaging all along the line and doing all we can to ensure we are not routed.

"Colonel Rossiter orders you and your men to retire immediately to Kirby Bellars, where you are to destroy the building and any fortifications that may serve Langdale's purposes. Under no circumstances is it to be a fit place for the enemy to install a garrison. They may have bloodied our noses this afternoon, but our defeat is not a disaster. But it will be if we yield our forts to them, particularly one so close to Melton."

It would appear my lack of enthusiasm to join in the fighting has gone unnoticed by my superiors. Time will tell whether that will be the case in the days to come, but right now, I am more than happy to carry out the Colonel's unambiguous instructions.

Collinson, who is now just an arm's length from me, and sitting astride a magnificent piebald stallion, leans forward and extends his bloodied hand.

"Ride safely, Francis," he says as he takes a firm grip of my numbed fingers. "May God be with you, and all of us, as we attempt to save our wretched skins."

By nine o'clock in the evening, the men and I have carried out our instructions, turning Kirby Bellars into a raging ball of fire. Even though our attempts are hurried and rushed, we carry out Rossiter's edict as efficiently as we can in the few hours at our disposal. Much of the structure is highly combustible, and we have little difficulty raising the old priory to the ground. When the sparks from the last burning ember finally die down, it is satisfying to know no enemy soldier will be willing to reside in this fragile and isolated place.

The dried beams crackle and spit as the inferno we have unleashed consumes them. Masonry falls to the ground; debris and ashes shower the well-tended grounds with the tell-tale signs of destruction. What was once a fortress to many quickly turns into just another scorched carcass littering this bleeding land.

My Company looks on, unsure how they should react, their pained expressions silhouetted as the flames continue to weave their merry and destructive dance.

It is dark. I look at my watch, breaking away from the spell cast by the fire. It is almost eight o'clock, and we have twenty long miles to travel to the safety of Leicester's walls, where we hope to be afforded a friendly welcome and discover the extent of our defeat this day.

I am emerging from my own thoughts and regrets when I hear Needham's distinctive voice calling out to me.

"Captain, do you really think we behaved with honour this afternoon?" he asks tetchily, pain and guilt dictating the tone of his clipped voice. "Should we not have gone to the aid of our comrades? Should we not have done something rather than just look on as good men were butchered?"

I pull on Bucephalus's reins, slowing my steed's trot so I can drop alongside Needham. As I do, I make sure none of the men can hear me as I whisper my reply.

"Cornet, in time you will learn that I am a Godly, honourable and loyal man, and I try to serve Parliament as faithfully as anyone can."

I speak slowly, as a kindly father would while scolding a favoured son.

"But I will never heed an order that is reckless or negligent. And I will not feel guilt or shame for doing so. Today, Colonel Rossiter took leave of his senses. He let thoughts of vengeance cloud his judgment and dictate his decision-making. It was plain to see. Why Gell chose to endorse the order, I do not know. It matters little. We were asked to guard the left flank, and we did so diligently. That is the truth of the matter, as God is my witness.

"I may face some criticism for not leaping to the defence of the main body, but what difference would fifty men have made to that slaughter? I tell you, any attack we had mounted would have altered nothing. The only thing that would have changed would be the number of dead, for many of our men would now be rotting corpses. And all for nought."

I can feel Needham's eyes boring into me as we both sway in the saddle. Our bodies are moving rhythmically, in time with our horses' legs as they carefully pick their way to safety in the blackness, guided by a handful of torches. Thankfully, the young officer is wise enough to know better than to continue with his line of questioning. He stills his tongue, and some semblance of peace descends once again. Strangely, none of the men are talking. They have been subdued by their shared experiences this day. Defeat has a chastening effect on all of us.

In the eerie silence, I see the far-off glow of Leicester. Braziers illuminate the city's walls and, as we get closer to the sanctuary we seek, I see the tower of Saint Martin's rising majestically into the night sky. Never has the sight that greets us been more welcoming.

After reflecting on Needham's words, I decide it matters not whether my subordinate agrees with me. What is of paramount concern to me is my men will now live to fight another day, and I take consolation and comfort knowing that while some may think I have failed Rossiter, I know I have fulfilled my obligations to them.

TWENTY-THREE

I AM NOT AFFORDED MUCH time to lick my wounds and restore what is left of my pride after the Melton disaster, for on Monday, the sixth day of March, I receive an urgent communication from Cromwell.

It is several weeks since I heard from the Lieutenant-General, and I confess I have been glad of the respite. The way matters concluded between us in London, particularly the arbitrary way Lord Grey was allowed to escape the executioner's axe, left me bewildered and full of rage. And Oliver is the person I have blamed for the sense of injustice that has racked my body and plagued my soul.

Wisely, the man I respect more than any other has chosen to leave me to come to terms with the events that so easily could have ended in disaster for him and Parliament. He knows his decisions caused me distress, but he also knows time is a healer and comforter.

Young Guy Goodman, one of the Militiamen in my Company, has been his eyes and ears at Stathern. Recently, he has had plenty of news to report to his master, not least my return to the Hall, which is where I headed two days after the calamitous and ill-judged clash with Langdale. He has also ensured the safety of my family, for which he has my gratitude.

I had hoped to be granted a period of extended peace to spend time with Isabel and the girls and rebuild my fragile morale. But, alas, war is a cruel and demanding overlord, always taking from you and the people you love and never being willing to give anything back. And so it proves once again.

Leicester's weakened state is the source of a great deal of vexation for senior Parliamentary figures – not least, Fairfax and Cromwell. They fear the city will soon be the target of a full-scale Royalist attack when the weather improves and the campaigning season gets underway.

With Spring just around the corner, such a scenario could confront us before we know it. With the city's walls riddled with gaping holes and just a few hundred poorly equipped and demoralised men to defend the ramparts and defences, it is ripe for the taking.

Thankfully, well over a year ago, Thomas Haselrig, my friend and fellow Committee member, spent time with me shoring up some of the areas of greatest concern. This involved the widespread creation of defensive ditches outside the crumbling walls and the erection of a series of raised banks, which form parapets at strategic points. These modifications allow a man to fire upon the enemy, step back a pace or two and be sheltered from any returning musket fire while he reloads his weapon.

While this was undoubtedly a step in the right direction, no progress has been made in plugging the many breaches that exist in the old Roman and Norman walls that encircle the city, despite numerous attempts to try and make this happen. Now there is not nearly enough time to make good the many repairs that are still needed, for the town's population is depleted, and it will take a considerable amount of time, effort and money to secure the stonemasons and raw materials that are required.

The loss of Leicester would be a huge setback. Its strategic importance cannot be underestimated: it is a critical communication and trade bridgehead for Parliament in the Midlands and a convenient thorn in the side of the King's formidable garrisons at Newark and Ashby. Yet Cromwell's dispatch speaks of the unthinkable, and the urgency in the Lieutenant-General's words is unmistakable. He writes:

> *"Francis, my dear friend and comrade.*
>
> *"I send you my warmest regards and affections. I hope you may have now started to forgive me for the cruel decisions I was forced to make that put State interests before personal considerations. I pray it is so?*
>
> *"I write to urge you to be wary, my young friend. Conspiracies are afoot in Leicester to make good the city to Henry Hastings. Since the defeat at Melton, prominent citizens have conspired with the Royalists to overthrow the mayor and alderman, allowing Hastings to take a notable scalp. Our spies tell us at least eight notable families are involved in the plot, which grows more serious by the day. Under no circumstances must their plans and collusions be allowed to succeed.*
>
> *"Please use all the means at your disposal to discover who the traitors are and, at the same time, start to make good the city's defences. In this endeavour, every*

day is precious.

"Report directly to me on this matter and, for as long as possible, ensure Lord Grey does not learn of this matter. We do not want him pursuing an opportunity that he could use to our disadvantage. I will be at Stamford in ten days, where I will seek a meeting with you. Expect further correspondence from me in due course.

"I remain your faithful and loving brother in Christ."

News of a plot doesn't surprise me. Indeed, the only shock is it has taken so long to come to fruition, for the good people of Leicester have been petitioning Lord Grey for the last two years, urging him to help restore security to the city. Much to their dismay, these pleas have been rebuffed at every opportunity. With anxieties now heightened after our defeat at Melton, it is little wonder some have lost confidence and are seeking to side with the Devil.

Discovering who the plotters are will not take long, of that I am sure. During desperate times, money talks, and the tongues of enough townsfolk will loosen when a few shillings are dropped into their greedy palms.

No, the real problem facing Leicester will come in April or May, when Prince Rupert will be at the head of the King's army, seeking to avenge Marston Moor and all the other victories that have gone our way in recent months. That's when our biggest test will come, and when it does, we simply cannot be found wanting.

"They have all been questioned and have confessed their part in the treason," reports Nathaniel Sydenham in his clipped Norfolk accent. "It didn't take much to get to the truth. Most of them broke down the moment we started searching their homes."

Sydenham stands to attention, looking straight ahead. He is a Sergeant under the command of Thomas Babington, one of the few men I can trust and the first person I turned to after I digested Cromwell's dispatch. That was a week ago. Since then, Sydenham and his small group of six trusted men have set about their business with an assuredness and efficiency that does them immense credit.

As he stands before me, I am acutely aware of the calmness and confidence exuding from him. He knows he is a cut above the riff-raff, yet there is a humility within the man that is rarely found. If Cromwell were here, he would say Sydenham is the kind of warrior all Parliamentary soldiers must aspire to be when the New Model Army establishes itself in all four corners of the land. And that would indeed be a compliment to hold on to.

"What are your orders, Captain. How shall we proceed?" enquires the man who has been the subject of my scrutiny.

I look directly at the Sergeant's ruddy face. We are in the Magazine, where the city's arms, gunpowder and munitions are stored. As well as being the main arsenal, it is one of the few places one can talk and not be overheard. And I certainly don't want an eavesdropper to hear the matters I am about to discuss with Sydenham.

"It is important this whole affair is only known about by those of us directly involved in it. If news of a plot gets out, matters could quickly get out of hand, and we are in no position to put down a riot," I say in an even voice. "Is that clearly understood?"

Sydenham agrees without hesitation. He blinks evenly, and I trust his word. The Sergeant will ensure his men stay silent. He is no idler, and his decisiveness is admirable. If he keeps his nose clean, this fellow has the potential to go far.

"Take the ringleaders to Nottingham and place them in the custody of Colonel Hutchinson," I continue. "Make sure they are kept as far away from the gaol's other prisoners as possible. I will write a letter to the good Colonel and give it to you before you depart. Make sure he appreciates the letter is for his eyes only. Not even his wife, the inquisitive Lucy, must be aware of its contents, not for the time being.

"When it is done, and you are satisfied with the arrangements, report back to me. But make sure you are standing before me within three days. By then, I will have consulted with the appropriate people about how we go about dealing with the main troublemakers and the other prisoners."

I bid Sydenham a good journey and leave him to do as he has been ordered. It is now time to meet Thomas and assess the weaknesses of the city's defences and agree what is to be done to bolster them in the short space of time at our disposal.

Good to his word, Oliver summons me exactly ten days after I received his original dispatch. It arrives late in the evening and requires my attendance in Stamford the morrow, the seventeenth day of March.

The town is some thirty miles away from Stathern, and the journey will require me to be in the saddle for a good six hours. But, thankfully, Cromwell cannot see me until late in the day. So there is ample time to enjoy break-fast with Isabel before bidding my farewells and making my way eastwards to the Lincolnshire Wolds.

I dread leaving my home. My anxieties have become more acute since the loss of Barbara and Isable. However, they are eased, somewhat, by the clear, fresh air, which helps purge my head of everything weighing me down. Before long, I start enjoying the freedom of the country-side once again and, for a few hours at least, I revel in the uncomplicated relationship I enjoy with Bucephalus and Mother Nature.

As we consume mile after mile of open countryside, I marvel at the never-ending beauty of the changing land-scapes that are seamlessly intertwined with swathes of woodland and forest. A myriad of colours flashes in front of my eyes. Then they are gone, replaced by blurred shapes and sounds I am unable to focus on, such is the speed at which we are travelling and the levels of concen-tration I need to apply.

When Bucephalus is content to conserve some of his energy, I look up and see foxes, badgers and deer aplenty. They lift their heads and watch as I ride by. Sensing there is no imminent danger, their interest in me quickly disap-pears, and they continue their business unperturbed by my sudden presence.

The route to Stamford is a relatively direct one, tak-ing me close to Garthorpe, Wymondham, Market Overton and Great Casterton. Nonetheless, the scenery is breath-taking, more so because I make sure I stay away from the many impoverished villages that litter these parts. I have no desire to visit places that spew disease and discontent like festering plague boils on a corrupted corpse.

Alas, no sooner have I started to relax than I see the rooftops confirming my safe arrival at my destination. The time has passed quickly, and now I am required to become an obedient and compliant soldier once again. Bucephalus senses my disquiet and unease, and he snorts in sympathy. I pat my steed's head appreciatively and spur him on as we set about completing the last couple of unfamiliar miles.

My room at the imposing George Inn, located in the Saint Martins area of Stamford and adjacent to the banks of the River Welland, is a lot bigger and grander than those usually offered to a Captain of Horse. It is the place of Kings, with Charles, and his late father, James, staying here in less volatile times – before brothers set about trying to slaughter one another.

It is not every day one of Parliament's great heroes insists I visit him and is determined to restore our association. So I give thanks where they are due, find the stables and pay a young boy some pennies to feed Bucephalus water and hay, and find him comfortable shelter for the duration of my stay.

"I will reward you further if he looks contented when I return for him in the morning," I say to the youngster, whose face beams at the prospect of adding more coinage to his tally. "But you will need to earn it. Bucephalus is a demanding master, as you will learn over the next few hours."

The lad chuckles and skips away to tend to his business. I laugh aloud, something I don't do nearly enough these days. I watch as he darts into the stables, a happy, contented soul. Oh, to be young once again, untainted by the evil of war.

My thoughts return to the present when a company of dragoons emerge from a side street. They are making enough noise to rouse the Devil himself, the metal shoes of sixty or so, large horses echoing off the cobbled thoroughfare. They are Cromwell's men, members of the New Model Army. They exude the confidence and power of the professional soldiery their master pledged they would be.

I watch them march up the street in two stern, disciplined columns. When the last of the men disappear from view, I reach for my pocket watch. It was a precious gift from Isabel, and I protect it as if it is a living entity. It sits close to my heart, nestled in the secure inner pocket of my leather jerkin. I look at the dial, and it signals it is almost four o'clock in the afternoon. I have several hours to kill before I sit down with the Lieutenant-General and begin to repair our broken bond.

Just as I wonder what I will do for the next few hours, I see the magnificent spire of All Saints Church standing tall and proud, looking every inch the beacon it is meant to be. I find myself pulled in its direction, marvelling at the construction of the sturdy tenement buildings I see in Butchers Street, Wollerowe and Byhindback. They are a far cry from the rotting, overcrowded slums that feature so prominently in Leicester's filthy streets.

As I reach Red Lion Square, I see the Guildhall on the south side. It looks just like every municipal building I have ever seen – aloof and self-important. For a moment, I feel compelled to darken its doors. Then I remember this town is not an enthusiastic friend of Puritanism, being close to Burghley House, the prized former home of the Earl of Exeter, which Cromwell took into Parliament's possession some two years ago.

So I walk to the doors of the church instead, marvelling at the quality and majesty of the distinctive sandstone masonry chiselled almost four hundred years ago in honour of the God we all serve. There is much to pray about, not least my reunion with Cromwell, the safety of Leicester, my brother's welfare, and what my Creator's plans are for me, his most humble of servants.

After paying my dues, I emerge into the late Spring sunshine some three hours later. My head is clear, my body refreshed, and my heart feels restored. It never ceases to amaze me how the power of prayer can have such a positive impact. It is a one-way conversation. I am not aware of God ever speaking directly to me. Yet, somehow he finds a way of communicating his thoughts. Thanks to his intervention, I now know how to conduct myself when I meet the Lieutenant-General in a little over an hour.

I amble around the square for fewer than ten minutes when I hear my name being called by a voice I instantly recognise.

"Captain Hacker! Captain Hacker!" It is the loud baritone of Robert Willoughby, a former officer in the Eastern Association. He has recently been commissioned to serve Fairfax and Cromwell in the New Model Army.

"Thank goodness I have found you," he says, gasping for breath. "I have spent the last forty-five minutes scurrying around this rabbit warren of a town trying to find you, Francis.

"Cromwell wishes you to attend upon him as quickly as you are able. His plans have changed, and he needs to leave Stamford sooner than expected. Dinner is waiting. I hope you have an appetite for eel pie?"

I chuckle aloud for a second time, for although the Lieutenant-General's culinary tastes are somewhat limited, as anyone who knows him will testify, serving Cromwell is never a predictable and dull exercise!

"Francis, it fills me with joy to see you looking so well," declares Cromwell, who oozes vitality and power as his bear-like hand crushes my hand as we greet one another in the main hall. "Life is clearly agreeing with you, my friend."

In comparison to my host, my tidings are polite but somewhat muted. For the first time in many years, I find myself overawed by the situation, unable to utter what I know I must say.

After Cromwell has complimented me on my appearance, apparent good health, and enquired on the welfare of Isabel and the children, a deafening silence descends on the room.

It is time.

"Oliver," I say as confidently as I can. "To restore our good relations and my steadfast loyalty to you, I need to say some things that may cause you some discomfort. But say them, I must, as you have always encouraged me to do."

Cromwell pulls up a chair from the large dining table that dominates the room. Then, without saying a word and with his gaze fixed firmly on my face, he encourages me to do the same.

"Speak plainly, friend," he instructs, his smile friendly and encouraging. "You know the esteem I hold you in. We have experienced much together, far too much for there to be a barrier between us. My rank should not be an obstacle, so forget I am a General, and you are a Captain. Tell me what is on your heart, and let's see what can be done about it."

So I do.

Almost an hour later, I am finished. And Oliver's portion of eel pie is cold and untouched on his plate. I have said all I came to say, and I have clearly given him plenty to think about.

"Thank you, my dear brother in Christ," he says. "You are one of only a handful of men whom I trust and whom I know will always be truthful. So, I am grateful. You have given me much to consider and ponder.

"I want to reassure you about one thing this evening, and that is my own motivation in doing the things I do. Quite rightly, you have challenged me, particularly in relation to the matter of Lord Grey. Be assured, this man will never be a friend of mine, nor will Parliament trust his motives. But he will be a useful puppet, and because of him, lives will be saved, and things will come to pass that would be denied to us if he had received the punishment his crimes warranted."

Cromwell pauses for a moment and reaches for the bottle of claret sitting imploringly on the table. Then, he looks at me directly, grins and pours two full glasses of wine, pushing one of them in my direction. Only after he has quenched his thirst does he continue.

"In London, I had to behave in a manner that was decisive and very challenging," he admits. "But, I had to do the right thing for the cause you and I serve. So I prayed. And I believe it was God who gave me the wisdom and tolerance that spared Grey's miserable life. It was not what I had wished for. I sought divine intervention that made it acceptable to execute the man. Yet, I received a sign telling me to do the exact opposite. And who am I to go against the wishes of the Lord?"

Oliver abruptly stops talking. His eyes start to water, and at that moment, I know him to be sincere. As one, we stand and embrace. There may be a score and five years between us in age, but we are brothers in Christ. And we are committed to doing His will.

"Forgive me," I say to him when we are seated once again. "My anger has got the better of me these past weeks, and I found myself judging you when I had no right to do so. Several years ago, I promised I would trust you, and I have failed in this regard. But I won't let you down again. You have my word."

Oliver takes a handkerchief from his pocket and wipes his eyes. When he has got his emotions under control, he speaks again as the General he is.

"My friend, that is good to hear. So now to business: I need you to take control of Leicester. The King will attack the city of that there is no doubt. Our agents don't know precisely when the assault will come, but they suspect it is a matter of weeks, not months.

"When it comes, the city must be able to withstand anything Charles and his army throws at its defences. Leicester must not yield. You do not have long to make the essential repairs that are necessary and knock the garrison into shape. So much depends on this, and you are the only person I know who is capable of making it so. Will you accept my challenge?"

Without hesitating, I reply: " Aye, Oliver. I will."

A brilliant smile flashes across Cromwell's taut mouth, but it is gone the moment he speaks again.

"Francis, holding Leicester is important," he says with steel in his voice. "But should the city fall, and we must acknowledge there is a likelihood this may happen, be sure to save yourself. Under no circumstances are you to be a martyr for the cause we serve. I need you. Parliament needs you. If Leicester is lost, that will be a setback. But if you were to die, that would be an altogether far more serious matter. Do I make myself clear?"

I say nothing as I nod my head in agreement. A gauntlet has been thrown at my feet, and I do not underestimate the size of the challenge. A force of up to ten thousand men could be sent to lay siege to Leicester, where a demoralised and poorly equipped garrison of fewer than four hundred men is all that stands in its way.

It is only as I ride back to Stathern the following morning that the enormity of Oliver's words hit me fully: I must not allow Leicester to fall!

Time will tell whether I am equal to the task.

TWENTY-FOUR

SEVEN WEEKS OF BACK-BREAKING toil and sweat follow my meeting with Cromwell, as the people of Leicester start shoring up the city's crumbling walls and pulling down the many timber-framed buildings that have the potential to offer protection to the enemy.

A simple, desperate desire to live drives us on.

Despite continued Parliamentary military successes all over England, news reaches our ears about the battle-field victories enjoyed by the Marquis of Montrose north of the border. The Scots may be hundreds of miles away, but the prospect of a Royalist resurgence in the north acts as a timely spur. As a result, hundreds of townsfolk, partic-ularly Leicester's women, heed the pleas to join the cause. They work around the clock in a bid to ensure the city has a chance to repulse the most significant danger it has ever faced.

Throughout these worrying times, all commanders do their utmost to improve the spirits of the garrison and recruit fresh blood to the ranks. More than a hundred and fifty men are added to our fighting strength from the county, courtesy of the impressment powers granted to the Committee by Parliament only a few weeks ago. Although they are far from enthusiastic about the uncertain future that has been forced upon them, these men will fight with every ounce of strength they can muster. I am sure of it. We all will, for none of us wishes to succumb to the afterlife prematurely.

The likes of Thomas Babington return to their family estate in Rothley, a village to the south of Loughborough. There willing farmers and estate workers – able-bodied men who don't need encouragement to fire a musket or plunge a sword into the gut of a Cavalier – are recruited. The Mayor and Alderman also make a notable contribution, identifying almost nine hundred men, aged between sixteen and sixty-five years, who will do whatever they can to protect their homes and families. And slowly but surely, our army grows.

As I continue about my business, I am comforted knowing I am equipped with a letter written by Cromwell commissioning me to "do whatever it takes" to protect the city. Accordingly, without seeking Lord Grey's permission, or that of Colonel George Booth, the governor, I enrol several Companies of Horse and Foot from the Midlands Association to the roster of defenders. I also ensure Needham and the Kirby Bellars Company of Horse I command are given new responsibilities.

When he discovers I have deprived him of some of his best men, Lord Grey is furious. He tells me so several times in a series of dispatches he writes to me, complaining of my "arrogance" and my "recklessness". But he is impotent. He knows it, as do I. So the works and the soldiery training proceed at the pace I dictate, unobstructed by the traitor who continues to reside in luxury at Bradgate House.

I inspect the progress we are making daily. When appropriate to do so, I offer encouragement to many and an occasional dose of chastisement to any unfortunate malingerers I see dawdling. Time is short. We must all pull together and do what is required. There can be no tolerance of idleness. Too much is at stake.

Thankfully, with the Lord watching over us, we achieve a lot in a short space of time.

Most of the walls, which stretch for three miles, are strengthened thanks to the unselfish hard work of the masons and women labourers. Morale improves, too. But nagging doubts persist, not least with the condition of the city's south wall, by the Newarke. Here, despite our best efforts, we struggle to make good the many rotting timbers and stonework that has been allowed to erode for far too long.

This is our weakest point, and should Prince Rupert, that most astute of Bohemian war dogs, discover our Achilles heel, I fear our best efforts will be undone and our cause lost.

One matter has been dominating my thoughts ever since I returned from my meeting with Cromwell in Stamford: what kind of justice should I mete out to the plotters who planned to open the city's gates to 'Blind' Henry Hastings in the wake of Parliament's defeat at Melton Mowbray?

I have thought about the right course of action on many occasions since the conspirators were arrested. I am in favour of clemency, but I don't trust my instinct. I understand the fears of these townsfolk and appreciate fully why they momentarily lost faith in Parliament's ability to defend them. Alas, my indecisiveness in this matter proves to be my undoing.

Colonel Hutchinson, unhappy at being required to provide dungeons and food for the conspirators I sent to Nottingham, has brought the matter to the attention of Cromwell. The Lieutenant-General has not been slow in offering me his opinion on what should be done. Fears have also been heightened by the arrival of a turncoat King's man, one Henry Purefoy, who brings tidings from Bristol confirming Royalist plans for an assault on the city are well advanced. The revelation creates a new wave of concern that treachery is still very much in the air.

"They must be hanged without delay," writes Cromwell in a private communiqué addressed to me. It is dated the twenty-third day of May and has taken two days to reach Leicester. I received it less than three hours ago while attending to my affairs in the Guildhall, and I am deeply troubled by its tone and content.

"We cannot prevaricate or show weakness in a matter as serious as this," continues Oliver. "As much as it pains me to say so, the men who would have betrayed the city to our enemies are nothing more than traitors. As such, they must be subjected to the severest of punishments. But be discreet. This act must not become common knowledge.

"As for the others, you are at liberty to exercise as much discretion as you deem wise. I can see no merit in executing the women. But their husbands are a different matter. If we don't show a strong hand, more troubles will flow from the cabal that bred this abomination."

I have no choice; the die is cast. There must now be a blood-letting and, as the man who is required to carry out the orders of Cromwell, I feel wretched about what I must do. Not wishing to dwell on things any longer than I have to, I write an order for the eyes of Colonel Hutchinson. It reads:

"By the express command of Lieutenant-General Cromwell, and with immediate effect, it is ordered that those prisoners arrested for plotting to betray the city of Leicester to the King's men at Ashby Castle are to be summarily executed. To maintain order, their crimes and fates are not to be recognised publically, and their bodies are to be buried in unmarked graves."

I hesitate momentarily, acutely aware I am sanctioning an act of infamy, one I am sure to be held to account for on my own day of judgment. Yet what choice do I have? I think hard and search for an opportunity to ignore Cromwell's wishes, but I cannot find a strong enough reason to ignore this harshest of edicts.

Despite my deep unease and reservations, I quickly authorise the instruction by adding my own name and signature to the document. At a stroke, I have condemned four men, who only sought to protect their families and businesses, to a cruel and painful death. Such is the evil of war.

Two pieces of news reach me on the twenty-seventh day of the month. Before breakfast, I learn Hutchinson has carried out the executions at a quiet place in West Bridgford. The revelation sends a shiver down my spine. My conscience has been awoken. Shortly afterwards, amid much consternation and excitement, word reaches Leicester that the King has departed Burton and is heading to Ashby with a formidable, ten thousand-strong army.

I am left feeling desolate by both pieces of information. My head is spinning. The hope that doomsters like Purefoy and even Cromwell may be wrong about the King's intentions is shattered. External forces are now firmly in control of my fate and those of everyone else. For the first time in a while, fear has a firm grip on me.

A distinctive East Anglian voice snaps me out of the stupor that threatens to become overwhelming. I look up from the desk I am sitting at in the Magazine. Men are hastily dispersing hundreds barrels of gun powder and a considerable amount of match to agents who have promised to safeguard the precious munitions. I see the reassuring face of Sydenham. He is talking to the other soldiers.

The Sergeant looks in my direction, nodding his head in acknowledgement before seeking to return to his duties.

"Sydenham," I shout just loudly enough to be heard above the commotion as the metal rims of a score of barrels skip off the slate tiles as they roll towards a host of eager, outstretched arms. "Over here, man. Quick. I need to talk to you."

The soldier does as he is ordered, and within a few seconds, he is standing directly in front of me.

"Yes, sir," he retorts, his voice unhurried and composed. "How can I be of service, Captain Hacker?"

I look up and quickly explain my predicament.

"The prisoners you escorted to Nottingham have now been executed," I say, noting the surprise on Sydenham's face as he absorbs the admission. "I was unable to intervene. Their fate was sealed the moment they chose to conspire with Hastings. But I can influence what happens to their accomplices, particularly the women and children you seized. Where did you take them?"

Although the arrests took place several weeks ago, Sydenham has little trouble recollecting the prisoners' whereabouts.

"I took them to the County Gaol in Highcross Street," he confirms. "It was the only place that could accept so many people. In total, we put twenty-three men, women and children into that rat-infested hovel."

I scratch my beard, long restored since my traumatic journey to Newark, before replying: "Go now, speak to the prison governor and order their immediate release. I will join you at the gaol within the hour. Make sure you don't allow any of the prisoners to leave that place until I have had a chance to address them."

Good to my word, I pass through the gates of the gaol within thirty minutes. My route enables me to check on the work being done to the defences. I find it hard to see beyond all the opportunities the enemy will have to gain the upper hand. Many buildings earmarked for demolition are still standing, and a long stretch of wall in the Newarke remains unfortified because a landowner refuses to allow the field that stands beyond it to be cut up. I sigh and pray these oversights do not cost us our liberty, or worse, in the hours and days to come.

My reservations are momentarily forgotten when the barred gate of Leicester Gaol emits a rasping noise as it is closed behind me. I am escorted to a courtyard, where a group of filthy men, women and children sit silently, staring vacantly into the void. Four guards and Sydenham are present. When they hear my approaching footsteps, they snap to attention, and the tension that already fills the air takes on a near physical form.

I waste little time with pleasantries. I need to be gone from this unhappy place as quickly as possible.

"I am here to grant you your freedom," I say. "You can give thanks to our Creator that you are being released after such a relatively short period of incarceration. The punishment for treachery is death, and you deserved this fate. But God is good, and today you have been saved from facing the hangman's noose, and now your liberties are fully restored.

"I will allow you to return to your homes and collect some possessions and whatever valuables you can carry. An armed escort will accompany you. Then, at four o'clock this evening, you will leave the city, and you will not return until the war is over. If you do, you will be executed. I hope I have made myself clear?"

Gasps and cries fill the air. Several mothers clutch their offspring and hug them dearly. Their joy at being set free is plain to see. Then a stark, lone voice rises from the back of the quadrant.

"What about my husband?" enquires a woman, gripping the hand of a child that is barely more than two years of age. "When will you release him?"

I pause, unsure of how I should respond. Sensing my discomfort, the woman presses me again for the information she is seeking.

"When can I see him, Captain?" she asks impatiently. "Where is he? What have you done to him?"

Before I can think of an answer, Sydenham steps in.

"Your husband has been hanged, as have the other men who were taken to Nottingham," he says, without any trace of emotion betraying his true feelings. "There can be no mercy for such men. Conspiring with the enemy is a capital offence. Remember that the next time you consider plotting against the good people of this city. For that is the fate that awaits when your plans are undone."

I sleep well that evening, finding solace in a bottle of port. It serves me well, ensuring my conscience is suppressed and kept in check.

I have slumbered longer than I intended, and it is eight-thirty before my bloodshot eyes open. The sun is shining brightly, forcing delicate rays of light through the small window and onto the polished wooden floor of The Red Lion Inn. They shimmer before me as I rise from my mattress, shaking my head in a forlorn attempt to clear the fog that is blurring my vision. It is my penance after consuming one glass too many on a night when I have fallen victim to the stresses and pressures of soldiering.

As I put my boots on, there is a sharp rap on the heavy door. The percussive noise makes me feel nauseous, so I instinctively reach out and grasp a chair in a bid to steady myself.

"Captain Hacker, you are needed urgently," says an invisible messenger. "Colonel Booth asks for you to meet him and the other officers at The Guildhall on the hour. No later, sir."

I rise slowly and go to the door, but by the time I have unlocked the latch and drawn back the heavy oak barrier, the speaker is gone. An eerie, empty silence greets me as the world forces its way into the small, square room that has been my resting place for the night. Shutting the door quietly behind me, I quickly finish dressing. It is time for me to confront the rigours and challenges of the day.

"The King, Prince Rupert and the massed ranks of the Royalist legions have spent the night in Ashby," states Colonel Booth to a cowed audience. "And this morning, they are making their way in the direction of this fair city. Gentlemen, there can be no doubts about the enemy's intentions. They mean to raise the royal standard here, and they have brought a mighty army with them determined to accomplish the task."

Booth, a relative of Lord Grey of Groby through marriage and by all accounts a decent enough fellow, lets the magnitude of the news sink in before continuing.

"By my reckoning, Langdale and the King's cavalry will be upon us within four hours, and the infantry is likely to get here sometime tomorrow," he says. "Therefore, we have little time to finalise our preparations. Every minute is precious.

"You know what is required. Each and every one of us needs to perform it in an exemplary fashion. If we use our cunning, guile and the terrain to our advantage, we have a chance of besting the foe. But if we allow Charles's forces too much freedom to carry out their plans, they will win the day. And be assured there will be a heavy price to pay if that eventuality is allowed to happen."

I look around the main chamber of the Guildhall. Ten men are present. My light-headedness has gone, replaced with a determination to play the fullest of roles. But I am not confident all my fellow officers share the same resolve. I look at the likes of Sir Robert Pye and

Major Innes, two experienced commanders who have served Parliament well in the past and have been tasked to lead the defence of the Newarke wall. In their tired faces, I see something I recognise as the resigned look of defeat. Thankfully, resolute souls like Babington, who will stand with me and defend Saint Sunday's Bridge and the North Gate, share the view that we must fight until we drop.

I can only pray that the stance to be taken by Thomas and myself will prevail on this most fateful of days.

By midday on the twenty-eighth day of May, in the year of our Lord, 1645, more than five and a half thousand Cavaliers have surrounded Leicester.

Escape is now impossible for those of us inside the city walls. We are here until the bitter end, and we will either survive or die. The outcome is that stark.

The enemy's brightly coloured standards flutter in the warm Spring breeze as Sir Marmaduke Langdale and fellow knights, John Campfield, William Blackstone, Richard Willys, William Vaughan, Robert Crane and Thomas Dalyson gaze at our defences. They seek out our weak points where they can send their human battering rams – the heavily armed Foot – against us. Also sitting in the group, astride fine-looking war steeds, are the likes of Lord Molineux, the Earl of Northampton and Lord Loughborough, the man we have called 'Blind' Henry Hastings ever since my skirmish with him at Bagworth Heath.

After suffering so many reversals in recent times, I sense the glee in their hearts. Before them stands a broken city, its garrison weakened and demoralised, and its citizens close to breaking point. If ever a place was ripe for the taking, this is it.

From my vantage point at the top of the Magazine, I look beyond the principal commanders and identify up to twenty different regiments and brigades that will soon unleash their collective might against myself and my heavily outnumbered comrades.

My hands start to shake. At first, I don't notice it. Then it starts to get worse. I seek to control the trembling by putting them behind my back and clenching my palms tightly together. Although I can still feel my heart beating wildly and the dryness of my throat, the tactic seems to work. I reproach myself, for I mustn't show weakness at this darkest of hours, nor must any of us who are charged with leading men to their doom.

I realise this is a solemn moment, and I seek to commune with the Lord. I reach into my coat and retrieve the Souldier's Pocket Bible that Cromwell gave me when it was first published some two years ago. Comprising sixteen pages, it contains one hundred and fifty specially selected quotations from the sixty-six books of the Holy Bible. As I thumb through its delicate pages, more and more enemy riders spill onto the ground some four hundred yards away, well out of the range of our drake cannons. I return my attention to the abridged version of the Good Book and find a quotation from chapter fourteen of Exodus that is ingrained in my memory. It reads:

"Fear the Lord your God, and he shall deliver you out of the hands of your enemies."

I close my eyes and recite the verse several times. If ever there was a need for my prayers to be answered, it is now.

TWENTY-FIVE

FOR THREE LONG HOURS, THE deafening sound of cannons unleashing their deadly wares drowns out all other noise as Leicester's principal line of defence – the fragile Newarke wall – is bombarded incessantly.

It is Friday, the twenty-ninth day of May, and negotiations between the two sides finally break down at two o'clock in the afternoon. It is at this moment Prince Rupert's brittle patience snaps. Two hours earlier, most probably against his better judgment, he offered the city quarter, pardons for the Mayor and other dignitaries, and free leave for Major Innes and his men if they departed immediately. But, to Rupert's growing frustration, his generous offer was not accepted. Nor would it ever have been, for we have been determined to fight, not bow to the demands of a King who has lost the right to rule.

By the time the Royalist guns start belching indiscriminate death, a few more precious hours had been bought. This gives us more time to disperse the few men we have more effectively and prepare many of the townspeople who are willing to continue the fight in the streets and fields.

Should we suffer an inglorious fate, we are determined Rupert and his kind will pay a high price for their victory. For we are sure they will seek to exact the harshest of retributions for the toil and losses they will be forced to endure this day.

I have just left another meeting at the Guildhall, shortly after the pounding starts, determined to hold the line to the last man. Those of us committed to Parliament's cause swear to do so without hesitation. Some present, including Pye and Innes, remain silent. That is their right. But as they are the two men who have overall responsibility to guard the city's main wall, I fear they may not have the heart for personal sacrifice when the massed ranks of Royalist infantry make their move, as they most surely will, when the cannons fall silent. When that time comes, I can only pray our Maker will intervene and keep us safe, for, at that moment, we will be firmly in his hands.

As I weave through the compact streets, making my way to the North Gate, and the men now under my command, a drake wreaks devastation close by. As it hits an unlucky target, the concussive impact of an eight-pound missile throws me to the ground. Although uninjured, my ears are ringing, and I am covered in debris. It takes ten minutes to compose myself and to be able to hear anything other than a high-pitched whistling. Finally, when I am ready, I look to my right. Where once stood a butcher's shop, timbers are now ablaze, and splintered masonry is littered everywhere. And the bloody corpse of a youngster hangs limply from the remains of an upstairs window.

I close my eyes and offer a silent prayer to the heavens. It is all I can do. There is little point dwelling on this savage tragedy, for I fear much worse is yet to come.

It takes me thirty more minutes to reach the position where Captain Babington, Cornet Needham, and I will defend the North Gate and the ancient Saint Sunday's bridge. The crossing spans the River Soar and is a gateway to the Abbey and Saint Leonard's church.

As I get closer to the front line, intermittent musket fire punctures the air. The lethal leaden cargo penetrates the wooden frames of the surrounding houses. Involuntarily, I find myself ducking my head far too often for my liking. By my crude reckoning, twenty enemy guns are being discharged for every one of ours.

"Francis, my goodness, it is good to see you, my friend. Unfortunately, I fear this time we may have bitten off more than we can chew!"

Thomas Babington hails me from the doorway of the bakery we commandeered at the start of the day. Despite his gloomy words, he is smiling, waving animatedly and keeping a watchful eye on proceedings. He is less than fifty yards away from where I am standing. From this juncture, we intend to manage the defences of this crucial area, and thwart the intentions of the three thousand vengeful foot soldiers Lord Jacob Astley, who has overall command of the King's infantry, will soon let off their leashes.

"What is the mood?" enquires Thomas as he holds the wooden door open and beckons me inside, while Needham sits nearby at a small desk listening intently and making notes. "Pray, tell me they are up for the fight?"

I take my hat off and run my left hand through my

hair. Sweat trickles down my forehead and drips into my eyes, the stinging sensation forcing me to blink several tears away before the discomfort starts to ease.

"It will be a miracle if we survive the evening," I say as evenly as I can while securing my hat to my pate once again. "We are heavily outnumbered. Our defences are still weak, and some of our senior officers would appear to be more interested in self-preservation than they are in putting the enemy to flight. But this was always going to be the case, my friend. We knew it would be so. Men of courage and conviction emerge at such times, while in others, vanity and selfishness also come to the fore. You can be assured we will see all these things and worse before the last shot is fired."

Just as I finish speaking, a sharp cry warns bystanders that grenados – small explosive clay pots comprising gunpowder and nails – are being hurled from various enemy positions close to the wall. Within moments the distinctive cracks of small explosions reverberate. Then we hear the pitiful shrieks of men who have been cut down by the tightly packed shrapnel that makes this device so prolific.

"Cornet Needham," I shout, buoyed by his presence and that of the entire Kirby Bellars garrison. "Put your quill down for a moment, my friend, round up six good men and root out the enemy grenadiers who are responsible for the carnage. Give them no quarter, and when you have finished, man the walls with enough competent musketeers to ensure the Royalists are unable to catch us by surprise again."

Ashen-faced, Needham stands, buckles his sword belt to his waist and marches out of the building. "Aye,

Captain," is all the Cornet says before he is gone.

I stare at the bare entrance, half expecting the young man to return, armed with a limp reason not to carry out my order. His first taste of close combat was at Melton Mowbray towards the end of February. It was a chastening experience – one I fear my comrade may not yet have fully recovered from.

Thankfully, after a good thirty minutes have passed and Needham has not returned, I accept my misgivings about my subordinate may have been harsh and unfair. Nevertheless, I make a mental note to congratulate him on his endeavours as soon as he returns.

With Babbington and myself hard-pressed to protect the bridge and the North Gate, we decide to concentrate on the latter. We pull the men we have into a defensive line and make preparations for our concentrated fire to cause the greatest damage when the enemy's massed ranks descend.

Our muskets are at the ready, prepared to unleash a deadly crossfire when the first of the King's infantry show themselves. It is now almost an hour and a half since I left the Guildhall, and so much has already happened. I take a moment to collect my thoughts and admire the bravery of the enemy, for these men know death awaits them. Yet on they come, their fears and anxieties suppressed. Astley and the tyrant Charles are indeed fortunate men to have so many loyal souls willing to spill their blood for such a tainted cause.

Several lines continue to edge forward a yard at a time, and soon I count more than a hundred martyrs making their approach. They are pensive and wary and know what is coming. It is time to give the order to unleash hell.

"Fire," I bellow, watching in macabre wonder as two hundred guns bark violence in unison. "Fire," I shout again, and the hundred guns of the Kirby Bellars garrison that form the second wave of defence leave more men dying, their guts and vital organs spilt onto the rough ground.

"Shoot at your will," I command when the acrid, smoke-filled air starts to disperse and I can see the enemy once again. "Make sure you hit your targets. We don't have enough ammunition to waste it on thin air."

Regular spurts of musket fire are confirmation my men have understood my orders and are obediently carrying them out independently. Even though we are a much smaller body, outnumbered by more than ten to one, the unrelenting wall of lead, ripping through unprotected flesh and bone, does its work. After fifteen minutes, with the area in front of the Gate littered with the bodies of the injured and recently departed, I give the order to cease firing.

An eerie silence greets my words. All I can hear is a ringing sound in my ears. It lasts for a minute, no more. Then the first of the pitiful cries of the wounded is heard. An enemy soldier is sobbing and praying to his God for the miserable life he has led. Then another voice calls out, and another. And so it goes on until Astley orders his troops back into the fray.

At that moment, the pleas of the dying are instantly forgotten as five hundred more men press forward, determined to break our brave resistance.

This time, rather than provide target practice for the defenders, a change of tactics sees Royalist grenadiers hurl more lethal explosive devices in our direction. The grenados are similar to those thrown over the walls just over an hour ago. Alert to the threat, we seek cover wherever we can find it, as the bombs fall short and their venom is neutralised by the peat and long grasses that run adjacent to the city wall.

As the enemy continues to gets closer in the hours ahead, I doubt we will be so lucky the next time their projectiles are put to use.

For the first time, enemy sharpshooters try and pin us down, so I command the men to return the compliment. Volley after volley of musket fire silences the attackers and buys us yet more time, for which I look skywards and express my gratitude, particularly as it is the men of the Kirby Bellars garrison who are working feverishly to pin down the Cavaliers. Once again, I thank the Lord; the limited training has not been wasted.

Absorbed in the life and death scenarios being played out in front of my eyes, I am surprised to feel a firm hand suddenly rest on my shoulder. It belongs to Thomas, and when he has my full attention, I see he is trying to hand me a folded sheet of paper.

"Booth wants you at the Newarke as quickly as you can make it," he tells me. "There is a serious breach in the wall, and he needs you and the Kirby Bellars Horse to drive off the Royalists while he attempts to make the repairs."

I shake my head in disbelief.

"You can't be serious?" I say. "We are at a critical point. I can't reduce our strength here by a third. It's tantamount to condemning you to certain defeat, and potentially far worse."

Thomas laughs stoically. "You have no choice, Francis," he cautions me. "You are needed. So go with God's speed, and ensure you and your men teach these curs a lesson they never forget. And don't worry about us. I am not a fool, and neither are these men. When it is right to do so, we will fall back to the agreed position, and I will see you there."

As we talk, I am conscious of the muskets continuing to be discharged as the heavy smell of death hangs in the air, for both sides are now losing men at a steady rate.

It is time to go. I extend my hand and grip Babington's spade-like paw.

"Stay safe, my friend," I urge. "Join me at Saint Margaret's, and we will show these dogs how men of conviction fight."

Buildings reverberate, and soldiers and townsfolk of all ages perish as the enemy keeps up its indiscriminate barrage on our brittle defences and the dwellings beyond. By six o'clock in the evening, four predictable lines of attack have emerged – at the Newarke wall and the East, South and North Gates. And every time the Royalists press forward more brave Parliamentarian men, women and children are ground into the dust.

Bodies are scattered everywhere. I briefly visit where the fighting is fiercest and count more than thirty corpses where the breach is at its widest. Most of them are women who have desperately tried to fill the gaps with the wool packs brought from a workhouse yonder. While the efforts of these brave souls have bore fruit, and some of the holes in the wall are now repaired, there is still too much to be done; and their sacrifice is for nought.

I realise our time is almost up. It won't be long before Prince Rupert and Colonel Lisle force us to flee the rubble and devastation, and then each of us will be fighting for our lives.

"Where is Hacker?" yells a voice I have little trouble recognising as that of George Booth. "Captain Hacker, where are you?"

I make my way from the men and horses I have brought with me to where the city's disconsolate governor is waiting for me. We left Babington and the other defenders some fifteen minutes ago and are now resting in the garden of the ruined Crown and Crane inn. It is located in Loseby Lane, just a few hundred yards away from where the most brutal of the fighting continues.

Flushed and breathing heavily, Booth stands before me. His once ornate coat is ripped and spattered in mud, and he looks like a man who is incapable of outwitting and outfighting a vastly superior force. Nonetheless, he is a man whose bravery and doggedness has earned the respect of all around him.

"I am here, Colonel," I say, hoping my own demeanour is measured and composed. "How may I be of service?"

Booth needs little encouragement to unburden himself. "Lisle has sent his infantry forward, and there is every chance this may be the moment they breakthrough," he warns. "I need you and your men to lead a charge that repels them. They won't expect a company of horse to descend from nowhere, and you may just surprise them enough to break up their attack. Can I count on you, Captain?"

On cue, the distinctive noise of steel biting into steel and the guttural gasps and groans of men locked in mortal combat reaches our ears. It sounds like the brutal fight for survival it is.

"Don't worry," I say with feeling. "We will cut down as many of the enemy we can and seek to buy some time."

I immediately turn and face the men whose lives I have had responsibility for since the beginning of the year. I tell them all I know, and I bless their courage. Then, after we have said a short prayer, we mount our steeds, draw our sabres and make our way out of the inn's courtyard. Fate is calling us, and the urge to go to war has never been stronger.

The fighting has now been raging for six long hours. Much of Leicester is in ruins, particularly the walls that have borne the brunt of the onslaught. Yet, miraculously, the city's garrison is still holding out, much to the frustration of the King. What he and his commanders hoped would be an easy conquest is proving anything but.

As Booth had hoped, the Kirby Bellars Horse emerges out of the South Gate at precisely nine o'clock in the evening. Before us, seeking to force home their advantage, Lisle's men are focused on overwhelming the defenders holding the breach. They are so confident of success, nobody is protecting their rear.

The beating hooves of a hundred horses bred for battle make a lot of noise, and as we get into our stride, the earth shakes underfoot. But the over-confident enemy infantrymen don't hear us until it is far too late, such is the vigour with which they are pressing home their attack. By the time they are aware of the danger they face, it is too late. We are upon them.

"Make every thrust and cut count," I shout as we plough into the ranks of Lisle's foot soldiers at the rear of the press. "Take as many as you can. Don't think, just kill."

The men bellow Parliament's cry of "in God's name" and then the dying begins.

Fear is a curse to any commander. When it sets in, you can do nothing to halt its advance. And this evening, as those committed to Parliament fight valiantly to contain a numerically superior force determined to crush them, I find solace in releasing my pent-up anger and frustration by committing acts of acute savagery and brutality.

As I slash, cut and impale, I become aware of a great panic rippling through Lisle's regiment and the enemy starting to disengage and break away. They are desperate to escape to the lunging, murderous thrusts of the ghostly horsemen I lead. And that is their undoing. My men, untried and inexperienced as they are, are now able to feast on the defenceless backs of Cavaliers as they flee towards the safety of their own lines. Moreover, they see me wading into the enemy and dispatching men indiscriminately. This gives them the confidence and encouragement they need to do the same, cutting and cleaving without any need for precision.

Many enemy soldiers escape, but sixty do not make it back to their comrades alive and scores more writhe in agony on the ground, their wounds rendering them defenceless. As I look on, men are hacked down. Their skulls are shattered or separated from their shoulders, and their limbs and bodies are mutilated by our vengeful weaponry. For the fortunate souls who have taken their last breath, death is mercifully quick, and their blood will be a temporary stain on the lush green grasses of Horse Fair Fields. For those who have lost limbs or had their guts ripped open, a crueller fate awaits, one that sees gangrene corrupt healthy skin until the body can withstand the agony no more. And I feel no pity.

As we return to the sanctuary of the great North Gate, I realise it has taken only a few short minutes to execute our orders.

In truth, I only know we have been successful when I hear a great cheer echoing around Leicester's ruined Norman wall. I look to my men; many carry the beaming smiles of victors only seen in the immediate aftermath of battle after a soldier has stared death in the face and emerged victorious. Caught in the moment, they also join in the jubilation, just as the last of the fleeing enemy reaches the Royalist encampment.

Then, as the last light of the day succumbs to the all-enveloping dusk, flames roar out of the mouths of the King's cannons yet again. And so the carnage starts once more.

The order to fall back is sounded an hour before midnight. The Royalists have succeeded in overpowering our men at the North, South and East Gates, and they are now descending on the Newarke's brave defenders – the only line of organised defence that remains.

"We need to fall back immediately, Captain," urges Needham, who has been by my side throughout the fighting. "The situation is deteriorating rapidly. If we leave it too long, we will not be able to get the men out of here."

We dispensed with our horses immediately after we

had crushed Lisle's ill-conceived assault. Since then, we have been on foot, bolstering the defenders committed to frustrating the King's main body. To my eternal regret, at least thirty of the Company have now paid the ultimate price for their defiance, their bodies left to rot where they have fallen.

As I rub the stubble on my chin, I stand by a brazier glowing brightly in the dark. It allows me to see the scale of destruction and what a gruesome sight it reveals.

"You are right," I say, seeking to hide my emotions, lest they get the better of me as I survey the scale of destruction and lifelessness all around me. "Round up the men, Cornet Needham. Let's get out of here."

Within a couple of minutes, we have left the ruined wall behind and are withdrawing to the church of Saint Margaret's, where we will seek to regroup with what's left of Babington's men. We hope to inflict more grievous losses on the enemy from our new position before we are overrun. As we pass the first of the tightly packed houses on Horse Faire Lane, unblemished by the sustained Royalist bombardment, a strong female voice calls out in the darkness.

"Are the King's men far away?" she asks without a hint of fear.

I look up, searching the evening sky for sight of my questioner. As my eyes adjust to the blackness, I see a pale, determined face looking directly at me from an upstairs window.

"Prepare yourself and your family, good lady," I say briskly. "They will be upon you within minutes. All is lost at the Newarke, and we must now make a stand elsewhere in the city."

Defiance bursts out of the woman as she comprehends the magnitude of my warning.

"Do not worry on my account, dear sir," she says. "My sons and I are preparing to give the enemy a surprise. So, too, are many of our neighbours. If we have our way, and the Lord is kind to us, we may buy you and your men some precious time."

As she finishes speaking, windows up and down the street are opened, and women and children lean out and beat the wooden slats as loudly as they can. I look on in wonder as these brave souls applaud my men and me as if we were conquering heroes, not the desperate and weary defeated wretches we are.

"We have boiling water and roof tiles, and many a Royalist head will feel the anger of Leicester's womenfolk before this night is over," declares our most unlikely of guardians. "God's speed to you and the rest of these men. May His strength and grace shield you all."

As one, we raise our hands in gratitude.

I am about to say something else when one of my men spins round, clutching his throat. Even though he is some distance away from where I am standing, I can clearly see the torrent of blood spurting from the mortal wound in his neck. Then we hear the familiar crack of musket fire as four more of my men are sent to the afterlife.

It is time to take flight. We are exposed. To fight here, where there is no cover, and we are easy targets, would be a folly that aides the enemy's cause and not our own. My men know it, so they press on without waiting for the order to run.

When we are free from the immediate danger, I pause for a moment, looking down Horse Faire to see if the Royalists continue to follow us. Surprisingly, I see nobody, only the prostrate bodies of two more of my men who have fallen to the muskets that were loosed on us. But out of my vision, I can hear a great commotion. As they pledged, the city's womenfolk are screaming obscenities, and there is the unmistakable sound of roof tiles and pots being smashed on the cobblestones.

A wry smile passes across my dry and tight mouth. I bow for a moment and pray, hoping these brave actions will delay the Royalists long enough so we can reach Saint Margaret's unmolested and prepare for what is sure to be our last stand.

Against all odds, Babington's men and the Kirby Bellars remnants put up strong resistance in the church grounds, repulsing three attacks in quick succession.

Taking advantage of a lull in hostilities, I conduct a quick count that reveals fewer than a hundred of our men are fit to fight. A similar number have been forced to take refuge in the church building, where their wounds are tended to by the Minister and his wife.

We cannot hold out for much longer.

As my pocket watch declares the time to be three o'clock in the morning, on the thirtieth day of May, the men who can stand and fight are exhausted. They have had little rest for the last fifteen hours, and most don't have the strength to thwart the enemy when they come again.

"I can't believe we are still among the living," says Thomas, the fatigue he is feeling all too evident in his voice. "It is a miracle we have been able to keep them at bay for so long."

Amid the glow of the burning houses surrounding

Saint Margaret's, where I can see the enemy Companies' silhouettes preparing to test us again, I look at my friend, Thomas Babington. Until recently, Abijah had been a constant presence at my side, always seeking to protect my back from the thrust of the unseen assassin. This evening, Babington has filled the void, saving my life on at least two occasions as the enemy sought me out.

"If this proves to be our final hour, let me tell you of the honour I feel in sharing this solemn moment together," I say to Thomas. "Even in defeat, we have won, for our men have proven themselves superior in thought and deed to our enemy.

"Tonight, I tell you, the King will be cursing the day he chose to ride against the city of Leicester. We have made his commanders' look like fools, and their men are clearly unequal to the brave souls we are privileged to lead."

As I finish speaking, the war cry of the Cavaliers echoes off the slate roofs. They are coming once again.

"Promise me something, Francis," demands Thomas as we draw our swords in unison. "Promise me that when all is lost, you will save yourself from the slaughter that will most surely follow our defeat?

"Allow me the privilege of staying with our men until the end. Knowing you are safe; knowing you can still protect your family will be an immense source of comfort to me. Please don't deny me this wish."

As our men let off a vicious leaden volley into the centre of the approaching enemy troops, I shake my head.

"My friend, I cannot possibly agree to your request," I say, walking forward. "I must fight. Only our Maker has the power to decide who lives and who does not."

Knowing we all face a potentially painful death spurs many of the men on. Tired muscles become rejuvenated, reflexes are sharpened, and flagging energy levels are restored. And they need to be. For the enemy doesn't give us any respite, bearing down on us from all sides, using its superiority to surround us and cut off any opportunity for escape.

For many of the men standing alongside me, there will be no tomorrow; their names, and maybe even that of my own, will become nothing more than a fading memory once the hungry carrion has grown fat on our remains.

As I think these dark thoughts, Bartholemew, to my left, collapses and crashes to the ground. He has been stabbed through the eye, killed by the first of Lisle's men to reach our threadbare line. This most faithful of men, who was once a farmer, doesn't make a sound as Paradise beckons.

Close to me, Potter, a man ten years my senior, fights valiantly when surrounded by three confident Cavaliers. He knows it is the end, and so do they. As one of the assailants tests his swordsmanship, the other two lunge at him from either side. He stands no chance and is gutted. I hear his death rattle long after his eyes have ceased seeing the horrors that are being committed all around the churchyard.

Much to my regret, I can do nothing to help my men as my swordsmanship is being put sorely to the test.

A beast of an infantryman lunges at me with an axe. I successfully parry the first thrust and then his second swipe. But as I attempt to go on the offensive, my boot slips on blood and intestines. I lose my balance, and before I can do anything to right myself, I have toppled over, losing my weapon in the process. The fall stuns me, just long enough for my conqueror to pin me down with the shaft of his weapon and prepare to deliver the killing blow. I close my eyes and say a final prayer of repentance as the Cavalier lifts his weapon. Yet, miraculously, I find myself spared, as Thomas emerges from nowhere and slices open the shocked man's throat with a powerful cut. A crimson tide from his severed artery drenches me as his lifeless body falls headlong into the grass.

"Get away from here, Francis," shouts Thomas as he violently pulls me to my feet. "Leave this place while you still can. Save yourself, man."

I look Babbington directly in the eye, and before I can respond, I feel an indescribable force take hold. Suddenly, I find myself running away from the fighting, towards the back of the church, where I know the enemy to be at their fewest. I have gone no further than a hundred paces when I stumble. As I pick myself up, a voice issues a challenge and two brutes emerge out of the night. The men appear to be guarding the perimeter. Before speaking, I look behind them and see the silhouettes of at least a score of fighting men. I need to be careful.

"What is your business?" barks a stern voice as I rise to my full height, the darkness making it impossible for my face to be recognised.

Without hesitating, I state: "God and the Prince." It is the call of the King's men.

Seemingly satisfied by my answer, the guards melt into the shadows and a pathway to freedom opens up before me. Needing little encouragement, I run as fast and as far as I can: through the ravaged and burning streets; past once-happy homes where womenfolk are now being abused and raped; side-stepping the many bodies that litter the ground.

Eventually, I lose track of time. Mixed feelings of elation and guilt grip me, and by the time I stop, I am tearful, exhausted and in urgent need of oxygen and rest.

As dusk rouses itself from its short slumber, streaks of early morning sunshine break through the gloomy skies and help me recognise my whereabouts.

It would appear I have found my way to the village of Braunstone, some three miles from Saint Margaret's, where I pray for Babington and our men. My hope is they have managed to survive the ordeal of the last few hours.

I find an outbuilding in the gardens of a prominent manor house and conceal myself as best I can. Inside there is straw aplenty and some water, which I drink as if I am a marooned sailor who has been cast adrift for two weeks or more.

The liquid eases the burning sensation in my lungs. As it does, fatigue claims me, and I embark on a deep and troubled sleep.

I awake to find the tip of a sword at my throat and five men staring at me.

Their hats all sport Peacock feathers, and a sense of dread threatens to suffocate me.

"Good afternoon, Captain Hacker," says a man who is clearly blind in one eye yet has the gait and confidence of a commander. "Your men said you had been killed, but it's hard to get rid of a wily old dog like you, isn't it?"

Lifting the tip of his sword away from my neck, my captor indicates he wishes me to stand. I am in no position to play the spirited martyr, so I do as I am instructed.

"Bind his hands and take away any weapons he may have concealed on his body," continues the blind man. "And no tricks, Hacker."

A subordinate steps forward and ties my wrists together tightly. My surrender and submission is complete.

Up close, Henry Hastings is shorter than I imagined him to be. But what he lacks in height, he certainly makes up for in temperament. The man has no reason to show kindness to me, as I ruined his eye and good looks some eighteen months ago at Bagworth. Yet, despite the pain I caused him, there is no trace of hostility in his voice. Instead, he treats me with civility and the utmost courtesy.

As I leave my temporary refuge, surrounded by my captors., the sun's rays dazzle me for a moment. Suddenly a rough pair of hands grab me by the shoulders and push me in the direction of a larger group of men and horses. The same hands continue to push me on, not caring whether I walk or fall.

As I flail for a third time, a voice I have little difficulty in recognising speaks coarsely in my ear.

"If I had my way, you would be strung up from the nearest tree," says the guttural voice I first heard at Belvoir Castle many months ago. "Thank yourself lucky it is Hastings who has found you, and not I."

Suddenly, the cruel and contorted features of Gustav Holck appear before me.

The Bohemian catches me by surprise. He is close enough for me to smell his rancid breath and to see the pockmarks and lines on his greasy face.

I step backwards, seeking to escape his menacing figure. As I do, anger rages within me, as does despair. For I am defenceless, unable to protect myself against the demeaning sport this killer wishes to play. And I am unable to avenge my daughters and Abijah, which I have sworn to do.

Once I have recovered from the shock, I start to take consolation from the appearance of my enemy. Holck looks tired; the scar that runs down his cheek is livid; there are several traces of blood on his jerkin and hose, and his left hand is heavily bandaged.

I look closely at the man who killed my two daughters in cold blood, who hanged my best friend, and who mutilated my brother, and find I am unable to say anything. I cannot speak. So I offer the only act of defiance I can: I spit in his face.

Holck's fist connects with my nose as soon as he recovers from the surprise of my uncharacteristic act. Another blow catches me squarely on the chin. But although I feel the pain of his heavy punches, I also sense my nemesis is unnerved.

As I continue to watch him, Holck makes to throw another punch. But before he can strike again, Hastings intervenes forcefully, grabbing hold of his arm and suppressing the killer. He then orders the Bohemian to return to Leicester and report my capture to the King and his most senior officers.

"You will be lucky to live longer than three more weeks," goads the mercenary as he wipes my spittle from his beard and starts to walk to his tethered mare. "And be sure I will enjoy our next encounter far more than you, Captain Hacker."

TWENTY-SIX

SOME TWO WEEKS AFTER MY capture and the
capitulation of Leicester, I am awoken by the anguished
shouts of men and the braying of horses in the large courtyard of Belvoir Castle.

It is Thursday, the fifteenth day of June, and my
period of imprisonment has been surprisingly comfortable. I have been treated well by the governor, Gervase
Lucas, and allowed significant liberties, which include
enjoying a daily stroll in the castle's large and panoramic
gardens.

While I am grateful for the civility being shown to
me by my enemies, I am racked with guilt and sorrow. The
memories of our defeat at Leicester, particularly the brutal
slaying of hundreds of ordinary civilians and the ordeals
faced by many of the womenfolk in the aftermath, have
haunted me. I have lain awake at night, with my eyes
closed, and all I have been able to see are the faces of the
dead. I constantly pray for the nightmares to end, but God
has not yet come to my aid.

My decision to flee the siege has been a source of deep personal regret. While I didn't feel as though I was in control of my actions as I made my escape, my duty was to stay with my men until the fight was over. I had made such a pledge, and many will have perished that night, determined to uphold this oath, while I was found wanting. It is conduct I would not accept in any of the men I lead, so I cannot accept it of myself.

It is strange, therefore, that my captors have not exploited what many will regard as an act of cowardice and infamy.

Perhaps one of the reasons I have been afforded such hospitality and courtesy is explained by the events that occurred three days ago when I was approached by Lucas and asked to consider a matter of utmost importance to the King.

The Governor and I have spent a lot of time in the company of one another since my capture. If an eavesdropper could hear us talking, he would scarcely believe we were avowed enemies, committed to the destruction of the other. As Lucas and I talked about matters of State in the castle's splendid grounds, and the many misfortunes of war that have afflicted both sides, he suddenly presented me with a remarkable and unexpected opportunity directly from the mouth of Charles: would I consider abandoning Parliament's cause and taking charge of my own Royalist regiment of horse?

I was left speechless by the proposition. I was not expecting an offer to become a turncoat, and when I am caught off-guard, I am often found wanting, as my wife will surely testify!

To my cost, I have learnt that warfare can lead to

unholy pacts between the most unlikely of individuals. Cromwell and Lord Grey is one such alliance I struggle to comprehend, even though there are undeniable advantages to Parliament from the grand deception being played out. But I am no player of games. I never have been; I am far too simple a man to be involved in such chicanery.

My reply was curt and to the point, leaving Lucas in no doubt about where my loyalties lie, for while I would like nothing more than to be free once again, I will never betray the cause I serve. Only a fool or a desperate man could think I would be tempted to do the Devil's work.

The governor accepted my rejection well enough. As well as being a fine soldier, he is a pragmatist. He knew from the outset there was little chance I would accept. But he did his King's bidding, and he tried his best to convince me of the merits of becoming a turncoat. That he was unsuccessful is no reflection on him. We have not spoken of the matter since.

This morning, with the shouting outside getting ever louder and more frantic, I sense something dramatic has happened.

Judging by the tone of the frightened and angry voices I can hear, the mood in the enemy camp is sombre, almost defeatist, and I am eager to discover the source of the pain and distress.

I rise from my threadbare mattress and go to the large window that offers an impressive view of the castle's immense roof and little else. Two large chimneys block any view I may enjoy of the courtyard, preventing me from witnessing the numerous Royalist comings and goings. But while this vantage point may render me blind, its position does allow me to hear everything. And this morning, what I learn puts me in extremely good heart.

"Arthur," I call sharply, rousing my companion from the deep sleep he has been enjoying while I have eavesdropped on the enemy. "Wake up, man. Something important has happened."

A sleepy Stavely opens his eyes, quickly clears his head and then turns in my direction.

"Whatever is the matter, Francis?" he says groggily after I have broken the spell he has been under for the last nine hours. "I hope this matter is worth such a rude awakening?"

Arthur shakes his head one last time, an act he regularly commits when he is keen to stimulate his brain. He then props himself on his elbow and listens with his usual, Owl-like intensity. As I hoped, it doesn't take long for him to also detect something catastrophic has happened.

"My God," he exclaims excitedly after listening to a particularly animated conversation between a group of distressed Cavaliers. "The King has been defeated in a major battle, and his army has been obliterated."

My trusted friend looks directly at me. His craggy features are a picture of joy and amazement.

"Cromwell and the New Model Army have crushed the Royalists, and the men loyal to the King, including Prince Rupert, have suffered huge losses," he continues, breaking away mid-sentence to pick up yet more intelligence from the four men who are now talking directly under our window. "These fellows are talking about hundreds of men losing their lives, while Parliament would seem to have emerged relatively unscathed."

The news hits me like a bolt of lightning. My head spins, and I lean forward and grip a large chest until I am settled once again. With my head clear, I walk over to Arthur's mattress, squeeze his shoulder and sit on the edge of the bedding. For a couple of hours, neither of us says another word. We simply sit and listen as more disillusioned men return to the safety of the fortress and reveal their tales of personal tragedy and woe.

By midday, we have a good understanding of what has happened on the raised fields of a small Northamptonshire village that was insignificant until yesterday's momentous events. The King has indeed been routed; up to thirty of his most senior officers have been killed, and what is left of his army is broken and in complete disorder. And Naseby is a name that will enter folklore for centuries to come.

"I suspect you may already know why I have called you here?" says a subdued Lucas, sitting at the large desk that is the centrepiece of the opulent room once owned by the pompous Earl of Stamford. "Those of us who support the King are about to face some testing times. That is pretty obvious; now we know the full extent of what happened at Naseby on a calamitous day for his Highness."

It is now three days since the Royalists formally acknowledged Parliament's glorious victory, masterminded and executed by Fairfax, Cromwell and the New Model Army. Much has happened since, not least the influx of large numbers of exhausted and demoralised men who managed to escape the battlefield slaughter and outrun the pursuing Parliamentarian cavalry. In addition, Leicester has fallen once again, with Fairfax reclaiming the city for

Parliament less than three weeks after the King's men took it by force.

Such momentous events mean the castle is now full to the brim with frightened and vengeful Cavaliers, who would give anything to take out their anger and despair on Roundhead prisoners like Stavely and me.

"For the time being, I cannot continue to allow you the freedoms you have been afforded," continues Lucas. "Be assured, however, I will not allow any harm to come to you while you are in my safekeeping. You have my word on this. But to ensure your safety and maintain discipline in the garrison, I am afraid you will remain locked up for the foreseeable future.

"There are several reasons for this, not least the imminent arrival of a group of senior officers attached to Princes Rupert and Maurice. One of them is well known to you, I believe?"

Lucas lets his words hang in the air, but his expression leaves me in no doubt he is referring to Gustav Holck.

The tale of what the mercenary did to my two daughters is well known, even though few men are prepared to talk about the subject directly to my face. It is also known it was the Bohemian who sanctioned Abijah's execution. Therefore, it doesn't require an onlooker to possess the brains of a Bishop to realise the blood between Holck and myself is as corrupted as it possibly can be.

"I see," is all I am prepared to say in response to the revelation, even though Lucas makes it plain he would clearly like me to say much more.

"Fear not," he snaps irritably after the silence between us becomes uncomfortable to bear. "You have my word I will not alert our guests to your presence in the castle. There is no need for them to know. But I cannot vouch for the continued silence of my men, many of whom do not agree with the tolerance and latitude I am displaying towards you. We can only pray your whereabouts does not become known.

"From the little I know, Holck and his companions should not be staying long in these parts. They are simply using the castle as a place to regroup. And when they are gone, be assured we will revert to the civilities we have been enjoying thus far until our respective sides arrange a suitable prisoner exchange."

My presence in the castle doesn't remain a secret for long, as I discover when I am awoken violently in the early hours of the nineteenth day of June.

A sudden pain in my ribs leaves me rubbing my eyes and straining to focus on the three strangers now in the room, one of whom is pointing a flintlock directly at Arthur. Another sharp kick from the brute standing closest to me elicits a painful groan and makes me aware of the danger I now face.

As soon as my anguished cries have been silenced, the man in command barks: "Hebe ihn auf und wenn er sich weigert zu kooperieren, erinnere ihn daran, wer hier das Kommando hat."

Translation: "Pick him up and if he refuses to cooperate, remind him who is in command around here."

Two goliaths with deadpan eyes drag me to my feet, and I am powerless to resist as they forcefully take me deep into the bowels of the castle. One of them grips the base of my neck with his vice-like hands. At the same time, the other grasps my right arm and pins me in a painful arm lock as we descend several flights of stairs and are enveloped by the darkness of an ethereal, subterranean world.

"Hier drüben, und sei schnell dabei," booms a commanding voice I recognise as we approach a series of studded cells I make out in the dim glow of the torchlight. "Wir haben nicht viel Zeit."

Translation: "Over here and be quick about it. We don't have much time."

On cue, I am manhandled into a small cell, which is dark and from where a rank smell almost forces me to puke. I am thrown onto a stool, and my arms are raised while I am handcuffed to a rusting and rough iron bar. The exercise takes less than a couple of minutes to execute. When all present are satisfied I am held securely, the two Bohemian thugs leave me to stare at the gaunt, malevolent face of Holck.

"So, we find ourselves in a familiar place once again, Hacker, where you are my prisoner, and I control your fate," he states tonelessly. "The last time we faced a similar situation, I seem to remember you displayed quite an ability to withstand pain."

I look instinctively at my scarred fingers. There remains a redness where Holck used a pair of crude pliers to rip all ten of my fingernails from my hands before repeating the exercise on my feet. The memory of that November afternoon, which occurred almost two years ago, brings many emotions to the surface, including the intense hatred I feel for this man.

"Don't worry," he continues, aware of the helplessness of my situation. "I won't be repeating that routine today, although the questions I will be posing once again have the power to condemn you to the traitor's death you deserve."

I try to use my strength to pull the bar from the castle's cold stone wall. But my attempt is futile and is abruptly brought to a premature end when Holck's fist smashes into the side of my face. The blow stuns me for several moments.

As my head begins to clear, I become aware of my captor standing directly over me.

"If you try that again, I will slit your throat," he warns. "Resistance is futile. You will answer my questions, or you will die."

For the next hour, which seems like a lot longer, Holck interrogates me about Cromwell's whereabouts, the New Model Army's plans and strengths, and everything I know about Royalist agents. He talks animatedly about the Else's betrayal before quickly getting to the point: the Bohemian wants me to disclose everything I know about Cromwell's recent activities in London and any Royalist plots against the Lieutenant-General that may have come to light.

The man is clearly rattled. He looked so when I saw him at Braunstone at the time of my capture. The authority he once held with his peers and masters is gone. That was apparent when Henry Hastings dismissed him so abruptly. Could it be Cromwell's plan, the one that kept Lord Grey of Groby in situ, feeding tidbits of false and useless information to the King's web of spies, is actually causing the kind of mayhem and disruption Oliver intended all along?

I try to play dumb. Alas, it doesn't wash with my

interrogator, who is wise enough to know I am aware of a lot more than I am saying.

Violent blows rain down on my head every time I fail to answer Holck's questions satisfactorily. Blood spurts from my nose and mouth, and I am roused from a state of unconsciousness on two occasions by buckets of cold water that drench my beaten face. By the time I have recovered from another painful beating, I can see Holck is almost at the end of his tether. He has clearly had enough of my lack of cooperation, denials and attempts to mislead him.

Through swollen eyes, I can see the beads of sweat on his brow. I may be feeling the pressure, but so, too, is the assassin. He sees me observing him and laughs aloud into the bleakness; the force of his exhalation is such that the candle flame flickers wildly before it settles once again. As my gaze shifts back to Holck, I notice he is now holding a dagger in his right hand and running his left forefinger slowly down the blade. I can clearly see the action is drawing a thin line of blood from the cutting edge of the perfectly balanced steel as it displays its killing credentials. The intent is clear.

"You will not obstruct me anymore," declares Holck. "You will answer my questions truthfully, or you will die here and now. Do you understand me, Hacker; there will be no more second chances?"

As Holck prepares to put my resilience to the test one final time, a loud and sudden commotion erupts in the corridor outside.

"Open this door immediately," bellows the commanding voice of Gervase Lucas. "I am aware of what is happening in here, and I will not allow a prisoner of mine to be treated this way."

Holck is halted in his tracks. Confusion is written on his face momentarily, and then it is gone. He sneers as he bares his teeth and grips the knife with all his might, the knuckles of his right hand glowing white in the gloom. It is clear what he is about to do.

Just as the killer prepares to unleash himself on my defenceless body, the door of the cell crashes open, knocking the lone candle onto the floor and plunging the room into darkness. And then the only thing I see is Holck's knife, as it flashes towards my head.

I duck instinctively. It is a reflex that saves my life, for the blade flashes through the air and slices through my ear, missing the jugular vein in my neck by a whisker.

"You bastard," I yell as loudly as I can, as a sharp and grievous pain explodes across the side of my face.

I feel blood ooze from the wound. I wait for a further, fatal blow, but it doesn't come. Instead, chaos descends as several bodies rush into the cell, and Holck's attack is suppressed.

"Hacker, speak, man," shouts Gervase Lucas. "Tell me you are still among the living?"

Three hours later, I am sitting in the chamber Lucas uses to entertain his most important guests. My wounded ear has been stitched together by the castle's physician; a bottle of wine has been opened, and freshly baked bread and some cheese adorn the table. Just two of us are in the room.

"Please accept my gratitude," I say to Lucas sincerely. "I never thought I would hold an enemy of Parliament in high esteem. But you kept your word, which is a rarity these days for men on either side."

Lucas laughs aloud and moves closer.

"You and I have always behaved respectfully towards one another, for as long as I can remember," he says. "The war certainly hasn't changed any bond that may exist between us, Francis; it just means we are on opposing sides. Even so, we can behave humanely towards one another, even in these violent and murderous times.

"I gave you my word that I would not allow anything untoward to happen to you, or Stavely, while you were under my protection. And I am glad I have been able to keep that pledge and prove that my word means something."

I look across the table. Gervase is smiling, and his hand is outstretched, inviting me to grip it. Without hesitation, I do so – in the manner I would greet a friend.

"There is something you may be able to help me with," he adds, breaking the momentary silence that has descended as we comprehend everything that has passed between us.

I nod encouragingly. "If it is in my power, it will be done," I state without hesitation.

After clearing his throat and adopting a serious pose, Lucas adds: "The war is now all but lost. It is plain to see Naseby has finished the King's cause. It is only a matter of time before Parliament is victorious, of that I am sure.

"When that time comes, there will be a reckoning. Many men who have done the King's bidding these past years will be held to account for their deeds, and some, men like me, will be caught up in plots and intrigues that will see us used to settle feuds. I expect the Earl of Stamford and Lord Groby to seek my head for the grief I have caused them in recent years. Without someone to speak up for me and defend my honour, I am doomed. So, I ask that when the time comes, you will be the man in my corner who defends my good name. Is that too much to ask of you, Francis Hacker?"

I take a sip of wine from the full glass of claret that was placed in front of me when I first entered the room. I savour its full and wholesome taste, knowing already what my answer will be.

"I will be happy to speak on your behalf, should it come to it," I tell a relieved Lucas. "I am aware of much of what you talk about, particularly the impact the victory at Naseby is having on the state of the country. So have no fear; I will be happy to speak up for you should the need ever arise. You can count on it."

For the first time since I arrived at the castle, I see the flicker of a smile pass across Lucas's mouth.

TWENTY-SEVEN

I SLEEP FITFULLY THAT NIGHT. My wounded ear throbs and I have no balms or potions at my disposal to ease the pain. So I lie on my mattress and pray, in the hope my Creator will take pity on my wretched soul and grant me some peace.

After an hour of torment, my pleas are seemingly heard and I drift off into the black void. A welcome sleep claims me, and as it does, a recurring and vivid dream takes a firm hold. In my vision, which seems as real as anything I have ever experienced, I find myself on a remote beach in the dark of the night. I am fighting a man of superior strength, whose sword thrusts I struggle to parry. Yet by using a combination of cunning and guile, I find myself winning the vicious struggle that will result in the extinction of one of us. I draw on all my reserves of strength and visibly see my assailant's strength waning, and his desperation become more acute. But just as I am about to finish him off, I slip on a rock and crash to the ground. The fall leaves me winded, defenceless and at the mercy of my enemy. By the time I have recovered my wits, my foe, whose face I cannot see, has regained his poise. He has discarded his sword and is now pointing a loaded musket directly at my unprotected chest. Unable to fight back or flee, my fate would appear to be sealed: paradise and my Maker beckon, and so I prepare myself for the afterlife. But as my would-be killer's finger curls around the trigger of his flintlock, a brilliant ray of moonlight illuminates the beach, blinding my attacker and granting me a reprieve.

Alas, I do not know how matters are concluded, for I find myself awake, as I have done at this precise moment two times already this morning. On each occasion, I dream the same things and arrive at the same unanswered moment of truth. And so, my turmoil and torment continue.

Maybe my vision is just shock, a reaction to Holck's failed attempt to kill me? Such events can profoundly affect a man, particularly in the immediate hours and days after such an experience. I have heard similar things talked about on many occasions in the aftermath of battle. Yet, I have heard nothing discussed about an event such as the one I have experienced. So, I can only conclude that within this vision, there is a specific message for me. What it is, I am not sure. But I do believe I must work it out quickly, for I am certain it is a sign I must heed.

Even though my mind is overactive, I must have fallen asleep again, for the next thing I am conscious of are hands shaking my shoulders and gently drawing me out of my slumber. Unsure of the time, I open my weary eyes and see the earnest features of Gervase gazing down at me.

"I have something of importance to discuss with you," he says matter-of-factly. "Get dressed, Francis, and be ready to come to my chamber in ten minutes. There is much to go over, for I find myself able to repay my debt to you much earlier than I anticipated."

Before I can utter a word, the Governor is gone, and the cell door is slammed shut. Lucas's footsteps are brisk and urgent, just like his words of a moment ago. And as he strides away, a deep sense of foreboding washes over me.

I arrive at Gervase's chamber at eight o'clock, escorted by a pair of sullen guards. These men clearly resent a rebel prisoner being in their midst at this time of despair and fear. If they had not been obeying the explicit orders of Lucas, I would have feared for my safety. But thankfully, discipline has not broken down at Belvoir Castle, and subordinates still do as they are ordered.

"Come in and sit yourself down," commands Lucas after the guards have left us. "There is food to eat, a lot to say – and time is precious."

I look at my host. He is clearly an agitated man this morning, but his manners and courtesy remain intact. Set out before me, on the large table, is as much food a man can eat. A feast, no less! Alas, my stomach betrays my thoughts once again, and a succession of unnatural and strange noises emphasise my urgent desire to eat.

"What is going on, Gervase?" I enquire, pointing at the exotic fruits and freshly baked pastries. "Why was it necessary to wake me up and drag me here, and what is all this in aid of?"

Lucas stands up and walks to the large, stately window that dominates the room. From this vantage point, he has a clear view of much of the western side of the Vale of Belvoir. When the skies are at their most clear, he has told me he can often see the church tower of Saint Guthlacs in Stathern, which is less than a handful of miles away. Today is such a day, and how I wish my beautiful wife, Isabel, could be in my arms at this moment, her piercing opal eyes gazing into my own. Unfortunately, I have come to realise a man cannot have everything he desires. If it happens occasionally, then he is a fortunate fellow indeed.

"Holck left the castle at seven o'clock this morning," Lucas informs me coldly, without turning around. "His men are riding to Oxford, seeking to be reunited with the remnants of the forces loyal to Princes Rupert and Maurice. As for our friend, he has plotted an altogether different path; one that will take him to the coast and a French boat that will secure his escape to the Continent."

I rise to my feet, forcing the chair I am seated on to crash to the floor. In an instant, Lucas has turned and is facing me. The noise has startled us both.

"This cannot be so?" I say, desperation all too evident in my voice. "That barbarian cannot be allowed to escape. He must be brought to justice and pay for the atrocities he has committed."

Lucas stares at me as I slump to the floor. Spent. All sense of hope and purpose has deserted me.

"I agree," he concurs unexpectedly. "That's why I have called you here, Francis. You will be released within the hour. But there are strict conditions, which I will discuss with you in a moment. It may surprise you to learn that men like Holck disgust me. I have made my views known to my superiors on several occasions. But they have been ignored because Holck has been a valuable servant to the King, even though his methods are abhorrent. The reality is that his tactics have achieved results for much of the conflict, and for many, that is all that matters.

"But circumstances have changed. The war is lost, and I have no desire to be tarred with the same brush as men like Gustav Holck. So I am prepared to give you what you desire most – time to settle your account with this man. But you must not breathe a word of this arrangement to anyone. It is between you and me."

I run my hands through my thick, dark hair, seeking to comprehend everything that is unravelling at a rapid rate of knots. Devouring a large crust of delicious, freshly baked bread, which gives me precious thinking time, I ask: "Tell me, Gervase, why exactly are you releasing me, and what are the conditions I must adhere to for this to happen?"

My unlikely saviour walks around the table and pours himself a glass of ale. When he has tasted the intoxicating hops and adjusted the lapel of his jacket, he replies: "My reasoning is simple, Francis: I simply wish to survive this war and grow to be a prosperous old man. I have also lost faith in the cause I serve and have no desire to see men like Holck prosper. He needs to be held to account, as do all the murderers who cause so much misery. I am prepared to offer you that opportunity if you so desire it? Give me your word that you will return to the castle within a month, so you can continue your confinement, and I will give you leave to do whatever you wish, wherever you wish to do it. What say you, is this proposition of sufficient interest?"

I nod my head slowly, confirming my assent, aware there is much I can achieve in thirty days, not least claim the justice my daughters and best friend deserve.

"As the Lord is my witness, you have my word. I will comply with any conditions you attach to my temporary release," I say to Lucas. "All I ask of you is one further thing: tell me where Holck is going?"

TWENTY-EIGHT

IT TAKES ME FOUR LONG days to ride to the fortified town of Dover, a place that once welcomed the conquering Julius Ceasar and for sixteen hundred years has been a haven for all seafarers.

Although only a few hours separate our departures from Belvoir Castle, I have no way of knowing whether my quarry has made good time or altered his plans. The information that came into the possession of Gervase Lucas was the result of a vigilant member of the garrison overhearing the Bohemian when he was talking to one of his men. It could still be highly accurate, which means my efforts will not be in vain. But it could also prove to be erroneous, leading me on a fool's errand. Either way, I will not know what my Maker has in store for me until I reach my destination. And after many hours in the saddle, the omens aren't promising, and my spirits are low. Holck has not been sighted by anyone I speak to. This is unusual, for, on such long journeys, a man can rarely hide and cover his tracks – particularly someone as distinctive as the mercenary.

Self-doubt and agitation become my constant companions. As I eat up the miles, there is plenty of time to know fear, acknowledge my many failings, and constantly dwell on my plan's numerous flaws. But one crumb of knowledge spurs me on: the belief my thirst for vengeance will be sated, and I constantly pray for the justice I believe I am due. This grain of comfort is all I need. And it sustains me.

As I work my way through the country, I enjoy the company of the Parliamentarian garrison at Newport Pagnell on my first evening of liberty. This is where young Oliver Cromwell met his untimely end all those months ago, albeit his death is nought but a distant memory. In the garrison, no questions are asked of me. The officers know me to be Parliament's man, someone whose character is unblemished. I am provided with a comfortable room and fed well before being asked to recount the tale of the siege of Leicester. Silence greets my words, and many battle-hardened veterans find the atrocities I witnessed by the King's men hard to countenance. As I speak, I see their resolve to hold Charles and his generals to account hardening in front of my very eyes. Heads shake. Fists tighten. But thankfully, the melancholy mood evaporates when the port is uncorked, and we share a glass, or two, before retiring to our chambers.

I awake early on the morning of Thursday, the twenty-first day of June. I am on my way by seven o'clock in the morning – after I have said my prayers and bid my farewells to the men and officers on guard duty. Their parting gift is a loaf of bread and a large chunk of locally produced cheese, which is secure in the panniers attached to my saddle.

My journey southward is slow and ponderous. It takes me twelve long hours to reach The Ruddy Duck hostelry in Bromley, where I will spend my second night on the trail of Holck's ghostly figure. I have never visited the town before, which is located a score of miles away from London. Here I find myself watched by people who eye me with suspicion and open hostility. Strangers do not appear to be liked in these parts, so after enjoying some over-cooked Goose flesh and a handful of potatoes, I retire to the small room I have been offered for the night.

As I undress, I reach for the letter handed to me shortly before I departed the Belvoir stronghold by a guard in my pay. I have already read its contents several times before nestling it in the inner pocket of my leather jacket. As I hold the vellum once again, I bring the sheet close to my nose, seeking to smell the lingering scent of the author. I am not disappointed, for it was written in the hand of my beloved wife just two days before my release and contains news I have long wished to hear…

"My dearest Francis

"Life in Stathern continues, my heart, but it is a lonelier place without you by my side. I think of you daily and pray the Governor and his men continue to treat you with the respect you deserve, and no ill fortune afflicts you. The children continue to miss you too and are eagerly looking forward to the day their Papa returns.

"However, home life is not the reason I pen this letter, albeit I could write for hours telling you of the happiness that has returned to the lives of Josiah and Ursula and the renewed optimism of the villagers, now the defeat of the King at Naseby is known by all.

"But I have something better to tell you, for your beloved brother, Rowland, has been released from his prison cell. He is a free man once again, and his reputation is unblemished.

"A messenger arrived at the Hall an hour ago bearing these tidings, and I had to inform you, as I know how grievously you have suffered these past weeks, tormented by Rowland's incarceration, deprivations and a real fear for his mortal well-being. Be assured your brother is now safe, my love, and he has been restored to the rank of Captain.

"I know nothing more other than this joyous news. And I want to share it with you as quickly as I am able.

"Stay safe, my dearest. Come back to us soon.

"Your loving and faithful wife, Isabel.

Tears trickle down my weary cheeks. But I am not sad. Joy has taken hold of me. A weight has been lifted, and emotions buried deep within have been released.

My mind remains overactive for much of the night. Eventually, my tiredness overcomes me. But I do not enjoy peace for long, as the gruff voice of the innkeeper rouses me from my slumber at eight o'clock in the morning. I have missed breakfast, and weariness racks my body. I pour some cold water into a bowl and splash my face. The cold sensation acts as a slap, and I find the fog of fatigue lifting.

Thirty minutes later, I am in the saddle and riding hard to make up lost time. Little do I know that the last leg of my journey will be the one that taxes me most and takes more than thirty long hours to complete.

By the time I pass Maidstone, every bone in my body aches. Yet, I am unable to sleep; such is the torment that consumes me. So I ride through the night using the stars and moon to navigate as I venture further south. With every new mile I travel, long-buried feelings surface that I have kept at bay for many months. I am unable to hold back my malevolence, feelings of anger and hatred, as well as a sense of grievous loss, and I find myself sobbing frequently. Thankfully, I am on my own. My weakness will not be exposed to others, who might expect a man of war, piety and faith to display a much stronger character and fortitude.

Eventually, after I have covered two hundred and fifteen miles of England's green and fertile fields and populous towns, and six powerful horses have been pushed to their limits of endurance, I see the turquoise-blue of the English Channel, hear the cries of Herring Gulls and Terns and stare in awe at the famed white cliffs. And as I look to my right, the slate rooftops of the town of Dover glitter in the sunlight, and I feel the destiny urging me on.

With little difficulty, I find the Flower of Luce Inn, located prominently on King Street.

Before I left Leicestershire, Gervase Lucas recommended the hostelry to me, claiming it is well known for the warmth of the welcome it affords all Parliamentarians. Before arriving at the seaport, I was unsure whether Lucas's words would be conjecture rather than fact. But I am not disappointed, as the innkeeper, a certain Richard Dawkes, picks up my bag and prepares to escort me to a modest room overlooking the harbour. Before he does so, Dawkes subjects me to rigorous, ten-minute interrogation as he seeks to establish my bona fides or unpick holes in my story. Such are the times we are all living through.

The time is just before midday on Saturday, the twenty-third day of June, and I am in desperate need of rest. It is a fact that has not gone unobserved by Dawkes, whose powerful figure exudes confidence and intelligence.

"You look as though you could sleep for a week," he says to me after placing my belongings on the large mattress that fills the sparse room. "Have you travelled far, good sir?"

A burst of involuntary laughter escapes through my lips before I can suppress it.

"That is something of an understatement," I reply. "I have been in the saddle for the best part of four days. And I fear I will not be able to enjoy the rest my body so desperately craves, such is the urgency of the business I must attend to. Can you please wake me at six o'clock this evening, Master Dawkes? My recuperation can wait. There are important matters I need to address in this town."

Dawkes looks at me directly, his curiosity raised by my intensity.

"As you please, sir," he says. "You have my word; I will wake you in six hours. Best get your head down as quickly as you can. From where I am standing, it looks as though you need as much shut-eye as you can get."

True to his word, the large knuckles of Dawkes's right-hand rap on the heavy-set door to my quarters at precisely six o'clock in the evening.

"Master, there is a bowl of stew and a tankard of the house's finest ale waiting for you downstairs," he says comfortingly. "Bide your time, by all means, but don't leave it too long before attending on us, as the food will go cold and my good wife will be most displeased with you, and her wrath is not a thing of beauty."

Before I can respond in the affirmative, I hear the innkeeper descend the wooden stairs, leaving me to wipe the crusts of sleep from my eyes and collect my muddled thoughts.

After a couple of minutes, I rise and stretch, first extending my aching arms until the tips of my fingers tingle. I then transfer my attention to my legs, where I am pleased to feel a similar reaction being generated in my toes. With every shake, my surging blood energises my tired sinews and muscles. After a short period, I find myself sitting upright, focusing once again on the task at hand. I reach for my sword and leather jerkin. It is time to take Richard Dawkes into my confidence and tell him of my purpose.

"That's what I call a hearty appetite," says Dawkes approvingly, as he watches me spoon down the last of the beef stew prepared by Martha, his wife. "You have eaten that like a man who hasn't seen food for a month of Sundays!"

Without waiting to be invited to join me, Dawkes pulls up a chair and sits down at my table, and I feel his unceasing gaze doing everything it can to tease out my innermost secrets. Eventually, when I have said nought, he relents.

"So what is your true business and purpose in these parts, sir?" he enquires, a large dollop of salty inquisitiveness and intrigue on his tongue. "You do not bear the appearance of a man who is a casual traveller. If anything, I would wager you are a soldier, a man of some substance who is in sore need of some assistance. Am I right?"

A wry smile passes my lips. Lucas was right about Dawkes: he misses very little.

"You are a perceptive man," I say while continuing to appraise the innkeeper. Eventually, I make my mind up and decide I must take my host into my confidence. In reality, I have little choice. I must find an ally.

"Allow me to appeal to your public spirit, for I need men who are loyal to Parliament and will help me bring a Royalist murderer to justice. Are you such a man?"

I am afforded the briefest of nods, and it is all I require to continue. So begins the unburdening of my soul and the hatching of a plan…

"That is quite a story," says Dawkes, as he leans back and rests his head against the rustic brickwork that props up the Flower de Luce. "Lesser experiences would have crushed most men I know. You are a rarity, Captain Hacker. And I will, of course, do all I can to help you find this evil-doer."

The innkeeper then proceeds to spend the next twenty minutes outlining all he knows about the comings and goings of strangers, particularly men of continental appearance. When he has exhausted the inner recesses of his mind, he looks at me pleadingly, hoping that something he has said resonates. Alas, nothing he mentions is useful.

"Damn," he snorts, hitting the table with the palm of his hand. "Be assured, captain, I will do my utmost to help you find this man. If he has travelled to Dover and has a roof over his head, I will find him. You have my word on the matter.

"No ships have left the port or entered it in more

than two days. The sea fog we have endured has put paid to any sailings. So if the man you are seeking is here, someone will have seen him and, in all likelihood, know his whereabouts. I will speak to some of the loyal men I know immediately so the search can begin."

Hope, a feeling I have not known for weeks, is suddenly alive within me.

"There has been fog here?" I ask, surprised by Dawkes's revelation. "But the visibility was crystal clear when I arrived. Surely, the sea mist can't have been that bad?"

Dawkes looks at me with his hound-dog eyes and waves his hand in my general direction.

"You are not a seafarer, are you, Captain Hacker?" he snaps. "If you were, you would know fog is the curse of any mariner. The channel can be clear one minute, and then a mist can descend from nowhere and envelop everything in the time it takes for a man to blink his eye.

"Sailing in such conditions is a risky business. And believe me, there have been some who have chanced their luck only to founder on the killing sands and secure a final resting place for themselves and their crews on the Varne, South Falls and Colbart banks. Only a fool would countenance such a reckless course of action.

"These are deceptive places that devour ships, even when visibility is good. So I say with absolute confidence: if your man has reached these parts, he will still be here. And I will do all I can to ensure he is snared like the cur he is."

TWENTY-NINE

POUNDING FISTS AWAKEN ME ON the morning of Sunday, the twenty-fourth day of June. The noise is loud and repetitive. Such is the determination of their owner to shatter my peace that the thick, oak door visibly recoils every time it is struck.

"God's strewth, I am awake," I shout in a bid to appease whoever is responsible for the commotion. "I am coming and will be with you in a moment."

It is enough. The noise ends, my visitor seemingly placated. As I rise from the weathered mattress, I look at my pocket watch: it is almost ten o'clock in the morning, and I have slept soundly for more than twelve hours.

I dress quickly to hide my modesty, and I am still pulling back the iron-restraining bar when the door bursts open, and an animated Dawkes barges into my room. He is sweating, his face is flushed, and his eyes can barely conceal their excitement.

"We have him," he exclaims breathlessly. "Your man, Holck; he has been sighted in Folkestone. And it is exactly as you say: he is seeking safe passage to France. I have just received the information from a trusted associate. He is very confident the man is whom you seek. He fits the description you gave me, even down to the scars on his cheek. And he is keen to leave our shores as discreetly as he possibly can."

I am struggling to grasp everything I am hearing, so I quickly close the door and focus my bleary eyes on the rouged face of Dawkes.

"Are you sure there is no mistake?" I ask the innkeeper as soon as I have regained my composure. "Can the word of your informant be relied upon?"

Dawkes strides over to the large window that dominates the room and opens the wooden shutters. Golden rays with an ethereal quality fill the sparse space. They highlight the many dust particles that were displaced when the shutters were forcefully opened. And as Dawkes speaks again, he looks more a Saint-like figure than the earthly, rustic soul he is.

"I will vouch for him with my life," he asserts boldly. "My man is brother to my wife and a good friend to Parliament and me. If your description is accurate and he says he has seen the man you are searching for, then you can be assured he has."

As the crow flies, Folkestone is nine miles to the west. Like Dover, it is also a port town that depends on fishing and trade with France for prosperity to flourish and a controlled peace to exist in these troubled times. Once a sovereign town, it now stands against the King and all who serve him. For three years, it has pledged its allegiance to the cause supported by rebels like me, albeit there is some resistance to Parliament's attempts to maintain order, particularly among those suspected of smuggling. However, on occasion, its citizens help Royalist fugitives wishing to flee England, especially if they are willing to pay gold to secure their flight to safety.

Tom Reynoldstone has lived in the town all his life. He and Martha enjoyed happy childhoods in the place, and now he is one of the many men making a threadbare living fishing for cod and scallops in the strait.

According to Dawkes, a little more than a day ago, Tom received word a mysterious foreigner, presumed to be a fighting man, was urgently seeking a boat to take him to the French coast. His demands were simple: he desired to dropped as near to Calais as possible, and he is willing to pay a high price for the right vessel and the continued silence of any would-be Samaritan.

"Tom knows a thing or two about these things," explained Dawkes, without elaborating on how his brother-in-law has become aware of such sensitive and compromising information. "He is one of a handful of boatsmen who have been approached by the man you are seeking. He has told him he can't help because his craft is too small and won't withstand the rigours of a Channel crossing. But he put the man we believe to be Holck in touch with someone he trusts, a sailor who is experienced and willing to countenance such a hazardous journey. And it would now seem a crossing has been agreed and is to take place tomorrow evening at high tide."

I let out a loud and involuntary gasp of breath. After all, I have endured, it seems I am to have the chance I have craved – to hold my nemesis to account.

"Thank you, Dawkes," I say appreciatively. "There

is much to consider and a lot to be done in a short space of time. I will make for Folkestone later. Before I depart, I need to speak to several people, including the Captain of a frigate anchored in the harbour. Do you have the connections to be able to make the necessary introductions?"

The local man's eyes glitter once again. "I certainly do, Captain Hacker," he says. "And it would give me great pleasure to broker such a meeting."

Evidence of the celebrations that heralded the Summer Solstice a few days ago is still evident in many of the thoroughfares that crisscross Dover. Broken ale bottles litter some of the pavements, the smell of piss and shit assaults my nostrils, fresh, crude graffiti adorns several walls, and over-painted women, who don't look as though they have seen soap in days, attempt to prostitute themselves to any man who looks their way. Yet I barely notice any of these distractions as I make my way back to the Flower de Luce after my meeting with Percival Hamilton, commander of the Leopard, a thirty-four gun, third-rate ship that protects England's chalk-encrusted cliffs and hops fields.

Captain Hamilton – a veteran navigator of the treacherous currents around the Dover and Folkestone coast – needed little persuasion to come to my aid. He listened intently as I listed my credentials and told him about the enemy we will be pursuing. Without raising a single objection, he agreed to allow his ship and men to be at my disposal the morrow, providing I can give him the details he requires before midday so he can make his own essential preparations.

After an hour in his company, during which we agree on everything that is necessary, I clasp hands with

Hamilton and bid the good captain farewell at three o'clock in the afternoon. He is an imposing figure, with a pate as bald as the finest hen's egg and skin more the colour of a Saracen than an Englishman. As I take my leave, I realise how lucky I am to have him as an ally.

It is as I walk back to the inn, where I have agreed to share a tankard of ale with Dawkes and apprise him of the outcome of my meeting with Hamilton, that a deep sense of unease consumes me with every step I take. I stop suddenly, reaching under my leather jerkin for the dagger that is strapped to my belt. When it is nestled in the palm of my left hand, I spin around, expecting to see the source of my disquiet. My eyes dart from side to side, examining the fronts of the brick houses for signs of life, but there is nothing. The street is quiet. My shadow is the only thing darkening the grey of the cobblestones, and shrieking seagulls are the only creatures keeping me company.

I continue my walk at a brisker pace, feeling uneasy yet not sure why. Occasionally, I look over my shoulder, expecting to see a furtive figure staying close to the walls. But every time I do so, I am confronted with the same picture of emptiness. If the piercing noise of the gulls wasn't such an assault on my senses, I would half-believe I was sleep-walking.

Eventually, the gaudily decorated door of the inn becomes visible as I emerge from an anonymous street. Soon I am sitting at a large table, with the ruddy face of Richard Dawkes in front of me, his bright eyes brimming with inquisitiveness.

"Well?" he enquires after attacking the large tankard containing his ale. "Was your meeting profitable, Captain?"

Although I have only known him for a few fleeting hours, there is something eminently likeable about this man's character. He is direct, honest – and loyal.

"It could not have gone any better, Master Dawkes," I reply. "Thanks to you, a frigate is now at my service. Hamilton seems to be a man of some repute and standing, and he has agreed to support my cause. Now all I need is a company of dragoons to help me entice Holck from his lair. I don't suppose your influence reaches as far as the local Parliamentary garrison, does it?"

My confidante pulls forward, moving his head within just a few inches of my own. When he speaks, it is but a whisper.

"It's funny you should mention this, Captain Hacker," he says, in a voice laced with good humour. "As a matter of fact, I am well acquainted with Major John Boys of Fredville, whom I have already spoken to about this matter. He, too, has indicated his willingness to support you in bringing this Bohemian turd to heel. I hope you don't mind, but I have taken the liberty of inviting Major Boys here this evening, and he has agreed to call on you at seven o'clock. I hope that is agreeable, sir?"

I clasp the muscular shoulder of Dawkes, surprising the man. "Thank you," I say appreciatively and acknowledging I will defer my journey to Folkestone to the morning. "For the first time in many long months, I feel as though I am close to gaining the justice my daughters and dear friends."

Before I can say more, the sweet voice of Martha can be heard calling out to her husband. There is work to be done. Obediently Dawkes rises, taking his ale with him. But before he has gone three short paces, he turns around, yet more excitement etched on his features.

"Before I forget, Captain," he says, "a suave, foreign fellow called here today asking some questions about you and wanting to know your whereabouts. I meant to say something as soon as I saw you, but my dealings with the Major, and your own news, got the better of me. I don't know who the man was, and he left quickly when I said you were not here. But he carried himself the way many mercenaries do. He had a swagger and an air of confidence about him that you don't find in many men. I am sorry I forgot to mention it earlier. It is remiss of me, sir."

As Dawkes joins his wife in the scullery, I find my mind and body moving into a heightened state of alert. Who could the mysterious man be? I rack my brains but can't think of anyone who fits the innkeeper's vague description. Except for Gervase Lucas at Belvoir Castle, nobody is aware of my present whereabouts.

Rather than put me at ease, Dawkes's news alarms me, and I quickly depart the communal area and retire to my room. I need to do some thinking before Major Boys arrives.

Like all good military men, Boys is punctual. He arrives at seven o'clock precisely, and he looks every inch the fighting man his reputation would have me believe. He has a namesake – a Royalist – who has also earned a formidable fighting name for himself as the governor of Donington Castle, a stronghold close to Newbury. But there can be no doubting the loyalties of my man, whose handshake is as firm as my own and who has recently been appointed one of Kent's Parliamentary Commissioner, with orders to suppress Royalist sympathisers in the area.

"I know what you are thinking, Captain," says Boys jovially, reading my mind perceptively as we move towards a table and two chairs that are positioned in the spacious room far enough away to prevent anyone from listening to our conversation. "And no, I am not the rogue who has been leading Cromwell and Fairfax a merry dance these past couple of years in the King's name."

We both laugh. It is the perfect way for two strangers, united by the cause they serve, to break the ice. And two full tankards of the finest Kentish ale, provided to us by the attentive Dawkes, helps the conversation flow even more naturally as we share common experiences and news of the war in our respective parts of the world.

Eventually, when our small talk is almost exhausted, Boys' expression changes. He drinks the what remains of his ale, looks at me directly and says in all seriousness: "So, Francis, I understand you need my help in apprehending a man who has been the source of much personal distress for you – and a thorn in the side of Parliament to boot?"

I glance in the direction of the door, where I see Dawkes watching us while pretending to go about his duties. I do not mind the innkeeper's inquisitiveness. He has already proven his worth to me, so I ignore his close proximity and continue to focus my attention on Major Boys, who is awaiting my reply. So I tell him everything I think he needs to know. As I speak, furrowed lines appear on his youthful forehead. I have grown accustomed to the violence and depravities inflicted on my children and friends like Abijah and Peter and Marjorie Harrington. What they suffered no longer shocks me when I think about their grisly fates. But for Major Boys, it is a different matter. A mask of fury envelops his face as I reveal every gory detail, so much so that after less than twenty minutes, he can take no more.

"For God's sakes, man, I beseech you, speak no more about these abominations," he gasps, keen to erase the images of my daughters being slain in cold blood by Holck's murderous hands from his mind. "You have my support and that of the Dover garrison. Whatever you need, it is yours. This dog must be brought to heel. And I will do all I can to ensure he is caught so he can face the punishment he so richly deserves."

I retire to my chamber at eleven o'clock. My time with Major Boys yielded a lot more than I could have hoped for at the outset: two infantry companies are to be made available to me, as well as the company of dragoons I initially sought. In total, more than two hundred men will be at my disposal to hunt down Holck, while waiting in the Channel will be the Leopard and Hamilton, its formidable captain.

Within minutes I have undressed, washed and climbed onto the threadbare mattress. My body is still exhausted from the rigours of my long journey to the coast. But I find time to pray to my maker before deep sleep claims me, and I quickly drift off into a welcome black void, where treasured memories of my beloved Isabel sustain and embolden me.

I am asleep for less than thirty minutes when a hammering on my door awakens me, and once again, I hear the excited, booming voice of Dawkes.

"Captain Hacker," he shouts. "Rouse yourself, good sir. The man I told you about has returned and insists I awaken you. Can you please come downstairs as quickly as possible? He won't leave without speaking to you first."

The innkeeper continues to hammer on my door until I beg him to relent and confirm I will get dressed and come downstairs as quickly as I can. As I rub my sleepy eyes, the fog that frequently leaves me with a heavy head, unable to think decisively and clearly, takes a firm hold, as it so often does when I am surprised. But I do as I am instructed, finding my hose and breeches before sliding my feet into my dust-encrusted boots. Unable to focus properly, I leave the room and follow the candles that provide just enough light for me to see through the gloom. After a minute, I reach the stairs from where I clearly hear Dawkes's soothing and reassuring voice.

"The Captain will be down shortly, sir," I hear him saying. "He was fast asleep when I knocked on his door. But I did as you asked and awoke him. He has confirmed he will come down, so please be patient. He'll only be a few minutes."

I listen for a response, so I can identify my mystery, late night visitor. But no sound is forthcoming, and I remain none the wiser. With the exception of Captain Hamilton, the only other person in Dover who knows my identity and whereabouts is Major Boys. Why either of them, particularly Boys, whose company I enjoyed less than an hour ago, would call on me at this late hour is beyond me. So I descend the stairs, my curiosity and wariness piqued.

"Ah, there you are, Captain," says a clearly relieved Dawkes as I make my entrance in the tavern area of the inn. "I am sorry to have disturbed you, sir, but this gentleman was most insistent on seeing you."

Dawkes, who is wearing what appears to be a stained and filthy nightgown, points in the direction of the far corner of the room, where standing in the shadows, I see a pair of highly polished boots attached to two sturdy legs. I edge forward, eager to see more. And as I do, I hear the unmistakable rasping sound of a sword scraping the wall.

"Don't be alarmed, mon ami," states a voice I instantly recognise as that of an ally. "I am here offering help, not bringing harm to your doorstep."

In the short time I have known him, it is the third occasion I have seen Guillaume de le Croix lurking in the shadows. And never have I been more overjoyed to hear his rich and melodious Gallic voice.

THIRTY

GUILLAUME DE LA CROIX IS a throwback to the age of chivalry, when godly men of standing were merciful, placed honour before greed and self-interest, and sought to be a force for good in a changing and corrupt world.

He impressed me greatly when I first met him in the bowels of Wallingford House, where Cromwell's violent interrogation of Lord Grey led to an accord with the traitorous noble. Before that, my skull had a brief acquaintance with the pommel of his knife in the shadows of the notorious King's Bench Prison. His combative qualities were something I learned to respect on that painful occasion, as was his undisputed courage.

I have been talking to the Frenchman for more than two hours, listening to his every word. We are seated at the same table I shared with Major Boys just a few hours earlier. As we converse into the early morning, sipping wine liberally, I can see the wick of the candle getting ever closer to the hot liquid wax that eagerly wishes to consume its wildly flickering flame. Yet there is much to discuss and

ponder, and the precariousness of the fragile light empha-
sises just how little time there is before dawn when my violent destiny will be fulfilled.

As Guillaume talks animatedly, I learn he has been
tasked by Cromwell to be my unofficial protector. It is a
role he has been fulfilling ever since I left the confines of
Belvoir Castle. For he has been tracking me – at a discreet
distance – close enough to monitor my movements and
ensure my safety while staying far enough away to avoid
detection.

"But you so nearly caught me out," he says as we discuss my productive meetings with Hamilton and Boys.
"Thankfully, I was able to keep my presence undetected
until I had something of value to share with you. And
that's why I came here this morning and returned tonight,
for I have discovered where Holck is staying and where his
intended rendezvous will be with the ship that is now in his
employ."

I sit back and look at the speaker's strong and bold
face. As I do, I spill most of my claret on the table, soaking
my breeches in the process. My error solicits a raucous
burst of laughter from de la Croix, who revels momentarily in my discomfort. At this moment, he reminds me of
Abijah, and the thought starts my head spinning. Oh, how
I miss my friend. And as I recall his features and the
painful and lonely death he endured, the memories come
flooding back.

As a melancholy mood and guilt threaten to overwhelm me in equal measure, I consciously force myself to
concentrate on the present. So many unanswered questions remain, not least how Guillaume found out about my
temporary release and my intention to pursue Holck to the

coast. But after pressing him on several occasions, all he will say is: "Lieutenant-General Cromwell simply instructed me to be at the castle, informing me of the time you would leave and the gate from which you would depart. And you did exactly as he said you would. I am afraid there is nothing more I can tell you, other than my primary purposes, which are to keep you safe and assist your endeavours in any way I can."

It is plain to see that trying to elicit meaningful answers from de la Croix will be a futile exercise. Cromwell and Parliament have a nest of spies and informants located all over the land. And since the calamitous Royalist defeat at Naseby, the number of men and women swapping sides will have grown significantly now the King's prospects of victory in this bloody conflict appear doomed. So I try a different line of questioning.

"Your presence here is surprising and a welcome relief, my friend," I say earnestly. "But what I have planned may be a source of displeasure for Oliver, bearing in mind it was he who allowed Holck to escape unimpeded from London. For my intentions are to end things the only way they can be brought to a conclusion: Holck must perish, and I must be his executioner. There is no other way."

Guillaume takes yet another hearty sip from his wine glass. When he is done, he says nothing for what seems a long time. At this late hour, the silence is deafening. Eventually, when he does speak, he reveals some of his inner core.

"Francis, I am your comrade," he confirms reassuringly. "Being by your side is my overriding duty to the Lieutenant-General and to you. How I choose to assist you is a matter for me and nobody else. So have no doubts, I am with you in this venture. And you are going to need me, for your adversary is a fearsome fighter. He is a killer in a way you are not, and you are going to need all the help you can get if you are to succeed."

One final, graceful gulp sees the Frenchman sink what remains of his drink. Then, after his thirst has been sated, he wipes his mouth with the back of his gloved hand and belches. The explosion of noise catches me by surprise and echoes around the cavernous room. When a minute or so has passed, and I have contemplated his words, I realise Guillaume is right. I have already come perilously close to losing my life at the hands of Holck, and while confronting him does not unduly concern me, I know the odds are stacked heavily in his favour.

"You are quite correct in your assessment," I say emphatically. "If we are successful, Oliver is likely to be sorely tested by what he will perceive as our hot-headed-ness and insubordination. But so be it. Some things have to run their course, and this is one of them."

Looking to raise the mood a little and focus on immediate priorities, I change tack slightly and say: "So, what news do you bring about the whereabouts of Holck and his plans for escape? And, just as importantly, how did you find out about them?"

Guillaume lets out a nervous laugh before leaning towards me, adopting the air of the seasoned conspirator that he is.

"I think I have enough information to ensure you continue to feel confident about your quest," he says. "As for how I came by this information, you will simply have to trust me, my dear Captain Hacker. Je sais pas. The only person I can share such confidential information with is the Lieutenant-General. And that, my friend, is all I can, and will, say on the matter."

Before I have time to think about remonstrating, de le Croix leans forward and lowers his voice even further, so it is nothing more than a dampened tone. "Your quarry is staying at a remote cottage located on the scrublands that surround East Wear Bay," he continues. "A fishing boat will collect him from the beach at nine o'clock in the evening, just as the light is starting to fade. And to make matters even better for our united cause, it is likely to be a full moon, albeit we will have to be careful not to give away our positions."

My friend has confirmed everything and more that Dawkes relayed to me earlier. I am now satisfied with the veracity of the information I hold and believe Holck is almost within my grasp.

My thoughts are about to claim me when seemingly out of nowhere, de la Croix produces a second bottle of claret and proceeds to fill both goblets to the brim with yet more intoxicating liquid. I need little encouragement and lustily take another sip. As men plot the death of another soul, we need something to block out our fears and anxieties. And tonight, this cheap wine has never tasted better.

"Mon Dieu, you are indeed a thirsty man, Captain," observes my protector as he proceeds to refill my glass. "Let us toast success and the triumph of good over evil, for that is what this is. And let us pray for clear heads, for we will need all our wit and guile come the morrow."

Simultaneously, we raise our glasses to one another. It may be the last occasion I ever taste wine, so I savour the sensation, knowing that in less than fifteen hours, I will either continue to be in the land of the living, or I'll have been dispatched prematurely to the afterlife, and whatever that holds for a man weighed down by sin.

By ten o'clock in the morning on Monday, the twenty-fifth day of June, Guillaume and I discussed our plans with Captain Hamilton and Major Boys and agreed on our respective courses action. I come away from the meetings feeling as confident as I dare be. I have also thanked Dawkes and his good wife for their hospitality and loyalty. Without their considerable assistance, my efforts would have been thankless. Because of the help of the innkeeper, I now have detailed knowledge of the Folkestone shoreline, a very clear picture of the area where Holck is hiding, and what his route to the bay will be.

As we leave Dover Castle, where the Parliamentarian garrison is located, men are sharpening their swords, cleaning their muskets and pistols, and making scores of rounded lead shot. Their faces are hardened, and an eerie silence has descended throughout the fort. Judging by the mood, it would seem Major Boys has not yet informed his men about the precise nature of their task this evening. All they have been told is they are to prepare for combat. So they are going about their business with extreme thoroughness, making sure their weapons will not let them down at their most significant moment of need.

Our destination is a three-hour trek from the ramparts of the ancient castle. Boys has confirmed to me his men will take up their concealed positions on the perimeter of the dunes and surrounding hills and cliffs by seven o'clock. I am told there are plenty of places for men to hide in the dunes, gorse bushes and rock formations strewn across the expanse that forms this secluded part of the seafront. It's little wonder the place is reputed to be popular among smugglers. To put men in position any earlier would certainly alert an experienced campaigner like Holck. After all, it is hard for such a large body to maintain silence for such a lengthy period, particularly when at least eighty horses will be accompanying their riders.

Guillaume and I say little for the first hour of the journey as we continue to assess the merits of our plans. There is so much to ponder. We take our time walking our horses rather than riding them, such is the heat of the late morning sun. The silence and sea breeze are most welcome. If the truth is known, I am feeling slightly liverish due to the amount of wine I drank in the small hours before going on to endure a broken and troubled few hours of sleep.

I had visions of a church and a man directing me to go and unburden my soul to my Maker throughout the night. No matter how hard I tried to dismiss these uninvited thoughts, they kept returning, plaguing my mind so greatly that rest became a near impossibility. Yet, although my stomach feels delicate, I am not tired.

"How are you feeling?" asks Guillaume. We have already walked four miles and are rounding a corner and climbing a steep hill known as 'Stepping Down'. "Are you thinking clearly and feeling ready for whatever we will be confronted with?"

I eye the man walking by my side. "If I told you I have never felt better, would you believe me?" I ask tetchily. "In all seriousness, I feel more apprehensive and nervous than I have ever felt. At times such as these, when you know there will be trouble, and you are at risk, I am normally quite philosophical about things. But today, I am not my usual self, and the wine you plied me with last night has nothing to do with it. On the contrary, I feel troubled because I somehow have to find a way of defeating Holck. And he is a man who should have the besting of both of us."

As I speak, I catch sight of my scarred fingers. The tissue is still red in parts, particularly around my thumbs – and the memory of Holck using the pliers on me at Belvoir Castle, under the watchful eye of Prince Maurice, comes flooding back. Almost immediately, my fingers start to tingle, as do my toes. Both were equally brutalised by the Bohemian as he sought information for his master that I didn't possess. The experience was chastening and incredibly painful. It demonstrated the delight with which the Royalist killer and torturer applies his skills, revelling in the pain he inflicts. From that moment, I became acutely aware of his power and cruelty, and although I do not fear him, I am conscious of how my own limitations as a fighter may be exposed when I eventually confront him.

A cough from my protector forces me to return to reality. I look up instantly, and as Guillaume readies himself to say something, a half-naked man emerges from the dense woodland less than ten yards away. He appears to be blind drunk, filthy and his eyes are overflowing with insanity. I recognise the signs, having seen too many urchins in a similar state in the streets of Leicester, all of them shorn of hope and dignity. Whatever clothing remains on his leathery body is ripped, torn and soiled. The poor fellow is in a sorry state, cavorting wildly in the middle of the track while singing one bawdy song after another. He must be at least seventy years of age if he is a day. We try to find our way around the stranger's wildly flailing arms, but every time we do so, he blocks the thoroughfare and forces de la Croix and myself backwards, pressing us against the dense and prickly Hawthorne bushes that snake upwards, following the path that leads to the hamlet of Hougham.

Suddenly, the man stops flailing and wailing and looks me squarely in the eye.

"I… know… you," he bellows. His words are slurred, and spittle and snot spray from his foul, toothless mouth. "I know your face, and I know why you are here. But beware: grave danger awaits you if you continue to follow the road you are taking. You need to ask for His forgiveness and help. Only He can help your quest."

I glance nervously at Guillaume, who is carefully scrutinising the crazed fool before us. We look at one another, not knowing how to react.

"Listen to me," shouts the old man, whose body looks every inch the frail shell it is but whose voice is surprisingly coherent. "You need to get on your knees and seek His guidance and strength. Only through your repentance can the cause you represent be recognised as just."

The last sentence is barked out as a painful rasping fit takes hold of him. And as he falls to his knees, clearly in significant discomfort, we become aware of several voices behind us calling out the name of "Henry". Within moments, three men round the corner and come to an abrupt standstill. They quickly take stock of the scene being played out before them, and eventually, their inquisitiveness forces them to speak directly to us.

"What is going on here?" demands the bravest of the three, a ruffian of no more than a score of years. "Why is old Henry on his knees?"

Before I can explain, de la Croix starts to speak. "We have done nothing to your friend," he says, with his right hand placed on the hilt of his sword. "We were just going about our business when he accosted us, blocked our way and started shouting at us. He had just fallen down when you appeared on the scene. That's all there is to say of the matter. But I would like to know where you are from and what you are doing here?"

The confidence oozing from Guillaume clearly unsettles the small group. So too do our swords – and the muskets we are carrying in our panniers, which are clearly visible. To simple country folk, we look what we are: fighting men in their prime.

"We mean you no harm, good sirs," assures the most vocal and coherent member of the three. "We were drinking at the Three Horseshoes over yonder with old Henry here when he vanished. We thought something might have happened to the old devil, that's why we started looking for him. He has a habit of disappearing when the innkeeper demands to be paid."

The comment forces a nervous laugh from all three men, and the humour visibly eases the tension.

"Who is this man?" I say. "Hasn't he got a home to go to and someone to look after him and keep him out of mischief?"

Momentarily my question leaves the strangers lost for words. Then the ringleader speaks again. "His name is Henry Hannington, and he is the oldest man in these parts," he informs Guillaume and me. "He has been a drunk for thirty years or more. Everyone in Kent has heard of him and knows of his antics."

The prolonged silence of de la Croix and myself

encourages the man to continue speaking. "Henry used to be the Minister of the church of Saint Laurence, which is on the brow of the hill about half a mile away," he continues. "He is from a wealthy family and became notorious for getting pissed and doing everything a churchman should not do. Eventually, the wardens and parishioners had enough of his antics. They threw him onto the streets, even though their decision provoked a bitter clash with other members of the Hannington family. That was just before the start of the war. Ever since, he has been living off whatever charity he can find and drinking himself to oblivion whenever he has a penny, or two, in his purse."

All five of us look once again at the frail figure slumped on the ground. Aware of our scrutiny, Henry Hannington rises to his feet, taking in all before him. Once erect, he glares belligerently in my direction, never dropping his gaze. Then, abruptly, he points his left index finger directly at me and slowly walks forward, one small step at a time, until he is standing directly in front of me, so close his rancid breath washes over my face. He then starts jabbing his bony finger into my chest.

"You... are... Hack-er," he says breathlessly, the stench of stale ale and puke almost forcing me to retch. "You... must... make... your... peace."

THIRTY-ONE

AFTER THE EXCITEMENT OF MEETING Henry
Hannington and his associates, Guillaume and myself
make the short journey to Saint Laurence church, where I
hope to rest and pray before commencing the serious business of apprehending Holck.

Almost five hundred years old, the church is a hidden citadel, surrounded by a forest of pine trees that conceal its whereabouts from the naked eye. Its bulky tower,
made from local flintstone and almost as thick as the body
of a fully-grown man, is drenched in daylight. Overhead,
Jackdaws and Magpies call out like sentries alerting a resting army to an approaching threat, as slowly and surely
Guillaume and I make our way towards the entrance.

"Will you join me inside?" I ask de la Croix as we
tether the horses together. It is almost two o'clock in the
afternoon. "As the old man said, we certainly need to make
our peace with the Lord before tonight, regardless of the
outcome. And now would appear to be the perfect opportunity."

The Frenchman shakes his head. "No, my friend, I will stay outside and rest up," he says. "The Lord and I have become strangers to one another in recent years. I continue to fear and revere Him, but too many evil things have been done in France and England for me to want to drop to my knees. So please take your time and do whatever you need to do. I will still be here when God has had enough of you."

Inwardly, I am pleased to enter the church on my own, although I would not have objected if Guillaume had joined me. For the last forty-five minutes, ever since the old man spoke to me, I have been deeply troubled and trying to comprehend everything that has happened. I was left numbed by my dreams of the early hours, but meeting Hannington – and hearing him utter my name so clearly and precisely – has left me dumbfounded and in urgent need of answers. I tried to speak to him after his finger stopped striking my chest, but he could not talk as the drink-induced stupor consumed him once more, leaving me to wonder about the significance of his words. And while the old man is unable to help me, I now have the chance to ask a higher authority.

The slate floor of the church is cold, but despite my discomfort, I feel heartened to be in the house of God once again. It has been a while since I last visited Saint Guthlacs, so I find myself immersed in thoughts and prayers as I search for forgiveness for every wrongful thing I have done and am about to do.

When a man faces the prospect of death and realises he is mortal, the vaults within his mind suddenly open and events and deeds that have been locked away for many years come to the fore. For me, it is as though a dam has been burst as I remember so many of my misdeeds. Indeed, as I recall events buried for a decade or more, I start to believe I will be forced to relive every misdemeanour I have committed. Thankfully, I have my prayer book with me, and I turn to Psalm Eighty-Six, which King David wrote so many centuries ago. Right now, its meaning resonates powerfully with my mood and needs, so I recite the first few verses aloud:

> *"Hear, O Lord, and answer me, for I am poor and needy. Guard my life, for I am devoted to you.*
>
> *"You are my God; save your servant who trusts in you. Have mercy on me, O Lord, for I call to you all day long.*
>
> *"Bring joy to your servant, for to you, O Lord, I lift up my soul."*

As I mouth the words, committing them to memory, I sense my heart is beating wildly. I feel the sweat on my brow, the tears in the corners of my eyes. I realise the emptiness and brokenness I have felt for longer than I care to remember is being replaced with renewed feelings of gratitude and purpose. I also hear soothing words being spoken, yet there is nobody in the building to converse with. I feel strange; I feel euphoric; I feel blessed – and I gradually start to understand why.

For the next hour or so, I come to terms with a wide range of emotions, and I share with the Father my fears and concerns about the murderous quest I am on. I speak openly about my hatred for the man I am pursuing. I also tell him of my intentions this day, and I sincerely ask for his forgiveness and direction in my bid to defeat Gustav Holck.

At some point, I blackout. I awaken some minutes later and become aware of something I can only describe as a supernatural presence. It is not physical, nor is it frightening. But it is all-embracing. How long I am out cold for, I do not know. But when I do come round, my emotions are in a heightened state, and what I am experiencing is a lot more than mere feelings. Something is happening within, and I am not sure what it is until I see Abijah standing before me, urging me to rise and prepare for the fate my Maker has planned for me. As I do as instructed, I clearly hear the words "look to the moon".

And at that very moment, I know exactly what is happening to me.

Eventually, I leave the church and find Guillaume soundly asleep. His head is propped against his sturdy saddle, the horses are restful, having been fed and watered by my companion, and there is calmness now the birds have gone to do their squawking elsewhere.

"You were a long time, mon ami," splutters Guillaume as he observes my re-emergence through two hooded slits that conceal bloodshot eyes. "If you had been any longer, I may have been forced to come in and get you, for it's time for us to get to the bay and rendezvous with the Major and his men."

I say little in response, not because I don't wish to, but because I cannot do so. The events of this afternoon will live with me for a lifetime, as I struggle to comprehend everything I have just experienced. I pull my cherished watch from my inner pocket: the time is five o'clock. We have less than two hours to get to the agreed location. Under the circumstances, "let's be on our way" is the very best I can muster.

We walk the remainder of the distance on foot, making good time and eventually arriving at the bay twenty minutes ahead of schedule. There is no sign of Boys or his soldiery, so I decide to embark on a short reconnaissance of the area. As I hide between rocks and trees, I quickly understand why this is a smugglers paradise.

From the gorse tree line where I am concealed, I am able to survey an area known as 'The Warren', located to the east of Folkestone. According to the information provided by Dawkes and Guillaume, some of the houses in these parts join with as many as four secret passages used by smugglers to hide their illicit goods. It is one of these tunnels that Holck intends to use tonight to make his descent to East Wear Bay and then on to what he hopes will be his successful bid for freedom. For those of us who lie in wait, the difficulty is locating the exact whereabouts of the tunnels, as these are a closely guarded secret, known only to the men who risk their lives bringing ashore items and wares that evade the hefty taxes that now swell Parliament's treasury.

"Where do you think he will come from?" I ask de la Croix as we simultaneously scrutinise the sands, shore and sea. "Did your informant have anything more specific to say other than what you have already told me?"

Guillaume prods the smooth golden grains with the toe of his polished boot, drawing a long line in the sand. He then squats down and uses his hands to make a crude map of everything we can see. When he has finished, he points to one hard to reach place from where Holck could emerge: the base of the high cliff.

"You can be certain Holck will not take any unnecessary risks," says Guillaume. "He has not come this far and got so close to his escape to throw everything away by dropping his guard. Therefore, although the route through 'The Warren' is the simplest and most direct passage to the sea, my betting is he will take the hardest path, which affords him the greatest protection."

I think about things for a moment, looking all the time at Guillaume's handiwork in the sand and recalling my conversations with Dawkes as I do. Before I say anything, I go to the edge of the tress and scan the cliffs, finding the point my French ally has identified. It is indeed the perfect place – impossible to guard without being spotted and with a vantage point that affords a panoramic view of the whole bay. From there, you can see virtually everything that moves on sea and land.

"I agree. Holck will not worry about negotiating a few twists and turns and a steep rock face, not if it provides him with far greater protection," I concur. That is the place from where he will emerge if, indeed, our information is accurate. There is no doubt in my mind."

Guillaume and I exchange rueful smiles. While we have made progress these past two days, the greatest challenge was always going to be in the last few hours, when the trap is being set. And so it is proving to be.

As both of us contemplate our next move, there is a notable change in the temperature, and the coastal winds pick up. On the horizon, a thick line of malevolent black and grey clouds inch their way closer to the coast.

Appropriately, a violent storm would appear to be brewing.

THIRTY-TWO

FOR MORE THAN AN HOUR, heavy rain lashes East Wear Bay. Waves and spray consume the shoreline, sending the raucous Choughs fleeing to their nests along the cliffs and forcing Guillaume and myself to sit motionless in an anonymous covert, powerless to avoid being soaked. Overhead, semi-darkness cloaks the land as the unseasonal black clouds block out the sun. And all the while, a hostile wind rips through the dunes and trees, whipping up sandstorms that sting the face and subdue my optimism.

Worryingly, there is no sign of Major Boys and his three companies of infantry and dragoons. Guillaume believes the poor weather may have caused the delay. Yet, with the hour almost eight o'clock and Holck's expected departure getting ever closer, I am unsure what to think. So far, I have attempted to find the Major on two occasions, without success. According to the plan we agreed in Dover, he and his men should have been concealed in a wooded area some forty minutes ago, well away from the sight of anyone who may have braved the inclement conditions. But there is no sight of them, and as the time ticks by, I am becoming increasingly concerned my plan is doomed.

"I am going to try and find the Major again," I shout loudly, so de la Croix can hear me above the squalls. "He can't be far away now, and time is pressing. He needs me to be waiting for him so he can deploy his men in a way that is advantageous to us, for no matter how bad the conditions get, I am certain Holck will attempt to escape tonight. Too much is at stake for him not to want to flee."

I glance towards the shoreline once again, in the hope my prayers will be answered and there will be a sign from above that the storm will soon start subsiding. Then, on cue, a gap miraculously appears in the clouds and blue sky and sunshine break through momentarily, revealing calmer seas are close by.

"There you have it," I say, straining my voice once again and pointing yonder, so Guillaume follows the direction of my hand. "It is a clear sign we will soon be through the worst, and our efforts are not going to be in vain."

My companion leans forward and grips my arm with an intensity I am not expecting. "Let me be the one to speak to the Major," he pleads. "You need to remain out of sight. Only you know Holck's identity, so you need to be the one who is kept out of harm's way until the moment you are needed. I know our plans as well as you do, so allow me to be the person to find Boys and speak to him."

My initial reaction is to protest. But before I can speak, Guillaume is on his feet, busily adjusting the angle of his sodden tricorn hat. I pull out my pocket watch; we are almost an hour behind the agreed schedule. Reluctantly, I agree to his proposal.

"I will be back before you know it," he says reassuringly. "Boys will be in position well before our man shows his face. And when he does come forth, there will be no escape for him."

The muffled sound of swords clashing reaches my ears just a few minutes after Guillaume has departed. The whine of the howling wind affects my hearing, so the clash of metal on metal is indistinct and muted, but to the trained ear, the noise means only one thing; somewhere close by, men are fighting for their lives.

I crouch and grasp the rock directly behind me, scanning the scrub and sand dunes for the telltale signs of conflict and worse. But I see nothing, and then the noise I am convinced I have heard is suddenly silenced. I lean further forward, searching for movement and evidence of anything untoward and out of place. I am desperate to discover what is happening, convinced some evil is at play. Yet as the winds start to blow themselves out, I remain blinded and deaf… until it is too late.

After straining my eyes and ears to no avail for several minutes, a sixth sense alerts me to imminent danger. Alas, my instincts are not quick enough, and as I turn my body and raise my left arm, two heavy blows to the back of my head leave me stunned. Several powerful punches rain in on my head; I feel my nose explode and clearly hear my eye socket crack. Blood starts to ooze from my wounds, and I fall backwards, helpless and unable to defend myself. Needing little encouragement, my attacker arrows a brutal kick into my ribs. Its impact expels the air from my lungs and leaves me broken and gasping for air. In less than twenty seconds, I have been outwitted, outfought and left to the mercy of a wily and superior assailant.

Coarse laughter rains down on me from above, but the blood from my damaged eye prevents me from seeing who is enjoying my sorry misfortune. As I ravenously take in some oxygen, I prepare my prostrate and limp torso to experience further assault. And I am not to be disappointed. Two more painful kicks to my midriff leave me reeling and brings up the bile from my stomach, while a stamp on my right ankle yields the acutest pain of all. It's at that moment I remember no more.

When I reopen my eyes, I make out the stocky features of a fighting man standing over me, binding my hands with rope. He is dressed in black; his dark locks have been cropped the Parliamentarian way, a scar disfigures his face, and except for his haircut, Gustav Holck is just as I remember him.

"So you and the Frenchman have tried to outsmart me, eh, Hacker," he barks at me in his coarse, guttural voice while shaking his head and standing upright. "You are not the only one with paid informants in these parts. Do you really think I would leave anything to chance and run the risk of being outwitted by an imbecile like you, now the King's cause is dead?"

For a moment, Holck just looks at me; his contempt and hatred are clear to see. Only when he is satisfied I am harmless does he continue with his verbal assault while placing his studded boot on my throat.

"You must think me a dullard, Hacker?" he states. "But as you have once again discovered, I am far from being the fool you would wish me to be. I have been aware of your presence since the moment you arrived in Dover. I knew where you were staying, and I was aware of your meetings with Boys and Hamilton. You barely concealed your tracks, so convinced were you that you were the hunter and I was your prey. Yet all the while, I have had my eyes firmly fixed on you, just waiting for you to slip up."

As the Bohemian eases the pressure on my throat, the hat he is wearing is lifted off his head, and lank strands of sodden hair are conjured into wild, snake-like figures. As they cavort and twist, I find myself thinking he has the look of Medusa rather than that of a man. It is a fitting image. As I ponder its meaning, once again, Holck's ugly voice brings me sharply back to my senses.

"Remember the drunken old man you met earlier today, close to Saint Laurence's church?" he enquires. "It didn't take much to persuade Hannington and a few of the men he associates with to wait for you and spin you and your accomplice a yarn that would delay your arrival. The ruse helped me create enough time to do what needed to be done. And you, like the amiable sop you are, took it all in, believing it to be true. How anyone can be so gullible is beyond me. But there it is. I must confess, I am grateful for it being so."

Before he stops speaking, Holck raises his right leg and propels his heel violently into my groin. An agony greater than any I have experienced so far explodes throughout my body, and I puke uncontrollably over my leather jerkin and on the damp and darkened sand. My head rolls to the side, and I find myself unable to move. Such is my misfortune that even more laughter comes out of my captor's embittered mouth.

When I can speak again, I rasp: "Where is my companion. What has become of Guillaume?"

Holck looks triumphant, just like he did when I first met him all those months ago when the course of the war was undecided, and he was all-powerful. "Your whelp of a friend found me to be more than his equal," he says. "After all, I have been filleting enemies for more than thirty years, and his enthusiasm and energy were no substitute for swordsmanship. I finished your puppy within a couple of minutes, after he had begged for his life and surrendered your whereabouts to me."

The news hits me like a hammer blow, and I groan aloud. Tears form and I weep for Guillaume. His is another precious life lost needlessly to this vile conflict.

"You really do revel in death, don't you?" I shout at my tormentor. "Whereas others fight for their beliefs, or to right a heinous wrong, you kill simply for amusement and profit. Is that not so?"

The Bohemian walks around my prone body. As he does, in a bid to gain a more panoramic view of the bay, my eyes refocus and enable me to see the weather has become more settled. Even at this late hour, deep blue skies are returning, the winds are dropping, and I can no longer hear the waves battering the shore. The Lord has kept his promise. What a shame I have not.

"And if you think you are going to be rescued, then I urge you to think again," says Holck confidently. "This afternoon, two members of the garrison gave Major Boys a letter, purportedly written by you. It informed him that your plans have changed, and I am now in Ashford. Right now, a company of dragoons is bearing down on the town and will be led a merry dance by some friends of mine, which will take up what is left of the evening. As for the two Infantry Companies, they remain at Dover Castle, so don't expect any help from that quarter. For the next hour or so, it is just going to be you and me. And when I am tired of your company, I am afraid only one of us will be left breathing this fine air."

Despair threatens to overwhelm me as I comprehend everything Holck is saying. There is no ambiguity: he means to kill me. I am not surprised; after all, that is the fate I had hoped to be dispensing to him.

For long moments, I think of my beloved wife and two surviving children. Even though I haven't seen them for months, their faces form a picture in my mind, and I remember so much about them in a short space of time. I think of the happy times and the many occasions when joy gripped Stathern. And then I remember the grief that consumed my home when the bodies of Barbara and Isable, my youngest girls, were discovered in the church-yard at Elston. I vowed that day to hunt Holck down and make him pay for their deaths. But, alas, although he now stands before me, he is in control of my destiny, not I. Yet I must not give up; I must not allow myself to be defeated, even though my hands are bound. For while there is breath in my body, there is hope, no matter how remote and unlikely it may appear to be.

"It is a shame things have to end this way," adds Holck, as the sea-faring vessel he is expecting appears on the horizon, still some two hours away. At its sighting, a victorious smile spreads across his face. "I am going to enjoy finishing you off far less than that rogue Swan, the friend you gave up so willingly. At least he died with his dignity intact, looking me in the eye as the noose was placed around his neck. He swore you would find me and avenge him. Well, does this look like vengeance to you, Hacker?"

When I fail to respond, the Bohemian stamps down on my leg. The vicious motion is enough to force yet another agonised groan out of me.

"You see that masthead and sail out in the channel? That's the boat that is going to take me back to France, away from the madness of England and the reckoning that is coming," continues Holck. "While you rot and your name is forgotten, I will be among friends living a contented life as an officer in Phillip of France's army. And what of your family, Hacker, what will become of them? Who will care for your wife and children when you are gone, you foolish and over-ambitious man? Think on that in the time you have left as you seek the forgiveness of your Maker."

As the hour gets closer to ten o'clock, I sense it is time. The storm has abated, the night sky is once again settled, and the stars are starting to shine. The bay is now quiet, and as a flock of Oystercatchers screech their warning calls over our heads, and Holck plays with a sharp knife, I decide to spend my last few moments talking to my executioner.

"Will you tell me one thing?" I ask of him.

The King's man stops toying with the weapon and stares at me. He sighs before responding: "What is it? What do you possibly wish to know?"

Memories flood into my head. There are so many things I wish to ask of this man, whom I only met after I had agreed to do the bidding of Parliament less than two years ago. Before then, I had never heard of Holck. How I wish I had declined the impassioned pleas of Cromwell and the late John Pym, who beseeched me to broker a secret alliance with Princes Rupert and Maurice. Much would be different if I had chosen to decline their overtures. But I didn't. And now, there is one thing more than anything else I wish to know.

"Something within me understands why you butchered Peter and Marjorie Harrington and why you killed Abijah," I say. "In war, such things happen, and there is an understanding that ordinary men and women are expendable. That is one of the harsh realities we come to accept. But tell me, why was it necessary to kill my children?"

Holck's eyes gleam as he remembers the moment he extinguished the lives of my two innocent girls. Next, his breath becomes ragged, as it sometimes does when a man experiences physical exertion. Then Holck moves towards me, his eyes never leaving my own until his face is just a few inches away. Only then does he speak.

"I have killed for as long as I care to remember," he says impassively. "For men like me, it is what we do. And I have become accomplished in the art of the assassin, so much so that I rather enjoy it.

"In truth, once I had taken your children that night, you were never going to see them alive again, Hacker. No matter what our agreement was, they were dead the moment they left Stathern. I don't expect you to understand, for you are not like me. Whatsmore, your views are totally unimportant, particularly as you will soon be embracing those girls in the place you Christians call Heaven. But when you kill, as I do, there has to be pleasure in it. And that is why your daughters died that day; cutting their throats brought me satisfaction. It is as simple as that."

Fresh, stinging tears cascade down my cheeks as Holck speaks his abhorrent words, and it takes what is left of my self-control not to break down completely in front of my avowed enemy. If I had the means, I would gut the man and let him bleed to death where he stands. But my precarious situation requires me to show as little emotion as possible. Eventually, I am strong enough to speak again and retain what is left of my composure. "Is that it?" I demand. "Is satisfying your perverse blood lust the sole reason my daughters perished that day? If so, what are you?"

Holck's answer is lost as sixteen cannons erupt, their thunder-like noise shattering the tranquillity of East Wear Bay. So absorbed have Holck and myself been in our own cursed conflict, we have not seen the rapidly approaching Leopard as it pounces on its unsuspecting target. Plumes of spray straddle the undefended craft that is now less than a quarter of a mile off the shore – fired from the portholes of the twin-masted frigate commanded by Percival Hammond. The sound of a second volley of concussive explosions punctures the air as Holck and I watch on, mesmerised by the unfolding events played out in front of us. Shock and disbelief are etched on both of our faces for vastly contrasting reasons. Suddenly, one-shot finds its target and an almighty ball of flame engulfs the starboard side of the smaller vessel. As it lists, unable to withstand the ferocity of the unexpected attack, another cannonball slams into its belly, splitting it in two and sending wood and debris cartwheeling high into the evening sky. When the air has cleared, and visibility has been restored, we watch what is left of the ship sink rapidly to the seabed, taking with it the trapped men who willingly accepted a killer's gold.

I avert my gaze from the destruction meted out by Hamilton and his crew and turn my attention to more pressing matters. And as I do so, I hear Holck's anguished cry as he launches himself at me.

My wounds prevent me from putting up the strongest of defences. It is all I can do to raise my bound hands and prevent the cutthroat's knife from ripping open my neck. Mercifully, I deflect the blow, but I immediately feel a sharp pain as the tips of two of my fingers on my left hand are severed. The shock of seeing my hand disfigured is instant and indescribable, but at least I remain among the living.

As hard as I resist, it is futile to try and get the better of Holck. My weakened state is no match for his superior strength, and he quickly masters me. Successive thrusts rip open my shoulder and render my left arm useless. The fight, if that is what it can be called, is over within less than a couple of minutes.

"It looks as though you might be staying here a bit longer than you intended," I shout as I prepare for the fateful cut that will surely finish me off. "Do your worst and see that you make quick work of it."

I open my eyes and prepare to look at Holck one final time. But, as I glance upwards, an explosion of moonlight illuminates the bay, dazzling my attacker. Instinctively the Bohemian lifts his right hand, which holds the knife he intends to kill me with, in an attempt to shield his eyes. And as he does, I remember the prophetic words of the drunk Hannington and hear the pounding sound of hooves on the sand and the voice of Guillaume de la Croix shouting my name.

The distinctive crack of a flintlock rebounds off the cliff face, sending the roosting gulls and terns into a frenzy. Amid the commotion, Holck spins around and grips his back, dropping the knife at my feet. It would appear the sudden light from the moon temporarily blinded him and exposed his position to the advancing Guillaume, whose single shot found its mark. Clearly in pain, Holck spasms; the musket ball has ripped through his upper arm – but he is still on his feet and seemingly has plenty of fight left in him.

"Das ist noch nicht vorbei, Hacker," he yells at me in his native Germanic as he staggers out of the hole. "Ich bin wieder für dich da, sobald ich mich um deinen Freund gekümmert habe."

Translation: "This isn't over, Hacker. I will be back for you once I have attended to your friend."

And then he is gone. Moments later, I hear the welcome sound of a horse and its master. "Francis, are you out here?" calls Guillaume. "Speak to me, mon ami. I pray you are still alive and can hear me?"

I don't know who looks worse. Dried blood covers much of Guillaume's face; he has at least two broken ribs and has been stabbed in the thigh. Every breath he takes is laboured, and his limp is more pronounced. Yet he has saved me from certain death.

"He told me you were finished," I say after the Frenchman has released me from the bonds used to restrain me before he quickly starts tending to his own wounds. "I believed him, yet here you are. It is a miracle."

My companion looks at me earnestly. "I have come as close to death as a man can," he admits. "He surprised me as I approached the area where we had agreed to meet Boys and his men. I had just arrived when Holck confronted me. Before I could fight back, he had run me through and slashed at my stomach. I was saved by the bible I carry but never read. But for the book, it would have been a lot more than my ribs that were broken. But enough of this chatter, Francis; we are not safe here, for Holck is still at large. Even though we are in a sore state, we need to find him and finish this matter for good. He cannot be allowed to escape. The horses are rested. Are you strong enough to ride?"

I don't need a second invitation. I stand, wiping some of the congealed blood from my face. "Nothing will give me greater pleasure," I respond. "Let's finish it."

Although the hour is late and darkness has cast a shroud over the dunes and trees, the light remains strong. Broken sand, disturbed only a few minutes earlier, leaves a trail that tells us where Holck is heading and indicates the extent of his wounds. For such is the haphazard pattern of his footprints that the injury must be more grievous than we originally thought. The direction of his flight is towards the most concealed of the smugglers' tunnels – the one closest to the cliff face.

"He can't be too far ahead," I say to Guillaume, as our horses eat up the sand quickly and assuredly, and dense plumes of steam are expelled from their nostrils. "We will be on him shortly, so reload the pistol and be sure you are ready. As soon as you can, shoot him – and make sure you kill him. We don't wish to engage in any hand-to-hand fighting, which could allow him to reassert his advantage."

As we climb to the brow of one of the dunes, the silhouetted figure of a man slowly making his way to the rock face comes into view. Guillaume and I look at one another. No words are necessary; we know what needs to be done.

I dig my heels into the flank of my horse and coax him forward, but as we close in on Holck, there is a sudden cry of alarm to my rear. I turn around in the saddle to see Guillaume and his horse falling down the side of the large dune. The animal's legs are kicking wildly, and I can clearly see my friend trapped underneath its belly as it desperately attempts to right itself. Their cries become more urgent as the steed's head and front legs smash into a rocky outcrop. Rider and beast settle at the foot of the mound in obvious distress, and the only thing I can do is seek to offer whatever aid I can.

When Guillaume realises I have broken off the pursuit and I am now approaching his position, the resolve in his voice is unambiguous. "Francis, what are you doing?" he pleads. "I will be okay. The horse has broken its leg and is done for. Continue with your pursuit, and I will follow on foot as soon as I can. Do not allow Holck to escape. There will be no second chance."

I pause for a moment. As I do, I see Guillaume point his primed flintlock at the side of the distressed horse's head. A flash of cordite ignites the gun and finishes off the unfortunate animal. The explosion makes enough noise to awaken the dead. With the sound of musket fire reverberating among the cliffs, I kick my heels into my horse's exposed ribs a second time and resume the hunt.

I finally catch up with Holck when he is tantalisingly close to securing the refuge he seeks. Unfortunately for him, the broken rocks and pebbles that litter the ground make it difficult going. More importantly, they continue to betray his whereabouts and lead me directly to him. The sound of my pursuit reaches his ears shortly after he has come into view. He stops, turns around and waits silently. The exertion is plain to see as he gulps down oxygen, breathing hard as he realises the chase is almost over. As I approach, I can see his right hand gripping the hilt of his sword; he's readying himself, preparing to strike.

Some twenty paces from where he stands, I dismount. Although my body is bruised and weakened, the greatest discomfort comes from my throbbing left hand. But the nervous excitement pulsing through my veins neutralises the excesses and makes it possible for me to move fluidly. As I do, I never take my eyes off him. After drawing my own sword, I let the horse wander back along the track. I can feel my heart beating hard. This is the moment I have anticipated for a long time; a chance to avenge my children and my dearest friend. I don't doubt Holck is a superior fighter. But if David could defeat Goliath, I am happy to take the chance offered to me.

"So, you think you can best me?" he barks when I am close enough to hear his hoarse and ragged voice. "Your wounds are greater than mine, Hacker, yet do you really think you can defeat me and prevent my escape?"

Then he is on me, his good arm a blur of motion, power and precision. The onslaught takes all of my composure, strength and skill to thwart. Sparks fly as murderous thrusts are parried before I retaliate with my own equally venomous slashes as I seek to turn defence into attack. Miraculously, I find I can hold my own, and the pain in my ribs subsides with every thrust I absorb and forward motion I make. Whatsmore, after numerous attacks from Holck have been thwarted, I find myself able to see clearly through both eyes, as the blurred vision I was experiencing only minutes earlier is corrected.

Gradually, I realise I am in the ascendency. As my confidence soars, I feel the enormous guilt that has weighed me down since the deaths of Barbara and Isable start to lift. I am moving freely, and I can predict when and where Holck will attempt to strike. As I continue to repulse every one of his assaults, I see self-doubt written on the Bohemian's face as his confidence starts to wane. In contrast, I feel myself getting stronger as if a supernatural force has taken hold.

I don't know how much time has passed when I hear the reassuring sound of Guillaume's footsteps approaching. Like me, he is incapacitated. But an injured, tiring and demoralised Holck is not a match for us both. And so it proves when he launches a wild attack on my left flank. I continue to block his thrusts with ease before driving him back effortlessly and forcing his sword from his hands. Then he yields.

"I am done," he yells as he falls to his knees, spent; the fight beaten out of him. Only when Holck is subdued, do I see the damage Guillaume's flintlock inflicted on his shoulder. Blood continues to ooze out of the wound, and although the night sky has darkened, there is more than enough light to see the extensive damage to flesh and bone. Begrudgingly, I find myself feeling a degree of respect for the man, only to dismiss my thoughts immediately. In truth, he is a ruthless killer who does not give quarter to his enemies. I blink some sand out of my good eye and silently give thanks.

If Holck were a comrade, I would seek to aid him in any way I could. But as soon as he capitulates, a cold sensation runs down my spine. I have felt this feeling before, and I fully comprehend its significance.

"Get a rope and bind his hands," I instruct Guillaume. "I want this cur at my mercy, so he can't resist or escape."

As de la Croix carries out my instructions, the prisoner scrutinises my every movement; his dark eyes follow me as I walk to the motionless horse and drink some water.

"I am your prisoner," he says eventually, after both of his hands have been pinned securely behind his back by Guillaume. "I have surrendered to you; therefore, I expect you to behave like the God-fearing man and soldier you profess to be. You are not a brute, are you Hacker? Therefore, take me to the nearest garrison and allow me to await my fate."

I say nothing. My tongue is stilled. Right now, all I am conscious of is the battle now raging within me. So much of me wishes to slaughter the helpless beast slumped on the ground before me, a murderer who deserves no mercy. I think of how the Lieutenant-General would act in such a situation; he would string him up the instant he had him in chains. I have seen Oliver do it on many occasions "to preserve morale and in the interests of justice". Yet something deep within me is challenging this impulse, and its call is hard to ignore.

"I know what you are thinking," taunts Holck, as he claims to understand my turmoil. "You fear acting decisively and are driven by compassion, even towards a man like me, who has inflicted so much pain on you and your family. But, I tell you, this weakness will be your undoing,

Francis Hacker. So prevaricate no more, and let's be gone from here."

I take a step forward, searching for the small dagger strapped to my side. My hatred starts to burn deeply, and I struggle to control my emotions, but as I contemplate carrying out the severest of retributions, I find my hand unwilling to grasp the sharp blade. Instead, I take a deep breath, look upwards for a few, fleeting seconds and allow myself to marvel at the wonders of the moon and the universe beyond. As I do so, de la Croix quietly draws by my side. He places his left hand on my shoulder, whispers the words "pour toi, mon ami", and then plunges his own knife into the throat of Holck. At that moment, time itself slows down, and all I can focus on are Holck's flickering eyes, as the shock of the moment quickly becomes acute understanding. I blink rapidly, once, twice, three times. Then I, too, comprehend the significance of what Guillaume has done.

By the time I move towards Holck's convulsing body, it is too late; he is dying in front of me, trying to stem a gushing crimson torrent and clear his airwaves of the knife that has sliced through his windpipe and several arteries. As I watch the life flow out of him, and he claws desperately at the blade, I find myself thinking this is indeed a pitiful end for a man who never pitied anyone.

And then he is still.

THIRTY-THREE

GUILLAUME AND I DEPART EAST Wear Bay at five o'clock on the morning of Tuesday, the twenty-sixth day of June. As we make our way from this place, the heat is already rising as the rays of the early morning sun cast a holy glow on the becalmed waters of the English Channel.

Throughout the night, we have used Laudanum to ease the soreness of our wounds and our aching and bruised limbs. Unfortunately, the tablets can do nothing to prevent the intense itching sensation associated with the healing process. Yet despite these deprivations, we have never felt more alive.

For several hours, the Frenchman and I talk into the night about the events of recent months, trying to comprehend everything that has come to pass and how we have managed to survive for so long. We recall the treachery of Lord Grey of Groby, the duplicity of Cromwell and the great battles of Marston Moor and Naseby. And we agree the war is almost won. What we haven't discussed are the events of the last few hours. Nor will we, for that's how men deal with violence and brutality. Our goal is simple; we wish to serve Parliament faithfully and be better men for the experiences we have endured. And while it is easy to pledge these things, we realise fulfilling such ambitions presents a challenge for us both.

For me, that means returning to Belvoir Castle as quickly as possible and resuming my imprisonment under the watchful eyes of Gervase Lucas, when all I wish to do is return to Stathern and enjoy the warm and comforting embrace of my loving wife. I have more than two weeks left to make good my promise to the governor, and it's a pledge I fully intend to honour.

"Are you sure placing yourself at the mercy of the Royalists is a wise thing to do?" asks Guillaume, surprised by my declaration. "What can Lucas do if you do not return? He can hardly send the King's men after you and round you up. I urge you to think again, Francis. Parliament needs you, particularly now victory is so close. And you must also think of Cromwell's reaction, for he will be most displeased to be deprived of your services at such a crucial time."

I shake my head, unwilling to consider for a moment the prospect of breaking my oath.

"When a man's word is meaningless, and he is no longer trustworthy, then his life has no value. It merely becomes existence," I say to my protector. "I do not want that kind of life for myself, nor do I want it for you or any-one else who is dear to me. My friend, it is better to perish an honourable man than to live fourscore years dishon-ourably. Whatever more is said on the subject, neither you nor Oliver can convince me of pursuing any other course."

Guillaume shakes his head and kicks out at the sand, extinguishing the flames of the small fire that has kept us warm these past few hours. He knows further conversation about my intentions when I return to the Midlands is pointless. My mind is made up, and it is time to go.

It takes us just fifteen minutes to climb the steep cliffs and leave the bay behind. As we reach the summit of the brilliant white chalk outcrops, I turn around and take a final look at my surroundings. Right now, peace reigns. It is barely believable that such scenes of horror and depravity were played out here just a few hours earlier. The only visible signs are a broken masthead, and a few wooden barrels that have washed ashore as the vessel sunk by the Leopard went through its death throes. But to know what they represent means the observer must have witnessed the events of last night as they unfolded. And while the crew of the Royal Navy frigate will certainly be regaling whoever will listen with tales of derring-do, on land, there were only three men who understand precisely what happened. And now one of them is dead.

I become distracted, and my gaze diverts to the foot of the cliffs, some two hundred feet below. Away to my left, an ancient Oak stands tall and proud. It is close to here that Holck met his end, and it is now where he rests, strung up by Guillaume and myself and left to hang until the gulls have filled their bellies on his flesh. He deserves no less. As I tug on the reins, snapping the bridle firmly in place, several large birds start circling the tree, taking it in turns to swoop down into the branches. As they screech their approval, I turn in the saddle and look at Guillaume. Grim satisfaction is written on both of our faces.

I edge forward and look more closely in the direction of the old and weathered tree. As I watch the body sway in the gentle morning breeze and the birds compete for the juiciest morsels, an altogether more compelling vision of Abijah and my daughters distracts me. I shake my head, eager to clear the hallucinations and set about leaving this place, but when I open my eyes again, the vision is still vivid, as clear as anything I have ever seen. All three seem to be in good heart and are holding hands with one another. And then the moment is lost, and I find myself staring once again at the Oak and watching a feeding frenzy.

"Are you alright?" enquires Guillaume from behind, unaware of my thoughts. Without waiting to hear my answer, he adds: "Let's get far away from this hellish place, Francis. With luck, we might get close to Bromley by nightfall."

I nod my head in the affirmative. I don't wish to offend my friend, who is no longer a believer, but in my experience, there is no such thing as luck. All things happen for a reason. Within a few minutes, the wind is blowing through my hair, and our plucky steed is cantering comfortably through the populous hops fields of Kent. A calmness I have not felt for a long time starts to take hold of me, and I feel an irresistible urge to bellow "vengeance is mine" as loudly as I can. As I do, I feel Guillaume's grip tighten around my waist.

Holck may have perished, but there are others like him. So without further delay, it is time to fulfil my debt to Gervase and then renew the part I must play in this bitter, senseless and bloody war – until a tyrant King is finally defeated.

– The End –

EPILOGUE

THERE IS A BITTERLY COLD chill in the air on the morning of Monday, the twenty-ninth day of January, in the year of our Lord, 1646. Even with the brazier coals aglow, it is difficult to stand still for long and pay our respects to the departed without the frigid winter air attacking our bodies and minds.

But honour him, we must.

The war is still to reach a conclusion, albeit all effective opposition has almost ceased. Soon the killing will be over and a new kind of peace will reign. At that moment, all I will retain will be the memories and wounds that ache so grievously, reminders of all that is passed and has been lost.

But on this solemn day, I am joining Isabel and more than two hundred souls, including all the active members of the Militia, inside Saint Guthlacs, where we are making our peace with our Saviour and remembering Abijah Swan, our beloved comrade and friend.

They say time heals the most painful of losses. It

does not. Abijah was killed exactly a year ago at this very moment: at eight o'clock. He remained dignified to the end, when the noose of the scaffold on the Great North Road leading from Newark took him from us. And I have missed him sorely ever since.

This morning, I am barely able to say a word as the large assembly sings hymns and listens attentively to the Minister, a man I abhor, preaching about forgiveness, repentance and God's love for mankind. Yet, while I know this to be true, I am unable to forgive Gustav Holck for his evil-doing. I wish it could be so, but the pain I feel is too great; the guilt all-consuming.

Abijah's dying wish was for his Militia 'brothers' to remember his life and those of all the other men, women and children lost in this vile and cursed conflict. And we do, bursting our guts in praise until it is time to return to the world and continue the struggle that has turned Parliament's way.

Maybe, once the fighting is over and we are able to reconcile our wounded nation, torn in two by the King's reckless actions, then some good will come from the bloodshed that has scarred our once propsperous land.

Abijah would dearly wish it to be so.

And God willing, in the years ahead, I will do all I can to make it so..

HISTORICAL NOTE

AFTER THE CALAMITOUS EVENTS AT Naseby in June 1645, defeat for the King was inevitable. His weak and ill-disciplined armies and generals proved no match for the all-conquering New Model Army, commanded by Sir Thomas Fairfax and Oliver Cromwell. And as Parliament's forces set about crushing Royalist opposition throughout the rest of the year, support for the Monarch quickly evaporated.

By April 1646, the fight was effectively over. On the twenty-seventh day of that month, Charles was forced to flee Oxford disguised as a servant. To have remained in the Royalist capital would have meant capture, or worse, as Fairfax and Cromwell had started to surround the city. Seeking safety, the King travelled to Newark, the last major stronghold to recognise him as sovereign. Alas, after only a few days, he surrendered himself to the Scottish Covenant army, believing he could persuade its commanders to rally to his cause. It was a calculated gamble that failed. Charles underestimated the resolve and motivation of the Scots. He no sooner was he in their clutches and the town and castle of Newark under their control than he was made prisoner, and negotiations commenced with the English about the size of the ransom to be paid.

The Royalist's formal surrender took place on the twenty-fourth day of June 1646, when Oxford opened its gates to the New Model Army. On the same day, Princes Rupert and Maurice left the country under strict terms imposed on them by Parliament and James, Duke of York, was made a prisoner. But it wasn't until the first day of September that the Scots army left England, after spending the summer months negotiating the size of the ransom it would receive for handing Charles over to Parliament. Eventually, a figure of four hundred thousand pounds was agreed – with half paid before the Covenanter army departed England and the remainder handed over in fixed instalments. It was also decided Charles, now a King only in name, would remain under the 'protection' of the Scots, only coming South when the full ransom had been paid (which eventually happened on the first day of January 1647).

As for Francis, he was released from his confinement at Belvoir Castle on Wednesday, the twentieth day of September 1645. He returned immediately to his army duties in Leicestershire and Isabel and their two surviving children in Stathern.

A month after Francis's release, Parliamentary forces besieged the castle at Belvoir. Still, it would take a further four months before an honourable settlement was reached with Gervase Lucas (on 2 February 1646), enabling the governor to leave unmolested with his troops. Meanwhile, at the end of the same month, the Ashby garrison also yielded, with Henry Hastings agreeing to leave the stronghold at the beginning of March. Under the terms he brokered, he was allowed free passage to a port of his choice and unimpeded flight to the continent.

Yet while Parliament was now firmly in the ascendency, forces loyal to the King and his son, the Prince of Wales, were already preparing themselves for a new struggle. For two years, the plotters carefully built new alliances and rekindled old ones, so they could set about reclaiming the throne for the King. This duly came to a head on Sunday the fifth day of July in 1648, at the Battle of Willoughby Field in Nottinghamshire, when Royalist and Parliamentarian blood was spilt once more and the second English Civil War erupted.

PHILIP YORKE

MANY THANKS

RESEARCHING A BOOK OF THIS nature takes many hours, and would be considerably harder to produce without the help and goodwill of many wonderful souls. I offer my gratitude and thanks to everyone who has contributed to the stirring and evolving story of Francis Hacker.

In particular, I would like to offer my appreciation to Catherine Pincott-Allen and Richard Pincott, who run an archaeological group called the East Midlands Field Detectives. They have a particular fascination with the English Civil War period and got in touch shortly after *Rebellion* (the first book of The Hacker Chronicles series) was published. Their enthusiasm for the subject has been infectious, as has Catherine's willingness to sense-check the manuscript, dig away at the Hacker family tree and winkle out the occasional historical inaccuracy.

The Reverend Brian Williams, Vicar at Saint Laurence's Church in Hougham, has also been an invaluable resource and help, offering up the character of Henry Hannington, who makes an appearance in the latter stages of *Redemption*. Hannington was a well-known figure in Kent during the 1600s. Interestingly, he was a notorious drunkard while Vicar of Saint Laurence's, responsible for the church's affairs for more than 20 years. According to the church's most recently published guide: "Saturday seemed to be his favoured day for frequenting alehouses, when he sang bawdy songs… He encouraged parishioners to drink and dance on the Sabbath, giving them as much time as possible by performing a minimal church service. His misdemeanours were endless." Part of me feels I should have given the wild and unruly Vicar more of a voice in this latest adventure!

One of the most pleasing aspects of writing about events that, in part, are based on fact is making a connection with family members of the person whose story I am telling. Since Rebellion was first published in December 2019, I have been delighted to make the acquaintance of several direct descendants of Francis Hacker, who reside in West Virginia and Oklahoma in the United States. Two members of the family in particular – Paul von Hacker and Jim Linger (both great-grandsons of Francis several times over) – have offered me their support, information and kindness during the past few months. In return, I offer my heartfelt thanks, and I hope they enjoy *Redemption* as much as they did the first instalment of the series.

Throughout my latest writing journey, other people have offered constant support and advice, which has been equally valuable. They have been excellent sounding boards and have never complained when I have thrust a fresh draft in their hands and asked them for a 'no-holds-barred' critique. My friends Dean Yates-Smith and Keith Potter have duly obliged, and I am indebted to both of them in equal measure. In addition, my walking buddies Philip Bird, David Moore and Stuart Hardy-Taylor have also helped me concerning a host of faith-related matters.

Last but not least, I want to thank my wife, Julie, for her endless love, encouragement, positivity and willingness to always offer constructive advice.

Should any mistakes be found in this manuscript after so many have laboured to ensure the accuracy of my writing and research, then please point an accusing finger in my direction, for I am the sole architect of anything erroneous.

ABOUT THE AUTHOR

PHILIP YORKE has a very special interest in history – particularly the events in Seventeenth-Century England that directly led to the three civil wars (1642-51) and the establishment of the Commonwealth and Protectorate.

Residing in a quiet Leicestershire village with his wife of more than thirty years, Philip uses his time to support his family; raise public awareness of the growing problems associated with food poverty and food waste in the UK (via the third sector); play a part in developing the editorial output of *Sorted*, a men's magazine and website – and research and write historical fiction novels.

He is a committed churchgoer and a long-standing supporter of Leicester Tigers rugby team and Hull City FC. He also plays tennis and enjoys discovering forgotten places while walking through the quiet country lanes of Leicestershire and the wider East Midlands region.

Redemption is the second installment of The Hacker Chronicles, a five-part series about the role Francis Hacker played in helping to end the reign of King Charles the

First and secure the Puritan regime headed by Oliver Cromwell.

To find out more about Philip's books and his wider work, please visit: **philipyorke.org**

Coming soon...
The third novel in the acclaimed *Hacker Chronicles* series

Regicide

By Philip Yorke

mashiach publishing

philipyorke.org

Printed in Great Britain
by Amazon

19260818R10274